Wrath of t

The Unholy Witch Wars

Book 1

D.L. Howard

ISBN: 978-0-578-63096-0 (Paperback Edition)

Cover Image by: Eddy Shinjuku

Cover Typography by: Story Wrappers – storywrappers.com

For Mama Donia who always believed in me.

Mum, Puff, & Wendy. My very own tribe. Thanks for everything. Without you all, I would be screaming in a walled off room and this book would still be stuck in my head. You all are the best!

Chapter 1

"Quit running! You'll hurt yourself." The grim-faced guard growled at the little girl. The hollow sound of her feet pounded against the ground echoing against the stone interior, as she left in a flurry, waving her hands at him.

"I'll be fine, Ekon. I'm late for lessons," the young girl yelled back, already down the hall. A select few only was allowed in the area where they traveled. Deep inside the mountain, these halls were the sacred sanctuary of the High Priestess. Well-guarded and protected with spells if triggered, could render a person soulless. Ekon watched as the young girl's shadows elongated into narrow lines from the torchlights on the walls making the area emptier than it already was.

She turned the corner leaving the guard standing by himself. He would catch up with her. He always did. Her lessons was the priority. If she was late, the repercussions were dire. Her mother and grandmother were strict with her schooling. Under so much pressure at such a young age. The little witchling would never let the stress show. Being in the spotlight of Enyxias' elite had been something she's known since birth. And she relished the attention. Even if on some days it made her cry. He hated those days because her anger was quick and furious.

Ekon turned the same corner as the girl and knew which room she would be in. There was no need to go inside. He stood outside the door and waited. She was safe. His duty was to watch over and protect her. A duty he enjoyed since the child was born. The girl was full of spirit, cold flames and smiles. Everyone loved her. He loved her like she was one of his own daughters.

Nthanda stood just inside the darkened room. Took a deep breath before she went further inside. It was her last lesson before her birthday. She was excited and scared. This would be a similar test of what would happen when she became old enough to claim and study the stronger magic. A sample of what she might endure at her majority. She waited for this moment for the entire lunam.

"I know you're in here my Little Star. Come now. Time waits for no one. Not even those late to their lessons," a woman said from inside the room. A loud rapping noise accosted Nthanda's ears. The staff of her teacher hitting the floor, signaled that lessons had begun. Mama Jia'ka was strict, but she was the best tutor Nthanda ever had. She sprinted to her, not wanting to be later than she already was.

The High Priestess assigned the old woman to her after Nthanda kept surpassing her previous instructors. *"Who better to teach my heiress than our own blood? At a certain point in our instructions, we can only learn from those who bore us into this world. That is our inheritance from the Mother Goddess. Never forget that daughter."* The High Priestess words sounded in her head. She didn't want to let her mother or Mama Jia'ka down.

Nthanda went to her grandmother and stood before her. The old woman was proud and tall. Her long dreadlocks, now white, hung low down her back. Her skin like ebony, now wrinkled held her staff tight. Her milky white eyes bore into Nthanda's amethyst ones and smiled. "I won't tell if you won't, Little Star."

Nthanda shook her head and giggled. "I promise it's between us, Mama Jia'ka."

"Good." Jia'ka turned and shuffled to the center of the room. She stood next to a large, empty silver basin. She pointed to Nthanda and bade her to come to her. The girl went to the basin. She loved looking into the water mirrors. It was always something different when she peered onto its surface. Only this time she didn't know what to expect.

"Child, it is time. Your day of birth is tomorrow. Twelve lunams is a special time for us witches. Tis the age where our familiars choose us. A chance to receive their precious, lifelong gift. Gifts of loyalty, protection, guidance, and love. They are part of us. Part of our souls. We are part of them. If we die, they surely die with us because they can't live without their witch. They seek the powerful and you child, you are strong enough to have one choose you."

"Why must we wait? Why can't we go search for mine now, Mama Jia'ka?" the young girl asked. Anxious. She couldn't wait until she was old enough to get a familiar and now the time had come, she didn't want to wait any longer.

The old woman looked down at her. "We do the Ritual of Binding on the witchlings twelfth lunam during the witching hour. That time strengthens our magic. So we wait." Nthanda groaned and pushed her full lips into a pout. "I've said you were an impatient one since the day you were born. You came too early, but you were strong and survived. Little Star, learn some patience. Will do you well in the future. And stop your pouting. Doesn't become you." Jia'ka rapped her staff once more against the ground. Nthanda stopped and straightened her stance.

The old woman lifted a stoneware jar and poured the water from inside into the basin while she chanted a few words. Nthanda watched on while thinking about the ritual of binding. She wondered what type of creature would choose her. There was so many choices out there. A few of her friends already went through the ritual on their twelfth lunam and received a familiar. Her closest friend, Serea, was chosen by a huge Tindian Spider. Made her shudder just thinking about the large furry creature.

Jia'ka caught the moment her granddaughter's mind wandered off and sighed internally. Once Nthanda's mind fell down a foxhole, it was hard getting her focus back in line. Setting down the jar, the old woman stopped her chanting and tapped Nthanda on the nose. The girl glanced up, saw the scowl on Jia'ka's face and froze.

"You are here to learn. Not wander off while in my presence young one. If you cannot focus here and now, then there is no need for you to be here to study. And if you can't be here now, there will be no Ritual of Binding tonight." Jia'ka said. "What will it be?"

There was no way possible Nthanda would leave and give up her ceremony. The missed chance to receive a familiar.

Her mother, the High Priestess wouldn't go for it. She would skin her alive, put her back together and repeat. She saw her do it as punishment before to a member of their coven. It was a very plausible thing that could happen. There were no excuses for punishments. Especially being in her position as her daughter. Nthanda's gulp was loud in the still room.

"I'll pay attention. I am sorry for the disrespect, wise one," she said. The woman nodded and stepped back from the basin.

"Good. You always got the way of things quick. First things first. We will not go over anything new. Our time today is not to study but go through a cleansing ritual. I will prepare you for tonight. Once you complete this, we do not allow you to speak to anyone or see anyone. You will go into confinement until it's time for your ceremony. A perfect time for reflection of self. Speak with the Mother Goddess. Use it wisely. We honor her by being the best of who we are."

"What will we do about Ekon? He will wait for me all night till I am done?"

"Ekon do what Ekon 'spose to do, child. Don't worry about him. He knows his role as you should remember yours."

"Yes, Mama."

Jia'ka nodded her approval then took a few steps and picked a leather pouch off the table. She untied the small bag and peeked inside. Smiling, she returned to her previous spot.

"As I said before, this is a cleansing ritual. You can't offer yourself up to the spirits and the Mother without coming to her pure in mind and body. Undress and set your clothes aside."

Nthanda undressed. Never having done a ritual like this before, standing bare before her grandmother, made her stomach do flips. She set the clothes aside. Jia'ka poured black sand from the leather pouch, forming a circle then a triangle inside the circle. Nthanda was shocked to see her grandmother use a rare ingredient in abundance like she did.

Black sand was hard to get. Ancient tomes said the sand didn't come from the realm of the living but the realm of the dead. If one could get their hands on the precious commodity, it would be a great tool for powerful spell-casting. Only a pinch was needed and did wonders, but Nthanda watched her grandmother pour out way more than that. Had her curious about the type of ritual Jia'ka really was doing.

"Step inside the triangle, careful not to smear the sand," Jia'ka commanded. Nthanda did as she was told and stepped inside, careful not to mess up the sand. She cleared her mind. Whatever was about to happen, she needed to be prepared and ready. Jia'ka noticed Nthanda switching mind spaces and nodded her approval.

"You remembered your lessons. Always go into a circle with a clear mind and heart. If you come into a circle unprepared, disastrous things could happen. I believe in you, child. There is greatness in you and I am so glad I am here to see and be part of your foundation. Now, close your eyes and focus. Listen to me and follow silently in your mind."

Jia'ka walked dextral to the circle and said the words to close and protect the circle. Finished, she took a step back and eyed the young girl before her. She really couldn't describe how proud she was of her. She was prepared and ready for whatever came her way. The world was a dangerous place for the daughter of a High Priestess. Especially one from Enyxias.

The bones spoke to her when she cast them a lunam ago. Two paths emerged in the reading. The stronger path was full of glorious darkness. It spoke of danger around the star and if the star took that path, the world would tremble at their feet. She knew soul deep the star was her Little Star. The fear she felt that night still haunts her.

Jia'ka told the High Priestess soon as she could about the bone reading. With no hesitation, she believed her and immediately assigned her to become the young one's new instructor in the arts. Her Little Star needed training no other could give her. It was a demanding lunam but Nthanda took to it like a natural and absorbed everything she threw at her.

"Mother Goddess we beseech thee. Look down upon your daughters and fill us with your glory. Nthanda comes to you naked as a newborn babe. With an open heart and mind. Guide her upon these next steps of her journey. Her walk with you. Protect her and guide her. Many dangers are in this world, let her be quick of mind, fierce, and strong enough to do what she must do to survive." Jia'ka took the silver and steel dagger with a bone handle from her hip and cut her wrists. She let the blood pool before it ran down her wrists and hit the ground with a soft splatter.

"Open your eyes young one." Nthanda opened her eyes wide. Jia'ka licked the edge of her dagger's blade and tasted her own blood. Her smile could put the fear of death in anyone. "Take this dagger and cut as I did on your own wrists,"

Jia'ka told her. She handed the dagger over and Nthanda took it with shaking hands.

She looked to the old woman, "Will it hurt?"

"Eh, what is life without pain? Not life. It may hurt but it won't last. No pain ever last too long. Either it goes away on its own or you do what's needed to get rid of it."

Nthanda took a deep breath, followed her grandmother's example and cut her wrist the same way. She made sure not to cut too deep and gasped when the knife slowly ripped her skin apart. Pain shot up her arms and tears threatened to escape the corners of her eyes.

She willed the tears back and watched the blood flow like a slow-moving stream. She handed the dagger back to the woman. Jia'ka took the edge of the blade and then licked Nthanda's blood off it. The tang of power rushed over her tongue and right through her. The girl was stronger than she expected.

"Let your blood flow over the points of the triangle you stand in. I will reinforce the circle with mine," Jia'ka said. She walked the circle in the same direction as earlier while Nthanda marked her triangle going the opposite way. When they both finished, the old woman stood directly in front of the little witchling. "Give me both of your wrists."

Nthanda lifted her heavy arms. The blood loss made her light-headed and dizzy. Jia'ka touched her bleeding wrists to Nthanda's and chanted a spell under her breath. Nthanda felt the rush of power that was her grandmothers. It was so strong; she went weak at the knees. Jia'ka gripped her wrists tighter, keeping her upright. At the end of the spell, a bright light lit up the room then dissipated.

"From this moment on, no words should pass your tongue and lips. You are now under confinement. You cannot speak until your binding ceremony. Do you understand, child?" Nthanda nodded slowly. Jia'ka picked up a piece of cloth from the table and dipped it into the basin of water then cleansed Nthanda's wrist. She then took a dry cloth and wrapped both wrists to stop the bleeding.

"You may cross the sands now," Jia'ka said to her. Nthanda stepped over the black sand that was much duller than when they started. "Get dressed. There's a black slip of a dress folded next to your things. Put that on. I will have your clothes delivered to your room."

Nthanda moved quick and changed. Jia'ka took her time going to the door. She startled the guard standing on duty. He jumped high when she stepped out into the hall.

"Mama Jia'ka," he said. "How can I serve?"

"Take the child to the room of solitude. There we will confine her until her binding ceremony tonight. She cannot speak or eat. She's only allowed water. No visitors. I trust you will do as needed."

"Yes."

"Good," she replied. Nthanda had come to the hall and stood in the shadows of the torchlight while they spoke. "Go with Ekon, Little Star. I will see you tonight." Jia'ka kissed Nthanda's brow and went back into her chamber.

THE DOOR CREAKED OPEN on its own. A tall and dark woman glided into the chamber. Jia'ka didn't need to look up to see who it was. She felt the power coming her way from down the hall. Her daughter was a tremendous force. She was the calm eye in the middle of a storm. Power rolled off of her if one knew how to detect it. Others who didn't recoiled at its touch, not knowing why they felt the way they did.

The High Priestess stopped beside her mother, letting her eyes scan over the working chamber. The walls lined with shelves, full of jars filled with whom knew what. Leather pouches and bones scattered across the tables. At the altar, black flamed candles were lit to the Mother Goddess. It was the room of a seer and one you didn't want to cross.

"How did the cleansing go, Mama?" The High Priestess faced the old woman.

"The same as any cleansing go, daughter."

"Did you taste the blood? Is she stronger like I expected?"

"She is much stronger than you and I at that age. Great things are in store for her. You chose wise her sire you did. Even if you won't divulge who the man is," Jia'ka said, letting the last of her words linger. She put down the dagger she was cleaning and sat down on the mat in the corner of her room. She patted the ground in front of her, indicating for her daughter to sit.

No matter how old the High Priestess got, she always revered and respected her mother wishes. She sat down, and memories of her childhood rushed to the forefront of her mind. She remembered her cleansing night before her binding ceremony. Of how scared she was and how excited. She could only imagine how Nthanda must be feeling. Her daughter. The piece of her soul that was complete when she held her the first time.

Twelve lunams had gone by too fast. The last lunam had gone by much quicker. Which brought her to the reason she was sitting there in her mother's chambers.

"What does your bones say, Mama? Have they changed any or do they still speak the same warning?" The High Priestess needed to know what course of action she had to take to protect her soul part. She had enough to worry about with her people of Enyxias. Worrying about her daughter took precedence and put everyone else on hold. The humans and witches alike were loyal to the lands. But whispers started to reach her ears around the same time her mother first mentioned the bones. She had eyes and ears in those covens, reporting back to her. But unrest still rose with those groups.

"The bones say the same thing. No changes. We must stay alert for the unexpected. The winds of change are coming. Prepare yourself."

"You don't think we should wait and hold off on the Ritual of Binding? Until we curb the unrest among the covens."

"NO! She must go through it. Mother Goddess will watch over us all. What will happen will happen because it is meant to. Besides, the child needs a familiar. A guide to help her with her magic. One is out there waiting for her."

The High Priestess let out a loud sigh. "I know situations and moments happen in our lives for reasons, but I swear on the Mother Goddess and her children that if something happens to my daughter. I won't care who is responsible. I will raise an army of daemons to devour the souls of my enemies."

"No, you must stay strong Chanda. This is larger than us. Everything is in alignment and in order. There's nothing more that we can do but let it all unfold. We all have our parts to play for the bigger picture."

Chapter 2

Nthanda was bored. She could only pray so much to the Mother Goddess without feeling like a beggar. She wished Serea was there to talk with her. To at least tell her what to expect. She really hated being in the dark. The girl sat back against the stone wall as the cold seeped through to her exposed skin. Her black shift dress was thin and did nothing to keep her warm. She crossed her arms over her chest, hoping to keep what warmth she had to herself.

The full moon was high in the clear night sky. Its silvery tendrils of pale light, slipped through the slits of the only window in the chamber, giving Nthanda the only light in the room. Nthanda closed her eyes and began to sing a song in her head. *If no words come out of my mouth, means I'm still in the rights of my silence.*

Time passed slowly, she was sure only a few candlemarks had gone by. When she entered the room, the sun still burned bright in the sky. However long it has been, she was ready to go. Ready to find her familiar. And she was starving. Food was a forgotten thought at this point. No one told her about fasting either.

She stood up and stretched, tired of sitting, wasting away. In a short line, she paced back and forth, silently grumbling to herself. She didn't understand the point of this part of the ritual. Why did she have to go through silent confinement? Made no sense to her.

She glanced to the window to find the moon's position changed. Another candlemark had gone by. Nthanda wanted to yell and scream at anything. She didn't want to sit. She couldn't sleep because it was too cold. She wanted out of the room. To curl up in her warm bed with soft furs and covers. Her stomach took that moment to make loud noises and remind her she was hungry. What she really wanted was food.

The sound of the door opening startled her to stillness. Nthanda wheeled around to find her two maid servants come into the room. Ekon followed closely on their heels. Many questions formed in her head but mainly she wanted to know what was going on. She opened her mouth to ask when Ekon shook his head and promptly placed his large hand over her mouth, preventing any words to fall out. Thankful for the catch, she nodded and relaxed her shoulders.

"Witchling, it's time. The coven calls for you. They await your presence. Your maid servants are here to prepare you for the ceremony," Ekon said. Nthanda nodded. Her guard bowed his head before departing, leaving the servants with her.

Didn't take her maids long to help her get dressed. Everything they had brought was pieces she had never seen before and she couldn't stop looking at them. A beautiful collection of clothing, somebody knew what she liked.

First, they handed Nthanda a long, velveteen dress, black as the void. Once she had the dress on, the soft fabric flowed like waves to the ground. Nthanda gushed over the silver spider web embroidery that covered the skirt of her dress. It reminded her of the colors of her hair and perhaps, that is what whoever had in mind.

Her maids produced a pair of black leather boots with delicate silver webbed chained laces. She rubbed her hands over the supple leather and realized the boots matched her dress. Once she had everything on, they handed her a new silver grey cloak lined with bear fur. Soft to the touch, Nthanda couldn't help but constantly rub her hand over it.

Her maids adjusted the cloak once Nthanda put it on, bowed then left the room. Ekon stood in the doorway and looked her over. She looked as regal as her stationed afforded her. The corners of Ekon's mouth tugged upwards into a huge grin. "The High Priestess outdone herself this time."

Nthanda's head shot up, her nose scrunched together in a moment of confusion. Not able to speak, she couldn't ask what he meant.

"Don't tell her I told you but she made your dress herself. She had Sienna make the cloak just for you but everything else was her design. She wanted your ceremony to be special."

Nthanda's jaw slacked open. Sienna was the most desired dress and cloak maker in Enyxias. Then to find out her mother sewed her dress, she didn't even realize her mother knew how to sew. She touched the sleeve of her dress and glanced back to Ekon. A priceless gift she had no way to reciprocate. She honestly didn't think her mother would let her. But soon as she was able to speak, she would make sure that her mother understood how much she loved it.

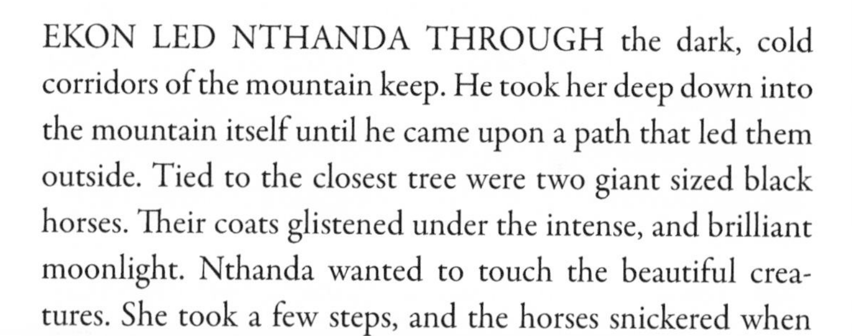

EKON LED NTHANDA THROUGH the dark, cold corridors of the mountain keep. He took her deep down into the mountain itself until he came upon a path that led them outside. Tied to the closest tree were two giant sized black horses. Their coats glistened under the intense, and brilliant moonlight. Nthanda wanted to touch the beautiful creatures. She took a few steps, and the horses snickered when she got too close, sidestepping away from her. She turned back to find Ekon watching.

"You ever rode before?" he asked the young girl. Her eyes were wide and lit with excitement. She shook her head with an enthusiastic 'no'. Ekon's deep chuckled filled their surroundings. He went to her, squatted and stuck his hands out for her to step on. "It's not too hard. Too dark to walk at this time of the night. The trails are quicker. Step onto my hands then hop on the horse."

Nthanda lifted the hems of her new dress and followed Ekon's instructions. Soon as she sat atop the beast, he snorted. She touched his mane and rubbed her hands through its silkiness. He visibly calmed at her touch. She loved the horses in the stables but never got close to one or let alone ride one. Now that she was on one, she couldn't wait until they moved. To feel the cold wind at her back. To be free from inside the mountain keep.

Her eyes followed Ekon's movement as he sat astride his horse. Once settled, he looked over Nthanda's saddle. He told her to pick up the rein and follow his motions. She was a quick learner and didn't take long for her to figure the basics out. Nthanda enjoyed everything about the ride. It was exactly what she thought it would be like. She hoped she could convince her mother to let her have lessons. That learning would be beneficial.

Time was of the essence and Ekon was running out. He led them down a slippery and rocky slope in a fast pace but their mounts held the ground fine. She relaxed a little when they made it to the bottom. The path out of the keep was too narrow and always made her nervous. When they reached the edge of the forest, he cut a path to the right and led them around the outskirts of the dark woods.

The night sky was clear and the light of the moon guided Ekon and Nthanda to their destination. A sharp blast of wind cut across the path, causing Nthanda to shiver. She pulled the cloak tighter across her arms and chest. Thankful for the warmth it provided. She was used to the cold, but this night was colder than normal.

Nthanda didn't know where they headed but Glass Lake glittering surface appeared in the distance from the path they were on. A place she wanted to visit but was never allowed to go on her own.

The lake was a dangerous mirror of ice and water, and many dark entities called its frigid waters home. A person could get lost if they stared too long into its mirrored surface, and too many people over the years had come up missing whenever they ventured near the shores.

Only half a candlemark had passed when Ekon and Nthanda came upon a small open space. A group of people gathered together, forming a half moon crescent. They hid their faces underneath the cowls on their black cloaks. Two people stood far away from the others. Obvious as night and day, Nthanda recognized her mother and grandmother based on how they stood. Confident, calm, and collect.

Ekon jumped down from his mare and tied it to the nearest tree. He helped the child down and led her to the center of the group.

"I brought the witchling as commanded." He touched Nthanda's shoulder and pushed her forward in the group's direction. She trembled beneath his hands and in that moment he felt sorry for her. The older woman nodded. Ekon was no longer needed, and he strode to stand near the horses.

"The hour is upon us, Little Star," Jia'ka said, removing her cowl so the child could see her. "At this hour our magic is stronger. We honor the Goddess tonight and in return she will bless you." She grinned, and Nthanda smiled back. The High Priestess motioned to the group, and they all formed a circle around Jia'ka and Nthanda. "Your time of silence is over." Jia'ka reached into a pouch and pulled out a powdery white substance. From her palm, she blew it into Nthanda's face.

The powder rushed over Nthanda's face traveling through her mouth and nose. It tickled which surprised her more. She opened and closed her mouth multiple times. Getting the motion back in her jaw. She didn't realize until that moment that Mama Jia'ka really put a spell of silence on her. She wouldn't have been able to speak if she had tried.

"My daughter just caught on that we spelled her." The High Priestess winked at Nthanda. "Everyone is silenced so your thoughts wouldn't get muddled."

Even if she was free to speak, Nthanda found she didn't want to. The whole situation seemed surreal to her. Finally, her turn to get a magical companion. She understood whatever awaited her had to choose her first. She was well aware of her strength and her magical ability. She didn't brook any argument that for her age she was powerful. Only the strong of their kind could handle a familiar spirit. Jia'ka trained her well this last lunam.

The coven encircled them and clasped hands. Their chanting voices were low as they began an invocation spell. Nthanda heard the same words repeated over and over again until it was stuck in her head. The High Priestess stood before her and Jia'ka stood behind her, placing her hands on her shoulders. High Priestess Chanda removed a silver bladed dagger from her waist, the sheen of its blade glimmered in Nthanda's eyes.

Jia'ka reached her arms around and pushed the cloak away. She pulled the top of Nthanda's dress down to her collarbone, exposing the smooth skin to the High Priestess. Right where Nthanda's bone protruded, Priestess Chanda cut deep underneath. The skin flayed apart like she was cutting a piece of meat. The shock and pain of the action sent the girl's eyes rolling back in her head. Nthanda didn't know what was happening. The burning sensation kept coming in waves, and felt like the priestess was carving a piece of art into her chest.

It didn't take long, but felt like an eternity. The sounds of the coven behind her, chanting still, was heavier. The thick swirls of magic formed around their words and Nthanda felt it as the power traveled through the grounds and crept up to her legs. The combined power encapsulated her. She couldn't remember when Jia'ka added her voice to the growling cacophony but her voice and power only made the spell stronger.

High Priestess Chanda placed her hand over the wound, whispering indecipherable words, letting her hand hover without touching it. The hand began to glow a bluish white color. When it became too bright for them to see, she pressed it against Nthanda's open wound.

"Mother Goddess and her revered children, we beseech thee. Tonight, we call out to you. Your daughters and sons are open to your wisdom," The High Priestess shouted. "This witchling comes to you whole and pure, seeking your gift. Guide her on her journey to find that which she seeks."

The chanting of the circle stopped. Nthanda wanted to but she couldn't scream. The searing pain only lifted when the High Priestess removed her hand. Gasping for air, tears escaped the corner of her eyes and rolled down her cheeks. Chanda's gazed pored over her daughter's face.

Chanda knew the girl wasn't prepared for the ritual yet she couldn't tell her what to expect. The Mother Goddess guided her and her hand. Every witchling ceremony is different yet similar. This one was none like she had done before. She reached up and touched her daughter's cheek and wiped the tears away. Bending down, she kissed her forehead.

"You did well, child. I am proud of you," Chanda whispered. The Priestess glanced down to the marking she had made, not knowing what it was she was carving. Lost in the throes of the magic, her hands worked on their own volition. Against Nthanda's dark brown skin was a luminescent marking in the shape of a full moon and a crescent moon with eight stars entwined in them.

"It's beautiful," Chanda said. "Look. You are favored by our most high."

Nthanda looked down at her chest where her mother carved her flesh. Seeing the mark, a rush of amazement escaped her mouth. "But... What? How?" She stuttered and quickly looked to her mother then her grandmother. Jia'ka was all smiles and patted her on her shoulder.

"I knew my Little Star was special!" Jia'ka said. "Now it's time for the part you have been waiting for!"

"Every witch has the chance to gain a familiar. Not all are blessed to receive the gifts of one. Now is your time to go out there and meet yours. I feel it on the wind, something is waiting. You have until dawn. As the sun rises and you haven't returned, your chance will have been lost forever. Go. Now! Everything you need the land and Mother Goddess will provide."

Nthanda pulled her dress up, covering her new marking. She would examine it later. According to the position of the moon, at least two candlemarks had passed. She didn't have too long before the sun rose. That surprised her. It only seemed like seconds. But when in the deep throes of magical spells, time ran differently.

Chanda's gaze never left Nthanda as she adjusted her clothes. "Go into the trees. Go towards the mountains. Travel by the river."

The girl nodded and took off towards the snow-covered trees. Nthanda was used to walking in snow but she didn't want to ruin her new boots. She stopped and spelled them from ruination. She didn't know what she was looking for or what to expect. She had put on airs around the High Priestess and Jia'ka but being alone scared her. All manners of creatures lived in the mountains and the woods. Bears and wolves mostly but spirits and creatures from the void also found refuge in the trees. She was always taught not to interact with them because they were tricksters. She could hear her grandmother's voice then, *"The world we live in is filled with all manners of people and creatures. Some harmless, some dangerous. A witch's job is to know how to treat each one."*

Nthanda found a barely noticeable path and took it going north. Following the river, there was plenty of light to lead her. The sounds of the night calmed her nerves as she trekked along the rocky path. In front of her face, little clouds formed from the heavy breath she took as she climbed an incline. Hearing the owls hunting in the distant night made her smile. She loved the birds and thought they were beautiful with their white and slate grey feathers. Creatures of the Mother Goddess as they all were.

Maybe I'll get an owl.

Nthanda didn't know how much time passed but she continued walking. Keeping her eyes open to anything. She didn't know how this part of the ceremony was supposed to work. Tired and thirsty, she stopped by a boulder near the river's edge and sat down. The sky was dark but the beginnings of dawn approached. The sun would make an appearance soon.

So far no luck in finding which she sought. She wanted to cry but crying was not for her. She refused to show weakness even if there was no one around. She would know. The animals would know. That thought caused her to giggle.

Nthanda took a deep breath and released. Rubbed her hands together to keep them from freezing. Her eyes went to the sky and her lips moved to speak but stopped. She didn't know what to say. Her mind was so confused with everything she thought she knew but didn't.

"I don't know what to think or do Mother Goddess. What do you expect of me? What do I need to do to show you I am a worthy daughter?" Nthanda spoke aloud. The sound of the rushing river was not too loud to cover the sounds of footsteps stepping on the tree needles. She froze and turned towards it.

"Who's there? Show yourself?" Nthanda jumped up and prepared herself for the danger that lurked in the dark blanket of the forest. She stood and waited. Her measured breaths was soft against the night. She took two steps forward to get a closer look. A perfect silence and a hushed stillness washed over everything. She waited and waited until she gave up and turned to go back to the boulder. When she turned her back, she heard the crinkling pine needles again and turned back toward the trees. What came out was not what she expected. A snow leopard cub with the brightest crystal blue eyes she's ever seen padded towards her and stopped only a few feet away.

Nthanda first thoughts were of its mother. If cubs were around, the mother was surely around too. She gathered her cloak closer and took off back in the direction she had come from. *I can't fight a grown wildcat!* Not hesitating, she walked as fast as she could without falling and hurting herself. Going downhill was much easier than her going up and she remembered where to step so she wouldn't fall. She glanced behind her hoping the mother didn't catch her trail and saw the cub further back stalking her. The cub stopped and let out a noise like a tiny mew.

"I don't want any trouble with your mama. Go back. I don't taste too good. Not enough meat on my bones. Shoo!" she shouted to the animal. The girl picked up a handful of snow and packed it into a ball. She threw it at the tiny cub but not far enough to hit the animal. The cub sat down on his haunches and tilted its head to the side. It made the noise again but didn't move. Nthanda turned away from the creature and continued down the trail, sliding a bit but caught herself and held on to the nearest tree branch.

Disappointment took root in her mind. Being out in the cold for all that time not to be chosen hurt her. Nthanda's spirit was deflated. She slumped to the wet snow, rested her head on the branch, and let the tears fall. She truly wanted it. She thought the ritual would mean something since they marked her. Pulling down the collar of her dress she examined the silvery marking on her skin. Touching it, thinking it would hurt but it didn't. She rubbed the new mark with the pad of her fingers but the scarring wasn't raised. It was pretty, and she wondered what it all meant. Transfixed at what she was staring at, Nthanda didn't notice the little cub sneak up beside her.

She jumped up and stumbled backwards. Her eyes widen as she searched her around. The fast-paced beating of her heart didn't once slow down.

"Why are you following me? Where are the other cubs?" The cub sat on its back haunches and tilted its head. "Where is your mother? I can't take care of a wildcat. I have no clue on what to do. Besides, I don't think the High Priestess would let me keep you," she said to the cub who watched her. Seeing the soft fur of the animal and its black and grey spots, she had a sudden longing to touch it. She stepped closer to the animal and thought it would move but the cub stayed put. She reached down and touched the cat's head and rubbed its ears. The cub's fur was extremely soft, and she continued to pet it. The cub purred from her attentions, and it made Nthanda laugh.

"You're such a cute thing. Are you lost? Is that why you are following me?" she asked the animal.

I like you. That's why I followed you.

Nthanda's hand stopped mid rub and looked around.

"Who said that?" She stood up searching and went to the edge of the trees to see who responded to her.

Hello. It was me.

The girl turned around and looked twice at the animal before her. She narrowed her eyes.

"Wait, is that you talking to me? How are you doing that? How can I hear you? Who are you?" she rapidly asked.

You ask a lot of questions, the cub said and licked its large paw before setting it back on the snow-covered ground.

"And animals shouldn't talk. Especially directly into my head."

Shows how much you know, Bright Star.

"Bright Star? Who is that?"

It is what I call you. In the ether, you look like a bright shining star. So I followed the light until it brought me to you.

Nthanda took a few moments, but it finally dawned on her. She realized what the cub was. There was no mother or litter of other cubs nearby. This creature came for her. She had no words for the emotions she felt. She was worthy. The cub was there for her. Because it was her familiar. She laughed out loud for missing the point.

Took you long enough. I'm hungry do you have anything to eat?

"No, and wait. How come I couldn't hear you when I first saw you?"

There was no link. Didn't form until you touched me willingly. Don't you know how these things work? The cub stood on all fours, padded to her, rubbed against her leg and purred loudly. Its tail swished back and forth, a sign of contentment.

"You're really here for me?" Still in disbelief. Nthanda had no words. "Ok. You're hungry. Me too. Let's head back and we can both eat."

Sounds good. Lead the way.

Nthanda turned back to the path. The cub beside her.

"Hey are you a girl or boy? Do you have a name? My name is Nthanda."

*I am female and I am called Kai. I will call you Bright Star. *

Chapter 3

Nthanda was so tired but she couldn't contain the excitement that overcame her. She did it. She completed her Ritual of Binding and now had a magical companion. The looks on Jia'ka and the High Priestess face when she made it back to the circle was everything a girl could ask for. Pride for her and her accomplishments.

The girl rolled over in the large bed. The furs, warm against her skin, warded off the cold in her room. Sunlight glared through the one window in her chambers, causing her to wince once she opened her eyes. Glad to have a free day. Free to do whatever she wanted now she was a bonded witch. Jia'ka told her to spend as much time as needed, bonding with the little cub because it would strengthen their ties, and her spells when she used them. Nthanda didn't have a problem with that. She wanted to learn more about her companion.

Nthanda stretched and sat up. Her hair was all over her head like an overgrown bush. Trying to tame her wavy curls as they did their own thing was pointless to her. The curls had a mind of its own. She turned her head towards the furball as she lounged on her bed snoring.

Bright Star. I'm hungry. I need to go hunt, the ball of fur said to her as she stretched its four legs.

Not surprised the cub was awake. "You're hungry again? We just had food before we went to sleep."

That was a long time ago. Besides, I'm a growing cub. I need all the food. Show me where to go and I'll figure out the rest.

"No. I will go with you. Maybe Ekon can take us. I wouldn't mind being able to ride the horse again," Nthanda told the creature. Remembering her ride the night before, she hoped her mother would allow for lessons. Riding was the most fun she had had in a long time. The last lunam had taken up most of her time with studies. She was already at the skill level with her magical abilities of someone way older than her. Someone who had finished their basic studies and was fully inducted into a coven. She wouldn't be able to join her family's coven yet. Not until her majority, and that was eight lunams away.

The girl hopped out of her bed, feet touched the cold stone floor. She had forgotten to heat the pipes when she came to her room. She kneeled down to the floor. Getting someone to do it manually would take too long. She placed both hands, palm down to the floor where the pipes were, and spoke the words for fire. Her hands glowed an orange red then back to its normal deep brown shade. The effect was instant. The floor already began to warm up.

Nthanda knew her faithful guard would be outside her door, standing like a statue as always. She sprinted to the thick door and opened it. Peeking outside, she noticed two guards but no Ekon. Her brows furrowed and her eyes darted between the two men. She pouted. The shorter guard of the two spotted her and stood straighter. The taller one slowly pivoted her way and bowed his head.

"Where's Ekon?" she asked. "I thought he would be on duty today."

"He is on duty today. The High Priestess summoned him not too long ago. We're here until he returns. Anything we can help you with, witchling?"

Nthanda huffed. She wanted to try the horseback riding again. Shaking her head, Nthanda retreated back into her room, closing the door behind her.

Kai lounged on her back. Her paws in the air, mouth opened with teeth and fangs bared. *I'm still hungry. We should go hunt. I can hear your stomach from here. You are hungry too.*

"I can hear it just fine. It's my stomach. We can't just go outside. Well, I can't. I have to have my guard with me at all times. Since he's with the High Priestess, we will have to improvise. Rules and all. But we can go to the kitchen."

What's a kitchen?

"A place where people like us get our food. Others hunt and bring it there. The kitchen staff prepare and cook the food for us to eat. I'll change and we can go explore the keep. You have to learn your way around."

HIGH PRIESTESS CHANDA stood at the head of the Blackwood table. To her right, sat Jia'ka, and her Council. To her left, high ranking coven members filled the remaining seats. She used to trust the council without reservation but for the last few months; she had reasons to change her feelings about them. Something was different about a few of the members and she couldn't figure out exactly what bothered her so much.

Frustrated, she was ready to end the meeting. Having been there since midday, she tired of their problems. Tired of hearing about their non-actions, not fixing any problems. She wanted alone time to collect her thoughts and to celebrate. Chanda's mind drifted but the arguments between two of her council, which hit peak levels moments before, kept bringing her back.

Done and couldn't suffer through the petty of everyone anymore she sat up straight in her chair. She cleared her throat getting the attention of everyone. Lord Winzi and Lady Savia had gotten to where they stood face to face. If Chanda didn't stop the two, they would destroy her space. Both were strong in the dark arts and their chosen craft. Chanda raised her right hand and a purplish light flowed from it. The wispy tendrils entwined and wrapped itself around both people, freezing them. Their eyes bulged out of their sockets and Lord Winzi turned blue in the face.

"I have more important things to discuss. Sitting here listening to you two bicker is tiring and old. Continue this and I will oust both of you and strip all titles. Am I understood?" The High Priestess loosened the bind she had on both Lady Savia and Lord Winzi. The color to Lord Winzi's face quickly returned. Together they nodded. Sitting down, Lord Winzi flashed Chanda a look that could kill before turning away. She didn't let it slip that she saw. He was a snake that she never trusted. Soon she would have to clear out the infestation.

"Nthanda went through the Ritual of Binding and the Mother Goddess saw fit to bless her with a companion. A strong guide for a strong, young witch. In honor of her recent accomplishments we will throw a gala. Spread the word. We will hold the celebration on the next full moon. Only a weeks' time from now."

Chanda anticipated the Council's objections, but she received congratulations instead. The tightness in her shoulders relaxed. "This meeting is closed. I'll see everyone at the celebration."

Jia'ka waited until everyone left before speaking to the High Priestess. She nodded to Ekon, who had stood guard just inside the room. He understood and left the two women standing alone. Humans were forbidden to be around whenever the dark crafts was being discussed. Anything about the arts were not for the uninitiated person. He didn't mind. He practiced the art of war. That was his magic.

"I am proud, daughter. The child, my Little Star, she is going places."

"Yes, she is."

"We are not in the clear just yet. The bones still point to danger. Are you sure we should have this gala? It would be no better time than at a festival for something to happen. I don't feel right. Doesn't sit well in my belly."

"Quit worrying. Everything will be fine. Ekon will watch her like he has for the longest time."

"I like him, that Ekon, I do. But Chanda, he is only human. What can he do that our males can't do? He can't protect her with his magic because he has none. If he goes up against a strong witch or lock, then what?"

"He could take his knife and slice their throats. He's well versed in the song of battle and I do not see why you're worried now. Why weren't you worried a long time ago when I assigned him?"

"It's obvious how much the human fascinates you." Jia'ka took a good look at her daughter. "He's your lover isn't he? That's why you keep him around?" Jia'ka gasped. "Don't tell me he's the child's father? You won't let anyone know who fathered her. Why?"

"No mama, that is not why I keep him around and he is not her father. She is pure witch. If she was part human, do you think she could even wield the power she does at twelve? Ekon is not her sire. Yes, at one point we were lovers but no longer. We are long past that. He is a good listener and a close ear to me. He keeps me informed on the humans."

"I see." Jia'ka stamped her staff once. "Something is on the wind and I trust no one but our own. The humans I suffer because they're useful. I would kill them all before they turn on us. We are not like those of the sun. We don't mix our blood with theirs and dilute our magic. Our power comes from this land and is ours alone. They look down on us because they don't understand who we are. We are better than them. Better than all of them and that is how it will always remain. You remember that Chanda. Never forget. Because there will be a time when the world will have its reckoning and it will start with us."

Jia'ka words didn't need a response. She left Chanda standing alone in the room. Chanda had a love and hate relationship with her mother. Most days they were okay, but she never forgot that her mother was an elitist. Her mother wasn't the only one. Most children of the Mother Goddess despised humans. Chanda was known for her powers and the coven turned an eye away from her views of mingling with the lesser race and kept her as High Priestess. They couldn't go against her power and win. Not when her mother was behind her too.

The door shut closed, causing the High Priestess to look up. Ekon stalked towards her. Face grim. A somber face like his meant Jia'ka spoke to him. Sighing, she rubbed her face and eyes. Chanda pointed to the closest chair and told him to sit.

"Thank you for coming," she said. "I have pressing concerns about the welfare of my daughter."

"I am always at your service, High Priestess."

"You know when we're alone together to call me by my first name."

Ekon leaned back into his chair. "I do, but there could be prying ears listening to what we're saying."

He was right. Chanda was careless and didn't check to make sure they were in the clear. Quick to rectify that, she raised her right hand and a blueish clear bubble formed in her palm. She whispered to it and blew it away from them. The spelled bubble grew larger and larger until it swallowed the room whole. There was a muted popping sound and then a deafening silence. Chanda turned back to Ekon and gave him a lazy smile. "We're good."

He nodded and visibly relaxed. "You must have a lot going on if you forgot the most basic tenement of our private sessions. What is bothering you?"

The High Priestess pulled out the chair next to Ekon and sat down. Her long tone legs stretched, caused her skirt to move to the side and showed her skin. She caught Ekon staring and pushed those memories away. That was a path traveled long ago, and she didn't want to go down it again.

"If you keep staring Ekon, your eyes will fall out of your head," she chuckled. Ekon cleared his throat and looked away.

"You're wondering why I asked for this meeting."

Ekon shifted in his seat and met her eyes. "I do. We meet every fifth day. It is only the third."

"There's a traitor in my coven."

"Do you know who it is?"

"No. Mother says not to worry but what else am I to do? I hear the whispers when they think I am not listening. There's unrest with the covens near the borders to the south."

"Always will be a few who grumbles about the hierarchy of things. You are wise and fair. What else could it be?"

"We witches are not inheritably bad or good. I can't say those of the sun are evil or good and find no ill will against those who have not done me harm. There is unrest in the lands beyond our borders. Their lands and the covens who live closer to the borders knows more about what is going on out there. They say we should take our soldiers and send them out to conquer those lands. Because I don't, they claim I'm weak and unworthy to rule them."

"Fools. All of them." Ekon crossed his arms over his chest. "You're the best thing to happen to these lands."

Chanda smiled at his words. Made her feel good to know somebody thought she was doing okay. "Thank you. Our armies are not all humans. You're a soldier. You know this. Witches fills those ranks and we Children of the Moon are stronger in our own lands. These lands amplify our magic because the lands are blessed by the Mother Goddess. If we leave to go conquer the other lands, we're strong but no extra blessings to help us. The same goes for those of the sun. We stay where we belong. The last war between us was dark times. We can't go back to those days. Those covens who are going rogue refuse to see and acknowledge this."

"Why are you telling me this? I shouldn't know this. It's dangerous and a death sentence to know a dark one's weakness. If I am caught, my captor can extract this knowledge from inside my head with magic. I've seen you do it to others."

Ekon didn't like what he was seeing in front of him. It disturbed him on too many levels. The priestess was acting unusual and for as long as he had been in her service, he'd never seen her afraid. Fearful. And there she was, showing all the emotions uncharacteristic to her. He didn't know what had happened but something had gotten to her and put the fear of the void in her.

"Listen to me my friend and listen carefully. Don't let my little Nthanda out of your sights. Ekon, promise me you'll watch over her. I trust my coven less every single day."

"You know I will do whatever it takes to watch and protect her. She is like one of my own daughters."

Chanda reached for his hands and squeezed them. "Thank you. That's all I ask. You're not like us but you have a strength that most humans in these lands don't have. You are different and I respect that."

Ekon didn't know what to say. His lips pressed into a firm line and he nodded. He squeezed her hands back. They sat together like that and let the silence breathe between them. It was comfortable for both. They always had that peace whenever they were in each other's presence.

Chanda eyes pierced his, and she smiled. The sadness and weariness in the way she carried herself, she tried to hide. He wished he could make everything all right but there was only so much he could do. Chanda touched his face gently and brushed her thumb across his jaw. His eyes closed at the intimate moment. No longer lovers, didn't mean he still didn't care for her.

The High Priestess moved closer to Ekon closing the space between them. Her lips brushed softly against his forehead and a breathy sigh escaped his lips.

"*Shaeza memorius lashka ti.*" Chanda whispered over Ekon. It was a spell she had used many times before. She knew he would never remember because she took them away each time their conversations became too dangerous. To keep him safe. She would remember and she cherished every single moment they had.

Ekon's face went lax then he frowned. He shook his head as he tried to clear the fuzziness from his mind. He didn't know what caused it but it happened more than he liked. He watched as Chanda leaned back into her chair as she bit her lower lip and fingered the circular pendant around her neck.

A nervous habit she had that he found amusing. She hated whenever he brought the habit to her attention.

"You're quiet, Chanda."

The High Priestess glanced at him. "You are my comfort, friend. In this treacherous world, you are always my comfort."

Chapter 4

Jia'ka stood next to the balcony at the top of the tower. Needing to get away from the noise and constant motion inside the keep, she found herself outside. The frozen lands lay before her. Where she stood, she could see Glass Lake and further out towards the Black Forest. Being that high up, the cold air still cut through her furs, but she didn't mind. She understood better than most that there was nothing better than the breath of the Mother Goddess to remind you she was always around.

High in the sky Jia'ka's gyrfalcon flew, circling her prey down below. They have been companions for many lunams and watching her familiar hunt always gave her a thrill. The gyrfalcon took a dive at top speeds, spiraling perfectly until she almost hit the ground. At the last second, she swooped, skimming the lake before taking to the skies again. Jia'ka knew without a doubt, she caught her meal. She almost felt sorry for the creature caught in the beaks of her friend. It was the way of life. Everything lives and die in a vicious cycle.

Being out there long enough for her bird to eat, ready to go back in, Jia'ka called out to the creature. The white and black plumaged bird flew to her and landed on Jia'ka's outstretched arms. Beaks red from her fresh kill, she screeched before settling down. Jia'ka rubbed the feathers on her back.

"Such a wonderful girl," she said to the bird of prey. Leaving the balcony, Jia'ka went back inside and followed the steps down to the next level. Soon as stepped into the hall a ball of fur ran into her legs. She looked down to find her granddaughter's familiar. Soon after, Nthanda skidded to a halt in front of her.

"I am sorry Mama Jia'ka. I didn't mean to disturb you," Nthanda said out of breath. She grabbed her snow leopard, now much bigger than when she first appeared, and backed away. "I tried to get her to stop but she wouldn't. She loves running through the halls." Nthanda sounded exasperated with her creature and eyed the young cub. No doubt chastising her through their special bond.

"It's fine, Little Star. I love seeing you with your familiar. In fact, I was just on my way to come find you. I have a gift to give you."

Nthanda's eyebrows rose, unsure if it was a trick or real. Jia'ka chuckled. She never gave a gift to anyone, including her Little Star. This time, the overwhelming idea came across her and was compelled to find the right gift.

"No trick. Follow me. Your mother should be there too. It was her decision just as much as mine. A gift from both of us, with the help from the rest of the coven."

Jia'ka went left and followed the corridor until an opening appeared. Near the entrance into the Grand Hall, stood two soldiers. Both with shaved heads and claw like scars under their eyes. Marking them as the elite, *Sons of Mynhit*. Followers of Mynhit. She who massacres. Behind them, an archway made of black basalt and obsidian stood. Glowing Nyxian script marked the archway all over. Pulsed like a living, breathing thing.

Nthanda rarely had the chance to go into the Grand Hall where the High Priestess sat. The look of awe on her face showed her lack of visits. The girl was wide eyed and slack jawed.

The hall was empty except for the High Priestess and her trusted advisors. They were in the middle of conversation when the High Priestess caught sight of Jia'ka and Nthanda as they walked in. Jia'ka clicked her tongue, and her gyrfalcon flew to the rafters. Nthanda had already set her cub down and Kai followed close to her side.

"Mama. Nthanda. Come. What brought you to the Grand Hall today?" The High Priestess sat straighter in her chair. The council members said their goodbyes and departed, leaving Jia'ka and Nthanda alone with the Priestess. Nthanda ran to her mother and gave her a hug.

"I ran into Mama Jia'ka and she said she had a gift for me." Nthanda turned and faced her grandmother, still eyeing her warily. She shrugged her shoulders and turned back to the priestess. "She said you both had a present for me. Tell Me!" Excited, Nthanda shifted on her feet.

You should be more patient, Bright Star. They will reveal it in due time, Kai told her. She sat next to the priestess chair on her haunches, licking the fur on her belly. Nthanda shook her head and huffed out loud.

"I take that you are getting along with your familiar?" Chanda asked, noticing the two having a bonded conversation. She reached over and pulled Nthanda closer to her.

Placing her face into her daughter's wavy hair and inhaled the black orchid scent that wafted off it. The smell brought her comfort in an otherwise crazy world. Holding a piece of herself in her daughter was the best thing in her life ever.

"Yes. She has a lot to fuss about. And she's always hungry. Why do she eats so much?"

I'm right here. I can hear you, Kai grumbled. She flicked her tail in annoyance. *I'm a growing feline. I need all the meats I can eat.* She turned her head away from Nthanda and curled up into a ball.

"Well, cats of her nature grow to be enormous. They need a lot of food to grow so they can be strong and sturdy. Especially if she will be there to protect and guide you. Child, you eat a lot of food too. You study hard, which is a way to feed your mind. Growing strong so you can protect yourself and your bonded animal with your knowledge. It is one and all the same. Do you understand, little one?"

Nthanda had a faraway look in her eyes, but Chanda knew she listened.

The child nodded. "I understand." Nthanda got quiet. She glanced to Jia'ka and saw her observing them with an amused grin on her face.

"Why do you stare at us like that, Mama Jia'ka?" Nthanda asked. She cocked her head to the left.

"I'm just looking at my beautiful family. My daughter and her daughter. The mother. The young maiden. And I, the old crone. We are all here. Everything in life is a cycle." Jia'ka took a step closer to the duo. Her bone staff clicking each time it touched the ground. "Everything in life has a time to live. And a time to die."

She took another step closer and went still. Jia'ka's milky eyes closed, and she swayed to the left and right, to a tune that only she could hear. Without opening her eyes, she spoke. "You, Little Star. A long time will come before you dine with Lord Athos but a difficult journey surrounds you. Just as you are the shining star in the night sky. You are the fire that burns bright in the day. Just as the cold winter ice fills your veins, the warm soil of the earth makes you whole. Mother Goddess watches over you." Jia'ka slumped over, keeping a firm grip on her bone staff. Her gyrfalcon screeched and circled ahead.

Nthanda looked at her warily. Scared and confused. Chanda stood up, and the young girl moved to the side. The High Priestess went to Jia'ka recognizing her mother's condition. The screeching became louder as the bird of prey circled closer over their heads.

"Nthanda, pay heed. We have been blessed with a vision from a seer. One from a powerful seer blessed by the dream messenger herself. Dreva, our Goddess of Dreams visited this one and gave a message to you. Remember what was said child. Perhaps one day it will make sense, as the message was for your ears only. Not ours." Chanda touched the center of Jia'ka's forehead with her palm and held it there.

"The message was well received, Seer. Come back to us now. We no longer need you here." A pulse of power radiated from the palm of the priestess into Jia'ka.

Slowly, Jia'ka came around. Limp and weak, she crumbled into herself. Chanda held her mother and eased her to the ground. Chills racked Jia'ka's body. *The vision must have been harder than most,* Chanda thought. Beads of sweat formed on her mother's brow and rolled down the side of her face. She was still in the throes of her vision.

The words spoken out loud was delivered to the person it was meant for but the rest; her mother would swallow into herself and not tell a soul. Chanda understood how those things worked. It would take a few moments before her mother came to. The High Priestess glanced up to see Nthanda and her familiar standing over them.

"Will she be okay?" the girl asked. Chanda nodded.

"Is this your first time seeing her wrapped in a vision?"

"Yes. I knew she had them but I've never seen one before. You sure she's okay? What can I do to help?"

The High Priestess smiled. The girl was fond of the old woman. "I am sure. Go! Bring me a cloth from behind the chair on the altar." Without hesitation, the girl took off. "Oh mama, I wonder what it was you saw. Come back so we can talk about what you told our Little Star," she whispered to the old woman.

Nthanda returned with the cloth in her hand. The High Priestess took it and wiped the sweat from her mother's face. The falcon above them calmed down. She stopped her screeching and landed beside Jia'ka.

"She will wake soon. The falcon has calmed down. Their connection is strong. When she is distressed, the bird can feel her symptoms," Chanda told her daughter. "Look. She's coming to." Her chin pointed to Jia'ka's eyes moving under her eyelids.

"Will my bond become as strong as theirs?" Nthanda asked. Curious about the relationships with familiars and wanted a better understanding of the bonding. She didn't know what to expect and Kai wasn't all that forthcoming. Nthanda believed Kai didn't know either and was too afraid to say so.

Chanda continued to wipe her mother's face. "Yes, because you are already a strong witchling. I can only imagine what your gift would be like once you hit your majority in eight lunams. I imagine, you'll be even stronger than me. Stronger than her."

Nthanda couldn't imagine being that strong. The two older women combined were the most powerful in their history. Known throughout their world and beyond. At least that is what the other witches told her. She wanted to believe because they were her family. The most important people in her life.

Jia'ka's milky eyes opened and a long breath escaped her lips. A small smile tugged at the corners of her lips. She looked to the woman holding her then to the child standing above her. The strong family of hers. A brief flash of the vision came back to her, and she stiffened. It was horrible. The worst she had ever seen, and would hunt her for a long while. She couldn't speak out loud without fear of repercussions from the Mother Goddess and her daughter, Dreva. Her patron goddess. Everything must unfold on its own. No matter how much she wanted to intervene, she couldn't.

"Little Star. I said that we had a present for you. No better time than now." Jia'ka sat up. She patted the High Priestess arms. "I thank both of you for your help. I haven't had a vision like that in a very long time." She gripped her staff and helped herself up.

Jia'ka reached inside the pouch she wore on her side and pulled out a shiny item. The glimmer caught the girl's eye, and Nthanda followed it. The old woman let the shimmering silver chain slip from her hand. Nthanda's eyes followed the motion and gasped. At the end of the chain was a pendant. In the shape of a crescent moon with opal and moonstone jeweled stars around it. Inside the crescent moon was pure amethysts, the same color as her eyes. The workmanship was beautiful and took Nthanda longer than she expected to understand that the necklace matched the marking on her chest.

Nthanda eyes watered. She reached for the necklace and stopped. She glanced to her mother and her grandmother's face before grabbing it from their hands. She held it close to her and examined the jeweled necklace. It was the most precious and beautiful piece of jewelry in her possession. Nthanda quickly put it around her neck and watched as it fell low to her chest.

"It's beautiful, Mama Jia'ka. Mama. I don't know what to say but thank you so much. Thank you from my heart. I love it. I really do." She couldn't stop touching the necklace. A large smile found a home on her face. Kai padded over to where they were and examined the gift.

It's beautiful Bright Star. I like it. There's power imbued with that. A good gift. I approve.

"She likes it too." Nthanda said to her elders. "She says there is power in it."

Chanda's brow rose. Her lips tugged into a smirk. "Your familiar is clever and smart. Yes, there's power in it. A protection spell from both your grandmother and I. Double spelled. Never take it off Nthanda. Promise me you'll never take it off."

Nthanda was confused on why her mother would ask her that but she agreed to never take it off. She picked the pendant up to examine again.

"It will guide you like the night star in our sky. I also spelled it that no one else can see it. Only us. And you. Your familiar is part of you, which is why she's able to. Happy birthday Little Star. I hope you love it." Jia'ka said.

"Yes, Happy birthday my little witchling," Chanda said.

"I will always remember to never take it off. Thank you so, so much. I will forever cherish this gift."

"Go now. Find Serea and get ready. Your Gala starts tonight. You must dress the part. You are my shadow after all," Chanda said.

SOON AS THE CHILD LEFT the room, Chanda glanced to her mother. "What was that all about mama? Are you okay?"

"No. I am not okay. I don't know what is about to happen but it will and I cannot stop what will go down. It's forbidden. The gods are at play and we are nothing but pawns."

"Why us?"

"I've taught you better to question the will of the gods. Pray you don't become in their way. Our gods can be harsh and unforgiving gods."

"I know."

Jia'ka turned her milky eyes towards her daughter. "The preparations are done. The courtyard and feasting hall are ready. Everyone will diverge onto this citadel and we will celebrate the child's birthday and celebrate her bonding. They are a good match are they not?"

"Yes, they are. The feline was a good choice for her. I am proud of our Nthanda."

Chapter 5

Inside the feasting hall, the people were loud and rambunctious. Filled with the privileged few revelers and her own coven, those who had come to celebrate Nthanda's birthday and bonding ceremony. Near the front of the hall, overlooking everyone, was a long table filled with Nthanda's favorite dishes and desserts. High Priestess Chanda sat in the center with Jia'ka on her left and Nthanda on her right. A place of honor being by her side. The retracted ceiling was open and nothing but the midnight sky, its diamond, glistening stars and the full moon shone down on the people. Perfect for the camaraderie. Outside the halls, in the courtyards, more partying took place and the laughter and pure joy reached Chanda's ears.

It wasn't too often the people was able to let go of everything and relax. Servants rushed between the tables, constantly refilling empty cups. When dishes of certain foods disappeared, they brought more to replace the newly empty ones. Chanda peeked over her shoulders to find Nthanda talking with her friend, Serea. They were all smiles and full of laughter. She approved their friendship. Serea was the daughter of her best friend growing up. Sadly, Serea's mother died in childbirth with her and she was left alone. Now living with her maternal grandmother, she gave them permanent quarters in the citadel. That was the way of the Enyxsians. Take care of the women and children. The men had no rights to the child unless the mother gave it to them.

Jia'ka leaned towards Chanda and whispered, "All goes well. The moon is still high. What else is on the agenda?"

"After the meal, I'll present her to the rest of the witches."

"Are you sure that is wise? She is still young."

"She is ready. She needs to be seen. She is their future. We are their current and past. I think it's time for Nthanda to step up and learn how things work around here. She can handle it, don't you think?"

"Of course she can, daughter."

"Then she will be presented. Her studies will resume in two days along with her martial training. I'll figure out a time where she can sit in on certain meetings."

"As you command, priestess."

Jia'ka sat back in her chair and cast her milky gaze across the hall. People thought she was blind, but she was far from that. She could see. Not in the way a normal person was able to, but she saw what was around her. The colors. The shapes. Everything was brighter with her sight. It was all thanks to the Mother Goddess. When her eyesight failed, she didn't expect the blessing of sight in another form.

EKON STOOD IN THE BACK behind the table close to the young witchling. The remaining food had been removed, and the tables was pushed close to the walls. The coven gyrated and danced seductively against each other to the musician's haunting and beautiful melodies. The flames from the torches lining the wall had dimmed to a flicker. A fraction of what they once were earlier in the evening. Moving shadows followed the direction of its owners and twisted into shapes that resembled monsters and creatures from lore. Everything and everyone moved as if enchanted and relished in the debauchery. Drunk off sharing power and drink, the celebration was in progress to take a turn for the darker.

He looked briefly at the young witchling. She was wide eyed and no signs of tiredness showed. She watched everything and everyone like her grandmother's familiar bird of prey. The little girl, Serea was already asleep at the table. Passed out a while back, not able to stay awake. Jia'ka and the High Priestess were deep in conversation with a council member, but still aware of everything going on around them. Ekon stepped to his young charge and bent down to her ear.

"Are you ready to leave, witchling?" He was used to being around those with magic but tonight was different. He was uncomfortable and ready to depart. The parties always became rowdy and the current one did not differ from others. It was no place for a mere human as himself and definitely no place for a child. The girl shook her head and told him to stand watch. Orders received, he stepped back to his former spot on the wall.

The night, no longer young, drifted as the moon moved across the dark sky. The crowd feasted but no longer on food. Everything was taking on a more carnal nature, and it was no place for a girl of only twelve winters. Chanda stood. A pregnant silence fell over the crowd and they watched their priestess with partially opened eyelids. "Nthanda is retiring. Let the festivities continue!"

Nthanda eyes lingered on Ekon as he woke up Serea. The girl always been hard to wake, it amused her at how hard of a time he was having. Ekon was tired of trying and lifted the young child and placed her over his shoulders. From the corner of her eyes, her mother said something to Jia'ka then turned towards her way.

"I will walk you to your rooms tonight. I'll return to the celebration later," she said. Nthanda was happy. It was rare that her mama took the time to spend with her like she was lately. Enthusiastically she nodded and placed her small hands in her mother's larger hands.

Jia'ka watched the small group retire from the feasting hall. Ever since her vision earlier, she was constantly on edge. It had something to do with what she saw and it was unclear, even to her. She didn't understand why it was so unclear this time when every other vision she's ever had was vivid and sharp. Jia'ka reached for her cup of *Toka,* the special drink they had on festival nights. She drank heavily from the cup and poured more once it was empty. She drank deeply from that too hoping it would drown out everything.

"DO WE TAKE SEREA TO her room or let her stay with the little witchling?" Ekon asked. Chanda glanced down at Nthanda. The girl was rubbing her eyes.

"She can stay with Nthanda tonight. Her grandmother is still in the hall. I will tell her."

Ekon nodded and turned the corner. Chanda and Nthanda was right behind him when a warm gust of wind swept in and pitched the hall into darkness. Unnatural and witch born. Ekon was on instant alert. There were no windows in the hall deep inside the keep. He had stopped to let his eyes adjust to the pitch black. Night blind he couldn't see anything. He didn't dare sit the child down. Fearing what was in the hall with them.

"Stay where you are, Ekon? We are not alone," Chanda said. Nthanda squeezed her arm and moved closer to her side. Chanda tried to comfort Nthanda as much as she could but even she didn't feel safe any longer. She rubbed her daughter's arms and reassured her that everything would be fine. She didn't want to let on that something was terribly wrong.

Chanda didn't like the situation they found themselves in. She reached inside and tried to relight the fires but her power didn't respond. Fear tried to rear its ugly head, and she pushed the unease away. She could see in the dark but there was nothing in the hall but them. She moved closer to Ekon. He jumped when her hand brushed against his back.

"It's only me, Ekon."

"High Priestess-"

"I can't see in this darkness but we are not alone. A heavy magical presence is here, and it is searching for someone. We shouldn't stay here. We must leave before it find and follows us."

"Mama, we should go back to the hall." Nthanda said. Afraid, she picked up her familiar and held the animal close to her chest. Before Chanda could even respond, loud and unearthly screams filled the halls. Flashes of light bounced off of the walls then dissipated.

Fighting had started from where they had just came from. Everything in her screamed to run. Chanda knew the guard would remember every exit and hidden passageway in the keep. "We can't go back that way anymore, Little Star. We have to get to safety. Ekon we need to reach the sanctuary. It is the only safe space. Which way is the quickest?"

"Grab on to the back of my tunic and follow me."

Both Chanda and Nthanda grabbed a piece of his tunic and held on tightly. "We're ready," the priestess said.

"This way," Ekon said with urgency.

He couldn't see but he remembered where they were before the lights went out. He reached out his hand to the wall and left it there for support and guide as he walked forward. The next turn wasn't far from where they stood and he led them there and moved into the passageway. It was an offshoot corridor veering off the main branches of the mazelike halls in the mountainside keep. He and the rest of the guards were the only ones who used it.

A quarter way in, the air became cooler and less oppressive. The braziers that stood in the corner recesses came to life as they passed each one. Away from imminent danger, Chanda took a deep breath and exhaled through her nose. Relief flooded her body. The passageways began to look familiar and after a few more turns; they reached the corridor that led to the safety of the High Priestess sanctuary.

"Thank you so much Ekon." Chanda reached out and hugged the guard. The moment she let go, a blast of heated air rushed through the hall like a raging storm and exploded.

Ekon and Serea was separated by the force and hit the wall to the left. Nthanda kept hold of Kai and was blown in the opposite direction from her mother. She hit the stone wall hard causing her head to bounce off it, and Kai flew from her arms. A high-pitched scream tore from her mouth. Loose stone and rocks fell down on her and the cub.

A piercing ringing filled Chanda's ears as she opened her eyes to dust and rubble clogging the hall. Her fingers trembled as she touched her scalp and her choppy breath caught when she realized they were covered in blood. Slowly, she got to her feet and turned, searching for Nthanda. Finding her, she moved in that direction when a streak of light flung her to the wall opposite of her. Without time to block it, she hit the wall again. Pain shot up her back, and warm blood flowed down her backside. Her eyes searched frantically, as she tried to find where the power came from.

Down the hall stood three witches she recognized from the border covens. Behind them, Lord Winzi and Lady Savia stepped forward. A moment of clarity dawned on her, realizing that Savia and Winzi weren't really fighting in their meeting. It was all a show, and they were working together. The savage smile on Lady Savia's face was terrifying when Chanda had figured it all out. She was a strong witch. A creative one with her execution methods but Chanda wasn't afraid of her. The High Priestess stood up and stepped away from the wall on shaky legs. Crumbled stone fell from her hair and clothes as she ambled toward the other witches. Waves of dizziness swept over her but she swallowed and kept moving.

"If you were smart, High Priestess, you would stop. Then listen to what we have come to say to you," Savia told her. She stood tall in the dark. Covered in a black cloak but her red hair gave her away. Savia looked down at her hands and picked at her fingernails, gloating at the fact that she could knock the priestess down to her knees.

"You are a disgrace to us, Chanda. You want peace with the humans when they are beneath us. They serve us! They are not to bed or love." Chanda eyes narrowed at Savia. The woman continued, "We know about your indiscretions with that *hoshta* scum. No one cares about that whelp you call a daughter. You don't even know who her father is because you are a whore. I bet she's half human since you whored yourself to their inferior males and love them so much."

Chanda bristled at the accusations. "My child's father is no concern to you or anyone else for that matter! He is much better at the craft than you could ever dream of."

The High Priestess hands and arms rose to her chest level. Her fingers moved in twisted forms, as she touched the Evernight and gathered its energies. She stalked toward the rogue witches and with each step she took the air became thicker. Her eyes rolled back in her head and charged words from the Evernight rolled off of her tongue.

Lady Savia and Lord Winzi watched as the three witches who came with them began to twitch and move unnaturally. A wave of unease washed over their group.

"You have challenged the wrong witch, Savia." Chanda's voice echoed and power rang behind every syllable she spoke.

Nthanda scampered to her feet, searching for her familiar. Finding her, under broken rock, she fell to her knees and removed the rubble. Praying she was still alive and breathing the whole time. Her mother's voice rose, and she felt the power rise with it. She glanced over her shoulders and the eerily white glow of her mother's hands caught her attention. It was as the light of the full moon manifested around them.

Chanda harnessed the power flowing around her and flung it to the rogue witches standing near Lord Winzi and Lady Savia. They couldn't counteract in time. The power wrapped around them like a cocoon. Their screams echoed as the magic squeezed the life from their bodies. Their screams cut off then dropped to the ground with a hollow thud. What remained was three hollowed out corpses that looked like they have been dead for years and not only seconds.

Chanda kept her pace and focused her attention on her two council members. She foresaw betrayal but not in the form she was seeing. Savia didn't bother to hide the smile on her face. Lord Winzi was the opposite. His eyes darted back and forth at the dead witches, and his hands shook at his side.

Before they could react, the High Priestess cast a silent spell, immobilizing Lady Savia while simultaneously she wrapped her fingers around Lord Winzi's neck. The councilman tried to move, but the spelled grip on his throat was too strong. Lost inside of her power, the whimpers from the man didn't bother her but gave her immense pleasure. Winzi was always weak minded and her actions was long overdue. All she wanted was the deaths of the two before her. The ones who dared to threaten her and her daughter.

"Any last words, Winzi?" she cooed. His eyes bulged from their sockets as she slowly squeezed his neck like it was a piece of fruit. He tried to reach for his power but Chanda had blocked his ability to touch it. He opened his mouth to speak but he couldn't form any words. The pain from her grip was agonizing and the rest of his body was going numb. He opened his mouth to scream and when he did, she clamped her mouth over his and sucked the air he breathed out.

She searched for the dark spot hidden deep inside his essence and destroyed the cage that protected it. His soul was as dark and foul as she expected. Bitter and rotten, she pushed the thought of his diseased soul away and inhaled it into herself.

Winzi's eyes turned red. Fear filled his mind, but he came to his senses and resigned to the fact that it was over. His body went lax as Chanda pulled the remaining bits of himself into her. She took his power into herself and replenished her own power with his death. No longer worried about him, she dropped him unceremoniously to the cold ground. She wiped her mouth with the back of her hand and fixated her gaze on Savia.

Savia didn't realize that the High Priestess was a soul eater. They were rare and extremely dangerous. When they briefed her on what she was to do, Savia's superiors casually forgotten to mention that part. Now she was in the grip of one of the most dangerous witches in Enyxias and couldn't even protect herself. When a soul eater wanted your soul, they could take it anytime they wanted. There was no protection or guards against one. They were the hounds of Athos, Lord of Death. Savia quickly came to the understanding that her coven leaders used her and her now dead partner as pawns. She wasn't ready to die; she wanted to live.

Stuttering, Savia tried to get her words out. "I-I- I can tell you whatever you may want to know my priestess. Just don't kill me. I can help you. I can tell you who sent us." She would do anything to save herself. If a soul eater took her soul, it was forfeit. She was no more. She didn't want the final end.

"And what can you tell me that I can't get from your soul and blood?" Cruel laughter escaped Chanda's lips. "You bargain for your life. You are not ready to meet your final death are you, woman?"

Savia violently shook her head. "I can give you whatever information you need High Priestess. I'm sorry. They promised things that is impossible. I see the error of my ways. I promise. Let me go and I will give you all the knowledge I know." Savia wasn't beyond her dignity to beg for something. Especially when her life hung in the balance. Chanda's grin sent chills down Savia's spine.

"Speak witch or die speechless." Chanda's voice brooked no argument.

"We- we were recruited by Winzi's birth coven. He's from the borderlands. His family promised him status and riches once we got you away from here. We weren't going to harm you. Well, I wasn't. I was hesitant about the plan the whole time. I really didn't trust his sister. She's the head of his coven. They sent him here as a spy. To learn the workings of your coven. The keep. Anything that could help them become stronger."

"What else. There's more. How many are there? Why tonight?"

"Their coven is forty strong. Good, strong witches. Some could probably rival you and your mother if they put their heads together. They have help with human soldiers and some can call the daemons of the Evernight."

"Why tonight, Savia?"

"Because you are distracted by that whelp of a child. She's not as strong as you all claim to be. We know it."

Without thinking, the High Priestess lifted Lady Savia up with her power and flung her against the wall. Savia's head snapped back off the wall and she slumped to the ground. The immobilization spell was still in place and she couldn't lift her head or move her body. Incoherent mumbled words flowed out of her mouth. The pain and hurt she felt was greater than she ever felt before. No one had to tell her she had multiple bones broken. She could feel the warm blood as it flowed down the back of her head from the impact.

The High Priestess strolled her way, bent down and lifted Lady Savia's chin with the tip of her finger.

"I think I am done with you. You have caused enough damage tonight woman. Tonight here, you die like the others."

"You promised that I would live. You have to honor your word."

"I promised nothing to you!" Chanda shouted. "Be lucky you die with your soul." Before finishing her last word, the High Priestess reached to her side and pulled out her bone dagger and sliced it across Lady Savia's neck. A spray of warm blood splashed across her face when she cut the woman's throat. She let go of Lady Savia's lifeless body and wiped her dagger on Savia's clothes before placing it back in its sheath. The High Priestess stood and glanced down the hall to where Nthanda stood with her familiar in her arms. Her eyes moved, searching for the guard and saw him getting up from the ground.

Chanda rushed to them, grabbing Nthanda's hand and reached for Serea who was now awake and shivering.

"We must get you two to safety. Get up Ekon. Let's go." The High Priestess stepped over broken stone. She sped down the hall with the two girls next to her and Ekon behind trying to catch up. It didn't take them long to pass the barriers of her sanctuary. She whispered to the wards, and it opened just enough for them to go through.

They entered a large chamber. A fireplace the size of the wall was lit with a roaring fire already. She let the girls go. Ekon walked in and stood at attention.

"What do we do now, High Priestess? What of the others?" He asked weary and tired.

"I will go check on the others. You stay here and protect my child. They said they were after me but I know they were lying. They are after her. I will do whatever I need to do to protect her. I have to protect my coven and more so, I need to find my mama. Promise me Ekon that you will protect Nthanda with your life if need be."

"I promise, Chanda. With all of my being. Now go. Help the others. We will stay here until you return."

Chanda went to her daughter and bent down. Her face was covered in Lady Savia's blood but it didn't matter. Her people dealt with blood all the time. Nthanda was not afraid of it. Blood was life and death. She looked into her daughter's amethyst gaze and watched the tears fall from the corners of her eyes. Chanda reached up and brushed them away, kissed her daughter's forehead, and smiled. She spread her arms wide and pulled Nthanda close, hugging her tight.

Nthanda didn't know why but the tears wouldn't stop flowing. Uncontrollable sobs escaped her. Something was wrong. Something was dreadfully wrong, and her mother was going into the danger. She didn't want to let her mama go. Nthanda wanted to keep her there in the sanctuary safe from everything. She loved her Mama Jia'ka, but she was strong and able to handle herself. But she rarely had any time with her mother and she didn't want her to go.

"Stay, Mama. Don't leave us. It's not safe out there. They will hurt you. Please mama, please stay."

"Child, I will be fine. I must check on my people. What kind of leader would I be if I didn't check on them? Not one fit to lead if I left them to their own devices. It is my duty to be out there with them."

"Don't leave me, Mama. Please stay!"

"Nthanda, look at me," Chanda demanded. Nthanda looked up. Her purple eyes were glazed from the tears. "Calm yourself! I am protecting you by leaving you here with Ekon. This is the safest place in the keep. You know this. Our people is out there dying and I must attend them. You will be okay. I am always with you. Remember that. I will always be here with you," Chanda said. She touched Nthanda's chest with her hand. "I am always here in your heart." She then placed her hand over Nthanda's head. "I am always here in your mind." She hugged the child closer. "I am always with you, daughter. You are part of me and I am part of you. We will always be bound. Do you understand?"

Sobs escaped Nthanda's mouth, but she really understood. "I understand. A great leader protect their own. They exact the revenge against those that do them wrong. You must protect our coven. Find Mama Jia'ka and the others." Nthanda recited. Ingrained into her by her grandmother and mother's teachings.

"I love you with all of my being and heart Nthanda."

"I love you too, Mama."

Chapter 6

The High Priestess stood and ran her hands over her black velvet dress. She had nothing else to say. Nothing that would keep her there. She turned without fanfare and headed back to the door. She reached for the handle and remembered one last thing. She glanced over her shoulders back to Nthanda.

"Never take the necklace off my Little Star. Never. The time will come at one point when you will truly understand and you will seek the answer and truth." Without another word, High Priestess Chanda left them alone in her chambers.

Nthanda refused to cry anymore. She would be strong like her grandmother and mother taught her to be. It was in her blood. It was her birthright. Besides, Serea wouldn't stop crying. She needed to be strong for her friend.

Nthanda looked over her shoulder and saw Kai watching her.

We are not out of danger, Bright Star. Trouble is searching for you. Your mother was right about that. They must not discover me. They would kill me if they did. I will hide if they find us.

"We will stay here and be on the lookout then? I can fight. You don't have to hide. I am not a helpless child. I know more than some of those other witches out there fighting," Nthanda told her familiar. *Let them believe that I'm half human and weak. Let them underestimate me. I will prove them all wrong if they cross me.*

"You will stay here, witchling. I promised the Priestess I would watch over you and Serea. I'll go and check when I think it has died down. It is not safe right now."

"Ekon is right," Serea agreed. She had stopped crying. Her eyes were puffy, but she stood there determined. "We should stay here. Your mother said these chambers are the safest place in the keep. She would know, don't you think? She is our leader and we must obey." She went to Nthanda's side and reached for her hands, placing them in hers.

"We are not blood but we are sisters in every way possible. Stay here. It's not safe outside this sanctuary. I've lost enough in my life. I can't lose you too."

Nthanda also thought of Serea as her sister. She didn't realize she cared so much. She rubbed her hands across her face, clearing her mind. She wanted to be out there but she would also listen.

"Fine, we will stay here until Ekon says it is safe to leave. Or when my mother or Mama Jia'ka return."

THE FEAST HALL WAS in shambles. Broken tables lay splintered and scattered everywhere. Shattered glass and stoneware crumbled under Jia'ka's feet as she moved closer to the door. It was happening. Just like the bones read. Just like her vision she had to swallow. No point in her trying to fight the rogue witches. The coven could handle them. She had to find her daughter and her Little Star. They were the most important thing to her at that moment.

Her people would recover but if they lost the child or her daughter, it would damage their core. She didn't want the headaches and responsibilities of being a leader to an entire group of people anymore. She did it once before. Once Chanda was old enough, she passed the title to her. Now, their lives were threatened by mediocre witches. She would not abide their betrayal.

Jia'ka stepped into the foyer not prepared for what was going on. The battle inside was nothing compared to what was happening in the corridor. Over a hundred witches were fighting for their lives. Screams of the dying filled the hall. The sound of metal swords and knives rang out. The coppery tang of spilled blood and its magic accosted her nose. Bodies hit the ground, and the groans slipped from their tongues. It was chaos and anguish mixed all in one.

She ducked when a dagger whistled passed her face, only mere inches away from taking her eye out. She twisted herself around to find the one who threw the knife. The witch stood only a few feet away with a smirk on her face. Jia'ka recognized the woman and shook her head. The woman showed no fear and Jia'ka grinned at the fool of a woman.

"Lord of the Evernight, Athos I call out to you. Grant me your strength and your ways to dismantle my enemies this night in your honor. Mynhit, She who massacres. Grant me your fire so I can call down and burn my enemies this night in your honor," Jia'ka yelled out.

Praying her god and goddess heard her, she reached for the witch who threw the dagger and released a blast of fire from her hands. The unfortunate witch screamed an unearthly wail when the fire struck her. All too late, she tried to cast a spell to put it out, but it was useless. Not when the fire of a goddess ravaged her body. There was no coming back from the flames and the woman screamed in horror, as her own skin melted off.

Jia'ka left the woman without a second thought as she crumbled into a burned pile of ashes. She weaved her way through the others, helping her people as she took down the enemy. When members of her coven recognized who walked among them, they showed her deference and moved aside, giving her room as they fought beside her. Reaching the intersection of the hall, Jia'ka conjured a large ball of burning witch light and flung it outwards to the renegade witches. The light was so bright, that everyone had to cover their eyes, but it didn't affect Jia'ka. She saw it the way no others could. How their enemies flailed and screamed when the light touched them. Their pain gave her strength. Rejuvenated her own stores.

From within the cries of the dying traitors, a faint noise touched her ears, and it sounded like Chanda. She pivoted on her heels and turned to her left. Her daughter ran towards her from down the hall with two rogue witches close on her heels. Jia'ka recognized them as Pelea and Zanji, relatives of Lord Winzi. Jia'ka knew exactly where they were coming from. Chanda led them away from the sanctuary. Jia'ka moved in Chanda's direction when Zanji pulled a long, curved blade from his hip and threw it at the High Priestess.

Jia'ka yelled to get her attention about the danger behind her but was too late. Chanda halted in her tracks. A small gasp fell from her lips.

Jia'ka couldn't take her eyes off the events that unfolded before. Chanda looked down at the blade protruding from her chest. Blood bubbled on her lips as words tried to form. Deep within Jia'ka, her power roiled like a turbulent storm. Without thinking, she flung out a protection spell to cover her daughter. She prayed to the Mother Goddess and hoped that it wasn't too late. The power inside her kept on building until she couldn't contain it anymore. She unleashed the power as it unfurled and flowed all around her. She didn't care if her own people got hurt, as long as her daughter survived. Pelea and Zanji disappeared from the hall before Jia'ka's magic reach the duo. She would worry about them later. All that mattered to her was Chanda.

She ran to her daughter and lifted Chanda's upper body from the ground. Surprised when the tears fell from her eyes. She placed her head near Chanda's mouth to listen for her breath. She placed two fingers on the side of her neck and checked for a pulse. Finding one, barely there, it was enough to give her a sliver of hope. The blade had to come out or else she would die. She reached behind the High Priestess, said a spell to protect her hand and grabbed hold of the blade's handle and pulled it out. Blood rushed out, covering her hand in a warm, thick liquid. Jia'ka chanted the healing words and placed her hand over the open wound. She could sense the danger her daughter was still in. She fused the cuts in and out with her healing magic but she already sensed the poison in her bloodstream. She needed an antidote, and she didn't know what type of poison Zanji used.

EKON COULD TELL SOMETHING was wrong. His soldier's instincts never let him down. He told the girls to stay put in the other room and he grabbed a short sword from the weapon room. He opened the door, poked his head through before fully stepping outside into the hall. It was dark and too quiet. The fires of the torches was unlit, and that was sign enough they were in danger. He moved further away from the chambers and froze when he heard voices. He tilted his head towards the sound and cautiously trekked down the corridor where the noise came from. He took only a few steps in when something jumped out of the dark and bowled into him. Vicious snaps and snarls filled his ears as he grabbed a handful of fur, trying to remove the beast from his chest. The animal bit into his left shoulder, scraping bone, causing Ekon to cry out. The pain was so intense that he almost blacked out. He tried to force the creature off of him but the beast wouldn't let loose.

Ekon remembered the blade in his right hand and shoved its tip into the side of the animal. The creature cried out and became relentless in its attack on the guard. Ekon felt when chunks of his shoulder ripped away and his bones crunched under the wolf's jaws. He was in agony but he shoved the weapon in further until the beast stilled.

Silence from the animal was a relief but brief. The cry of its witch was horrible and terrifying. He didn't have time to catch his breath; he had to move away from there. He shoved the animal off of him with his good arm and slowly got to his knees. Before he was able to stand, a crazed woman and her painful screams came from the same direction of the dead animal. The woman's short blonde hair, splattered with dust and blood ran directly at him. The braziers lit up as she got closer and realized it was Pelea. He stood and stumbled, moving backwards. She was in the coven with the witches who went rogue. They were too dangerous. He needed to keep the witchlings from them.

Her eyes fixated on him. "You killed my wolf! You will die for this, *hoshta*!"

Ekon straightened himself and got into his fight stance. "You will die trying, witch."

Pelea ran at him with her staff in hand. She twirled it in a fever pitch as her power drew upon the air they were breathing. Ekon chest heaved up and down, steeling himself for the impact. He could only do so much with use of one arm. But if it meant protecting Nthanda and Serea, he would do his best. He promised the High Priestess he would.

Ekon turned his good side to face Pelea right when she swung her staff at him. The impact jarred his whole body. He gritted his teeth as he tried not to bite his tongue. Ekon held his ground and barely moved an inch. Pelea rebounded back like something had knocked her out. The guard looked up and realized he was still in a warded area. Protected as long as he stayed within that area.

The witch woman got back up and came at him again. This time she slid to a stop before him and whip like strands of power unleashed from her and wrapped around his ankles. He looked down then quickly back up when Pelea motioned with her hands, like a puppeteer and pulled the ground from under him. She walked backwards, dragging him out of the safe wards. The maniacal grin on her face was clear the woman had gone mad.

"You. Will. Die," she said in a tone that stilled Ekon's heart. Fear was never really an issue with him. Not around the witches but this turn of events changed his mind. His stomach churned and his good arm trembled. A loud ringing accosted his ears and his eyes narrowed at Pelea. She chanted under her breath. Ekon tried to get up and move but found he could not. He had no control over his limbs and his heart beat out of control in his chest. Sweat beads popped up and ran down his head.

The witch stood over him and straddled his chest. All he could do was watch as she pulled the long, curved blade her coven was known for out of its sheath on her hip. The pupils of her eyes dilated and turned blood red. All of his thoughts went to his daughters back home. He prayed that they would make it out of the witchlands with the caravan he snuck them on before being on duty. He remembered their bright smiles and their infectious laughter. He grinned as Pelea ran the blade across his throat.

A loud scream filled the hall. The blade in Pelea's hand dripped blood to the ground as she glanced up. The child they were searching for stood before her. She glowed like she was in the pale light of the moon. Pelea wiped the blood on the guard's tunic shirt and sheathed her knife. She stood, smiling at the witchling.

"Don't touch the girl," Zanji said from a distance. "She is not to be harmed, Pelea. You know the rules."

"If it wasn't for her, my wolf would still be alive. If it wasn't for her, we wouldn't be risking ourselves, love."

Nthanda didn't know who these two were and didn't care about any wolf. All she saw was a witch who murdered her guard and she would make sure she paid.

"Just grab her and come on. We need to leave before the seer comes after us," Zanji told her.

He turned around and went back into the darkened hall, keeping an eye out for the seer or others of her coven. Pelea gave the child a once over and shrugged her shoulders. "Come on witchling." She reached for Nthanda but she pulled back when Pelea got too close.

"You killed Ekon!" the witchling growled. Nthanda was angry and hurt. Ekon was her friend. She loved him and she hated those who caused her loved one harm.

Pelea reached for the girl once more but this time Nthanda grabbed the witch's wrist. She looked into the woman's eyes and glared. "You are finished here, witch!" Nthanda's said as her hand heated and burned Pelea's skin. They both looked on as the burn moved at an alarming pace. With Nthanda's free hand she thrust it in front of Pelea's face and chanted words from the Evernight. Pelea didn't know what was going on but she could feel the fire inside her and she screamed so loud that her throat was raw.

Zanji came running back to the corridor and saw the witchling burning his love. He shouted to get their attention. But it was too late. Pelea was gone. He pulled his dart blower from his belt and placed the dart inside and shot it at the girl. It hit her on the side of her neck. Her head swiveled to him and was about to say something and stopped. He knew the potion worked when her eyes rolled to the back of her head, letting go of Pelea, she collapsed to the ground. He waited a few minutes before going to her.

The witchling was out, and he hoped the mixture would last until he could get her to the borders. He glanced to his lover, his wife as she lay dead on the ground, eyes staring at nothing. Blackened from the fires of the child. Consumed by rage. She was better off dead than alive. Her familiar was gone, she wouldn't want to live without him.

Zanji reached down and closed her eyelids and replaced the dart blower into its pouch. He pulled the dart from Nthanda's neck and checked that she still had breath. Satisfied, he lifted the girl from the ground and threw her over his shoulders. He needed to get out of the keep before they found him. If they found him with the High Priestess daughter on his shoulders, it would be bad for him and his whole coven.

Glad the girl wasn't too heavy, he shuffled out of the winding and twisted hallways till he came upon the hidden entrance on the side. It led him outside to where his and Pelea's horses were tied up. He placed the girl sideways on Pelea's horse and tied her to it so she wouldn't fall. Seeing that she wasn't dressed for the weather, he threw a blanket over her to keep her warm. As much as he wanted her dead for killing his wife, he had to abide by his coven's rules. He hopped onto his horse and grabbed the lead to the other, clicked his tongue and took off.

Being so dark, he had to be careful on the trail. It was treacherous and slick with ice and snow. Once at the bottom of the mountain, he could open up the pace on the clear terrain. He had to get back to their territories before Mama Jia'ka realized their precious witchling was missing. It would only take a couple of candlemarks to get to the borderlands and from there, his coven leader would take over. They made the dart concoction to last at least four candlemarks, so he was safe from the child's magic.

Checking behind him, assured they were not followed, Zanji spurred the horse, and the mare took off at a faster pace. He had to hurry because he knew that they were working against time.

Chapter 7

Jia'ka heard the wails of pain and of death but none of it concerned her at the moment. The only interest she had was that of her daughter. She needed to find out which poison they used to coat the blade to help Chanda.

"Hold on daughter, we will find you proper help," she whispered to the unconscious priestess. She needed to get her to a healer.

"How can I help?" a deep voice boomed.

Jia'ka glanced up to find Lenzo standing over her. He was a promising male witch strong with the healing arts. Seeing him, she felt relief.

He bent down and whispered, "Mama Jia'ka. How can I help? Tell me what to do to help her. She doesn't have long."

His words jolted Jia'ka senses. "What do you mean, she doesn't have much time?"

"My power lies in the healing arts, you know this is true. I meant nothing spiteful but I can see her aura. The light is getting dimmer as we speak. I can help. We just need to get her to the infirmary where my remedies are."

Without waiting for approval, he whistled to two others, and they came running to them. He pointed to the priestess and told them to take her to the infirmary. He picked up the blade by its handle that Jia'ka pulled from Chanda and peered at the old woman.

"Is this the blade that poisoned her?" Jia'ka nodded. He sniffed it. "Banesroot and Widow's Claw. Combined the concoction is lethal. The ingredients for the antidote is rare and hard to find, but my specialty is potions and antidotes. I have the ingredients in the infirmary. I should be able to heal her in time. Don't fret, Elder."

Lenzo helped Jia'ka up from the ground.

"Thank you Lenzo. We cannot lose her."

"I promise we won't. Will you come and wait or stay here?"

"I need to go find the child. Make sure they're fine. She is who they were after. We were the distraction."

"I understand. Come by the healing room within the next candlemark. I should know how she will fare by then."

Jia'ka nodded. She embraced Lenzo, hugging him tightly before going to find her granddaughter.

ZANJI WAS TIRED AND numb from the cold wind slicing at his face. But he was almost to the borderlands. He couldn't stop because stopping would mean death. Glad that no one was in pursuit, he relaxed a tinge. Not much. The girl scared him. A girl her age shouldn't have been able to kill his Pelea the way she did. And yet there she was still breathing and his Pelea was dead to the world. Visiting the gates to the Evernight.

Zanji kept his gaze forward and was glad when the large ice formations came into view. The ice field was magnificent and dangerous. Known as the landmark to search for when you entered or left the winterlands. He curved to the left to take them near the Night Forest's edge. He was to meet his people in the ruins of Azeyu'k, on the edge of the forest and the ice field.

Everything flew by as he tried to keep his tears at bay. Memories of her flooded his mind, and the deluge took up everything in his head. Before long, they arrived at the meeting spot. He slowed the horses down to a trot then to an eventual stop. He got down and rubbed his thighs. He wasn't a fan of riding and he always hurt after riding for an extensive period. He checked on the girl and made sure she was still out. After assuring that she was, he tied her horse to a broken stone arch.

Zanji took a flask out from the bag attached to his saddle and drank deeply from it. Letting the blood wine fill him and replenish the magic he spent that night. He found a grouping of rubble and stone, brushed the snow off and sat down. Taking another swig of the wine, he was able to finally collect his thoughts and clear the mad rush of everything in his head.

He let the tears fall that he had held on to for too long. He would miss his wife. His Pelea. He didn't know what he would do with her absence. Zanji sat there long enough to cry it out and then wipe the tears from his face. He replaced the wine and turned in a circle to find a group behind him, quiet and still. He didn't hear them approach. Their silence was like the dead and it unnerved him.

Lord Winzi's sister and their coven leader, Shasa, stepped forth, removing the cowl from her head. She was beautiful yet her features screamed cruel. There was always something about the woman that made him afraid. Her red hair danced in the wind that always seemed to surround her and her ice cold blue eyes pierced his. She looked nothing like her brother and that was how they got by so long with no one being the wiser.

"Where is Pelea?" She asked. Her cunning eyes scanned around the area. They grew up as close friends. Like sisters. "Zanji, where is she?" Her voice cut across pulling him from his trance.

"She's in the Evernight, Shasa. Ekon cut her wolf down then this witchling," he pointed to the sleeping girl. "She killed her. She killed my Pelea. I thought you said she was harmless. That she wasn't strong enough to take us on. You lied!" He shouted.

Shasa was shocked. Whispering, "I didn't know she was that strong, Zanji. I Swear. She was your wife, but she was my sister of the soul." Shasa quickly moved to where Nthanda was still on the horse and removed the blanket. Disbelief rendered her shock. *This girl couldn't have killed my sister,* Shasa thought to herself.

"This runt killed my sister? How? This girl is barely twelve winters old!"

"She's stronger than she looks, Shasa. I swear. I would be dead if I didn't use the dart on her."

"Then good riddance." Shasa snapped her fingers and two hooded figures from behind her came forward. "Load her onto the sleigh and ride fast to the borders. There should be a cave. Wait there. I will catch up. Now go."

The two hidden figures untied the girl and lifted her off the horse. They took her to the sleigh that Zanji didn't notice before. They secured her tightly and threw the blanket back over her. One stayed in the back with the witchling while the other got up front and took control of the reins and left them behind.

Shasa turned and embraced him in full. "I am sorry Zanji. You are hurting too. I didn't mean to lash out. Your information took me by surprise and it cut deep. I loved her as you do. Forgive me?"

"I will forgive you always, Shasa. You know this."

"I do but most important, Zanji. You must tell no one of what happened tonight. We cannot take any chances." Before she could finish her words, she shoved the knife hidden in her hands through Zanji's chest. Shock registered on his face. He tried to speak but the words wouldn't come.

"Why? Why Shasa?" he mouthed as he grew weaker by the second.

"Because you were never good enough for my sister. You failed her tonight. You don't deserve to live while she no longer takes a breath." She spat in his face. "May the Lord of Death take pity on your soul Zanji."

JIA'KA TRAVELED THE dark halls, stepping over stones and large blocks that fell down when she unleashed her power earlier. Now that Chanda was in good hands, all she could think of was of her little star. She moved with grace and avoided a few falls but she found the hall that would take her to the sanctuary. The closer she moved to the corridor she could feel the wards. They recognized her energy signature. She was safe, but the warding were unquestionably weaker. Bound by the high priestess life force, it made sense if she was weak that the wards would be weak too.

Jia'ka stopped and sniffed the air. Death rode the winds, and she coughed and gagged. Slowing down her pace, she carefully watched where she stepped and came across the first casualty. It was a wolf, and she knew that it was Pelea's familiar. But the man down next to it wasn't Pelea. She looked at the human and fear rose in her body. Ekon was dead. His blank eyes stared at nothing instead of guarding the girls. Anger flooded Jia'ka. She told Chanda they needed a male witch to watch the witchling. Not a human who couldn't hold his own. But to take down a wolf familiar, the man was stronger than she expected. She reached over and closed his eyelids. It was the least she could do for him.

She quickened her step and moved forward, stumbling but not falling. The shadows of another body was ahead of her. The closer she got to it, the more she realized it was too large to be Nthanda. Standing next to it, she scrutinized the crumbling corpse and could tell it was a burned woman. She squatted and examined the body. It didn't take long to conclude it was Pelea. But who did this?

Jia'ka recognized the witchfire and the remnants of the spell used after a few moments. This was Nthanda's handy work and she couldn't have been more proud. The girl was always a quick learner. She stood and ran as fast as she could to the entrance of the sanctuary chambers and burst through the doors.

"Nthanda," she yelled out. "Little Star. Where are you?" Frantically, she searched the room and continued to call out. Stopping only when she heard sniffling. "Nthanda, is that you, child? Come out now. It is safe."

Her granddaughter didn't reveal herself but Serea did. She shuffled from her hiding spot behind an armoire.

"She's, she is not here Mama Jia'ka. She left. She and I heard fighting. I couldn't stop her. She told her cat to stay with me and she would be right back, but she never came back. I- I was too scared to go out and check. Her animal went crazy and wouldn't stop yowling. She finally stopped moments ago but she won't respond to anyone," Serea told her.

Jia'ka saw the snow cub by the fireplace, watching her. If the animal acted that way, then Nthanda was long gone. Not dead but no longer in the keep. The soon to be dead bastards took her. She couldn't understand another's familiar but they understood her. She looked to the beautiful cat and got her attention.

"I know you can understand me. They took her. I have no clue where to but she must come back here. Go and find your witch. You can catch her scent once you're outside. Hurry before it's too late," she said with urgency.

The snow leopard cub didn't hesitate and darted out of the room. Jia'ka knew the animal would find their Nthanda. She would just pray to the Mother Goddess it wasn't too late.

Chapter 8

The cloaked figure in the back of the sled with Nthanda held on tight as the driver sped over hills and blankets of powdered snow. Fresh snowfalls covered their tracks as they glided across. The nickers and neighs of the horses filled the air, interrupting the dead silence. The moon still hung high in the sky, emitting pale light, giving them a way to see the nighttime landscape. It was clear for now but the clouds said it would change soon. Blizzards and snowstorms could happen anytime but this storm wasn't natural.

They raced against time. The mercenaries waiting needed to be away from the lands before sunrise. Enyxias was already a treacherous place for those not favored but by dawn, the land would be dangerous for all. Their coven knew the old woman would send the whole lands to the Evernight for their transgressions.

The driver didn't slow down when they hit the ice going full speed. The sled swerved dangerously to the sides as if it would tip over. Eventually, the driver slowed down, got the sled and horses under control. Close to the territory line, they wouldn't stop until they made the rendezvous point. The Ice Fields were frozen solid but sometimes spots would thin and had caused many accidents.

The witch guarding the captured child, checked to make sure she was still under. The girl's fingers were too cold and almost frost bitten. She grabbed another blanket from the pack she had and threw the woolly cover over the child, making sure her limbs weren't exposed.

It took another candlemark to cross the fields, but they arrived near the edge of the border and sighed relief when the sled landed back on the soft-packed snow. Near the trees, they searched until they found the hidden cave. Orders were to wait and meet the mercenaries. The driver jumped down and checked the horses. The other witch lifted the girl and took her inside the cave after checking to make sure it was empty.

Once inside, the woman dropped the girl unceremoniously to the ground. She started a fire in the back, far enough so the cold draft couldn't reach. The fire would do some good. Heat the area and not worry about being seen from outside. *The humans are late.* She removed her cloak and ran her fingers through her coiled twists and stretched. She didn't want to be there longer than she needed to be. She would rather be home in her warm bed.

She sat down in front of the fire and warmed her hands. She looked up when Pae walked in, shoveling snow off his shoulders. He removed his cloak and went sat next to the woman.

"How much longer must we wait for these humans? A storm is coming. The horses are nervous. We should be back on our way to safety."

The woman shrugged her shoulders. "They're late. Shasa said she would meet us here too. Maybe she can tell us when she arrives. She shouldn't be much longer. She was leaving right after we did."

"All of this is wrong. Shasa was wrong for this," he said.

"Doesn't matter. We are sworn. I don't care one way or the other."

Pae let out an exasperated sigh. His sister wouldn't listen to him. She was always stuck in her ways whenever Shasa was involved. "Patience is not my thing."

"I know. Here," the woman handed Pae a skin of water.

He took it, glad for the drink. He was thirstier than he realized and took long gulps before handing it back to her.

"If you want to take a nap, I'll stay up and wait until the others arrive. Keep an eye out on the girl. You need your rest to get us back home safe," she told him.

Pae leaned over and kissed the woman on the cheek. "You're the best sister ever. Have I ever told you that?"

"Only hundreds of time," the woman said. Grinning, she stood while her brother got comfortable on the cave floor.

Lae walked towards the front of the cave and peeked outside. Still no humans or Shasa. Alone with the child made her uneasy, even if the witchling was asleep. She was ready to hand her off and be done with the business. Something about the child screamed danger and she couldn't understand why no one else felt it.

Not wanting to be caught unawares; Lae placed a protection ward across the entrance, then placed one over herself and her brother. Hoping to keep the growing wind out of their makeshift shelter, she used the strength of the earth to help move the large boulder just inside the entrance to make a door. Blocking the falling snow and bone cutting wind, it was almost instant relief from the enclosure. Lae left only enough space for one person to fit through at a time. She didn't want to be completely closed off. Satisfied, she went back to the fire to wait.

IT DIDN'T TAKE LONG for Shasa to catch up. Riding with just one other made the trek quicker across the fields. She told the rest of the coven to find safety. Outrunning a brewing storm was too dangerous for any of them. Only one witch she knew of could brew a witchstorm as strong as what was coming. It was enough the old woman was a seer but powerful too. Mama Jia'ka could be brutal in her hunting.

Many days and nights, she prayed to the Mother Goddess, thankful and glad she wasn't the one who infiltrated the High Priestess's own coven. Thoughts of her brother should bring up tears, but to cry for a brother she had a love/hate relationship with, there was no point. He was dead the moment he went undercover. She mourned for him then.

A self-satisfied grin widened on her face. She couldn't believe her coven pulled the plan off. In the beginning there were too many disagreements. More people were afraid than what they were willing to admit out loud. Her faith never wavered. She didn't doubt they could do it. The job took a long lunam, but they executed it to their best ability. Shasa would do anything to get back at Chanda and her mother. *They may have the bloodline, the power, but they don't have the guile and strength to rule like a true child of Enyxias. I can and it was my right to take down the weak minded so only the strong could survive,* she thought to herself.

The driver of her sled slowed then halted. Shasa looked to the sky. The storm was coming in too fast. She jumped down and told the driver to be on the ready. The mercenaries weren't there, but they were very close. She could smell humans' clicks away.

She walked to the entrance of the cave and stopped. She tasted the tang of Lae's magic. Proud that she remembered to protect themselves. The warding was nothing to Shasa. She could easily dispel it but she would respect the other witch's boundaries as they're taught to do.

"Lae. Pae. Let me in," she said to the twins. Her voice was low enough not to give her position away. Lae heard the coven leader and released the warding and dipped her head in reverence when Shasa entered.

"You made it! We were worried with the storm coming. We should leave soon."

"The humans are close. Another half candlemark and we can leave. If not sooner. How is the child?"

"She is still out but the potion should wear off soon. She will need another dose."

"I can take care of that. I have extra with me. Bring me the bag from my sled."

Lae didn't hesitate to follow the command. She regretted not putting her cloak on soon as she stepped beyond the cave. Shasa's driver still sat at the head of the sled. Too cold to speak, she waved. She didn't understand how he sat there in the freezing cold.

The wind picked up, tossing the tree limbs around to the point of almost breaking. The once clear sky now ominous, covered with dark clouds that reminded her of faces and lightning for veins seemed almost sentient. The storm's fast pace wasn't natural. A witchstorm like none she had ever seen before and it was getting closer. Searching. Anyone found caught in the cacophony wouldn't survive.

She spied the leather satchel hiding under a blanket. She reached for it then jumped off the sled. She headed back inside when she heard a faint noise. Lae stopped and turned towards the sound. She glanced at the driver but he didn't move. When she took another step, she heard the noise again. She turned on her heels and headed in its direction, wanting to see what the noise was. Passing the horses and sled into the edge of the forest, the natural sound went quiet.

The crushed noise of someone who stepped on pine needles and broken branches broke the silence again. The sound of someone who didn't know how to be quiet in a forest of others. The hour of dawn approached but with the storm; it was almost like the sun wouldn't rise. She stopped at a large tree to block herself from the cutting wind when she spotted two males coming towards her dressed in brown and black leather and furs. Faces covered with snow contraptions on their feet. She was more than glad to see them. Yelling out to them, she got their attention and pointed them to follow her.

Lae waited until they were closer to move, careful as she rushed through the trees. The change of weather was worse, and they needed to be leaving. The two men caught up with her and trailed her steps as she made her way to the cave. She bade they waited at the entrance and went inside. She handed the leather bag over to Shasa who stood over the child and told her of the men she found.

Shasa opened the large pouch and pulled the concoction out. She had two more doses. Enough to keep the girl under until the men met up with the rest of their party. She opened the witchling's mouth and poured the contents of the vial down her throat and massaged the outside of her throat with her hand to make sure the potion went all the way down.

"Thank you, Lae. Tell the men to come in," Shasa said.

Lae, let the mercenaries inside the cave. She took a closer look at the men, after they removed their head coverings. They didn't look like the humans of their land. They stood like they were born of noble lineage. Their bearings screamed danger even if they were calm. Both were tall and smooth faced. They had long, straight black hair and their skin was like the color of golden sand. The man standing closest to her; he had eyes the color of grass while the other had eyes the color of molten amber ringed at the edges with black. The amber eyed looked her over before speaking to Shasa in the common tongue of the desert lands.

"Where's the witch? We must hurry. We can sense the witchstorm brewing and want to be as far away as we can when it hits," he said with an accent that Lae never heard before.

"You are late?" Shasa retorted. Her eyes narrowed at both of the men.

"We are here exactly at the time we are supposed to be."

"How do you know about the witchstorm coming?" Shasa sniffed the air. They surprised her. They smelled like humans but they weren't. "You're not human are you?"

Green eyes looked to the other and back to Shasa and smiled. "We are not and it does not matter what we are. But we will take what now belongs to us. Where is the witch?"

Shasa wasn't expecting witches from Namansii to take the girl but that was better than the humans. She just didn't understand how they were able to mask their scent to make them smell human.

Shasa pointed to the girl covered in blankets. "She's still under. I just gave her another dose, she will be out for a few more candlemarks. She is strong. I have one more dose if you would like, I suggest you take it. Once she is awake, she will be sluggish but still strong enough to give a fight. Or even kill. Never underestimate her. Her bloodline is powerful."

Amber eyes stepped closer to the witchling. He touched the center of her forehead, then touched the center of her chest. His mouth moved but no words ever came out. Shasa and Lae watched on, curiosity getting the best of them. The man removed the blanket then touched her wrists and continued to mouth words unintelligible to the winter witches. Once he was done, he pulled the blanket back over the girl and lifted her. Placing her over his shoulders.

"Thank you for the offer of the potion but I do not need it. The geas I placed on her is strong enough to last until we get back home. She won't be going anywhere or even able to touch her magic." He pulled the head wrappings back over his head and walked towards the cave entrance. He turned and looked at green eyes. "Pay her so we can be on our way."

Green eyes nodded. He reached inside of his furs and pulled out a scaly looking pouch. He pulled out twenty gold pieces and handed it to Shasa. "You will never see this child again and we won't tell you where we are going. Do not follow us."

Shasa took the gold pieces and placed them in a pouch on her hips. Green eyes covered his head and turned to leave then stopped. He faced Shasa again. "I don't know who you made mad enough to cause the witchstorm outside but whoever it is, is someone you can't fight and win. I pray for protection for you and your kin." Green eyes pivoted again and with an unnatural speed, he darted out of the cave.

Lae didn't know what to say. She turned to find Pae staring at her not realizing he had awakened. He stood and began to put his outer clothes back on. On alert and he didn't look happy. Lae knew her brother's moods, and she was sure they would discuss what just went on there in the cave later.

"We need to leave too, Shasa." Pae said to their coven leader and banked the fire in the cave plunging them into the dark.

"Very well. We will examine everything tonight. Let's leave this place. Destroy your spells. We want no trace of us being here."

Lae and Pae eyed each other the only way twins do before trailing after Shasa.

KAI PADDED CLOSE ENOUGH to the cave and watched the three witches leave. Glad enough that she made it that close to her lost witch. She hid behind a tree and waited until the rogue witches left before going inside the cave. She already knew her witch wasn't there. She couldn't feel her close, but she wasn't too far gone. She could still reach her.

The leopard cub searched the cave and caught the smell of two different people. They were the ones who took Nthanda. Memorizing their smells, she padded back out of the cave and followed the scent into the trees. Determined to find her witch before it was too late, she took off down the same path. The two others were quick but she could catch up. She refused to lose her Bright Star.

Chapter 9

"We are close to the others, Tovoz. Should we catch our breath before walking into the camp?" the green-eyed man asked his friend. He was tired of trying to outrun the witchstorm that plunged Enyxias into darkness soon as they stepped pass their territorial borders. Glad he wasn't on the receiving end of that storm. Winter witches always gave him the chills. The red-headed witch didn't understand the magnitude of a witchstorm that size.

Tovoz stopped and adjusted the sleeping girl on his shoulders. His companion was right about taking a minute. Not in the best of moods from his mission he hated going back to the camp. Everyone with him was in his father's pocket, except his friend. His father's personal advisor and a company of soldiers came with him on two of his family's ships. He told his father he didn't need all of them but his father being the man he was, insisted.

He had the package like his father wanted. He hoped his father would see he was ready to be trusted. Especially since he fulfilled the quest like he promised. Tovoz sat the girl down on the ground. She wasn't too heavy, and he was very grateful for that. Still under the cover of the trees, he needed a breather. A moment to rest and think before going back out there to the pit of snakes.

"You have always been the brains, Zeran. Rest but not for long. We must leave these forsaken lands. This storm won't stop at the border. We must be out on the open seas and on our lands to be truly safe."

The green-eyed man, Zeran nodded. He watched as his friend Tovoz handled the child. She was small. She was the same size as their own.

"She's nearly the size of Nessya and Tiabu. I wonder what is so important about this young girl," Zeran said.

Tovoz shrugged his shoulders. "I didn't know we were retrieving a dark witchling until I saw her. Father said he needed to retrieve a package that required my skills. Godspeaker Nelioz and his Seer read something in the sun. He and his advisors sought what they needed to make it happen." Tovoz looked up, "I just do my duty, Zeran."

"She is a dark witchling. Why are we bringing her back home? Her kind doesn't deserve to touch our blessed lands. Better to let her drown in the water deep."

Tovoz agreed with Zeran but he was told to bring the girl alive. He couldn't imagine what type of trouble the child must have been in. She was the same size and build of his precious Nessya but that is where the similarities ended. With a deep sigh, he picked the child back up.

"We must depart. Let's hurry. The quicker we are back to camp, the quicker we can leave." Tovoz patted his friends back. "We are almost done friend." Tovoz though tired, made the trek back to the camp quicker than he wanted to.

He hoped the advisors had the boats loaded and ready to leave soon as he arrived.

KAI WAS TIRED, BUT she finally had caught up with the men who had taken her witch. She was asleep but otherwise unharmed and it thrilled Kai. The men didn't notice she was behind them. Glad for the short break, she inched closer and listened to what they discussed. The language was strange and differed from the tongue of Bright Star.

She sat on her haunches and waited. She would continue to follow them again when they started to move. Kai didn't know where they were going but she was determined for them not to leave her. The men spoke in hushed tones, and they looked frustrated. The one holding her witch looked resigned and tired. There was more to him than what he showed. He picked Bright Star up. He and the green-eyed man took off into a jog. Once they were far enough, Kai stood on all four of her paws and ran after them.

It didn't take long for the men to make it to a makeshift area. Numerous men and women moved with purpose and focus. Many of them carried long weapons with metal blades at the end. Kai followed the two men into the camp, hid behind a tent and observed from the shadows to see where they would take her. Once the others saw the two men, they all cheered and shouted. Loud enough to where the ground shook.

Kai froze and her hackles rose. She thought the storm caught up, but it was only the reverberations from the stomping and shouting. A loud horn blasted about the camp enclosure. The men and women ran to the tents and took things down. She couldn't get caught. She ran, ducked and hid in shadows until she was close enough to smell Bright Star. Knowing she was close comforted her. Their bond was still strong. The closer Kai was to Nthanda the happier she was.

Soldiers walked to the shoreline where two larger-than-life vessels waited and floated. Kai never seen a ship up close and was in awe. The man holding Bright Star walked the plank leading to the first ship and disappeared up top. They were taking her away. The cub's thoughts went into a frenzy. She needed to be on that boat too. Jia'ka commanded her to find Bright Star, and she did. Kai couldn't leave her. She brought her out of the darkness to the light.

Kai waited until they paid no attention to who boarded the ship, darted to the plank and ran up the wooden platform. The cub kept herself hidden from the others. Once aboard, she followed Nthanda's scent to a small room where they had placed her. The door was ajar just enough to where she squeezed through and dashed inside. No one else was in there and was glad. Bright Star was still asleep under a blanket.

She was safe and unharmed. Kai hopped onto the bed and moved behind the witchling. She buried herself under the covers next to Nthanda and got as close as she could while keeping herself hidden. She would be there when her witch woke up.

JIA'KA PACED THE INFIRMARY. Too many candlemarks had gone by, and still no sign of Nthanda. The witchstorm she created, searched but her heart part couldn't be found. The child was no longer in Enyxias and that made her angrier than ever. The rogues would pay for their treachery. She will find out the mastermind and punish them as only deemed fit. They would die a painful and slow death.

There was nothing she could do. She had to worry about the daughter that was there. Lenzo created the antidote and gave it to Chanda but she still wasn't awake. The sun had rose, and neared midday and still no sign of hope. She kept on pacing and pacing, slowly wearing a depression into the stone cold floor.

"Mama Jia'ka." Lenzo called to her.

The old woman looked up. She was a mess. Her eyes were red rimmed and puffy from the tears she couldn't stop. She was showing weakness but her world was turned upside down and didn't care at the moment.

"Yes." A simple one word response. She didn't think she could form full phrases if she really tried.

"She's awake. Confused but awake. I haven't told her anything. That is for you not us."

"Blessed be the great Mother Goddess. Thank you Lenzo. You are a great wonder and if you need anything, come directly to me."

Lenzo nodded and grinned. Thankful for her support. "I will Mama. Thank you."

Jia'ka waited until Lenzo left the room. She wanted to talk to her daughter alone. She had to tell her about the witchling and the news would come best from her. Not secondhand. Her steps were slow to the point of almost dragging. Her breath hitched as if she would cry again. Jia'ka hands trembled the closer she got to her daughter's healing bed. She never wanted to face Chanda how she did then. To tell her High Priestess the terrible news, and yet it was her duty. As a guide. A mentor. A mother.

Chanda opened her eyes when Jia'ka shuffled to the foot of her bed. She could sense the strong aura of her mother from anywhere. She could also tell something troubled her.

Her lips tugged upwards in a slight smile, "I'm fine Mama. I still breathe. Thanks to your quick spell work. I felt your protection spell the moment my life force tried to depart its own cage. Thank you."

"I couldn't let you go just yet, daughter. I only did what any mother would do to protect their own blood. How do you feel?"

"A little weak but I guess that will subside as Lenzo's potion does its work." Chanda rubbed her chest. "I won't have a scar. No damage inside, just the phantom feeling of a blade being drove into my back and chest."

"Then you're still blessed. Honor the Mother."

Chanda could read her mother tell-tale signs. The way she kept looking around the room and not at her. She fidgeted with the blanket at the edge of her bed and how she wouldn't come sit down next to her. Jia'ka was off and that bothered her. It was unlike her mother's normal way.

"What is wrong, Mama? You are not yourself. Come sit next to me and tell me your problems?"

Jia'ka knew it was no better time to talk to her. She slowly walked to the side of the bed and sat down. She still had a hard time looking her in the eyes but she did. Concern creased across her daughter's face. The worry in Chanda's eyes. Jia'ka lifted Chanda's soft, warm hand and placed it in hers. She lightly squeezed and exhaled the breath she held. Jia'ka peered into her daughter's eyes and let the words fall from her lips.

"Your human, Ekon, he is dead." Silence. The only thing that alerted Jia'ka Chanda heard was the tightening of her hand squeezing hers. Jia'ka dreaded the next part, but she couldn't keep silent. "They took Nthanda. She is not dead, but they stole her away."

Chanda searched her mother's eyes as the world fell down around her. A high pitch scream erupted from Chanda's mouth. There was so much power behind the pain. The ground shook under Jia'ka's feet and the walls moved, raining dust and pebbles down on her. She expected more but Chanda's control of her magic and rage compared to no other. Tears fell from Chanda's eyes and the wails of anguish pulled at Jia'ka's heart. She understood the pain. Her Little Star was just as much her child as hers.

"Her familiar is alive. I let her go to find her. If she doesn't return, then we know she found our star. Or went back to the Evernight. We have a few prisoners. We will find out who did this. We will find out who betrayed us. Even if it's to my dying breath. We will have our vengeance," Jia'ka vowed.

Chanda didn't want to hear anymore. Her soul ached for the loss of her child. She wanted to be alone. She turned her head away from her mother. She didn't blame her. She couldn't. It wasn't her fault. Jia'ka would have done the best she could to protect not only Nthanda but the rest of their coven and their people. Everything was beyond them yet, it still hurt.

"Leave me," Chanda said so low that Jia'ka barely heard her.

"You need not be alone right now. I'll stay by your side."

"I said leave me. I don't want any company. I need to be alone. I say this as your High Priestess. Please go."

Jia'ka couldn't ignore the command no matter how much she wanted to. When the High Priestess speak, everyone listens. She stood up, her legs wobbly and tired. She stood over Chanda and wiped the tears from her eyes.

"When you are ready, come and find me. We have much work to do, you and I. It is time these lands recognize and respect those that lead them. We have been too soft and now we must show the hardened bone of our family's power. These fools have forgotten that we are of the Nightshade bloodline. They will regret the day they forgot." Jia'ka voice was strong, and she knew the words hit home. With nothing else to say, she left the room. Her daughter needed the time to mourn that for the one who is lost and yet to be found. On the next day, they will begin the work that should have been done years ago.

Chapter 10

T*wo weeks at sea...*

Nthanda opened her eyes to complete darkness. No amount of light entered wherever she was at. The swaying motion of the ship made her dizzy and nauseous. She swallowed the spit in her mouth and gulped for air, hoping the feeling would reside. She was confused. Not remembering much of how and why she was shut off from her gift.

You're awake. Finally! the cub said to her witch.

"Kai! Where are you? It's too dark in here, I can't see," Nthanda whispered. Her throat was scratchy.

Hush. Don't be too loud. They'll come back in here and put you under again.

"Who are you talking about? Where are we?"

We are on what you called a ship, crossing the seas. No longer in the land of your birth.

Nthanda shot straight up and hit her head against the wood frame above her. "Ouch. That hurts," she said rubbing her head. The pain slowly receded but it would leave a knot. "How did we get on a boat, Kai? The last I remember is I burned that awful woman. It was complete darkness afterwards. Kind of how it is dark now."

You were shot with a dart, filled with an elixir that put you to sleep. The bad witches who took you away from the place in the mountain shot you. The one you call Mama Jia'ka was furious. She told me to leave and come find you.

Nthanda reached over, searching in the dark for the creature. Her hand brushed against the fur of the small leopard cub. She rubbed her hands through its soft fur and relaxed. Her familiar was the only thing keeping her calm. She's never been away from home and she didn't know who these people were.

Still whispering so her captors couldn't hear her, "How do we get off this thing and escape? Anywhere that's not home is not where I want to be." The pangs of missing her mother and her grandmother had already started. Nthanda could only imagine how they felt. She was ready to hug them. To see and be near them. Everything hit her like falling snow in an avalanche. Her guard was dead. That was why she was out of the safety of the room and was burning the woman. They had killed Ekon. Her breath caught before she realized and tears fell from her eyes.

Kai could feel the rampant emotions her witch was experiencing and moved into her lap. The closer Kai was, the easier for her to help calm her. She didn't know what else to do. Nthanda pulled the leopard cub closer to her chest and squeezed gently before laying back down on the mat she was on. Not ready to be awake to face the unknown. Closing her eyes, she went back to sleep.

Kai heard the men before they made it to the door. She jumped down from Nthanda's arms and hid underneath the mat. Careful not to be found by them. For all they need to know, is that she doesn't exist.

"I THOUGHT I HEARD A noise. That's why I am checking on her, Zeran. She shouldn't be awake yet. My geas is supposed to keep her under until we get closer to Cebi Harbor."

"We don't want any power unleashed, even if it's from a tiny, dark witchling. Doubt she's strong enough if they caught her easily."

"You know as I do that sometimes witchlings can be just as strong as a witch in her majority. She comes from strong bloodline so they say. That is why father advised placing a geas on her. Except I don't think he or anyone was expecting a child. I don't like this."

"I get it. Really, I do. Still rubs me the wrong way we have a darkling aboard our ship. Either way, hurry up, I'm starving and I am sick of the same old fish we've been eating. Cook says he has something different for tonight. At least that makes dinner interesting."

"You're always hungry. If we have something different tonight, then I am sure you will be happy with the change," Tovoz said in a deadpanned timbre. Zeran scoffed.

"Such the funny man you are today. Ha. Ha. How much longer do we have on this godforsaken boat? I swear to the serpent gods and all things holy in our precious jungles, that I will not step foot on another boat for a very long time."

Tovoz didn't respond and only gave his friend a side eye. "Just give me a minute."

Zeran nodded and took up as guard next to the door. Tovoz opened the small door and stepped inside the darkened room. He conjured a ball of witchlight in the palm of his hand. The girl didn't need light as long as she was sleep but he did for the moment. The cabin was the smallest on the boat and perfect size for the girl. The only thing in the tiny room was the mat and a blanket. He didn't want to give her access to anything she could use as a weapon if she ever came to. He already knew that children could be creative in their choice of toys or weapons.

He stepped lightly, as he tried to avoid making a sound. He stood over the child and watched her chest rise and fall as she slept. The girl was just the size of his own daughter at home. He couldn't imagine what it would have been like if someone took his daughter away from him as they did to the witchling's parents. He strengthened the spell on her and made sure she would still stay unconscious. He would make sure a soldier would bring gruel later.

THREE WEEKS AT SEA...

Tovoz stood at the front of the ship on the top deck next to the rails and let the spray of water cool him off. The night was warm and humid, which meant they were getting closer to the land of sun. His shoulders were tense and his hands gripped the smooth wood too tight. Only a week away from making landfall and that had him on edge. His eyes followed the horizon line then moved up. Night had fallen, and the moon was high. A clear night and most of the crew were sleeping in turns. He needed a moments' rest away from everything and the tiny piece of solitude was a godsend.

Zeran also got on his nerves. Between the sour attitude for being on the ship and his hatred for the dark witch, Tovoz was glad for the few members of the crew who were still awake asked if he wanted to play a game of *Snake Eyes*. It was his friend's favorite game to lose coins on but Tovoz hated the game. It was a game for the commoners and their station was above that. Their laughter drifted across the air, tugging a small smile out of him. Zeran wasn't one who cared for the commoners but he loved their gambling games. Tovoz once asked why he liked the game so and his friend responded 'passes the time away in this hot jungle'. Ever since then, he never argued with him about the game.

Chio, a Captain in his father's guard came up from behind and placed his fist of over his chest. Tovoz heard the clinking of the metal on his clothes before the man could even reach him. "Sir. Noises have been reported by the room with the girl. What should we do?"

Curious, Tovoz turned his head to the man, "What type of noises?" He knew there shouldn't be any sounds coming from the room. Without waiting for a response, he pivoted and headed in the cabin's direction. Chio was close on his heels.

"Sir, my men have been hearing them more at night. They're scared. Says the darkling will be the death of them. She will sink this boat. What should I tell them?"

Tovoz didn't bother to stop when his deep voice carried over the sounds of waves, "This ship will be fine. No one is going to die, unless it's by my hands. Now, leave me be."

Chio stopped while Tovoz crossed the main deck before going back to where his men stood. They overheard the conversation and was not pleased. Tovoz didn't care. His father's men was a superstitious lot. More than a few came from the deep, what his people called the inner jungle. His family lived in the cities, closer to the waters and were part of the royal court. The type of thinking the soldiers did were eschewed in his circles. Tovoz thought his father needed to correct the backwards thinking of his soldiers. It wasn't a good look for the family.

Tovoz didn't take long to get to his destination. He slowed his pace and eventually stopped only feet away from the cabin with the child. He wondered if she only faked being asleep every time he checked on her. To be sure and safe, he masked himself to where he couldn't be seen, heard, or even sniffed out. A spell working he mastered growing up as a child himself. He remembered how he would terrorize his older sisters. They hated it but his father was proud when he first saw the spell himself.

Now, he stood there about to sneak in on a darkling child, never mind that she was truly a child, yet she was still a dangerous foe. Every precaution needed to be taken. Tovoz took a step. Dread filled his chest. He didn't know what he would find in the room. He took another step. He wanted to turn around and pretend that he checked on the girl and would tell the men they were overreacting. But he still felt their heated glares on his back. Pushing himself forward a few more steps, he arrived at the door and listened for any type of voices. Only the soft lapping of water touched his ears.

He breathed in and breathed out. Repeated the cycle twice. He was ready. Tovoz placed his hand on the door handle and went in. Only the light of the moon found its way into the room and he froze when he saw the girl sitting up in the dark staring at him. Her startling purple hued eyes caught him by surprise and he snapped his gaping mouth closed. She was awake and everything inside him dropped to the pits. He checked behind himself to make sure no one was watched and then closed the door plunging them back into the darkness. He didn't need the crew or his father's soldiers seeing this. He removed the spell he had cast on himself. Tovoz conjured a bright ball of yellow witchlight and let the sphere hover at eye level to the side of him. He stood straight as he could in the tiny space of a room.

The girl scooted back as far as she could to the wall. Still as the night, she eyed him like he was her prey. Not wanting to provoke her, he took a different approach.

"They call me Tovoz," he said in her tongue. It was a forbidden tongue in their lands but when he went to the deserts to study for a few years, he picked the language up there. He told no one, especially his father. Knowing and speaking Nyxian meant death. Learning their language was the highlight of his studies at the temple. He never once asked his instructor how he knew the tongue but he was grateful for the tutelage.

"You can trust me even if you don't think you can," he said to her in a lowered tone. He didn't want the others outside listening in or hearing what he said. "What is your name?"

The witchling didn't move. He sensed her fear, and he needed to reassure her she really was safe with him. He couldn't say the same for everyone else onboard. His father wanted her alive and well, not dead and rotting. Which is what she would have been with Zeran. He squatted so he could be on the same eye level with her.

"You can tell me your name, little witch child."

The girl spat in his face. "You are not worthy to speak my name!"

Tovoz wiped the spittle from his face. He needed to come up with a different approach. He smiled at her. "I have a daughter about your same size and age. She would be afraid too if she woke up to a new and strange place."

"Then take me home, since you are so understanding!" the girl said. "I don't belong here. You stole me from my home."

Tears fell from her jeweled tone eyes. He wanted to reach out to her to comfort her but he couldn't. "I didn't steal you from your home," he said to her. "Your own people did that."

"They may have taken me first, but you didn't bother to stop and think if it was right to follow their lead. You put me on this contraption and sailed away from my lands. You are just as much wrong as they were. In essence, you stole me away just as much as they did. But you are worse. You took me from my lands. One day, you will regret the actions you took. I promise you this."

The witchling turned away from him and all he was able to do was stare. She had a valid point, and it hurt him inside. There was nothing he could do or say to make any of what he did right. He was trapped just as much as she was. They both were bound in some way. Tovoz stood and his legs were glad for the movement. If he didn't leave soon, his people would begin to wonder what was happening.

"I will not put you back to sleep if you can promise me a thing or two," he said to her. He waited for her to turn back around. He knew he caught her interest when her head tilted slightly so she could hear him. She still didn't say a word.

"I will promise to let you stay awake if you will keep quiet. My people are scared of your kind. They say you bring bad luck to us all. I don't believe them, of course but still, you must stay quiet. The second is to never leave this room until I take you out. If you must do your business, there's a bucket in the corner. I'll make sure it is emptied daily. Also, continue to pretend that you're sleeping when the door open. Sometimes it may not be me coming through. They are dangerous to you, child. Trust no one. Not even me. Can you do these things?"

He waited. He wouldn't leave until he had her assurances. If Nessya was in the same predicament, he would want her to have an ally no matter how much it would hurt her to concede. His father had no good intentions with the girl and he wondered if he acted on behalf of their ruler. If the child was in sight of the Godspeaker, it would not bode well for anyone.

The girl's voice was light. Defeated but he heard the fire that burned underneath. She promised to do as he asked and relief flooded him.

"I'll make sure to bring food whenever I can. It won't be much, but I will do what I can," Tovoz said. The girl wouldn't say anything else. Her tears continued to fall from her eyes.

Tovoz left the witchling to her privacy. He couldn't take her back home, no matter how much he wanted to. He turned to depart, his burning ball of witchlight followed, bouncing along. When he opened the door, he extinguished it. He hated to leave her in the dark, but he had no choice. The others would see light coming from under the door if he wasn't in there and he didn't need any more problems. They were almost home.

Chapter 11

We are coming to a stop. I wonder where we are, Kai said.

Nthanda hugged herself. "I have no clue but it's not home. I can't even touch my powers. It is there, but I can't reach it. I've never felt this before. Almost like an emptiness. A heavy void." She stood up from the mat and stretched. "I'll check even though you have better hearing than I do."

I can't understand their words. Yours came natural to me. I have told you this.

"You come from the Evernight. It is natural for us to understand each other quicker than these people. Them, not so much. Now hush."

Nthanda shuffled across the tiny space and placed her ears to the wooden door. Even though the people outside was muffled, she still heard what was going on. There was a lot of commotion and yelling. People ran, but she didn't understand why. The ship had stopped so wherever they made landfall meant she would get off and get fresh air. She didn't know how long they were at sea but she stunk and was dirty. She wanted a bath and proper food. She only hoped they would give her that.

She kept on listening and heard the man's voice. The one who called himself Tovoz along with another man's voice head in her direction. His friend. Nthanda remembered he called him Zeran.

"Hurry and hide, Kai. They are coming to us." The cub now larger than when they first left their home, hid under the scratchy blanket. Nthanda ran back to the mat as well and laid so close to her familiar that they wouldn't be able to see her. She closed her eyes soon as the door creaked open.

"What are we going to do? How are we going to hide the girl, Tov?" Zeran asked. "Anyone that didn't make this trip can't see her. The people would go mad if they realized we had one of her kind with us."

Tovoz shut the door and conjured his witchlight. "We will keep her hidden. We need something to cover her with so we can carry her off the ship. I have to unload her to my father in secrecy."

"It would be so much easier to kill her. Less hassle and worry."

"She is important, Zeran. No one is killing her. Go find something to carry her in. Ask my father's advisor. This whole trip was courtesy of him."

"Fine, I'll be back. Strengthen the geas. We don't want any mishaps."

"I know what I am doing. You just do what I asked."

Zeran mumbled a few choice words as he left Tovoz alone. Nthanda sat up soon as she knew the other man was gone.

"I don't like him," she said to Tovoz. He looked at her bemused. "I don't like you either but he's different."

"Some days I don't like him either but he's not a bad person deep down. We were raised together like brothers, even if we are not by blood."

"None of you are good people."

"I can understand how you would feel like that."

"Where are we?" she asked. The heat made it obvious she wasn't home and because her power was still dormant. Her skin was warm and clammy inside the small box of a room and she couldn't stop sweating. She would not like whatever answer he gave her. She was used to the cold and wherever they were, was not it.

"The land of sun. Namansii. That part doesn't matter. You will learn soon enough. Before Zeran comes back, I will need you to lay back down and no more pretending you were sleeping. I must check the geas."

"I don't want to go back to sleep. I want to see where we are." Nthanda complained. Tired of hiding. She was angry and wanted to go back home.

Tovoz's head jerked up. He turned around and went back to the door, quiet as he listened to the crowd.

"I hate to do this but I hear the Advisor and Zeran," he said. Without warning, a bright light shot from his fingers and hit Nthanda in the chest. Her eyes widened, and a gasp escaped her as she tried to stop what was happening and failed. Soon as the light touched her, her eyelids became too heavy to keep open. She slumped over, mouth wide open.

"I didn't mean to do that little witchling, but I hope in time you will understand," Tovoz whispered to the unconscious girl. He went to her side and strengthen the hold he had on her. To keep her in the dream state, he placed her under. He took the dirty blanket and covered her to her neck. Soon as he removed his hands, Zeran and his father's advisor waltzed in like it was a room they owned.

"I found him on my way back," Zeran said, jerking his thumb towards the sharp-featured man. The advisor was a tall and a reed thin man with large, black eyes and an aquiline nose. He kept his thin and stringy hair long and down to the middle of his back. A giant wooden piece of jewelry pierced the bottom of his lip and went through his nose. Tovoz never liked him. He didn't like the way the man's aura was. His power was too sticky for those who are of the sun. But he did what he did for the man to stay on his father's good side.

"What do we owe the pleasure?" Tovoz asked.

"She cannot be seen. I've come to help with the hiding."

"We have it under control."

"Which is rarely the case. It took you two long enough to find and retrieve her. Those abominations almost discovered us! I told your father we needed someone else competent to do the job. One of your older brothers but for some ungodly reason he insisted on you."

"I do not need you here. Leave us, Ti'kal." The advisor sneered before storming off.

Once the man was out of earshot, Zeran looked to his friend. "I am glad he is gone. What are we going to do?"

"Keep her hidden until we reach my family's seat in Cebi. We will need a sturdy cart. Did you not find one? I told you to search for something to carry her in."

"Not yet."

"Then go find one. We must be on our way. I'll bring her down."

"Let me help wrap her at least."

"I am good. She's unconscious and will do no harm to anyone. Hurry. We must leave here before the sun is too high in the sky. You know the heat gets unbearable during that time."

Zeran sped out of the room and left Tovoz to his meanderings. Tovoz couldn't believe they were home. It had been over two long months out at sea and he was ready to hug his children and kiss his wife. The things that was the most important to him. His family. He glanced to the breathable cloth in his hands and wrapped the girl in it. The others would think she was a rug or something. He made sure that the shape of her small body wasn't noticeable.

It didn't take long to unload and leave the massive ship. Zeran had found a cart and a driver. Tovoz loaded the girl onto the back. He hopped on the seat next to the driver and told him where to go. He looked at Zeran still standing and watching and waved.

"I'll see you later, friend. Don't have too much fun with the ladies. Your wife waits for your return."

"She understands my needs. She will be glad to see me whenever I show up," Zeran said. His eyes twinkled and laughter came from him.

Tovoz shook his head. "May the sun forever warm your skin."

"Same to you, Tov!" Zeran turned and headed to the town that sat at the harbor.

KAI WAITED UNTIL EVERYONE was off the boat and followed Bright Star's scent. She discovered she had a new ability and was thrilled at the discovery. Kai was able to mimic other animals and creatures her size. Searching for a possible camouflage, she hoped wouldn't be too hard. She didn't like the landscape or the weather but was determined to find something suitable. There were too many trees but mainly it was too hot. Her fur was thick, and she needed a cooler climate. Kai's soft paws padded on the ground full of wild and flourishing flora. The upturned dirt from the path filled her nostrils with the local fauna's essence.

The place was huge and wet. A large, leafy fern slapped Kai in the face as she passed it. The scent from the others accosted her nostrils, and she knew she was getting closer. The cart carrying Bright Star moved at a snail's pace. The moss-covered path was difficult and dangerous to steer the cart on. The verdant moss and the steamy humidity made it slippery and extremely easy to fall or even break the wheel on the cart.

The jungle spoke to Kai. Welcoming her. Recognizing her otherness and accepting it even though she was from another land. It recognized she was kindred and not kindred. The place was full of songs sung by the inhabitants of the terrain. The trees stretched tall and reached for the sun. Kai heard its cry beseeching the sky. The animals and their voices were all different but together their cries raised up and created a song unique to the residents.

It was beautiful and deceiving. Kai remembered from the Evernight how beautiful things sometimes could be the worse things out there. She didn't remember how long she drifted in the place of eternal darkness. She didn't remember her time before her first breath like some others did. All she remembered was she woke up one day in a strange dark place and her spirit lingered. The other beings and even the daemons mainly left her alone but there was some who wanted to extinguish her completely. They wanted the bright light that made up her. Her soul. Many nights running and many nights sleeping, she hid from those. Prayed to the Mother Goddess to release the torment she was in or guide her to make things right.

She never thought the day that her prayers would be answered. Kai was very glad for what she had. She remembered how she heard a voice telling her which way to go. Then out of nowhere, the brightest starlight blazed in front of her. Lighting up the path. The others were hungry and craving the light. They all tried to rush to it but she was protected and blessed. The Mother Goddess watched out for her and guided her down the path to the light and prevented the others from following.

Before Kai reached the light, she recalled the Mother Goddess telling her to pick a form. Kai didn't understand what she wanted. Confused, she told the All Mother as much.

"Pick a form that you would like as soon as you step through. Look around and search your surroundings until you find something and take that form. There is a girl near the water, go to her soon as you find your form," the Mother Goddess said to her.

Kai understood then and when she went through the shimmering opening, she searched and searched until she found the cubs and took its form. Once she had all four legs, everything came to her, and she understood everything about the world and she didn't know how. Perhaps the Mother Goddess gave her the knowledge. She was strong in the body, the form she chose and began to jump around and play with the other cubs to adjust to her new motions.

Once she had full control of herself, she followed the sounds and smells of the water the Mother Goddess told her about and went to it. There she found her Bright Star. The one she wanted to go too since she was in the dark of the Evernight. Forever grateful to both her Bright Star and the Mother Goddess for the life they brought to her.

She would do whatever to protect the witch child. That is why she followed along, trying her best to not get caught by the tall man who stole her yet helped her. Kai eventually caught up when the men stopped to rest. They checked the wheel and the girl on the back of the cart. Kai kept hidden behind a large boulder.

The men got back on the cart and took off again. Kai ran to the cart and jumped onto the back next to the witchling and made sure to make herself look like whatever she was around so they wouldn't notice she was there. They must never know of her. They would kill her just as quickly as they would kill the witch if they didn't need her so bad for whatever reason that's unheard of.

Kai learned how to keep time thanks to the girl and it took them at least another candlemark to get to the gates of a large village. They moved through the crowds and went up an incline. The air was clearer the higher they went and, a large building came into view. She knew they had arrived to where they would be.

Chapter 12

Tovoz jumped from the cart and thanked the driver. He was happy to be back home. The oppressive heat he was used to, the cold not so much. Two guards stood ready for a command and Tovoz pointed to the girl.

"Take her to the cells. Unwrap her and lock her in," he ordered. The guards nodded and moved with swiftness to remove the girl from the back of the cart. Tovoz opened the pouch on his hip and removed a single golden coin and handed it to the driver.

"Thank you for the ride. Would you like to stay for a meal?"

"I will be all right Te'Mak. I need to get back to the harbor before it's too late. Traveling this deep in will take just as long going back. May the sun forever warm your skin, Tovoz."

"May Elios blessings fall down on you and your family, Zito." Tovoz spoke the Namansii blessing when a person departed ways with each other. The driver turned his wheeled cart around and went back down the path they had just arrived on. Tovoz took in all the familiar sights around him. He had missed it all. The comforting sounds of his jungle. Of the people outside of his home moving about. Tovoz breathed in the air, thick with moisture. Almost sweet and tasted like perfumed flowers. He was home and he was so thankful.

Surprised his family hadn't heard him come in, he went to the cells. Tovoz wanted to check on the girl. He couldn't figure out how he was going to explain to his wife and children why they're holding a young dark witch in their holding cells. His older children wouldn't like the situation at all. They were like most Namansiians. Hated the dark witches and their way of life. His wife, Tovoz wasn't so sure about. She grew up in the Kingdom of Roshan where both the Children of the Sun and Moon lived and intermingled. She would be a little more okay with the situation except that the prisoner was a young child. A young child the same age as their youngest daughter more than likely.

Tovoz pushed his family's feelings to the back of his mind. He would worry about the opinions of his family later. Since they weren't around, he assumed they were out with his father. He moved quickly up the path, past the gates, into the stone house built on the side of the cliff. A coveted area where the trees were cut down and left the cliff a barren open field that overlooked the Serpentine River. Tovoz's house was one of the very few in the district where he and his family resided. The compound had been in his family for the longest time, built by ancestors and passed down through his father's line. He had inherited the place when he had come into his majority. His father no longer wanted to be in the stifling heat of the deep and wanted fresh air and breezes on the daily. He moved to the coast, close to the sea, into another ancestral family home.

The Cliffside stone homes were called the 'Row of the Great Sun Elios'. The few homes on the cliff belonged to other high ranking nobles and distant members of the royal family. Soldiers and family guards were everywhere. All reported to the Godspeaker. One had to be careful what was said in the open for fear of reprisal by their God chosen leader. Tovoz always made sure to deal strictly with his family's guards and soldiers.

He didn't go in through the front door but around to the side where another door was located, hidden from unwanted eyes. He reached the wall and felt for the button and pressed. The hidden door slid open and a blast of rotten foliage, mildew and small animals hit his nose. Tovoz gagged and waited a beat before stepping on the set of slippery limestone steps. He stayed close to the slick walls and climbed down the stairs slowly, careful not to misstep and fall. The deeper into the earth he went, the darker it was.

Drips of water echoed off the walls and was the only sound he heard. The child was quiet. He had expected loud wails and cries. Screams for freedom and perhaps even sobs from crying. He didn't need to wonder if the guards placed the girl in an empty cell; they obeyed without hesitation. The end of the stone stairs had come to an end, and an open foyer opened up to Tovoz. The area fanned out into a giant circle to represent the sundial. His father always gave reverence to the gods, Tovoz was not as pious. Each cell position corresponded with the marks on the sundial. Every candlemark, the light from above would hit the mark and light up that particular cell. Above, the ceiling was a skylight that opened up into a closed off courtyard inside the compound.

It let in strands of light and whiffs of fresh air. Sometimes even rain during the rainy season.

Tovoz eyes immediately fell on the girl in the small chamber straight ahead of him. His footsteps made a tapping sound against the hard ground as he stepped over thick ropey vines and large stone pieces. He made a note of how the place was. Repairs and a deep cleaning was needed. Tovoz reached the cell and observed the girl who was sprawled out on the mat in the corner. Still unconscious, he opened the metal gate and went inside.

The guards had removed the blanket and cloth but her clothing was drenched. Not made for the oppressive weather of Namansii, he didn't think to have a change of clothes ready for her. Her body would take some time to get acclimated to the sticky heat. He honestly didn't know how long his father planned on keeping her, how long she would remain in their house or if she was to go to the Godspeaker.

Inside, Tovoz placed his hand on her temples and wiped the moisture away. He would have to find her clothes that would be more appropriate than the thick, heavy duty ones she wore. Tovoz touched the witchling's wrists and the center of her chest to strengthen the geas he had placed on her. Lifting his hand, he pressed his palm on her forehead and chanted a few words of his spell. He no longer needed to speak his words for his spells out loud but sometimes he found comfort in doing just that.

Tovoz stood and stepped out of the cell the moment the little witchling began to stir and move on the mat. He locked the gates and placed his hands on the bars. He stood back as she finally woke and looked around. Observing her new surroundings. She was smart. He could tell by her quick words just from the small conversation he had with her on the ship over. He only wondered how strong she really was. With his geas there would be no way to find out. He didn't even want to try to find out because letting a dark witch have her powers was asking for death to come visit.

"You're awake. Good," he said to her.

The girl turned her head slightly and frowned. "Where are we?"

"We are in my home. You are in the dens below. And there is where you will stay until my father have a look over you."

"Why does it matter what your father says? Just let me go."

"I can't do that. Before I leave, tell me your name? I won't ask again." Tovoz warned. He never got her name, and his father would want it. Tovoz also knew that knowing a witch's name could be used to bind a witch for good if they were in your thrall.

"As a witch, even one of light, should know just as much as I do that names have power. Why would I give you my name? I refuse to let you have complete dominion over me. I will never tell you my name and you will have to be satisfied with that."

"I promise on the Godspeaker and Father Elios in the sky, that no harm should come to you with your name."

"You kidnapped me. You spelled me when I refused to go back to sleep," Nthanda shouted. "That alone says I can't trust you. It won't happen again. Quit asking me."

"I understand. But know that we have ways to draw the information out of you. My father won't care that you're a child." The girl shrugged her shoulders. Tovoz was frustrated and didn't feel up to a verbal fight. "I will send two of my servants down with food and a fresh change of clothes. They will take you to the springs to get washed and cleaned. Do not make any funny claims or I will hear about it. Especially my father would hear."

Tovoz pivoted on his heels and left the girl where she sat. He jogged quickly up the stairs and out of the cells. He hated down there. The place was alive with memories he would rather keep locked up.

Nthanda's purple gaze followed the golden-skinned man as he left her in the horrid cells. She wanted to cry but didn't. She cried enough and refused to give these Children of the Sun anymore of her tears. She sat back against the stone wall and let the coolness seep through. She was too hot and her skin was clammy. He had mentioned a bath, and she prayed to the Mother Goddess he really meant what he said.

BRIGHT STAR, KAI SAID to her witch below.

Nthanda eyes opened quickly. *I must have fallen asleep*, she thought. She sat up and rubbed her crusted eyes. She hadn't seen her familiar since she woke up in the dirty prison. Not too worried about the creature, she knew that Kai would always find her. The girl stood and crossed the small area to the bars, searching the circular space. She didn't see the animal. Her shoulders slumped and her head fell against the warm metal.

"Now I'm hearing things." She hit the metal bars with her opened hand. The slap rang out and the sting of her hands resulted from her growing frustration.

"I just want to go home. I hate this place," she said to no one.

Up here, Bright Star. Look up into the hole.

Nthanda heard Kai again but she looked up as her familiar told her to. Blinded by the bright sunlight, but in the shadows she saw a welcomed shape. Kai's furry face came into view.

"I thought I lost you when I didn't see you after I woke in here. How did you get up there?" she asked.

I searched this place for an entrance but couldn't find one. I followed men who had your scent, and they came here. To this area up here. They're standing watch but they do not pay attention. I will find a way to you.

"I will leave soon for the waters to have a bath. Wait and follow me there. Maybe we can try to leave this place then."

We can't just leave! These lands are too dangerous. We must have a plan.

"I don't belong here. We don't belong in these lan-" Nthanda stopped mid-sentence and listened to the wind where the chatter of women voices and footsteps carried upon it. "Someone's coming, Kai. Find me outside and we will talk later," she rushed out. Kai bounded away from the hole leaving Nthanda alone again and she didn't like that. There were a lot of things she didn't like lately about her life and she hated she was only a girl helpless to it.

NESSYA AND TIABU WENT down the steep decline of the steps with Nessya's personal servants following her. She wanted to see the new prisoner. She overheard her father discussing it with her mother before seeing him. He stopped talking about the young girl soon as she stepped into the room. His smile lit up at the sight of her and she was glad he was back home. The two months was long without him. Her grandfather was harsh on the whole family. He was never in a good mood but for the last two months; it was worse.

He kept rambling about if her father messed up, the whole family would be in ruins and the great Godspeaker would sacrifice them to Elios. Nessya wouldn't let herself be sacrificed like that. She would run to the desert lands and hide before she allowed that to happen. She took on the ideology of her father, that their kind was too dependent on the God of Light, Elios. That they should be more reverent to nature and all that it offered. They were a broken people. Sadly enough even they couldn't see it.

"You two will stay here until I call you over. You can take her then to go do whatever it is that father commanded you to do," Nessya told the two women. They nodded and took a step back on the stairway. Tiabu smirked and with her nose up in the air, she went ahead of her.

"I want to see the one that has everyone riled up. She can't be that special." Nessya wasn't too far behind her and they both reached the cells at the same time. Tiabu's face scrunched up, and she almost gagged. "Elios above, what is that awful stench?"

"These holdings are old and rarely cleaned out," Nessya said.

"I think it is the dark one in there." Tiabu hit the metal bar with her foot. "Come here, girl. Show your face to your betters!"

Nessya hated when Tiabu thought she was better than everyone else. But she knew not to say anything. Tiabu always brought up the fact that she is a distant relative to the Godspeaker and that she is ninth in line to the throne. Every time Tiabu brought it up, Nessya rolled her eyes. She always thought being ninth in line was a polite way of recognizing that you were kin, but nothing will ever come out of the arrangement.

She touched her friend's shoulder, "Tiabu, leave her alone. She has done nothing to you."

"She breathes. That's enough. A dark witch is nothing more than dead to us. She is not worthy of being in the same space as us." Tiabu said with vehemence. She picked up a piece of stone, the size of her hand, and threw it at the girl in the cell. It hit Nthanda in the face and drew blood.

Nessya couldn't believe Tiabu acted like that. She shoved her to the side. "That is not who we are, Tia. Stop that. You are better than this!" She hoped her words reached her friend. But she was afraid they wouldn't. They never did. She loved her friend, they were almost like sisters but as they got older and Tiabu spent more time at court, her attitude had begun to change and it wasn't for the better.

"You need to get with the reality, Nessya. Dark witches all hates us. We are enemies. A good dark witch is a dead dark witch. If you keep one alive, it is an abomination in the God of Light's eyes." Tiabu stepped closer to Nessya to where they almost stood nose to nose and poked her in the chest. "Your family is going down a path that you won't be able to find your way back from. You shouldn't suffer because of the elders. Remember who you are. A Child of the Sun. My sister. I don't wish you or yours harm but know that they watch you. Your whole family is under scrutiny."

"You don't know that." Nessya replied, but she knew it was the truth. Her grandfather wouldn't be acting the way he was if something wasn't up.

"I do. I heard papa talking with others. War is brewing. Remember who side you're on. What you are. I don't want to be around this filth anymore. I'm leaving. Find me later when you had your fill of the monster in there." Tiabu scoffed and stormed out of the holding area. All Nessya could do was watch her leave.

Lately her friend was fickle, and she didn't know how to take it. Her mother told her not to worry that all young girls go through that stage at their age. She really hoped that she didn't go through that stage. She couldn't even see herself as cruel. Not in the way that Tiabu was turning to.

"Go upstairs and wait for me there," she told her servants. They bowed their heads and quickly took to the stairs, trailing in Tiabu's path. Nessya waited a beat before she turned back to the girl in the cage. She gestured to the girl, getting her to come to her but the girl wouldn't budge.

"I won't hurt you. Come here." she said but the girl still didn't move. She wanted to see what the witchling looked like. When she was eavesdropping on her parents, she heard her father say how unique the child was. Her curiosity was instantly piqued and couldn't wait to find a way to see her.

It was dark in the cell at this time of day, so Nessya conjured a bright yellowish ball of witchlight and sent it to hover just inside the cell. Enough to chase away the darkness so she could see. She wasn't expecting what she saw. The girl was unique and didn't look like any of her people there in Cebi.

She had heard tales of the different family of witches in the books she had read but none matched the girl before her. Her dark brown skin contrasted with the deep purple hue of her round eyes. And the girl's hair was completely white with the ends black like the Evernight. A blend of curly and wavy hair and it was wild, all over her head. The girl was beautiful to her in a wild untamed way. But it was her eyes that kept drawing her. Nessya remembered reading a forbidden tome by her father but her lesson instructor let her read whenever she visited. The tome listed the original witch families included their lines. Even the families that died out. Nessya recalled that some of the strongest families had traits of purple hued eyes. But she could have sworn the one she read about was a line that had died out. Now, she wanted to know which line had the purple eyes.

"My name is Nessya. You don't have to tell me yours if you don't want to," she said in the girl's tongue. Her father taught the language to her and swore her to secrecy. Tiabu and not even her own family knew she could speak in the harsh tongue of the Enyxians.

Hearing her own language, the girl perked up but still didn't respond. It would take time but Nessya would do her best to help when she could. She guessed the girl was just about the same age as her. *Maybe I can teach her my tongue in exchange for her friendship.* Nessya thought to herself.

"I am going to send my servants down to help you get clean. A bath should make you feel better. I will have papa send food down too. Eat and get strong again. You will need your strength." Nessya diminished the light until it was gone and left Nthanda in the darkness. The maidservants came down the stairs shortly after Nessya left. She made a vow right then to herself that she would not be like her grandfather or even Tiabu. The girl in the cage didn't ask for what happened but everyone could always use a friend. That would even include dark witches turned slaves.

Chapter 13

One year later...

"Tovoz!" The man yelled. "Send the girl away from here. We must talk." Te'Mak Paku said to his son. Tovoz didn't know what had come over the old man but the crazy antics his father always pulled exhausted him. He couldn't believe it had been a year already since they stole the witchling away from her lands. She proved to be most difficult. And some days she was compliant. On those days, he was very thankful for the compliance. He had enough to deal with by being a Te'Mak with his father on his back.

"Why, she's doing what we trained her to do, which is to serve us. Leave her be."

"She needs to go away, she cannot hear what we say."

"She does not speak our language, father."

Te'Mak Paku had a limp when he walked but it was more pronounced when he moved too fast. A gift from battle during his younger years as an elite warrior for the Sun Prince, now turned Godspeaker. Even the best healers couldn't repair the damage done. Dragging his left foot slowly, Te'Mak Paku reached the girl and grabbed the bicep of her left arm. She sucked in air through clenched teeth. She knew not to make a sound. If she did, punishment would ensue. The elder

Te'Mak always found reasons and excuses to beat her. She hated the elder more than the younger.

"Girl! Go away. We no longer need you!" He yelled in her face. His foul breath accosted her nostrils and phlegmy spittle hit her cheeks. The Elder pointed to a guard close by. "Take her to the cells."

The guard nodded, yanked the girl from Elder Te'Mak's hand and shoved her in front of him. His spear poked into her back, as he yelled at her to move faster. The guard herded her to the doorway that led down to the cells and practically shoved her in. Soon as they were out of reach, Te'Mak Paku turned back to his son and told him to sit. Tovoz didn't hesitate and sat down. He didn't like the way his father looked and didn't get a good feeling about what would probably happen next.

Paku moved and sat in front of his son. His head hung low and for the longest time, he refused to look up. The quietness was unlike him and it had unsettled Tovoz. "The Godspeaker wants to see the girl."

No reaction came from Tovoz's way. He couldn't react because he had expected the summons soon after he arrived home with the witchling, but it never came. It still didn't mean he wasn't worried.

Paku continued, "He wants the entire family to visit him in the Golden City. We have been officially invited as his guests to stay for the festivals. We have two weeks to arrive."

"Two weeks!" Tovoz shot up from his seat. "It takes nearly that long to get to the Golden City if not longer at this time of year. How long have you known about this father?"

Elder Te'Mak hissed at his son's insinuation. Te'Mak Paku's snake familiar slithered from its hiding spot and wrapped itself around his left arm. The solid black serpent with a blood red belly eyed Tovoz. Its forked black tongue tasted the air before resting its large head back on the elder's arm. Tovoz never liked his father's familiar, there was always something different about it and he could see the intelligence in its slitted pupils. Watching and judging him.

The Elder Te'Mak rubbed the scaly creature that found comfort on its arm and they both visibly calmed down. "The messenger only arrived this morning. We will leave at dawn. No exceptions. Make sure that girl is properly caged and not free ranged like you have her do around your house. We are more respectable than that."

"You know that my house will be in order." Raw anger thrummed through his veins but he had to know. "Before you leave, I have a question for you." Tovoz said. He stood up from the chair he was in and puffed his chest out. His long hair cascaded down his back like a waterfall. Tovoz's amber eyes narrowed and pinned his fathers.

"What is it?" Te'Mak Paku pressed his lips tightly together into a grimace.

"Why did you have me do it?" Tovoz asked. "Why did you need the girl? What's so important or special about her?"

"Does it matter why? If I told you to do something that would benefit the family, I expect it to be done without questions or complaints. You did excellent. You excelled where I thought you would fail. And for that, I am very proud of you. There's a first time for everything is there not?"

Tovoz never heard his father say those words in all of his life. That he was proud of him. Even if it did come with a backhanded insult. Hearing it now made him feel a type of way. The little boy that always wanted his father's approval deep within himself was elated but there was also sadness. It came too late and there was no pride in stealing a young child from her home. Tovoz's emotions were in turmoil but showing the confliction he had within would be showing weakness to the man who ruled with fear and strength all his life. The anger still smoldered but Tovoz's grin was the complete opposite as he tried to set it aside.

"But, why do we need her?"

"The oracle said we needed a Child of the Moon. A strong one. Is she not one?"

"She is but why did we need a dark witchling and not an adult?"

"You said yourself, the witchstorm was powerful and horrible in its darkness. That you didn't want to be the one on the receiving end of it. Tov, who would create a storm that great for one child? What would do that? She is not just some child, my son. Open your eyes!"

Tovoz thought back to the year before when he took control of the girl. How the storm was oppressive and sentient. He could feel the presence searching. He could feel the anger and the hope rolled up into one during that storm. It was a dark storm that he never wanted to be on the receiving end. His father was right about that part.

"I remember but that still doesn't tell me who she is. She doesn't speak our language. She doesn't understand our words. We can't even get her name."

"Dark witches don't have kings and queens like we do. Their leader or ruler. However you want to call it is chosen by being the strongest of them all."

"Yes, I know this. We were taught this early on."

"The only one strong enough to brew a storm such as what you told me is the current High Priestess or Jia'ka," Te'Mak Paku spat at the ground. "She is their seer. We are not sure but we think this girl is related to them or she is only being trained to become the next High Priestess. Whoever she is, she is a precious commodity they did not want to lose. Lucky for us, it was their own people who betrayed them."

Tovoz froze in place. It was as if someone stuck their hands into his chest and pulled his lungs and air out. He couldn't breathe. No wonder the girl acted the way she did, he thought to himself. She was practically royalty if she was in training by the High Priestess herself. They stole the Children of the Moon's next leader. He knew there was no way his people would get away from his actions unscathed.

His father's grim face matched his own. "What else is it you're not telling me?"

Te'Mak Paku didn't want to tell his son, but there was no way he couldn't tell him. Especially with the family leaving for the Golden City the next day. He would no doubt hear about it at court. He took a deep breath and exhaled.

"They are searching for her. The girl. Our people are dying left and right and the people who live across the seas in the desert lands are not safe. That includes your wife's people. Even on our shores, we have heard of the news. The outer islands is being plagued with strange sightings and creatures. Some say daemons from the Evernight," Paku spat at the ground to ward off the evil and continued, "They search for the child. We cannot come back here. Not at least for a while. Not until this dies down."

"We should be safe in our homes. We shouldn't run for fear of being hunted down by daemons and the dark. We are strong too. We can protect our own."

"I don't think you truly understand. That witchling's family is a pure bloodline if she truly is the daughter of the High Priestess and that foul woman Jia'ka. Direct through the women of that line. They are direct descendants of one of the original witch families. The Godspeaker has all of his trusted scholars and cabal searching, trying to determine which house but the going is hard. There are unfriendly eyes everywhere. It is unsafe. We cannot stay here. Especially with the girl being used as a servant. She is distinctly not one of us."

"Direct Descendants? I didn't think there were any pure bloodlines left except for the Godspeaker's family?" Tovoz said.

"It would seem we are wrong. And between you and me, his bloodline isn't all that pure like he makes out to be." Te'Mak Paku glanced sideways. "There is a lot about those abominations that we don't know but we will. Our education starts with that vile creature in the cells."

Not wanting to talk anymore, Tovoz needed time to think and away from the man before him. "I understand, father. We'll be ready at sunrise."

"Good. Only your most loyal servants should come. Sacrifice the others to the great Elios. Ask for protection and favor. We will need it." Te'Mak Paku said. He stood and reached out his arm. Tovoz embraced it then watched the man leave with relief. Tovoz needed to see his wife, and he knew exactly where to find her. There was too much to say and do with not enough time.

KAI FOLLOWED THE SPIRAL staircase until she reached the bottom. Before she even padded down them, she knew the cells were empty except for her Bright Star. Over the last year she had become an expert at hiding herself in broad daylight where no others could see her unless she wanted them to. Night had fallen and Kai didn't need to hide anymore. She walked freely with no worries of being caught.

Streaks of moonlight filtered through the windows and through the skylight above. Its pale fingers tried to reach its daughter, but it wasn't enough to make it to her. Nthanda sat alone in the corner of her cell. Curled into a fetal position on the dirt-packed floor in the complete darkness. Drowning in its abyss and the loneliness gripped her soul and squeezed it tightly. She missed her family so much. She even missed Serea, her sister by choice. Tears escaped, and she found no reason to wipe them away. Let them fall as she had fallen.

Bright Star. I am back, Kai said through the bond.

"I am glad you made it back safe," Nthanda replied. Her voice was coarse, instantly alerting Kai that she was not okay.

Kai padded to the metal bars and contorted her body to fit through them. Wanting rubs on the top of her head, she nudged Nthanda's hand. Kai wanted her to feel better and hoped she could help by forcing her to pet her.

Nthanda obliged and gave the young cat what she wanted. She sat up, hoping to make the movements easier and her body protested in response. "What have you learned today?" Nthanda asked her familiar. Over the last year, they agreed to let her roam and gather information. They needed whatever information they could use as they planned to run away.

The old man we dislike talked to the younger. We are to leave in the morning. The whole family is to leave and travel to some place called the Golden City and meet someone called the Godspeaker. The servants not worthy, will be sacrificed to their sun god Elios.

"The Godspeaker. That doesn't sound good, Kai."

Yes. The Godspeaker is requesting to see you. It is why we are going. I don't like this.

"We will play it by ear. Stay in the shadows tomorrow. They cannot know about you."

I will. If they try to catch me, I will take my claws and rip their throats and bellies open and feast on it for breakfast, lunch, and dinner.

"Feeling a little violent today are we? No, no killing my jailers for now. There will be a time when it will be necessary but not yet."

Well, when?

"When I get my powers back."

Your powers are gone, Bright Star. They locked the power up so you can't use them. Remember?

Nthanda glanced around to make sure they were alone. She picked up the heavy feline and held her close to her chest with Kai's head resting on her shoulders. Nthanda whispered into the cat's ear. "I felt something today. Earlier. It was only a trickle but I know what power feels like, Kai. It was different and warm. Not cold. I don't understand but it's there. I will do what is required and try to reach that font of power. Once I tap into it, maybe I can even use it."

Are you sure it was power?

"I am positive," she said. She rubbed the spine of the cat and Kai's purr was loud and content. Nthanda didn't understand the feeling either but she would work with whatever the Mother Goddess would give her.

Chapter 14

Three years later...

On the dais, the High Priestess sat at the seat of power. No longer in the citadel, she moved to the Black Keep at the southern borders where her daughter was last seen. She took only those she explicitly knew she trusted. She refused to go through another betrayal like she did before. The land of Enyxias was still paying for that mistake. And they would pay for it until her daughter walked the Winterlands again.

Jia'ka stood beside Chanda. She placed a hand on her shoulders. The gesture comforted Chanda and made her glad to have her mother by her side. It had been hard for them both. The last few years was spent searching for Nthanda. She would receive leads and information but none panned out to their liking. Then Chanda turned her searches to a more localized area. To Enyxia. She sought out the mastermind behind the upheaval at the ill-fated celebration to no avail.

Now she and her people would get peace at least for finding the culprit. The High Priestess stood, and a hush blanketed the room, alerting all the witches and their covens in attendance. The Hall of Shadows was spacious and filled to the brim with women and men. Young and old. All her people. Chanda raised her hands and plunged the hall into complete darkness. The living and breathing shadows that lingered against the walls and floor spread across the entire hall, chasing every inch of light away, obeying the priestess command.

"Into the darkness we are born. Into the darkness we die. In life, we live and thrive in the shadows. The in between life and death, it is there where we worship our Goddess and her children. Tonight we honor them all." The High Priestess voice rose into a fever pitch. The crowd's quiet anticipation swelled like a pregnant woman's belly ready to give birth to chaotic glee.

A flame bearer near the recessed wall waited for the signal before he dipped his flaming torch into the waiting holy oil. Like the fire snake of the gods, the brilliant orange and red flames danced across the oil as it chased its own tail, burning all around the hall, illuminating with its holy fire. Chanda's fixed her piercing stare to all in attendance. Their gazes met hers and never wavered. No one spoke. To speak was to be in contempt. Silence reigned in her presence instead. She could feel their fear. Their anticipation. She tasted its sweet nectar from the air. Thick, oppressive, and it fueled her well of magic to its core.

"Bring them in," She commanded. The guard who stood the closest to her, head snapped up and faced her. Fist over chest, he pivoted on his heels and left the hall. Chanda sat down, her back against the chair. Rigid and hard like her heart had become.

The thick wooden doors to the hall opened, letting in what little light it could then quickly diminished once the doors was closed again. The guard along with two others strode into the hall. Each followed the path to the dais escorting and dragging chained prisoners. The prisoners' eyes were wide and round. They searched the crowd but found no smiling faces or allies amongst them.

Chanda and Jia'ka took three years to flush Shasa and the rest of Shasa's coven out. Long and tedious but worth every bit of information they pulled from the minds of the rogues. Chanda glorified in their pain and demise as she sent their souls to the Evernight. The guards dropped the last three people who caused her heartache to the ground at her feet.

Below, the fallen three didn't bother to look up at the High Priestess. Chanda recognized the young man and woman. She had heard all about the sacred duo. The twins were Shasa's left and right hand. They were Shasa's prized students, and she took care of them like they were her own. Chanda hated that a fellow sister in the dark would lead sacred twins down to ruin. The whole complicated affair was a shame on Shasa and her line.

Shasa was full of pride and refused to show weakness. She didn't know when to stop and that was her downfall. Chanda remembered from their childhood how the woman was always jealous of her. Shasa's jealousy had gotten worse as they grew older and into their majority. Many times, the High Priestess wondered if she only had took the time to know Shasa better than maybe they wouldn't be in the predicament they were in. Now it was much too late. Her misdeeds must be rectified. Everything was above and below her and these three would finally pay for their actions. Justice demanded it.

"Do you all have any idea why you are here? Kneeling before me?" The High Priestess asked. Her voice was smooth and unperturbed. The twins' scraped knees touched the smooth stone with their heads hung low. Their beaten bodies trembled under the strain, causing the chains wrapped around their ankles and wrists to shake. Creating an out of sync off key song of wrong notes and chords. The strong essence of their fear was even more delectable to Chanda.

"I didn't think I was talking to myself. I asked a question and any of you can answer. Shall I repeat myself again but this time much slower? Maybe you will understand me then?"

Shasa remained quiet with her head lowered. The twins, Lae and Pae raised theirs, having already incurred the wrath of the High Priestess, they didn't want to make things worse. Pae nudged his sister's shoulder. Lae shook her head, refusing to say anything. Chanda watched as the tears fell from the young witch's eyes. There was no point in crying and watching the pain of the fallen witch made her despise the girl even more. Tears were for the weak. You cry in solitude not in the face of your enemy. Not in front of others. The woman deserved her fate. She wasn't worthy to be a Child of the Moon.

Pae turned his head towards the priestess and opened his mouth yet no words came out.

"You have something to say, Pae?" The man nodded and opened his mouth to speak again but no words wouldn't come out.

"Oh yes, I almost forgot. The cat has got your tongue. Well, let me fix that for you."

The High Priestess waved her hand in a fanlike motion and Pae's face tightened then relaxed. "Now speak or I'll rip your tongue loose," she threatened.

He stuttered as he tried to get a few words out. "We are here because we were wrong and betrayed you. I swear, we did not want to. Our Coven leader, Shasa forced us. She said we had to do it or they would oust us into the cold."

"We are from the land of ice and snow. The land of the cold. We thrive. We live. We survive. We embody all that is winter. You should not be afraid of the cold weather young Pae. Now tell me, what is the real reason you did what you did? Why did you and your sister partake in this foul play instead of coming to me? I am your High Priestess and by right you are obligated to warn of the treachery that would happen?"

Pae kept silent. He didn't know what to say.

"Then let me tell you why. They promised you status. Riches untold. Things that Shasa could never or would ever give you. Even if she was the High Priestess, she wouldn't even be the bug under my shoe as I crush it. She has never been worthy. Or strong enough. You are all weaklings. Now tell me. What happened and in details? I won't ask again."

Lae chewed on her bottom lip. Her eyes darted back and forth between her brother and Chanda. "Shasa came to us in one of our lessons," she interrupted. "Said we had potential and that she was in her right to grant us favor within our Coven. With our natural gifts and talents, we can be so much more if we were to follow her without question. That what she had planned, if all went accordingly, we would be the pinnacle of our people. Pae and I never had much, we came from a poor witch family and Shasa was like our family too. We thought nothing about it until she told us the pla-"

"Foolish girl, shut up!" Shasa cut her off. "Don't you get it? She will kill us all if you say anything more."

"I was going to do that anyway, Shasa," The High Priestess said. There was no point in pretending that was not what she had planned. Better the inconvenient truth was out in the open, where everyone understood what was going on. She turned back to Lae. "Continue on."

Lae didn't know if she should or not. She didn't want to die. She wasn't ready to die. "My brother and I wasn't part of the attack."

"Yet you knew about it. You knew what your mentor had planned, and you still didn't come and tell me. Or even Jia'ka."

"I- I- We were afraid, High Priestess. We were afraid for our lives if we didn't obey or follow her commands."

"Perhaps if you would have asked for protection if you two would have come to me, then maybe you would be in a better predicament."

Lae was jolted by the finality in those words. There was no coming back from their deeds. She was blinded by status and riches. She and her brother were at the bottom for so long; without hesitation they jumped on the chance to seek out and become something better than they were. The only redemption they sought now was a quick death and a chance to move on to the next life.

"You are right. We should have come to you," Lae said. She ignored the harsh words and curses coming from Shasa. The woman she respected and trusted and now hated. She wished her and her brother would have said no all those years ago and ran away. Given the time in the dungeons to think about everything, she understood it really. Longtime jealousy fueled Shasa. And it was that same jealousy she held on for years against the priestess that led over one hundred people and their families to ruin or death. She didn't care, she could tell by her facial expression even now. Shasa was only mad that the High Priestess and her soldiers caught her and that angered Lae.

"Where is my daughter?" The High Priestess demanded. She was tired of the games.

"I don't know."

"Weren't you there when she was handed off?"

"I was."

"Then how come you don't know?"

"We didn't ask who they were or where they were going. They gave Shasa a bag full of coins when they were satisfied with the girl and left. Said something about a storm brewing and they didn't want to be caught in it."

Shasa's head snapped to the girl. "Shut up Lae! I should have killed you and your brother when I had the chance. But I took pity on you instead."

"And now no one will take pity on you, Shasa," Chanda reprimanded.

The High Priestess looked once more at the man who was quiet. His chest rose and fell with rapid breaths. She had no doubt that he knew more than what was said. Chanda slowly rose from her black vine covered chair and moved with preternatural grace towards Pae. She lowered herself to his eye level and with her pointer finger; she lifted his chin so her eyes pierced his. He was like a small wounded animal trapped in the hunter's grasp and his body shook in her hands.

Chanda wrapped a cocoon like mist around him and her, blocking everyone else from seeing them. Pae eyes darted around but couldn't find anyone but him and her. No one could even hear them and she told him as much.

"It is just you and I in here."

"Where are we?" He asked.

"We are still in the Hall of Shadows, but I took us away from everything and everyone. They do not see us even though we are still here." Chanda stood, helping the young man up. "You know something young Pae. Don't be like your sister or even be like your mentor. Your sister is only talking because she doesn't want to die. But I can feel something within you. You're not like those two. They're greedy and hungry for power. You truly was just following along."

"I was. I didn't want to let my sister or Shasa down. But I didn't want to do it. I knew it was wrong. She was only a child and had no business mixed in the affairs of Shasa's gross plans. I am truly sorry, High Priestess. There are no words to express how sorry I truly am."

"I don't need words, I'll take the images from you myself. Do not move." She wanted to know the truth. Not the truth in parts. She knew that Lae's words were truths as she wanted them to be but she felt no remorse in her words. And for that, they would pay.

Chanda touched Pae's temple with her hand. "Close your eyes. This won't hurt if you open yourself to me."

Pae nodded and relaxed. Letting his mental barriers down, allowing the High Priestess to have full access to his most inner and sacred space. Chanda was new to walking through the minds of others but she picked it up quickly and was very successful at it. Inside Pae's head was a jumble of mess but she knew what she was looking for.

"Think back to the days before your covens' attack on mine. Back to the secret meetings when plans were made," she whispered to him. Like a flower in bloom, his mind opened wide and vivid for her. Full of color, she could see everything like she was there at the time it happened.

"Yesss, I see it so clearly now," She said more to herself than him. She could see Pae during the meetings with his coven. The moment when Shasa approached them. She could see the pure gleam of excitement from his sister while his smile barely tugged upwards. His emotions were embedded deep in him. He was not for it. She searched around and found him discussing it with his sister and how he wanted to leave and not do it. Hide but he knew that their mentor had eyes and ears everywhere. He also knew his own twin would tell on him if he did.

His sister was Shasa's prodigy, he was just the extra. His heart was better than she expected and for that, she felt like being benevolent to him. But she needed the whole story. The whole truth of the matter before she made any hasty decisions.

"Show me the night of the attack," she demanded of him. The scene in his mind change and he groaned out loud. It was taking longer than she wanted but she needed to know. She didn't want his mind destroyed, so she fixated a thought on who she wanted. Nthanda. She searched for the girl and gasped when she saw her daughter wrapped in blankets, dead to the world.

She kept her cool as she found what she was looking for. The transfer. Pae was sleep and woke to find two males in furs talking with his sister and Shasa. Confused, he didn't understand what was going on. He knew they were waiting on humans to take the girl but the men before them were not human but witches of the sun. She could see their faces the way he had that night. One with green eyes and the other with molten amber. They were not rough with her child but they took her all the same. The one with molten amber eyes is the one she knew was the leader. He was the one who needed to pay for stealing her child.

The High Priestess released Pae from her grip and released the shadows that kept them hidden from everyone in the hall. Reappearing suddenly out of nothing didn't shock her people but, the only sounds came from Lae's screams. Calling out for her brother. Pae collapsed to the ground, unconscious. He still had breath in his body and for that he was lucky.

Lae turned her vicious gaze to the priestess, "What have you done to him?"

"Nothing more than have a mind to mind talk."

"Liar!" Lae yelled. "He lay there barely alive."

"I wouldn't be doing that if I was you. Calling your betters," she paused, "Liars. Young Pae is alive and will be well. My walk through his memories took a toll on him and exhausted his body. It taxes the person just as much as it taxes me."

Lae stopped her yelling and accusations. She had never met a dream walker before. They were just as bad as soul eaters she thought.

"You learn quickly. Just as I learned a lot on my short journey. You are not what you seem."

Lae swallowed then turned her head to look at Shasa. Her longtime mentor ignored her instead and she lowered her head. Shoulders slumped.

"I have told you how it started. It was her fault." Lae pointed at Shasa. If she had control of her powers, there was no doubt in Chanda's mine that it would have shot out and hit the woman. The chains the three prisoners had wrapped around their hands, chest, and feet were created by her mother. Designed to keep the powers at bay. There was no possible way they could touch their wells.

"I know better. I saw into your brother's mind. It is amazing what you can find when you know where to look. You had so much potential Lae if only you were part of the right coven. Shasa is a rot that poisons everything she touches. She has poisoned you, your brother and many others. It will end today. I have made judgement," Chanda said.

The High Priestess found the crowd full of terrifying grins. They knew what was coming. Vindication for what happened to them and their own friends and family. Vindication for the betrayal. But this was only the start. There were more in the world to pay. And they would find them all.

"Lae. You are guilty of treason against your own kind. You willingly betrayed your coven and your High Priestess. The crimes are easy to stack up and relive but I'd rather we move on. Your heart is just as diseased as your soul. Avarice and greed found root there and flourished to your mind. You are not what we Children of the Moon are supposed to be. The Mother Goddess would not be pleased. As a speaker of the gods, I banish your soul to Athos, Lord of the Evernight. The God of Death. May you find redemption before your rebirth into this world!"

The High Priestess didn't move from where she stood. Stretching her hands and arms in front of her, the lingering shadows in the hall answered the witch's call. They danced around the shackled woman wrapping around Lae like fingers wrapping itself around a fragile glass. Lae was lifted into the air, while swirls of grey and black smoke encircled her. She hovered above the basalt stone ground, her feet pointed downwards, the rags of the barely there cloth hung off her frame, exposing her flesh to everyone. Lae's face was a mask of indifference but the High Priestess could practically feel the fear roll off the young woman.

"Any last words?" Chanda cooed.

"I hate you, Shasa. May your soul never find peace," Lae said as she spat down at the woman on the ground beside her. The woman who mentored her. The woman who was like a surrogate mother to her and her brother didn't even bother to look up at her. To acknowledge her or her words. "What will happen to him? He really didn't want any part of this, Priestess. And for whatever it is worth, I am truly sorry for my actions during that time." Lae's voice cracked.

She never thought they would get caught, but they did and she regretted everything she did. She wasn't ready to die. She wanted a family of her own but it wouldn't happen now.

"I know he didn't want to but the love of a sister is strong. The sacred ties that binds twins like you, it will do many things to a person when loves come into play. Don't worry about him. He will have to face the punishment for what he did," The High Priestess stepped towards the young woman and whispered to her so only she could hear, "But he will not die. His actions don't warrant death. He did not want what you did, and he was remorseful for his actions. I don't feel as much with you." The High Priestess grabbed Lae's wrists and sliced them with the bone dagger she wore at her side.

Chanda then took the dagger and drove it into the chest of Lae and slashed down to her belly. Warm blood coated her hands and arms. She smeared it across her face as if it was war paint then licked it off her fingers. She released the hold on Lae. The woman was on the brink of death when she drove the knife into her chest. The latter was just for the pain they had caused her family. Lae's lifeless body fell to the ground and formed into a crumpled pile.

The High Priestess faced her coven. Her people. All of those harmed or hurt because of the actions of the three before them.

"Take her remains and feed them to the hounds below," she told the guards near her. Without hesitation, they moved fast, picked up the not yet cold body and removed it from the room.

"My people," Chanda called out to her covens. "We have waited three long years for this moment. Three years of searching and looking for the ones responsible for the horrors they inflicted on our own. Wondering why they would hurt us when we all should come together against our true enemies. They were greedy and wanted which wasn't theirs to have and for this many of them paid. But we have here tonight one who hasn't paid for her deeds. For her transgressions against us. She will suffer and wish for death but will we grant her the release?"

The noise in the hall was deafening. The jeers and shouts resounded and bounced off the walls. Her people were hungry and thirsty for revenge and she would give it to them. The High Priestess went to Shasa and grabbed her at the throat and lifted her into the air.

"You will not die this day. Or tomorrow. Or even the next day. You will wish for death. Pray for death but the Mother Goddess and her son, Athos will not allow it. Mynhit, she sanctions your pain and your screams will be payment in abundance. When you think you can't hold on any longer and try to slip from us, I will grab hold of your soul and place it back into its cage. You will only die when I say and I don't feel too generous towards your plight anytime soon."

Chapter 15

"Since you won't tell us your name. Will you at least tell us your age? You've been here for three years now and we know nothing about you," Nessya asked the girl. She wanted to know more about the girl she had come to like. She wasn't one of them, but she was still interesting. Her views and her beliefs were opposite of those who lived in the land of Namansii. Even her looks differed from those of the Children of the Sun.

Nthanda was chained to the wall in a small earthen styled room. Made from a combination of stone, packed earth, and metals. Her captors had to relocate and now occupied a home in the Golden City. No longer residing inside the palace, Te'Mak Tovoz had a private compound but still on the royal grounds.

She hadn't gave up on trying to find a way out of the grasps of the ones who held her in chains. Nthanda hated all of them. Lately, Tovoz rarely let her out to have fresh air or to even walk. She no longer served the family or was allowed in their presence. Tovoz and his family had standards being a noble and all. Having a dark witchling serve in his household didn't look good for him and his children. No, in a moment's time once they moved to the current location, Nthanda truly had become a prisoner. The only joy she had was news of the well-planned attacks on the coastal cities and its shores. The Namansii islands were no longer safe, and neither was the human desert lands. Nowhere was safe if you were a Child of the Sun.

It was a relief for Nthanda to know that her family hadn't forgotten about her. That they still searched for her.

"Why does it matter how old I am? Knowing my age won't change anything. I will still be chained to these walls. Still a slave to your family."

"You are more than just a slave. You're important. I overheard papa and grandfather."

This wasn't news to Nthanda. Plenty of times she overheard the elder Te'Mak discuss with Tovoz that she was important. That the Enyxians didn't give up looking for her. They couldn't understand why they refused to give up. Knowing this, the Godspeaker became even more curious about Nthanda.

"What do you mean I am important? I am just a girl you stole away from her home. I can't even touch my well. There should be no worry for me causing harm."

"You can do more harm without than a person with their gifts. Don't discount yourself."

Nthanda was curious about what the girl meant. Wondered if she saw something or if she had seen Kai. "What is this news you've claimed to have heard so you can leave me be. This is the only reason you come down here. To taunt me. I grow tired of the games. I just want to be alone."

"If I give you the news, you promise that you will tell me how old you are." Nessya hoped the girl would give in.

Nthanda eyed the girl warily. They would never find out her name. Not until she was ready for them to find out, but what harm could come from knowing her age. "I would clasp your arm the way your people do to seal the deal, but I can't." She shook her arms and wrist. The sound of metal clanked against each other in an off pitch, out of tune song. "These chains keep me from doing a lot of things, I'm afraid."

A spark of hope lit inside of Nessya, "So you will tell me how old you are?" She wanted to make sure she understood correctly.

"Yes. You tell me the news first and I will tell you my age. But once I tell you my age, you can tell no one else."

"I promise I won't," Nessya blurted out.

"No need for promises. Oddly enough, I trust and believe you. You're not like the others. For one, you taught me your tongue so I could understand. Two, you told me to keep it a secret that I knew the language and keep it a secret that you know mine." Nessya grinned. "Wipe the smile off your face. I can tell you are different. That is all. Don't make me regret my decision here tonight."

Nessya nodded, giddy with excitement. "I overheard papa and grandfather talking in the men's room. Women aren't allowed in there at all."

"So you were eavesdropping? How so if you couldn't get in the room?"

"I have my ways and I wasn't eavesdropping." Nessya defended herself. "I collect information because knowing important information is power. Eavesdropping is such a bad word." Nthanda's brow creased and her nose crinkled. "Like I was saying, I overheard Papa and Grandfather talking. They spoke of how our kind were dying in larger numbers. More so recently than in the last three years. Something must have happened. When we came here two years ago at the request of the Godspeaker, it was because there were rumors your people suspected we knew your exact whereabouts. It's why our holy Godspeaker ordered us here. To protect us from the dark witches."

"That's obvious. But go on," Nthanda said, fully invested in the girl's story.

"No, you don't understand. Your people knows. Somehow, they discovered the identity of my father and Uncle Zeran with our soldiers who took you away. Somehow your High Priestess found out. She searches for you."

Nthanda's stomach dropped when her mother was mentioned. She shrugged the unsettled feeling off. "Why would the High Priestess be looking for me? A nobody I am. I never met her in my entire life."

"I have no idea honestly. I was kind of hoping you would tell us."

"Us? Who is us? You keep saying 'Us.'" Nthanda's eyes narrowed and her mouth twisted.

"I meant me, not us. You know what I mean."

"I don't know what you mean. If you are spying on me for your elders, tell them to come ask me themselves if they are not too afraid!"

"I offended you," Nessya said. "I didn't mean to offend. I apologize."

"You didn't offend me but you are insulting my intelligence. I am not dumb. I see far more than what you may believe. Just because I am locked up in here, doesn't mean I still can't listen." Nthanda moved from her crouched position and sat on her backside. "Can you at least unchain me? I won't run. I won't do anything. I swear."

Nessya looked nervous. "I'll ask papa when he is alone."

Nthanda didn't like the look she had. The girl was hiding something, and she was determined to find out what. Times like this, she wished Kai was around but ever since they began to chain her up in the burrows, her familiar kept to the wild.

"If there's nothing else, can you leave? I *enjoy* sitting here in the dark in my filth."

"First you tell me your age. We made a deal you and me." Nessya insisted.

Nthanda exhaled a long sigh. There was no getting out of it. "Fine. I am fifteen winters old. Now will you let me be?" Nthanda huffed out. She flopped back onto the packed earthen walls and closed her eyes. She knew she was alone again when the girl didn't say another word.

Nessya closed the door and followed the corridor until it took her to a cramped stairwell. She climbed until she reached the entrance that led outside. She glanced around before darting through the lush courtyard and slipped inside her home. Soon as she stepped through the door, the scent of fresh *falis* bread and roasted fish made her mouth water. She didn't realize how hungry she was and she followed the wafting scent of hot food.

"There you are. Where have you been?" her mother asked. "We sent Tiabu to search for you."

"I wasn't far. Just enjoying outside." Her mother gave her a look that said she didn't believe her. Nessya glanced to her father as she sat down and his head moved into a nod that was barely perceptible.

"I smell my favorite. Roasted Tarp fish." Nessya said trying to break the tension. She looked around the table and found only her parents and her Uncle Zeran. "Where is Tiabu? Shouldn't she back if you sent her after me?"

Zeran was the one to speak up, "She'll be back soon enough. She probably was looking for you in all the spots where you two hangout." He picked up his cup, smiled at her, then took a long drink.

Nessya didn't like the way he grinned. The older she got the more she noticed that Zeran wasn't trustworthy. Plenty of conversations in secret with her father, she tried to warn him but he refused to listen. The man sat there and never let his stare wander too far from her. No one had to tell her, she could sense it. He knew something and wasn't telling.

She grinned back even though she didn't feel the emotion behind it. She didn't want anyone to think she was up to no good. The food on the table looked delicious and she couldn't wait to dive in. Eating would be her priority. Soon as she reached for the food, Tiabu walked in. Her friend gave her a hug and sat next to her.

"I've looked everywhere for you. All the usual and unusual spots."

"You didn't look hard enough," Nessya chuckled.

"I even checked in your getaway from everything hiding hole. You weren't there either so I gave up and came back. My stomach was making all sorts of noises."

"I don't have any of those get away from everything spots." Nessya knew she did but couldn't figure out how Tiabu would know.

"Oh, but you do." Tiabu faced the table and ignored the look that Nessya gave her. "This smells and look delicious. I can't wait to taste everything, Te'Ma."

NTHANDA WAS HELD BY two guards while Zeran stood with his feet apart and arms crossed before her. Taller than Nthanda by a head he had to look down to face her. The beautiful green that was the color of his pupils was full of malice and hate. The scowl was almost a permanent fixture whenever Tovoz wasn't around and he was alone with her.

Standing tall, Nthanda stood defiant to him. She already knew what was coming. His mouth moved and words came out but she pretended she didn't understand. It made things easier even if it was hard. Thanks to Nessya, she understood the curses and the jeers. She understood how he hated her for being someone different. A dark witch, his blood enemy. That's all he ever saw her as. To him, she was not a person. When the back of Zeran's hand connected with her face, she understood why too. It didn't make it right, but she had been in their clutches long enough to know how the jungle dwellers operated.

Pain blossomed across her cheeks. This was the way it always started. It wouldn't leave a mark on her skin to show what he did to her, but it left a mark on her soul. Her face stung and the coppery tang of blood filled her mouth. She aimed his way and spat it out. The fluid mixed with her spit and blood landed in the center of his tanned chest and she watched as it dripped slowly down his smooth skin.

"You bitch!" he yelled. Instead of an open palm, he balled his long fingers into a fist and punched her face. The blow was hard, and the force of it knocked her head back. A darkened sea of black, dotted with white stars filled her vision. A loud ringing sounded in her ears and before she could stop herself she kicked the man. When her foot connected with his rock hard legs, the contact jarred her. He didn't respond, but contained his assault on her.

Zeran called for another set of guards and told them to hold her legs. Unable to move, she took the beating. This was an occurrence that Te'Mak Zeran had done too often. Nthanda knew she would have bruises the next day. He had figured out Tovoz's schedule on seeing her and when the next time he would show up to inspect her. He made sure to always pay her a visit, when Tovoz wouldn't be visiting her again soon.

Most days he came alone. Sometimes he brought his guards. Then on the truly horrible days, he would bring his daughter, Tiabu. Those were the worst days and she was grateful it wasn't one of those days again. Zeran would have Tiabu practice on Nthanda. Vicious type of spells that did physical damage. Unable to protect herself, she always came away with scars. Then Nessya would sneak in afterwards and work what little healing magic she knew and healed it enough to where she wouldn't scar. Many nights Nthanda prayed to the Mother Goddess asking for a way to protect herself from those two. She prayed that Tiabu and her father would die a gruesome death and be sent to the Evernight.

Nthanda never got a response but it didn't stop the prayer from falling off her lips.

The witchling didn't realize that she was lying on the dirt floor of her cell until she tasted it in her mouth. Not able to move, it was almost as if she was paralyzed. Every time she took a breath, a searing, sharp sensation stabbed her in the chest. Her left eye was swollen shut. Nthanda's head throbbed a steady staccato beat and the drumming got louder. She wished she would have died but instead, she succumbed to the sweet relief of darkness.

Chapter 16

Nthanda wore thick white furs around her shoulders and warm winter boots on her feet. The mare she rode was quick and flew across the trail that cut through the trees. Dodging and ducking from the snow-covered pine tree branches as she blazed through brought her immense joy. Her smile was bright as the full moon that shone down on her and her laughter, infectious as it was, echoed across the night sky. She was happy. It was the first time she felt the emotion in years. She was finally home. No longer a prisoner to the Children of the Sun.

Streaks of spotted fur, slipped in and out of the woods, as it kept pace with her and her horse. She could feel through their bond how much Kai loved the run. The thrill of the chase and of being home. It was something she never thought she could do or see again. Serea's and her mother's banter caught up to her, letting her know they were not too far behind.

Nthanda rounded a small curve, and the opened expanse of flat lands spread out before her. She slowed the horse down to a trot then an eventual stop. She twisted herself around, looking back while still on her mare. Nthanda's mouth gaped opened. Kai was nowhere to be found. Serea and her mother was like they were never there. Gone. No trees. No dirt paths like the one she was just on. Looking forward again, all around her was an endless field of ice. Crystal blue and dangerous in its beauty surrounded her. Nthanda eased down from the horse and carefully walked to the edge, refusing to go any further. She didn't understand why the landscape had changed. It was not natural; it was wrong. It wasn't supposed to do that.

Nthanda's eyes darted back and forth. The vice grip that had an iron hold on her chest tightened. She was weak in her legs and wasn't able to catch her breath. She closed her eyes and counted to three. The pressing need and desire to depart washed over her. She had to get out of there. This was a trap, she thought. She turned to go back to the mare she rode, but the horse had disappeared too. The world around her had changed again and had become bright white. Flat lands of nothing but soft, powdery, blinding snow. The temperature was dropping, and she shivered against the cold air. No longer unsure of herself and what to do. She didn't know which way to go or turn. Afraid to go in circles, because if she did, the world would change again. She screamed for help.

"Do not trouble yourself, daughter," a woman's voice said on the wind. Nthanda turned towards it but saw nothing. The sound was familiar to her ears, but it was a sound she hadn't heard in almost seven years.

"Mama?" she called to the wind. "Is that you? It can't be. Show yourself whoever you are. Quit playing games with me. This has to be a trick."

"I assure you it's not a trick," the woman's voice said as she materialized in front of Nthanda.

The High Priestess wore a sleeveless midnight blue gauze dress that flowed around her curves like a river. The neckline plunged deep between her breasts in the form of a V. Glistening symbols the color of silver from the Evernight, marked her arms and her burning gaze never left Nthanda.

"You have grown so much. Nearly a woman." Chanda observed. She could see the burgeoning features of womanhood on her daughter and other things. "You are thin. Do they not feed you?"

Nthanda was in shock. She couldn't understand how her mother was before her. Talking to her. "How are you here? You're not real!"

"I am as real as you are real," Chanda said and stepped closer to her daughter. She wrapped her arms around Nthanda and embraced her missing heart part. Nthanda remembered the warmth of her mother's arms and let the tears slide down her cheeks.

"How are you here? How am I here? Where are we?"

"You still ask a lot of questions, witchling." Chanda chuckled. Her sad eyes roamed the landscape before finding her daughter again. "This place, I created. It kept changing because I couldn't hold the landscape down to one. These flatlands are easier to keep. I thought you would like the snow. That you would miss it by now." The high priestess smiled. Nthanda was confused. She didn't understand.

"But..." Nthanda said.

"I can walk in the minds of men and women and search their dreams."

"You can dream walk now?"

"I am not a true dream walker. Your grandmother and I have been doing a lot of reading. In my sanctuary's library there are old tomes from the first witches of our bloodline. They are filled with information about dream walkers. Some of our an-

cestors were born with the skill and the traits are passed on to their children and so on. We will always have the trait, but it's up to the Mother Goddess if that trait manifests and bloom. In those sacred texts, we discovered a way to use the skills without being a true walker. It spoke of ways to reach the ones we search for that carry our blood. With the right ingredients, we can find them in their dreams. We've been searching for you. Searching a long time now. All of my trying has paid off it seems."

Nthanda knew they wouldn't have forgotten her. "I want to come home but I don't know how. They blocked my powers from me."

The High Priestess form flickered in and out.

"Mama!" Nthanda cried out. "Please don't leave me. You only just came."

"This is all new to me. I can't keep this place long. I've been trying so hard to reach you but I wasn't strong enough. I'm barely holding on now. I don't know if I will be able to come back again anytime soon so we must be quick."

Nthanda nodded. She understood. Her mother was strong but the casting must have been life draining. "How do I remove this geas on my powers? I miss the cold fire that always sat low in my belly. Now, here I am always hot and sticky. Sometimes there's a spark of fire in my chest and it scares me. For the last seven years, since I've been in these lands, I felt it now and then."

Chanda caressed the side of her daughter's face. She wondered for years if it would happen. Now she knew it to be true. "I know they have hidden you deep in the Golden City. It is a sacred place to them. Their lands are holy and our powers can't touch there. I can't remove the geas that have you chained like an animal. Perhaps you can. That fire. That spark. It is a type of power too. Nurture it. Let it fill you. Remember, you are your mother's daughter but you are your father's child too. There will be a reckoning for what they have done to you, love. Stay strong. We will see you soon. You will break free of their chains and come home to us. The Mother Goddess demands it. Never lose faith in the goddess."

Nthanda tears were heavier and flowed like a raging river down her face. "Don't leave me. Please don't leave me. I can't stay here any longer."

"I wish I could but I can't stay longer either. I don't have the strength. There is a cost for everything. I love you. Come home," Chanda said. Her voice was faint, and she was fading away. Soon enough, she too disappeared from Nthanda's presence. "Come Home..." Remnants of her voice echoed in Nthanda's ears.

Nthanda fell to her knees, and the dam broke. She couldn't contain the sobs that racked her body. She was glad to see her mother, but it opened up fresh wounds of when she was first taken. The despair and loneliness she had endured. The physical pain over the years. And losing something so important to her. Her powers.

NTHANDA WOKE UP TO a rough tongue licking her face. Kai had come back and was beside her, comforting her. Nthanda knew that Kai could sense her pain that leaked through their bond. Her familiar would always be there, especially in her lowest moments, she could count on the creature and for that she thanked the goddess many times over.

Kai was the only piece of home she had besides the necklace she wore around her neck.

She sat up from the itchy, straw mat they gave her for a bed. Not able to stop scratching her arms and legs, welt marks rose where her fingernails dug too deep. Kai, now full grown and strong, took up most of the space on the bedding they shared. Once Nthanda discovered that her familiar was special and able to become invisible, she kept her closer to her more than ever. Kai still preferred to roam in the jungle to feed, listen, and to learn about their captors. She was Nthanda's ears when she couldn't use her own.

"Kai, I need to tell you something," Nthanda whispered to the large cat. "I had the weirdest dream. I saw my mama. She said she was dream walking. That she have been searching for me."

Walking the dreams of men is for the goddess and gods. Is your mother a goddess?

"No, but she is a favored speaker of the Mother Goddess. Besides, dream walking is something my ancestors used to do."

Then your line is blessed. No wonder she sent me towards your path.

"That wasn't all, Kai. My mother said some things. She said that we need to leave. She said that we need to come home."

I do prefer the snow over this heat. Kai licked her front paws.

"Kai."

Bright Star.

"You know what I mean."

Kai chuffed in a way that Nthanda could tell it was her familiar's way of laughing.

"There was other things remember," she said

I remember. Tell me, what was it?

"The warmth I feel in my chest. That spark, it is there constantly. It reminds me of my power, but it is wild compared to the cold fire that chilled low in my belly."

Have you tried to use it?

"No. Should I?"

Why ask me when you already know the answer to your own question?

Nthanda became quiet and retreated to her thoughts. Kai curled next to her, even though it was warm, she still didn't mind too much. She had to try it but she wouldn't do it just yet. She needed help and the only person she knew would help would be Nessya. The only problem Nthanda had with that was trusting her. Was the girl trustworthy enough to divulge that information? Nessya is after all, the daughter to her captor. Nthanda was only a prisoner to them.

"We need to test Nessya."

Why?

"She can help me with this spark if it is my magic power manifesting in another way, then I should be able to touch it and use it. We could escape. We can run and be free from all this."

The girl is the only one I believe would be trustworthy but I still don't trust her. She would have to prove herself an ally. If you say we must test her, how should we do it?

"Give me some time and I will figure something out. I don't know, mama sounded like it was urgent we find a way home. She said something else. Something about my father. I have questions. She has never once in my life, before they took me away, mentioned the man who sired me."

Nthanda for the first time felt like she had a plan to get away from her captors. From the pain and hurt they inflicted on her. That spark inside her chest flared as her anger rose. They would pay and they would pay dearly for what they did. The beatings. The many days of no food and no water. Being placed on parade in front of their Godspeaker and nobles. Laughed at. They would regret the day they let a Child of the Moon into their midst.

Chapter 17

Winter Solstice, Eight years later...

Bright Star.

"Yes."

I remember many things. On this night eight winters ago, I found you.

Nthanda smiled as she remembered that night. She was so excited to find her familiar.

"I remember. The weather was so cold that fateful evening. Wrapped in that beautiful silver cloak lined with bear fur, I was able to stay warm and not freeze to death. My mother had Sienna make that for me. I loved that cloak." Nthanda turned her head towards Kai. "I did everything they told me to do and still couldn't understand why my familiar wouldn't show. I had given up. Then I saw the most beautiful cub with spots on her back. She followed me you know."

I do.

"Then I figured the cub was lost, so I tried to make the animal go back from where it came."

The cub was stubborn.

"That cub still is stubborn. Just grown up and bigger now," she chuckled and fingered the necklace around her neck. "Imagine the surprise when I first heard that cub's voice in my head after touching her. The ramifications didn't dawn on me that she was there for me, and I was there for her. That night Kai, we found each other. I thank the Mother Goddess every night for you. This place is bad but you make the misery at least bearable."

I feel the same way. Happy day of birth, Bright Star.

Nthanda didn't realize it was her born day. In the jungle, winter didn't show up like it did back home for her. It was a bittersweet moment. She hit her majority all the while in the lands of her enemies. In their hands. She should be home, excited, as her family prepared for a huge celebration. Her rising moment to join her coven as a full member. Instead, she was in the jungles of the sun witches, far away from proper civilization. She wanted to cry, but she couldn't even force a tear to fall. The only emotions she had was anger and hatred towards those who stole her away. She wanted them to all die.

Orange and red flames from the torches outside the cell door crackled and roared to life. Nthanda stood and moved closer to the light like a moth to fire, squinting at the sudden brightness. She could hear voices but couldn't tell who they belonged to. Too far away, deep and soft sounds echoed down the hall reaching her ears. The thick smoke curled into twisting slated gray spirals as it caused her to have a coughing spell. The flames flickered back and forth forming harsh shadows through the narrow slits of the iron bars keeping her from freedom. She stepped back into the darkness of her cell and watched the shadows as they danced on her wall, twisting into monstrous shapes and forms. They reminded her of the monsters of her dreams of late.

"Someone is coming. You should go, Kai."

Nthanda's familiar could somehow come and go through the spelled bars without hindrance unlike her, they were designed to keep her in. Her captors didn't know about her familiar who had been by her side since they took her and it would stay that way. Kai's growling sound and in that instant she knew who it was. Kai didn't like Tiabu just as much as she did. The girl now a young woman was always horrible, but it was worse. Ever since Tiabu became engaged to the Godspeaker's youngest son, her cruelty knew no bounds. Nthanda carried reminder scars of her cruelty on her back. Even Nessya didn't get a pass lately.

"Fine, you can stay but you must hide."

You worry too much. Have you done your kicking routine today?

"What does that have anything to do with you hiding?"

You should practice on the loud mouth. Kai grinned with her large fangs showing. Nthanda thought it was a grin. Whatever it was, it made her chuckle.

"Come on, Kai. Please." She rubbed the giant cat ears and kissed the top of her head.

I hate what she does to you. Let me rip her throat out.

Nthanda could hear people coming closer. If Kai didn't hide right then, they would find her. "I promise you one day soon, you will have the chance to go wild on these jungle dwellers. Today is not that day!"

Kai chuffed and disappeared from sight. *I'll hold you to your words, Bright Star*

They no longer locked Nthanda in chains. No longer afraid she would run away or do anything to harm them. They thought she was defeated, docile and tamed. Relaxed in their imprisonment, their concern wasn't much anymore. Spelled so she couldn't touch her powers, they took comfort in that. All the while, her captors lived safe above in the Golden City as if the world was the same day to day. Safe away from the constant attack on their shores and inland cities. Away from the daemons that her mother and grandmother sent to search for her.

The Children of the Sun laughed and got drunk while she roamed deep below, in what they called the burrows. A deep underground network of tunnels and dens that ran underneath the royal palace complex and its connecting noble houses. In those burrows, each home of a noble has an entrance that takes them down to the earthen prison. Each family have its own area with a set of cells connected to them for their use. Locked by spells and chains, Nthanda could never get the fire spark in her chest to work right enough to break them.

She had plenty of space in her den, but still it was unfavorable conditions. If it wasn't for the Te'Mak's daughter, Nessya, she knew it would have been much worse. The only plus side to being so far underground was the colder air. It reminded her of home and all that she had lost. She missed the light of the moon at night and even missed the warmth of the sunlight during the day but the cold was a comfort. They didn't let her out much, but she made sure she kept strong. On the days they didn't feed her, Kai would bring foodstuff, so she could hide it in the hole she made in the packed earth floor close to the wall. Nthanda thanked the Mother Goddess every night for her familiar.

The voices were louder and Nthanda knew they were closer. She sat down on the cloth and feather bedding, rested her head against the wall and closed her eyes. Her chest rose up and down in a steady rhythm as she tried to find her center. The sour smell from being unwashed burned her nose. The white and black wavy tresses that covered her head was now brown and limp as layers of dirt and grime coated her skin and hair. She would do anything for a bath and clean clothes. It had been too long since the last time they even gave her that.

The chains unraveled and Nthanda's body went rigid when she heard Te'Mak Zeran's voice. He was the other person with Tiabu. The father and daughter duo were beasts. She thought her own mama was bad when she was a child, but now a woman; she had come to the understanding that those two were a different breed of an animal. Her mother did what she did to teach a lesson. Used as punishment. These two got enjoyment from it. They were cold and cunning and to her, they perpetrated the stigma against her people more than her own people did.

Clinking metal and the citrus tang of controlled magic hung in the air. Nthanda eyes shot opened. For the longest time, she could not smell the tang of other magic users. When they had placed a geas on her after capturing her, it blocked her own magic and her ability to sense others. She remembered and knew what it was. She had missed the slight burning odor. If she could smell the scent of magic, there could be a possibility she could use her powers in full.

She still didn't feel the cold flames inside of her, but that warm spark still held steady in her chest. A grin lifted at the corners of her lips and when Zeran walked into the room with his swaggering gait; she was still smiling.

"Looks like the *hoshta* is happy to see me." Zeran laughed. "That is what your people call humans isn't it? Never mind if they did or not, you are lower than human and don't deserve breath. You lived eight helions too long."

"Papa, you know we didn't come down here for fun. Well, maybe I did. I still don't understand what is so important about her. Why is the Godspeaker so fascinated with her? The prince keeps me informed, and she's the reason our people are dying on the coasts and the islands."

"Hush girl. You say too much." Zeran scolded his daughter. Tiabu stepped back without another word.

Nthanda didn't know their people were dying and that small piece of information filled her with glee. It wasn't much, but she would take what little she could get. It was enough to keep the grin on her face.

Zeran stepped closer to her. His smooth chiseled jaw tightened and his bright green eyes hardened. The hatred he harbored radiated off of him and Nthanda could feel it. "You will learn to respect your betters." He backhanded her quickly, she stumbled backwards, head bouncing off the hard-packed earth. She didn't see that coming and the sting from his hand bloomed across her face.

"You will regret that," she said to him in her native tongue. "All of you!"

"Look papa. She can talk. Too bad she doesn't speak our tongue like a proper witch."

"She's no witch. She is the scum at the bottom of our death pits," Zeran responded. He didn't give Nthanda time to compose herself, he grabbed her neck and slowly squeezed. "The only good winter witch is a dead winter witch."

Tiabu giggled like a little girl behind him. She looked over her shoulders before she stepped closer to the others. "Please papa, let me try. You know I am a favored daughter of the Elios. He sanctions my actions this day."

"All the reason to let me do what I came to do. You are to marry Prince Alios when the sun is high in the sky today. You should be preparing and not down here following me."

"I know."

Zeran sighed. His shoulders relaxed and his hands around Nthanda's neck loosened. He turned his head towards Tiabu, "Do your best. Show me how much you have learned." He shoved Nthanda against the wall and moved to allow Tiabu room.

"I will leave her unbound. Make it quick. We need to leave before Tovoz come down."

Tiabu nodded and stalked towards Nthanda. Yellowish light formed in her hands and her lips moved silent while she recited a spell. Nthanda didn't know any protection spells to use against the sun witch. The light in Tiabu's hands twisted into two small daggers, and she flicked them at Nthanda, piercing her shoulders. A grunt escaped Nthanda's lip and blood welled up in the small cuts.

Bright Star, Kai called to her through their connection.

Nthanda shook her head. "No. Not yet."

"What are you saying? You should speak our tongue not that abomination of yours." Tiabu grabbed Nthanda's jaw and forced her to face her. "You are nothing special. Never have been. Your own family doesn't even want you or else they would have come for you long ago. You are worthless!"

Nthanda was over it all. Without thinking, she moved with quickness and hit her head against Tiabu's, forcing the young woman to the ground. A loud scream erupted from Zeran's daughter mouth, and he rushed his broad shoulders into Nthanda's chest, knocking the wind out of her lungs.

The warmth in Nthanda's chest flared hotter and took her by surprise. She didn't know what was going on but the return of her magic felt good to her as it rushed through her veins and limbs. Nthanda didn't have much time to think about the revelation because Tiabu was up again and the look on her face said she was pissed. The Te'Mak's daughter took out a small glowing blade, imbued with her magic. The blade burst into flames and before Nthanda could do anything to protect herself, Tiabu lunged from her spot and attacked. Nthanda didn't realize the woman had even moved.

Tiabu was on her so fast with the flaming knife and plunged it deep into her shoulder. With a twist, Nthanda felt the fire burn her inside. She couldn't keep the screams from escaping her mouth no matter how hard she tried. Tiabu held her down and forced more power into the blade inside of her shoulder.

"Se Elios te'zho nesvia te maka voz na o," Tiabu chanted over and over. Her eyes glazed over and her pupils turned a solid white. Nthanda tried to remove the woman off her but it was the same as trying to move a large boulder.

"If she doesn't shut up, Tovoz alarms and forces will be alerted and head down this way," Zeran shouted.

Tiabu stilled with her head facing upwards. Her lips moved faster, and her chanting was fevered and grew louder. The pain was more pronounced in Nthanda's shoulder and it spread across her body, keeping with the speed of the chanted spell. Nthanda couldn't do anything to stop it. She couldn't move her limbs. They were too heavy to lift.

Bright Star! Kai could feel what her witch was going through, and she was doing her best to restrain herself from interfering.

Don't, Kai. Stay wherever you are at. Nthanda commanded her familiar through their bond. The command hit Kai like a branch to the face and had no choice but to obey.

Fine. Don't make me regret this decision, Kai grumbled.

Te'Mak Zeran watched with pure pleasure in his face. He had stepped further away from the two young women and checked the gates to make sure Tovoz or his guards didn't show up.

"Finish it," he shouted. He knew the spell too well. The air was thick with its charge. The spell needed a release, or they all would feel the blowback. All it needed was the final execution and Tiabu was holding off. He kept looking behind towards the halls. That much magic would cause any of the families above to come check it out.

Tiabu eyes returned to normal and glanced down at Nthanda, "You should prepare to meet your pathetic and useless goddess, witch!"

A blast of blinding white light emitted from Tiabu and filled the small chamber. The burning sensation inside of Nthanda grew until she couldn't contain it anymore and exploded from her. It met the bright light from the woman on top of her and collided into a spectacle of black and purplish tendrils wrestling with tendrils of light like the sun. The power of both witches met with a concussive sound and threw Tiabu backwards into the wall. She slid to the floor.

Arms, legs, both weak and sore. Nthanda slowly got up and stood there. Her body trembled all over. She gulped for air trying to catch her breath. She searched the room and found Kai safe. She faced the two people who had tortured her for years and slowly moved their way. Every step she took, her body ached. She didn't know what happened, but somehow her magic broke free and protected her.

Bright Star. Look at your hands and arms, Kai told her.

Nthanda stopped her movement and looked down and saw how a thin film of the same dark blueish energy wrapped around her. Her power never was that color before and she didn't know what it meant but it coursed through her body and she refused to let it ever get locked up again. The rush of it all made her remember her youth before it turned sour.

From the corner of her eyes, there was a motion that caught her attention. The pushback from their power colliding had blasted the cell door to pieces. Te'Mak Zeran and his daughter stilled breathed and was sitting up. Blood dripped from the cuts on their heads and arms. Zeran placed his head in hands, disoriented. Tiabu glanced around before locking her gaze with Nthanda's.

Standing up, her face twisted into something monstrous. Without warning, she flung a spiked orb towards Nthanda hoping to catch her off guard, but Nthanda could feel the surge of Tiabu's power before she released it. Nthanda dodged and pulled deep from the voided Evernight and ran towards the young woman. She shaped the energy she was manifesting and formed it into a long dagger with a blade so black it looked like it came from the god of death itself.

Tiabu set her feet apart and prepared herself for the full impact of Nthanda but it never came. The only thing she felt was the sharp pain in her chest as it radiated outwards to the rest of her limbs. She looked down to find a blade sticking in her chest with Nthanda's hand still on the glowing handle. She glanced back up to the woman who shoved it there and grimaced. Dark reddish blood that looked black in the shadows of the chamber, bubbled over her lips and streamed down her chin. Her steps faltered as she staggered backwards.

"May the Lord of the Evernight watch over your soul. May it find no peace and rot in the bowels of the void for eternity," Nthanda whispered to her in Tiabu's tongue. She made sure she could understand the words that flowed from her mouth. Nthanda released her hold on the dagger and made it disappear as Tiabu slumped to the ground.

All she heard was Zeran shouting and yelling. Nthanda knew the moment Tiabu took her last breath, and all she felt was sweet relief. For too long she suffered torture at the hands of her cruelty and Nthanda relished in the payback. Too sudden, a wave of dizziness hit her and Nthanda stumbled backwards. Everything was blurry as her vision left her.

The encroaching darkness hounded her. More voices entered the fray. Deep and angry men voices. They argued and shouted at each other, each voice rose over the other. The one voice she remembered was Zeran's and the anguish in his tone was enough to make her smile.

Bright Star. What can I do to help you? Kai panicked.

Nthanda heard her familiar but couldn't respond. She was tired and had no energy to move anymore. She fell to her knees. The jarring upon hitting the hardened earth still couldn't get a reaction from her. She tumbled onto the ground and let the sweet darkness take over her.

Chapter 18

"Why are you down here, Zeran?" Tovoz shouted. Frustrated, he ran his fingers through his long tresses. He didn't know what the huge release of power meant when they felt it above but he was determined to find out. With his trusted guards by Tovoz's side, they quickly made way into his family's area of the burrows. The scene before him was not what he had expected. His prisoner unconscious and his friend hovered over his daughter crying. Tovoz was more than angry. Hurt and afraid was what bothered him the most. Once the Godspeaker and his favorite son, the Prince, find out what happened, they would be in a world of trouble. All of them. Tiabu was dead, and it was by the hands of his prisoner. That much he could get out from Zeran. Tiabu was to marry to Prince Alios and he would demand retribution for his former betrothed. Days like this he wished his father was still alive to deal with the problems and not him.

Tovoz paced back and forth beside his prisoner. So many scenarios and thoughts ran through his head. He had no clue how any of this even happened. Zeran or Tiabu shouldn't have been down there. He stopped in his tracks as disjointed memories pieced together to make the puzzle whole. He remembered Nessya over the years as she tried to tell him, or warn him about Zeran and Tiabu hurting the girl. He never listened, instead he shrugged it off. He never could understand why the girl would end up with bruises and cuts all the time. He assumed it was self-inflicted. Then one day it stopped. Now, he saw the truth of everything.

He bent over her and checked to see if she still lived. He almost wished she had died instead of Tiabu. She had brought nothing but trouble and scrutiny to his house and family. Letting out a frustrated shout, he checked the girl for the geas. Not finding it, panic set in. *No wonder she had the power to do what she did,* he thought. Tovoz didn't realize his geas didn't work any longer. If the Godspeaker found out, he would be sacrificed because of his negligence. He placed it back on the girl and poured as much of his power into the geas as he could. Hoping it lasted this time.

He snapped his fingers at his guards, motioning them over. "Take her to the next cell and lock her in. Timo. Suya. You stay and stand guard. Make sure no one come near her or into her cell. I don't care what they say. If it's not me or Nessya, turn them away."

Timo and Suya crossed their arms over their chest and bowed their head. They lifted the girl and left. Tovoz turned on his friend and stalked towards him. He picked Zeran up and threw him against the wall. He didn't care if he was already hurt. This was all his fault. Tovoz balled his hand into a fist and punched his longtime friend in the face and repeated the motion until it tired him. Zeran didn't fight back. He took all the blows Tovoz gave him. Panting and short of breath, Tovoz wiped the perspiration on his brow and pointed at his friend.

"You are the reason she is dead. Not that girl in the other room. You! If you would have left her alone like they ordered us to do, Tiabu would still be alive. Now you have brought the might of the Godspeaker down on my family and I will never forgive you, Zeran. Take your daughter and leave from here! I want nothing to do with you!" Tovoz shouted, stepped over the dead girl, and left Zeran on the ground crying.

MUTED LIKE SOMEONE had stuffed cloth inside her skull and pounded it with a stick, she wanted to scream. The pain didn't get any better. Nthanda sat upright with her hands on both sides of her head and groaned when everything began to spin. She closed her eyes, hoping it would all go away. Through the bond, she could feel Kai and reached out for the cat. The leopard padded softly to her and placed her head in her lap.

There are guards at the door, Bright Star.

What happened? Last I remember was shoving the knife in Tiabu's chest.

The girl is dead. You did well.

Nthanda sensed her familiar's amusement and pride and shoved it aside for later. *Then why are we still in a cage?*

You passed out and I couldn't get you awake. I stayed hidden and followed those who carried you in here.

"Aaaagh," Nthanda cried out and doubled over. She swallowed to keep whatever down that tried to come back up.

Suya, a woman with short raven black hair and eyes the color of a summer storm cloud turned and hit the bars to the cell. "Quiet in there," she shouted.

Your powers are free again. I can tell through the bonds, Kai said. *But the man. The one you call Tovoz placed another spelled geas on you. I watched as he did it.*

I feel it. The geas, Nthanda said as she rubbed her chest. *It didn't work. His magic is warring with my magic. Fighting for control. I think he knew it wouldn't work. It's almost like an illusion spell. Penetrates deep enough to seem like it is there but its not.*

Nthanda wasn't slow and understood the implications of his actions. Tovoz was afraid. If a stronger witch, one who could sense the magic spells of others, checked for the geas, he would be in trouble. His entire family would be in danger from the Godspeaker. If they were in trouble, no doubt her life was in perilous danger. Her time had run out.

Those two were talking about you having to go before Godspeaker Nelioz and his son. Bright Star, we can't go before them.

You mean I can't go before them. My captors don't even know you exist.

They almost found out before your magic broke free. Lucky them.

Yes, lucky them. Either way, I'm not surprised. I killed the prince's bride. Of course I'd have to go before them.

You can't. He and his son is strong but I know why he has that cabal of witches as guards. They are the real power behind the Godspeaker. You can't fight them all and live.

What do you mean?

Exactly what I said.

The Godspeaker is strong. You can match his strength. His son is strong for a half-breed bu-

Half-breed? Nthanda interrupted. *Now you must explain, Kai. I'm lost and still dazed from this pain in my head.*

I've learned a lot about this place when I roam. Godspeaker Nelioz bloodline is diluted. No one knows, but members of his cabal suspects. That's why he keeps them on a tight leash and they watch his every move. It's an abomination for the leader of their people to breed with the humans. They see them as playthings and that's it.

How in the Evernight did you find this out?

I listen. Heard him talking with the mother of his youngest one night. The oldest son is full witch. The rest including his heir is half witch. If it's found out that the heir and favored son of Godspeaker Nelioz is only half witch, there will be a rebellion. He was happy when his son showed signs of power and he only wanted him to marry that awful Tiabu to make sure the children came out strong. He is trying to hide and erase the human part of his son.

Does the prince know? Nthanda asked.

No. He is clueless.

Nthanda's hand stopped petting the cat. If anyone knew what she was just told, the royal line would be sacrificed and the Godspeaker with them. They are okay with humans and get along well with them from what she saw, but breeding with them. The nobles wouldn't go for it.

That is unexpected news.

Yes, it is. I must hide, the man and his daughter are coming. Kai stood on all fours and her tail swished back and forth. *I am tired of hiding. One day soon I won't have to hide anymore and the world will tremble at my might.*

Nthanda rolled her eyes and grinned. *You can be so over the top.*

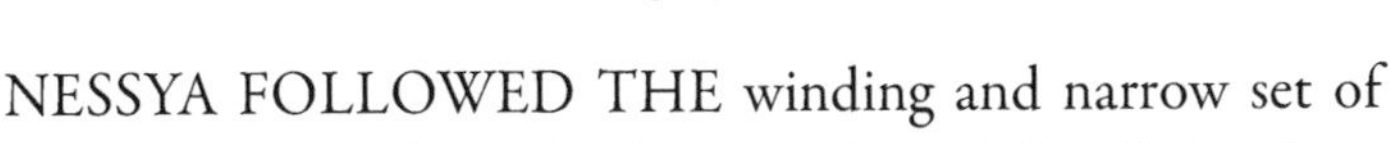

NESSYA FOLLOWED THE winding and narrow set of stairs before reaching the bottom. Ahead, her father kept a quick pace full of purpose. The colorful beads he wore around his neck and arms, letting others know he was head of his house, clanked together in a high tempo cadence as he moved. Tovoz had received the awaited summons to the palace with the prisoner. Fury vibrated through his being and Nessya was afraid to even speak to him.

The Godspeaker found out courtesy of Zeran who blamed Tovoz and his family for Tiabu's death. Being the daughter of a noble and the future bride for the heir, justice moved swiftly when called for. Zeran and the Prince demanded retribution. Nessya didn't have to be told, she knew her entire family lives were at stake.

Over the years, she warned her father of Zeran and Tiabu's actions, but her father never believed her. She loved her Uncle Zeran, but he was like any other Child of the Sun. His hatred was deep and pure for any dark witch. Sadly, he taught his daughter the same ways. Nessya, she thought herself more like her father. He would never admit he had a soft spot for the young witch but she saw.

Nessya caught up to her father, and they walked side by side in the semi-dark hall. She let the pregnant silence linger between them. Flickers of light bounced off the wall from the Te'Mak's witchfire. Tovoz suddenly stopped, turned quick on his heels, faced Nessya and grabbed her shoulders. In a low tone, so his voice wouldn't echo, he whispered to his daughter. The words fell off of his lips and dug into her head through her ears. She heard his words and nodded. As quick as he stopped, he moved again not stopping again until he was in front of the two guards.

"You're good to leave Suya. Timo. We'll take it from here," Tovoz said, pointing to the space between him and his daughter. "Eat and enjoy the evening."

"Thank you Te'Mak," the two guards said simultaneously before departing.

Tovoz removed the locks to the cell and stood still. The girl now a young woman followed his movements from inside. Her purple gaze always unnerved him but that day, they were brighter than other days and he didn't know what to think. He prayed to Father Elios that the geas worked.

"Why do you watch me? Afraid?" the young woman grinned.

"No. Why should I be afraid?"

"Then come in," she said and stood up. She spread her hands wide. "Welcome to my lovely home, Te'Mak."

Tovoz watched as the woman bowed her head in the ways of his people. Nessya touched his arms and shook her head. He understood. He would not rise to the bait, instead he would let it go.

"Can I come in? You can trust me." Nessya asked. "Have I ever done anything to harm or hurt you?"

Nthanda paced her cell and stopped. She turned her head towards the wall where her familiar stood camouflaged.

We cannot go before Godspeaker Nelioz, Kai. We must run old friend. We can take these two easily.

We have not thought this through. Listen to what they have to say. They haven't done to you like the others. How can we navigate these trees without their help? Listen to them.

Don't you know the way?

I know enough. Instincts say we need them. At least her.

Nthanda sighed. "Fine. You first," she said, pointing to Nessya.

Nthanda went and sat by the earthen wall. She pulled her legs and knees up to her chest and wrapped her arms around them. "What do you want?"

Nessya pulled the metal bars opened and stepped through. "We have to take you to the Golden Palace. Uncle Zeran says you killed Tiabu. Claims we failed in our duty and didn't keep you bound. But I know Papa. If anything, he is loyal. Tell us what happened."

"Why would you listen to me? Listen to what I have to say?"

"Because the fate of our family relies on what you tell us."

"Help me," Nthanda whispered to her. A soft demand. A plea to leave the place that suppressed her for too long. She reached up to touch the necklace around her neck and stopped. They would wonder what she was doing since they weren't able to see it. She placed her hand on her chest, next to the pendant and rubbed in slow circles. She had to soothe her nerves somehow.

Nessya heard the plea and knew she couldn't answer the way she wanted. She twisted around and looked at her father. He stood next to the metal bars as a lookout of sorts. She turned and faced the dark witch.

"I can only do so much. You know this. But I swear on the sun god himself, that when the time comes, I will do whatever it takes to help you."

Chapter 19

Not wanting to face the people just yet, Tovoz followed the less-traveled underground tunnels to the palace. There, his family along with his wife, would wait for him and Nessya as they brought the girl to court. He didn't want them showing up late like he would. The Godspeaker's anger was enough; to incur more would make the situation worse.

Uneasy quiet steps was what the small group had between them. Still sensing the geas on the white-haired woman, he prayed it was strong enough. Fear crept in his mind and its spidery legs took root, digging into his skull. Tovoz was afraid that Godspeaker Nelioz would take his longtime friend's side. He rubbed the nape of his neck and exhaled the breath he didn't realize he held.

His mind kept going back to the time before he took that fateful voyage to the land of ice and snow. Excited that his father chose him to undertake the secretive duty he had asked of him. Tovoz should have known it was a bad idea sneaking into Enyxias but a person can be blinded by which they seek the most.

He should have stood up to his father and said no to the whole voyage. The moment he saw the package he was to retrieve was not a package at all, but a young witchling from their blood enemies, he should have left the girl there and turned around. Should have gone home and suffered the consequences. The young woman had brought nothing but trouble to his household. She was nothing but a foul, living curse. Yet, he couldn't blame her. She was an innocent, caught in the pit of vipers. In the end, his family was more important. *As long as his family was safe, Godspeaker Nelioz could have the girl* he thought.

The small group came to an open space and stopped. Three tunnel entrances faced them. Tovoz turned back to his daughter. "You remember what I've told you?" He asked.

"Yes."

"This is that place. Now go to your mother and siblings. I'll find you shortly."

Tovoz eyes didn't stray from Nessya as she left. She glanced back one time before disappearing into the entrance on the far right. Without looking back or saying another word, he entered the darkened space to the far left. His captive was close on his heels behind him.

It didn't take long to reach their destination. Tovoz and Nthanda embarked on an incline that eventually became stone stairs. The coolness that kept him comfortable dissipated with each step he took higher. The heat wrapped around him like a lost lover and momentarily he wished he was back in the burrows in the cool underground.

He stopped at the top of the steps when the sounds of two men talking reached his ears. He waited until the voices faded before he poked his head out from the hidden entrance. The way he went took him to a hidden closet not far from the Golden Hall where the Godspeaker sat. No one was around. Tovoz twisted around to come face to face with a hardened amethyst gaze. Nthanda's lips pressed together, forming a line while her jaw tightly clenched.

Tovoz jerked his thumb behind him, towards the hall, and told her to follow. Every step he made towards the Golden hall, the heavier they became. The air was thick, oppressive, and the beads he wore stuck to his skin. Everything in him screamed to run but he wouldn't. He couldn't.

Sunlight shone off the gold-lined mural walls, lending a yellowish light to everything. Lush greenery complemented the sunlit metals and painted images. Vines with blooming blood-red flowers made its home as the plant crossed the ceiling and clung to the walls. In the corners, trees and its branches integrated into the design of the palace. Tovoz always thought it was a masterpiece of beauty and architecture. Blending nature with the desire to be sheltered from the outdoors.

The corridors to the palace typically full of motion, now lay empty. A desolate wasteland, nothing or no one lingered in its maws. Not even the guards. He frowned. The silence alone made Tovoz uneasy. If there was no one in the halls, then they must have been in the Golden Hall, where they waited on him.

The long walk took them to the great doors where two guards stood with spears in hand. Tovoz would have thought they were statues if it wasn't for the slow rise and fall of their chest. Tovoz stepped back, grabbed Nthanda's wrist and spun her around with their backs to the guards.

Tovoz stood behind her and pretended to check the geas he knew was there and whispered to her in her tongue. "I am sorry for everything. I hope my Nessya was better to you than I ever have been."

NTHANDA DIDN'T RESPOND to his words. There was no need. Tovoz turned to the guards and let them know he was ready. Over the past eight years, she hated the man who stole her from her home but over time; she grew to understand that duty had him do what he did. She understood duty. Sometimes there was no way out of it.

What did the man say? her familiar asked. Hidden from plain sight but never once left her side.

The large doors to the Golden Hall opened and a whoosh of perfumed air accosted Nthanda. She shook her head to dispel the cloying scent. The bright light that lit the room to give the hall its name hurt her eyes for only a short bit.

I'll tell you once we are safe from here and alone. Stay close. Let no one touch you.

Nthanda stepped through the threshold with her head held high and eyes forward. She remembered her first time in the blinding hall and even now; she was not afraid. She ignored the gazes of everyone as she made her slow approach behind the Te'Mak. Distorted and angry face glared in her direction. Every step she took, their heated whispers and their useless curses reached her ears. She grinned a fierce and dangerous grin. *She was better than them and it was time they figured that out;* she thought.

Nthanda was taught as a child to always keep her chin up and eyes forward. Her shoulders were back and never slumped. No matter how dirty she was. No matter how unclean her hair was and how bad she smelled. She would never let it show it bothered her. The dais where the Godspeaker sat with his son beside him loomed closer and closer. The Godspeaker's cabal of witches stood behind them in their thin cloth long sleeved black tunics and matching pants. The mark of their elite group. Multicolored snake familiars slithered around their arms and necks while their witches observed her.

Nthanda shoulders tensed. She didn't take into account everyone familiars and creatures. *Can other familiars sense you Kai? Even if you're hidden?*

No one can see me unless I allow it.

Nthanda didn't trust anyone there and didn't know what would happen if they discovered her. The Te'Mak before her stopped at the marked line on the floor. It gave sufficient space between the man on the throne and the person before him without being in any danger.

Nthanda stopped just behind Tovoz, clasped her hands in front of herself and let them rest lazily near her waist. She caught glimpses of Nessya standing with her family. Her mother and older siblings stood beside her and all of their eyes were on the man who was head of their family. Whatever transpired would determine the fate of their family. She hated that Zeran and his horrible daughter caused the family trouble but it was not her fault and she hoped that one day they would understand.

Godspeaker Nelioz rose from his throne and took a step down but no further. He was a tall and fit man, no older than Tovoz or her own mother. Shifting red and gold tattooed markings snaked across his shoulders, biceps and legs. They told a story and was part of his power as their leader. His long, bone straight black hair, parted down the center, fell down his back and framed his face. It brought out the hazel color in his eyes that missed nothing. His features were strong and Nthanda thought he was a beautiful man. Deadly no doubt but beautiful nonetheless.

Tovoz bowed his head as did the rest of the crowd. Nthanda didn't move. He was not her leader and refused to bow to any man.

"Tovoz. Lift your head," the Godspeaker said. His strong voice didn't need amplification. Tovoz raised his head and stood straight before Nelioz. He smiled as he touched Tovoz's shoulder. The revelation hit Nthanda then. No justice would be served. Her being there with Tovoz was all a farce. It was clear in Nelioz's eyes that he already had decided and it was not in their favor.

"You are one of my faithful servants, Te'Mak and what I have heard recently is disturbing to say the least. The accusations and charges brought against you by your own friend. The man who is like a brother to you," he said. His enchanting voice was almost like a spell, entrapping everyone who listened. "You who would do whatever I ask."

"Yes, Godspeaker Nelioz," Tovoz responded. "I understand the charges."

Godspeaker Nelioz turned to the people and spoke to them directly. "Before we move on to the reason, I gathered us here today, I must first explain how we even got here."

A hush descended upon the crowd, attentive to every word Nelioz spoke.

"Eight years ago, the oracle here in our temple came to me. They saw something and said I needed to speak with our Father God, Elios. To gain clarity and direction. They spoke to me. Our God, Elios, he spoke to me. They told me of danger to our lands. Our ways, his people. The only way to protect us was to be preemptive and strike at the enemies who sought to destroy us. One of my most trusted advisors, and I came up with a plan. I entrusted the deed to one family. The late elder Te'Mak Paku and his son here, Tovoz, didn't let us down."

Whispers started again, and it didn't pass Nthanda's ears that the Godspeaker didn't add Te'Mak to Tovoz's name.

"They were to take a child from the land of our enemies. The ones who sought to destroy us. Take this child and bring it back to me. We are to sacrifice this child. This offering to Elios after eight years at the wedding of Prince Alios. So it was I who left the child in their household. She was not to be harmed or killed." King Nelioz turned to Tovoz, "And you did a fine job of what was asked of you but tell me, Tovoz. What happened? Why are we here now when we should be celebrating my son's nuptials?"

The lump in Tovoz's throat bobbed up and down as he swallowed. "I don't know what happened Godspeaker. My family and I was preparing for the events when we all felt and heard the loud explosion below us. It couldn't have been the prisoner because she cannot touch her magic. She doesn't even speak our tongue. She is dumb and worthless. The perfect sacrifice for our Father God," he said.

His voice wasn't shaky like she thought it would be. He meant part of what he said. A man would do or say anything to save their family. She wasn't his family, but a burden brought on to him by his father and his leader.

The Godspeaker kept silent and eyed the Te'Mak. His eyes fell back on Nthanda and his smile slipped before he picked it back up. Nelioz walked towards her and everything in her screamed for her to run in the opposite direction. Just like the familiars of his trusted cabal, he was a snake but with two legs.

They were almost of the same height as he stood directly in front of her. He grabbed her chin and squeezed tightly. His power coursed down from his hands as it searched for the geas. If he discovered it was merely an illusion on Tovoz's part, their family was more than just dead. She didn't know what she was doing but the flames that burned in her chest, she willed it to strengthen Tovoz's illusion. She refused to cause an entire family's demise no matter that they were her captors.

He leaned over her and inhaled her scent. She stopped the flow of her magic, not wanting to be caught using it. The moving tattoos on Nelioz's body slithered around and then stopped. He let go of her chin and stepped back. His watchful gaze followed her from head to toe before he turned and sauntered back to his throne. Tovoz turned towards her and let out a long-held breath. She could see in his eyes he was thankful.

Bright Star. I don't like that man. He isn't saying something. Something is very wrong.

I know, Kai. I know. Stay alert.

Nelioz leaned back in his chair with a slight closed-lipped smile. An eerie silence blanketed the Golden Hall.

The gathered people looked all around. Prince Alios slimy grin matched his father's.

"Te'Mak Zeran, step forward," Nelioz commanded.

The grieving man came forward from the crowd on the opposite side of Tovoz's family. His hair was a disheveled mess and his clothes were unclean by their standards. He didn't look like the man that came to her over the years and beat her. Tortured her and abused her. Who taught his daughter his sadistic ways. She saw him and the flames in her chest burned. The hate she felt in that moment grew exponentially and she wanted to rip his throat out. He was a horrible man, and he deserved to be dead like his daughter was.

"Kinsman, come closer." The Godspeaker beckoned Zeran closer to him. "We all grieve with you. Losing a daughter of the sun is a loss to us all," he cooed.

"Father," Prince Alios called out. "We all grieve with our kinsman, but Tiabu was to be my wife! We had become close, and I loved her. Let me get vengeance on the one who took her life." He turned towards Nthanda. He flexed his shoulders and moved towards her.

"Stop, Alios! Wait."

Prince Alios spun on his heels and moved towards his father. "Why?" he shouted. "I should be standing here getting married before you, our people and Father Elios. Instead, we are here. Standing trial for something that doesn't need a trial. This witch is only here to be offered up to Elios. Let me sacrifice her!"

"In due time, son. In due time. We must follow the order. You will get your time. Now, stand back and learn some patience," Nelioz said to his son.

"Zeran, what happened? You said this girl here killed our Tiabu. A promising and strong witch of the sun. This girl has a geas placed on her and I can tell that it has been on her for a long time. She can't even reach her power and I am sure all this time it was suppressed. She probably doesn't even remember how to use them."

"I swear by all things holy, Godspeaker. She killed Tiabu. She used her powers. There were no geas. He must have reapplied it before coming here," Zeran stammered.

"I assure you Godspeaker, we followed your command." Tovoz pointed to himself and gestured to his family in the crowd. "I have chained this girl since the moment she came into my possession. I never once removed it. I wouldn't dare let one of her kind have that type of power in our lands. I never once abused her like Zeran and his daughter, Tiabu. They who snuck into the burrows and did what they did. You said not to touch her. I only did what you instructed. He disobeyed you not I," Tovoz said.

"Liar!" Zeran yelled.

"Enough!" Nelioz shouted. He snapped his fingers at two of his cabal witches. "Bring the girl forward," he commanded.

The two burly men moved quickly, and they each grabbed Nthanda's arms and drugged her to the bottom step and dropped her. Nelioz glanced at his son, "Do your best or do your worst. Just don't kill her. That is my job. And she will die today by my hands." Nelioz hard gaze turned to her. "You have caused enough problems in this land and it all ends today."

Nthanda fumed. She was over all the accusations they flung her way. They blamed all their problems on her when she had done nothing to them. She was so tired of everything and everyone. She took a step forward and stopped. Prince Alios sauntered her way. The biggest grin she had ever seen him wear spread across his face. His hands raised and greenish fire bloomed from the palms of his hand.

"You will suffer for your deeds you foul and soulless daemon." Prince Alios flung the green fire at Nthanda's head. She dodged his flames and fell into a crouch. He growled and ran at her and was upon her before she could react. With force, he hit Nthanda with an uppercut to the jaw and she flew back. The jarring pain stunned her. She landed on her backside and slid across the floor.

The flare in her chest was a constant burning sensation, and she yearned for a release. Prince Alios didn't give her time to think about anything as he let loose a mixed barrage of powerful hits and punches at her. She could barely dodge him but she did. When she last fell to the ground, she lay on her back, eyes to the ceiling.

Nthanda gasped for air. She ached all over from Alios onslaught of hits. Lack of food and water had made her weak but she wouldn't give up. Slowly, she rose after the prince stepped away from her. He gloated to the crowd as their voices rose and praised his prowess.

No one noticed when Nthanda stood straight, even though the pain in her limbs screamed for her to rest. They still didn't pay attention when she prayed to the Mother Goddess to guide and protect her. Through the bond, Kai prepared for what was coming. Prince Alios, who looked so much like his father, turned back around and faced Nthanda. The smirk on his face never moved. It was a permanent fixture on him.

"She dares stand to face me. I should be ashamed to do what I do towards a woman who can't even fight back. But you killed my Tiabu and you will suffer for it." He reached to his hip and grabbed the thin vine like weapon and let it unfurl. Alios charged his weapon with his magic and sharp, metal daggers formed at the edges of it.

She gathered the fire in her chest and let the cold flames in her belly ignite within. A welcomed feeling that had been missed for years. She didn't care if these people knew she could touch the Evernight but they would learn. Prince Alios eyes widened at the sight of Nthanda and she didn't understand why and didn't care. Lost into herself. She moved with a preternatural grace. Both of her arms were low to her sides and outstretched. Her palms faced upwards and a dark purplish black flames hovered over it.

"You have no dominion over me. I am done with this. You cannot control me any longer and you all will regret the day you brought me to your lands," she shouted. Tovoz looked at her in horror then to his family and ran towards them, getting away from her.

She fashioned the flames in her right palm into a thin wiry rope and with the flick of her wrist; she had it wrapped around Prince Alios neck. She dragged him to her and his small whimpers amused her. Prince Alios clawed at the rope around his neck but no matter how hard he tried, he couldn't remove it. His magic kept repelling off the rope whenever he tried to force it.

The crowd cried out, but they didn't come any closer to her. Instead, they stepped further away. The moment Nelioz stepped down the dais, his cabal immediately moved and surrounded him. They wouldn't let him get in harm's way, not even for his favorite son. His eyes pleaded with her but she looked past them. Past that. The rage and fury she had kept bottled up inside herself wanted a release. Wanted to be free like her.

Alios was on his knees, still clawing to remove the rope around his neck. His golden tanned skin turned gray and ashen. His eyes were bloodshot. His perfect mouth gaped open, trying to get air to no avail. Screams pierced the once silent room and two of the Godspeaker's cabal marched toward her. With her left hand she flung out the flames towards the two witches. The flames grew larger and larger and hit both cabal members in the chest. They went down screaming. Their power of the sun couldn't touch her powers of the Evernight and the flames ate through them.

Nthanda looked down at the prince on his knees. The rope around his neck slowly burned as it choked him. He was almost dead. The furious shouts from Nelioz was louder and closer. Her head shot up to find Nelioz stomping towards her with the light of the sun blazing around his entire body. She squinted and moved back.

"Foul woman, let my son go!" Nelioz shouted. He conjured a ball of witchfire in his hands and fashioned it into the blazing spear of Elios. "It is time you die," he said and took off into a sprint towards her. The hall was in hysteria. Everyone tried to leave and get to safety but the doors were blocked.

Without thinking, Nthanda snapped the rope around Alios's neck and his bones cracked. Instantly, he went limp and his body slumped to the ground. Nelioz watched it all play out in slow motion before him. The sickening sound of cracked bones echoed loudly in his ears. The favored son of the Godspeaker fell to the ground. Alios arms splayed out unmoving. His head fell to the side, facing Nelioz with wide opened dead eyes and his neck at an unnatural angle. Nelioz was dumbstruck. He turned on her with reddened eyes like the flames that burned around him.

All the spells and teachings from childhood rushed to the forefront of Nthanda's mind and she let it fill her. She moved without thought and fought the King. She too fashioned a staff that was black as the Evernight and brought it around right as the Spear of Elios came down on her. The force behind it jarred her weakened arms but Kai strengthen her through their bond and she sent her a silent 'thank you'.

They attacked each other relentlessly. When one person looked as if they would fall, they would somehow be granted strength to continue. Nthanda tired, and would fall if she didn't end the battle right then. Nelioz jabbed at her with the spear, and she dodged it by a hairsbreadth and rolled to the side. She jumped up behind the Godspeaker and quickly raised a ward around him, blocking him from moving anymore. He shouted, but it did no good. Nthanda's power grew in strength the longer she fought and Nelioz couldn't remove the ward with his magic of the sun. She felt the presence of the Mother Goddess and her children at her side.

There were still a few nobles around watching and waiting for the outcome. Tovoz and Nessya was still there along with Zeran lurking around like a panther stalking his prey. Nthanda turned in circles and caught everyone's eyes. Nessya mouthed to her and pointed her thumb over her shoulder. It didn't take much to know that she wanted her to follow her. Nthanda turned back to the Godspeaker and grinned.

"You and your lackeys always wanted my name. Today you can do no harm to my name because I am not in thrall to your people any longer, Nelioz," Nthanda said in their tongue as she paced in front of him. The look of surprise on his face made it better when he realized she spoke their language.

A few of the cabal members crept closer to her. Nthanda quickly pivoted and sent a giant size ball of witchfire at them. Some dodged it but the rest couldn't avoid the path of the witchfire and was caught in its flare. They burned where they stood. The flesh sizzled like an animal over a fire pit.

Nthanda whipped her head back around to the Godspeaker. "Nelioz, I know Tovoz and his father acted on your orders. Ultimately, it is you who is at fault. You and all of your people will regret the day you came into Enyxias and took her favored daughter away. You, who is in the business of stealing children will regret the day from now until you die. I curse you and your direct line, Nelioz. Your family shall have nothing but daughters and they will be weak and endure the same pain you put me through." Nthanda's grin grew wide.

"Remember this," she said and pitched her voice so that all could hear. "I am Nthanda, daughter of Chanda, daughter of Jia'ka. A true daughter of the Nightshade line and you will remember this day and my name!"

She raised her arms and closed her eyes. Her fingers moved and danced to a tune only she could hear. She was deep into the Evernight pulling her power. The cries of the crowd as they screamed and shouted fueled Nthanda's heart. A ferocious roar of flames drowned out their pained pleas.

Nthanda opened her eyes to see the Golden Hall ablaze. A conflagration of black wildfire she conjured from the deep ether. Thick smoke was getting thicker and hovered like clouds of death over everything it touched. Nelioz's eyes were void of any emotion and he mumbled to himself. Nthanda looked over to where Nessya stood alone and ran to her. Halfway there a loud growl caught her ears. She twisted around to find Zeran running after her with a long blade raised. Kai made herself visible to everyone and jumped towards the man and latched her sharp teeth around his throat, bit down and ripped it out. Zeran didn't see the leopard coming and couldn't stop it. His death was instant.

"Come on!" Nthanda shouted to her familiar.

Kai's big pink tongue licked the blood that smeared around the white and spotted fur by her mouth. She leaped over the dead man and followed her witch.

I've been wanting to do that for a long time, Bright Star. Thank you for fulfilling your promise.

Nthanda chuckled, "Anytime, friend!"

Chapter 20

Nessya ran fast as her legs would take her from the Golden Hall. There was no need to check over her shoulders to search for the girl, Nthanda and her familiar was on her heels. Clouds of dark gray and black smoke drifted across the ceiling, slowly squeezing the breathable air from rooms. Every time Nessya inhaled, the vapors burned her lungs. She covered her nose and her mouth hoping to lessen the damage. The best thing for them was to get fresh, clean air. Godspeaker Nelioz and his people wouldn't be able to put out that fire. That fire was otherworldly and would die out when the Gods saw fit.

Nessya took them through the hidden passageways that her father showed her earlier. She hoped he, her mother, and the rest of her siblings got away safely. They took off when Prince Alios fell, realizing an opportunity when they saw one. The moment their captive, now Nthanda proved she was no longer beholden to them any longer, they left in the crowded fray. Nessya's father tried to get her to come with them but she refused. She couldn't leave the girl there alone. It wasn't her fault. It was her father, grandfather, and Godspeaker Nelioz's fault.

Deeper and deeper into the earth they went. Following the stone paths that turned into packed earth. It was too dark to even see but Nessya had a plan. She lit a ball of witch-fire in her hand and told Nthanda to do the same. The winding path became narrower, and they were to the point where they had to squeeze to move through.

Once Nessya had gone through, she turned to find the woman and her large cat stopped. "Come on, we can't rest yet. We have further to go," she pleaded to the girl.

"I don't know if," Nthanda turned to Kai then back around. "I don't know if the giant cat can fit."

I can fit, Bright Star. Go. I am right behind you.

Nthanda nodded and squeezed through the jagged rocks. The blade sharp stoned sliced her skin, causing her to cry out. Once she pushed through and was safe on the other side, she folded over. The magic she unleashed earlier had drained her, and she had no more energy to even stand straight.

"I can't go any further. I am too tired. I need to rest."

"We can't stop here. Maybe another half a candlemark and we'll be safe to stop for the rest of the night. We have to get away from the palace grounds and the extended part that's spelled. Once off the royal grounds, it'll be harder for them to find us and easier to hide. The Godspeaker and his cabal will hunt us down. Especially for you. That can't happen," Nessya said.

"Why are you helping me?" Nthanda asked, curious.

"Because I want to. It doesn't matter if you are a Child of the Moon or a Child of the Sun. We are all witches. We are the same and should stand together." Nthanda stared at her. Speechless and surprised at the response. "Come on. You have lasted this long, you can last just a little more."

Nessya moved at a slower pace to help Nthanda along, but they still moved quickly. The palace complex was deep in the jungles and they had to move carefully out of them or else they would find themselves lost. The small group trailed behind each other in a single line through the narrow passages till they came into a large, dark, cavernous opening.

Phosphorescent greenery covered the ground like a soft blanket as far as Nthanda could see. While its luminous insect counterparts, blinked in and out of existence. Large natural crystal formations glistened in multiple colors from the ceiling and walls. Casting small rainbows all over the cavern. It was surreal to her, and she had seen nothing like it before.

Nthanda took a step forward, wanting to touch the inviting scene but a firm arm blocked her path. Nthanda looked down to find Nessya's arm outstretched before her and with the other hand, the girl pointed down. Nthanda followed her finger and realized that they stood on the edge of a cliff and if she had taken one more step, she would have fallen below into the darkened abyss.

"Thank you," she said. "I didn't realize that was there."

"It's a small crevice, but goes down forever. There's a path we can take to cross just over there," Nessya said. Her head nodded in the opposite direction.

"After you then." Grateful for the woman. Nthanda was ready to sit down somewhere. Only way for her to recoup all the energy she lost was to sleep, and she needed that in abundance. To be without her magic for all those years, missing a piece so vital to her, now back again was fulfilling. But it depleted her as if she was a new witch and the thought made her smile. *At least her gift was back*, she thought.

Nessya moved towards the thin rock shelving that crossed over the abyss. Only one person was able to traverse the narrow stretch at a single time. She tested the strength of the path before taking a step. Feeling confident that it was stable enough to hold her weight, she moved forward. Three quarters of the way, she stopped and twisted around. She raised her voice loud enough for Nthanda to hear her.

"It is safe and sturdy. Come on. The cabal knows of this place."

Nthanda didn't like the narrow strip, but she listened and let her feet move her forward. Barely able to move, she took a step, then forced another step. The price of freedom she knew wouldn't be easy but being out of the loop of the world for so long, she just wanted to cry.

She felt a wet nudge on her skin and stopped to find Kai behind her, helping her across.

Go Bright Star. We can do this. Nthanda nodded and pressed onwards. She tried not to think about the pregnant darkness on both sides of her and that even a slight misstep could have her falling to her death in the vast emptiness of the unknown. Once she made it to the other side and ambled over to Nessya, she released the long breath she held. Nthanda's hands shook so hard, she clasped them together to stop them from moving.

Kai was still out on the ledge. The large cat moved at a slower pace than the others. Being three times the size in weight bigger than Nthanda or Nessya made the trek more dangerous. The muscles rippled through her spotted fur as she crouched low to the ground and slow crawled. Halfway through, Kai stepped on a sharp and jagged rock that cut the padding on the bottom of her paw. A loud and pained growl escaped her mouth. She slipped. Kai's lower half tumbled over the edge and she hung on with all of her might.

Nthanda screamed. The thought of losing Kai jolted her senses. She ran to the edge and slid to a slow stop, scattering loose rocks, not knowing what to do. The need to help her soul part was dire.

"Stop!" Nessya shouted and ran next to her. "It's all coming down. Too much weight. If you go out there, I'll lose both of you. All of this would be for naught."

"Well, what do you expect me to do? Leave her? If so, that is really out of the equation. I have to do something."

"You don't have the strength, I'll help." Nessya, touched Nthanda's bare shoulders. "Step away. I'll help your animal."

Go Bright Star. I believe the witchling.

"Fine," Nthanda huffed. She didn't want to, but she listened to the others. She had no choice but to stand and pray to the Mother Goddess. She watched as Nessya ran away from them further back into the cavern and came back with a rope made of strong entwined vines that was found in the jungles above. Her mouth moved as she touched the rope. The gentle tug of Nessya's magic swarmed around the rope as it imbued it. A faint glow grew stronger before it disappeared.

Kai struggled to keep her grip. The more she moved the more the rocks fell around her. The sound of a whip cracking alarmed the two women to only realize it was much worse. The first part of the rock cropping crumbled and fell into the darkness. Large masses of the narrow strip slowly broke away and made its way towards Kai.

"You must hurry!" Nthanda forced out between sobs.

Kai held on but her strength waned. Nessya took the rope, made a loop at the end, and swung it a few times over her head before casting it out to the big cat. Missing, she brought the rope back in.

"Hey cat, I will not hurt you. I will throw this at you. Try to maneuver the rope over your head or hold on to it between your teeth." Kai nodded her big furry head. Nessya threw the rope out again and missed.

"Crap," she whispered. Nessya stilled her nerves and swung the rope one more time. Kai snapped at the twisting vine and held onto it with her teeth. Soon as she caught the rope in her mouth, the land mass near her broke and fell. Close to the ledge, a rock formation jutted from the ground, thick enough to support what Nessya needed it for. She quickly ran to it and tied her end of the rope around the formation. Time was of the essence and she didn't have much more of it. Once the rope was secure, she went back to the ledge to find the large cat scramble upwards as the land fell from under her.

Everything happened quickly and moved slowly, almost as if time had stopped itself. The animal had grunted but never let go of the rope in her mouth and held on for dear life. Nessya didn't know what to do. Her eyes darted around and at the last second, she grabbed the rope and held on. Kai swung along like a pendulum and hit the side of the stone wall hard. She was the only light spot in the dark that surrounded her.

Nessya couldn't hold on much longer but refused to give up. She kept her position. Kai scrambled for purchase against the side but couldn't find it. Her large paws slid across the slick rock and kept her dangling.

"Hold on," Nessya said between clenched teeth. Kai looked up to find the woman peering down at her. Her hands glowed a bright yellow as she picked up the rope and pulled. "I can only pull you up so far. Keep searching for a hold alongside the wall," she grunted out. Nessya pulled the rope as hard as she could. The creature was heavier than she expected. She poured more power into her imbued hands and continued to pull.

Kai knew the girl wouldn't be able to pull her all the way to the top. She kept touching the side of the wall, looking for any depression so she could grab and jump. At a gradual pace, she moved higher and higher. Suddenly, the rope began to tear. Nessya couldn't do anything to save the rope. She tried to grab above the rip before it fell away and didn't make it in time. Kai slipped, losing all the progress they had made. At the last moment, she found a small hole and stuck her back right paw and her front left paw into the second opening. She wouldn't give up and leave her witch alone in the world. She poured all her strength into herself and leapt as far she could upwards towards the woman looking over the ledge.

The woman didn't move away in time and Kai bowled into her, knocking her down. She landed on top of Nessya, covering her. Kai was slow at getting up but she did when Nthanda wrapped her arms around her neck. Nessya shot up and took a deep breath of air, no longer suffocating on animal fur.

Twisting around, Nessya found the animal being hugged by the dark witch. Both of their eyes were closed, and Nthanda's face was buried into the animal's fur. She was glad the animal made it but looking over the area they just had come from, there was no way they could go back in that direction. They had to continue to move forward.

Nessya stood, went to move then stopped. She tilted her head towards the way they just came from and listened to the wind. The sound of footsteps moving at quick speed touched her ears. A group of muffled voices came next. She knew who they were and why they were down in the tunnels. They needed to hide. Nessya raised both hands up, palms out. An iridescent stream of wispy, thin tendrils of magic poured from her hands. She directed the way the wisps went, letting them flow towards the ledge to the left and right of her. She directed the wisps to move up far, reaching the ceiling. The iridescent wisps of magic spread as far wide and up as it could and once they encompassed everything, she clasped her hands together, held them like that for the span of a breath and released them.

She had created a wall that no others would be able to see at first glance. But she put nothing pass the Cabal. They were the elite of their lands for a reason. Nessya turned around to find both the cat and Nthanda watching her.

"An illusion spell. I am coming to think your family's specialty is in trickery," Nthanda said with a smirk on her face.

"Something like that," she shrugged. "We need to move. The Cabal is coming. They're not far. Hopefully, the wall I put up will reflect an emptiness. They won't be able to see us or what is over here. We need to rest. Especially you. But we can't stay for too long. They will get suspicious and come back round."

Nthanda got up from the weird crouch she was in, keeping her hands on Kai's head. They followed Nessya, going further into the cavern. The soft moss under her feet was a relief compared to the hard surfaces of the rocks she walked on. The woman led the small group to the very back. Hidden from the ledge, along with her illusion spell, if someone came into the cavern, they wouldn't be able to see them. A brief respite, but well needed.

The group found a small overhang with crystalized formations all over. They were able to hide behind them. Kai was the first to lie down, and Nthanda lay next to her, as close as she could. Not only was she hidden from searching eyes, she was warm from the heat the big cat emitted. She closed her eyes and let the silence of the cave rock her to sleep.

I'll watch over everyone. Sleep. Kai said to her.

Chapter 21

Startled awake, Nthanda's heart raced a tapping rhythm in her chest. There was no light, just the dark even though her eyes were open. Disoriented, she tried to get her bearings straight. Soft fur covered her face, and she picked out a few pieces that was in her mouth. The push and pull of Kai's chest calmed her nerves, and she remembered where she was. Who she was with.

Rubbing her sleep crusted eyes, Nthanda sat up. She didn't know how long she slept but her body wasn't as sore and didn't ache too bad as it did before she crashed. Kai's round furry head turned inwards and nudged Nthanda.

You're awake. Stay quiet. Something is wrong, Kai warned.

What do you mean?

The girl jumped up too. She is lurking near the edge, hiding behind that rock.

Nthanda head turned towards the area that her familiar spoke of. Nessya crouched low with her ears and side of her face touching the ground.

What is she doing? she asked Kai.

She's been like that for a while.

Nthanda went to stand but stopped when Nessya looked her way, held up a hand, and motioned for her to stop. She didn't know why or what was wrong so she did what the woman wanted and crouched low to the ground. A bone deep growl came from Kai's chest that Nthanda felt it in her bones.

"What is wrong?" Nthanda whispered.

The Godspeaker's witches are close. We should leave this place.

Dread filled Nthanda's belly and though she rested, she was still tired. After everything she had gone through, she refused to give up. She couldn't let the Cabal catch her or her companions. She looked all around letting her gaze fall on the wall of light magic. The iridescent barrier Nessya placed shimmered pearlescent shades of pinks, reds, blues, and greens. Nthanda prayed that it kept them hidden from searching eyes.

Nessya jumped up from the ground, wide eyed, and dashed towards the others. She grabbed Nthanda's arm, turned and went in the opposite direction of where they were, practically dragging Nthanda along. "The Cabal knows we are here. They must have discovered my magic while we slept."

"Are you sure?"

"Positive. My spelled wall can detect when another magic user touches it."

Nthanda's mouth formed a perfect 'O'. "Okay then."

I sensed nothing, Bright Star. Kai said. Troubled that she failed in her protection duties.

"You're fine. You didn't fail," Nthanda responded. Kai's guilt flooded their bond.

Nessya's head turned to the side but never lost her stride as she continued to pull them away from danger. "The animal is your familiar? How? Father would have said something. He wouldn't have kept that from the Godspeaker."

"He didn't know. No one did. And I pray to the Mother Goddess that you do not speak of my familiar to anyone."

Nessya gently squeezed Nthanda's arm. "You have my word."

The group moved along in silence. Afraid to speak out loud or make a sound. Not wanting the hunters to find them. Nessya took them through the ethereal caverns until they reached two dark entrances.

"Where do these lead to?" Nthanda asked.

"One leads to more underground tunnels," Nessya pointed to the one on the right. "This one leads up. To a small hole that leads into the jungle. Once we're up there, our tracks will be harder to find, but not all the way."

Nessya led the group to the right and down a tight, narrow space. They passed through large spider webs, and damp walls, showing no one had been that way in a long while. The air, once cool, was now warmer the further up they went. Cautious about where they stepped because spelled traps was a real thing. After a candlemark, they emerged from the oppressive darkness into the blinding light of the jungle. Though not as dark as being in the earth, the little light that cut through the trees was enough to make it feel like they stood directly under the sun.

Sounds of cawing birds and rustling leaves from being stomped on by small critters underneath, filled the area. The silence of the Burrows and the underground tunnels drove her crazy most days, where she longed for any noise. Finally, free from that torment, Nthanda welcomed the symphony of the jungle to her ears. The cloying scents of beautiful yet deadly flowers wafted all around her and the wet heat accosted her skin. Instant beads of sweat formed on her brow. She wiped the moisture off with the back of her hand, knowing the act was pointless. More beaded balls waited to replace the ones she destroyed.

"I need food," Nthanda said out loud. Her stomach made grumbling noises and her mouth, devoid of moisture, was to the point of choking her whenever she tried to swallow. "And water. I didn't realize how thirsty I was until now."

"I have some dried foodstuffs stored. There should be two packs around here buried. Look for a large tree with weird markings."

Nthanda's eyes roamed to all the trees nearby. "We are in the middle of the jungle. Marked trees are everywhere. I will need you to be a little more specific."

"We're looking for my family's sigil with a sunburst and a snake entwined into it. Should be near the bottom of the tree's trunk."

"See, much better." Nthanda didn't let the moment go unnoticed that Nessya was thoroughly prepared. The planned escape route. Knowledge of stored goods that they would need. Nthanda knew a precious gift when she saw one but her curious mind needed answers. "How come you knew to come this way? How did you know to have food stored?"

Nessya didn't hesitate with her reply. "Because father told me. He had all of this prepared long ago."

Nthanda's full lips formed the perfect O again. She noticed the action was becoming a regular occurrence. Her feelings were mixed regarding Nessya's answer. She hated the man who spirited her away from her motherland and yet he was the one who set her on this path to get away from there.

"Did he know that I would use the items? That I would follow this journey?"

"Yes. You are the reason he did this. Father felt nothing but confusion and guilt since the day he took you. I was a curious child and wanted to know more about the dark witch in our house. I came to you on my own and father discovered my treks and didn't stop me. He took me aside one day after seeing you and told me one day that I will need to be there for you. That you will need a friend in these lands. I've considered you my friend for the longest time." Nessya gently touched Nthanda shoulder then she went in the opposite direction.

Did you know any of this, Kai?

No. But it makes sense why the girl kept coming to you.

Can we trust her?

You already know the answer to that question don't you, Bright Star?

Nthanda sighed. She wanted to hate the girl because of who she was but the girl never cared about who Nthanda was. She even taught her the language of the light witches tongue. Somewhere deep inside herself, she considered Nessya more than just her captor's daughter. The young woman cared for her and saw her as a person. *Did she dare call her a friend?*

Nthanda went to the right. Away from everyone, avoiding their knowing gazes. How she must have looked like a fool. So caught up in the hate in her heart, she didn't realize that the Mother Goddess had sent her an ally. Someone to be there for her when things got too hard for her. Nessya was there for her. She even fought her childhood friend to protect her. Nthanda turned her head around and could see Nessya from the corners of her eyes. She was bent over, searching the trees. Nthanda smiled. The girl ran with a fugitive. She will no longer be welcomed in her own lands for helping a blood enemy. Twisting back around, Nthanda decided she would think about everything later. Measure the ramifications when she was able to properly think everything over.

Nthanda stopped near the closest tree to her. She looked up and gawked. The tree was massive. The trunk was wide as eight people standing side by side. She checked the bark for the sigil and found none. Not giving up, she checked all the ones closest to where she was at. Frustrated, she kicked the tree nearest her and yelped when broken bark fell down her leg and onto her feet.

You okay, Bright Star? Kai asked. Feeling her frustration through their bond.

I'm fine! she squeaked through the mental conversation. Kai chuffed and turned back around. Kai sat on her haunches, facing the cave entrance. She refused to move anymore. She kept watch while the women did their searches. Keeping the two in her eyesight, never letting them wander too far. She didn't want to have a repeat of what happened earlier.

Letting out a rugged sigh, Nthanda wiped her face then slapped a flying bug off of her arm. Frustration reared her ugly head because she couldn't find anything that resembled a snake entwined sunburst. Wanting the dead insect gone, she flicked it off her when a shimmering, glowing light caught her eyes. Coming from the direction of the small tree she had kicked, Nthanda moved closer to the light and squatted low next to the sapling. Near the bottom, close to the ground she found a marking. Not burned into the spot like she thought it would be, but placed there by magic. She could feel the small spell. Whoever created the mark, made it barely noticeable.

She reached her hand out to touch the glowing sigil and thought better of it. She raised her voice loud enough for Nessya to hear her but not loud enough to where they would be discovered. "I found something. I think it's what we're looking for."

"Oh good. I couldn't find anything over here," Nessya responded. She jogged to where Nthanda squatted and peered over her shoulder. Her long, raven black hair fell over her eyes, and she pulled it back behind her ears. The glowing mark was exactly what she was looking for. She bounced on her feet, "That's it!"

She grinned and moved into the spot that Nthanda had just vacated. Gently brushing her fingers over the marking, she could almost taste the residual of her father's magic. A small spell but powerfully packed. "The bags should be under here. This sapling hasn't always been here. Maybe a year or two. We need to dig under the roots after I dispel it first."

Nessya went to work on the spell. Kai padded over to where they were and watched the light witch work her magic.

I heard that you need to dig up something. Do you need my help?

Perhaps...

It will be faster if I did it. Less time wasted. Those bad people are coming. I can hear them a distance away. They split up. Some went down the other tunnel and a few followed our scents through the other one.

"That's not good," Nthanda said out loud.

"What's not good?" Nessya asked just as she finished removing the sigil and spell and burned it so it couldn't be traced back to her family.

"They got pass your illusion. We need to hurry. They picked up our scents."

"Crap, that isn't good. Well, let's start digging," Nessya said.

"Go on. Do your thing friend," Nthanda said to Kai and patted her shoulder. "My familiar will dig, just tell her where."

Nessya pointed to the spot just below where the sigil was and with two swipes of her large paw, Kai had dug up the packs that was hidden for them. Nessya opened both, checking what was inside. Relieved to find everything including coins inside a small leather pouch.

"Good. We have a change of clothes, dried meat and *falis* bread. Some coins if we may need them. That's everything."

She handed the other pack to Nthanda. "That one is for you."

"How do you know?"

"There's a letter inside and it's not for me. Read it later once we're safe again. We have to be at the coast in three days so we will move fast. I know some people who we can stay with tonight but we must hurry if we are to get there before nightfall. Never want to be in the trees at night. Daemons are still running amok in our lands."

"Are they trustworthy? These people you speak of. Would they care that I am from Enyxias?"

"We can trust them. There is no love lost for the God-speaker and his nobles with them. My family is the only exception. They believe in the old ways. They believe in balance. But so does my father to an extent," Nessya replied. She got up and placed the leather bag around her neck and shoulders. Nthanda did the same.

The small group took off at a fast pace, leaving the cave system and their hunters behind them. Nthanda was still tired but slowly she regained her strength. The cacophonous screeches from the monkeys that swung from the thick vines to the branches above made her want to pull her hair out. The jungle floor was wet and soggy and Nthanda's feet were slippery against the leaves.

Jumping over fallen tree trunks and dodging poisonous flowers, Nthanda wanted to collapse into a pile. She huffed loudly; moving through the dense trees at a grueling pace drained her faster. Nessya didn't slow down for anything and Kai kept behind, watching their backs. What seemed like days, only took two candlemarks. Only stopping to rest near old temple ruins.

Nessya took the group inside a door and called forth her witchlight. The walls were painted in bright colors and depicted a scene of mass sacrifice and worship. Nthanda touched the wall, examining the bloody scene with mild interest.

"What is this?" she asked.

Nessya looked up. "That's a scene from the first war. To gain favor from Elios and his banished son, the Godspeaker of the time demanded blood sacrifices in their honor." She shrugged, "This was one of those times."

"And I thought my people were bloodthirsty," Nthanda chuckled. "What is that sound?" A loud rushing, roaring sound covered everything.

"We are near the falls. You will fully see within the candlemark. The people we are to meet lives near them."

Nthanda slid her pack to the front of her and opened it. She touched the sealed letter, tempted to open it but waited. No one had to tell her who the sealed letter was from, she already knew. The Te'Mak had words to say, and proved that he knew the entire time that his own daughter taught her to read, write, and speak their tongue. Maybe she was wrong about the man. Maybe not. He still took her away from the only place she knew and brought her to these dangerous and treacherous lands.

Chapter 22

Loud bumps and shouts from the room above seeped through the wood of the house where the group slept. Nthanda eyes shot open while Kai's menacing, low growls vibrated against her. All she could think about was the Cabal found them. She looked around the small room and searched for the missing member of their party.

"Kai, where's Nessya?"

She's upstairs in the other rooms. She's been gone for too long.

"Why didn't she wake me?"

You needed your rest. You were courting death. I can tell through the bond. Kai moved closer to her witch and licked her face with her rough tongue. *You made it this far, don't need you dying off because you got excited killing people with your magic.*

Nthanda feigned surprised, and a smirk turned her lip upwards. "Well, I won't deny that killing the prince wasn't satisfactory."

And Tiabu?

"Oh all right, her too. Once I realized what I did," she said as she bumped her shoulders into Kai's side. The large cat chuffed, her form of laughter.

Heavy footsteps coming down the stairwell disrupted their playful banter. Both witch and leopard stilled before they relaxed when Nessya stepped into the flickering low light. Her wide-opened eyes pierced Nthanda and Kai. She rushed to the two and dropped to her knees in front of them.

"The Godspeaker's Cabal is up there," she whispered, pointing above. "They are searching all the villages looking for you and your beast. They're looking for us."

"How did they find us?"

"They can't tell we are here. The Godspeaker sent all of his Cabal after us. The ones in the cavern, this group is not them. But the ones upstairs, they are just as strong. We are lucky that our gracious hosts are stronger than them," Nessya said.

Nthanda internalized the information and no clue what to do with it. She would die before she would go back with them to their King. Her brows furrowed in deep concentration as she thought about how they could run away from the hunters upstairs.

"Do not worry. We are in a spelled room. I tried to tell you last night, but you were too tired and passed out when I was talking to you."

What she says is true. You were exhausted, Kai chimed in.

Nessya continued, "Our hosts built this secret room and spelled this shelter for times of necessity. I am very thankful they had it for our use."

Nthanda nodded and shoulders relaxed a fraction. As long as the Cabal roamed above, she wouldn't be safe. She trusted the woman, but she was still cynical. Still in disbelief that she was free yet on the run.

"How much further do we have to go until we are safe? You haven't said. Why are you keeping everything to yourself? I need to know these things too."

"Yes, you do. Wait a moment and I'll explain everything. Right now we must be quiet. Their footsteps is closer to the door above. I'd be more comfortable if we are silent just in case," she said, shrugging her shoulder.

Nthanda leaned back into the wall, pulled her knees to her chest and rested her chin on them. She closed her eyes, inhaled then exhaled the stifled air. She searched for her center, found the spot and prayed to the Mother Goddess to lead her out of the lands to safety.

The group stayed in perfect silence while voices rose, and things broke above. Heated words flittered to them down below but in the end, no one came to their door. No one opened and discovered them. They were safe, and they were grateful for the generosity of their hosts.

"Who are these people we stay with, Nessya?" Nthanda asked once it was safe to speak again. "You are so confident and trust them explicitly but you never said who they were except people who believed in the old ways."

Nessya twisted around to face her friend. "They believe in the old ways. They really don't care if you dabble in the Evernight or even pray to the dark mother. They believe in balance. Without one we can't have the other," she said. Crossing her legs, Nessya rubbed feeling back into her thighs and continued. "We call them old family friends, but they are distant relatives on my father's side. They have been teaching me the old ways since I was a child. While with my immediate family, I would still learn the ways for the daughter of a Te'Mak. My father always thought I differed from the other children."

"I see."

"Yea, he said I was the child of his spirit. I am how he wishes he could be if he didn't have his duties. For him, that could never be broken. When I came along, the youngest, he refused to let me grow up like him. My older siblings followed in his steps, but he would let me be free." Nessya stopped speaking and thought about the letter in the bag for Nthanda. "Did you read the letter yet? The one left for you?"

The sealed letter had been on Nthanda's mind since she saw it. She wanted to, but couldn't pull herself to read it yet. Her emotions were full of conflict and too muddled for the Te'Mak. She hated the man and yet; he sacrificed his daughter to help rescue her. He could have tried to kill her a long time ago, but he didn't. He wasn't cruel like Zeran and Tiabu but he did what he did because he had to. Familial duties. She could understand oh too well but she didn't want to pity the man either.

"No, I have not. It's still in the bag. I know the letter is from your father but why would he write me? How did he know that I can read and write in your tongue?"

"He knew what I was doing and didn't stop me. He encouraged it, actually. He was remorseful for his actions. They weighed heavily on his mind. Especially after my grandfather died. Everything my father did was to please him. I wasn't sad the day they found him dead."

"I knew he died but what happened?" Nthanda asked.

"Daemons."

"I thought daemons were only on the coastline?"

"They are. My grandfather was visiting a coastal city on business and couldn't protect himself quick enough. They left his face untouched, but they ripped the rest of his body to pieces. There was an uproar. It was the first time a well-loved noble was harmed by those foul creatures. The God-speaker's favorite Te'Mak was murdered by the daemons from the voided Evernight. The only safe place for our people was within the borders of the Golden Palace and its courts." Nessya picked at the hem of her clothes. "It was your family who sent them. Once you gave your name before setting the palace on fire, the answer became obvious. Your family is one of the first families."

Nthanda said nothing. She wouldn't confirm that information. If the person know of the first families, then they know the answer to that statement. She let the girl continue her talking but what she wanted was to be alone. Her heart was missing those close to her. Even her sister friend Serea. She really missed her. She wondered what she would be like along with her Tindian spider.

Nessya observed her reluctant friend. Sadness permeated her colors. She couldn't help her there but she would do whatever to make sure the girl got back home. She didn't belong in the jungles of the people who hated her for just being born the way she was. Her people was pathetic and needed to go back to the old ways. Where witches' both light and dark were one and didn't want to kill each other on sight.

She reached out and touched Nthanda's hand. Picked it up and squeezed it. "I'll go find us some food. I think it's safe to go back upstairs. We will leave when the sun is at its zenith in the sky. We need to be at the coast by nightfall tomorrow. We won't stop anymore until we reach the harbor."

Nthanda nodded and watched as Nessya left and went back up the stairwell.

What is wrong? You are sad, yes? Kai asked.

I will be fine once we are back on lands full of bright snow and cold enough to freeze a limb off.

I miss the snow too. I am better made for the cold weather. This heat is not for me. My coat will look better in the snow too. Shiny and softer.

So vain, my dear cat.

Somebody has to be! Kai chuffed. *Read the letter. Find a semblance of peace.*

Get out of my head, animal!

I can't, we're bonded remember. I am in there all the time.

Nthanda hugged the snow leopard. "I know and I am very thankful you are."

It didn't take much persuasion to read the letter. It had to be done but for whatever odd reason; she was almost afraid to read the thing. The subtle pressure from both her familiar and Nessya was the push she needed. All done for her sake. Perhaps to ease the hurt in her heart and soul. She opened the bag and pulled the letter out. Sealed with the Te'Mak's family sigil, the sunburst entwined with a snake; she slid a finger under the wax and broke it. She opened the thin paper and found the words was not in the Te'Mak's tongue but in her native language. It felt good to see a piece of her home. A piece of her own language. Tears welled in her eyes. Nthanda wiped them away before they fell and smeared the words.

WITCHLING,

If you are reading this, then you are no longer a prisoner in my clutches. I praise the Sun God for that news. Too long have you been my prisoner and too long have I wished things were different. I must clear things between us. This is the only way without your heated, and rightfully so, words. Foremost, I am sorry. I am so sorry for everything I have done to you. I regret it every minute since that fateful day I took you away from your homeland. When I realized you were the same age as my daughter, I knew what they tasked us to do was wrong. Yet, I didn't stop or protest.

My duties have always come first because it's how my father raised me. I was too afraid to falter and do what was right in that moment. I figured if I did my duties like the faithful son, I can offset it with introducing my daughter to you. I expected my youngest would take a liking to you so I didn't stop her from seeing you. From teaching you. From befriending you. In fact, I encouraged it. I spied from afar as that relationship grew and I was proud of her.

I understood there would come a time I would have to present you to the Godspeaker for the final time, and I set upon a plan to prevent that from ever happening. I know if anyone could help you get home it would be my little one. I hope you open your heart to trust her. She won't betray you and she is nothing like I am.

She is strong both of character and power. Not weak minded. She will protect you with all she has. She is my gift to you and I hope you appreciate it. I wish you a safe journey and if we are ever to meet again, I won't stop you from whatever you need to do. I deserve it all.

May your Mother Goddess watch over you.

Te'Mak Tovoz

Chapter 23

"Thank you for the food and supplies," Nthanda said to the friendly old woman and her husband. They were a short couple and never stopped smiling. "I will remember this kindness you favored upon us."

The woman reached over and hugged Nthanda. "Don't worry. We only did what was right. The Godspeaker and his followers are corrupt. We don't condone what they do at the Golden Palace. We eschew their ways and follow the old way."

"What exactly is this old way you speak of?"

The woman's gaze looked her up and down, as if she was coming to some conclusion on her own without saying out loud what it was. She reached her wrinkled hand to Nthanda's face, closed her eyes and hummed. They stayed that way for what seemed forever but only for a few minutes. A surge of heated power flowed from the woman's hand and Nthanda stilled.

"I see why they search for you," the woman finally spoke. "You are more than what you seem, yes." She removed her hand from Nthanda's face and stepped back. "When you reach the temple, seek Zizia. She will help you when you need it the most. Now go. Those who seek you and Nessya is not long gone. They were suspicious but couldn't break through my illusions. Stay in the shadows. The daemons won't hurt you. They search for you and protect you by order of the ones who summoned them."

"How do you know all this?" Nthanda couldn't help but to ask. The woman knew and saw too much.

"I see it all."

"You are a seer?"

"Something like that," the older woman responded. Her smile widened to where all of her teeth showed. "Go. Do not hesitate or wait any longer and remember what I have said to you."

"Will I ever meet you again?" Nthanda couldn't help but ask.

The woman clasped her hands in front of her. "Perhaps, perhaps not. Only the Gods and Goddess knows what is in store for us. May the sun forever warm your skin."

The girls embraced the older couple one last time and then left them. They heeded her words and took to the shadows in the trees. The jungle wasn't as dense as it was when the left they palace complex but it was enough to keep them hidden from the more severe dangers hunting them.

Nthanda wasn't quite at full strength, but every time they stopped, she'd gotten better than she was before. Nthanda's spirit was lighter every step they took away from all that she left in the burrows.

I need to feed, Bright Star. Kai said. *I was too worried about you and haven't been eating like I should. I am not at full strength either.*

Night had fallen, and it had been four candlemarks since they left Nessya's distant relatives. They moved at a grueling pace without stopping. Nthanda could use the rest and told Nessya as much.

"We can stop here," Nessya said louder so her voice could be heard over the sounds of the rushing river. Nessya sat her pack against the large boulder close to the water. "We'll eat, then figure out a way to cross."

Nthanda walked closer to the edge and watched the water snake across the land. The forest's life blood that gives and takes. Thundering crashes of waves against the standing rocks in the center of its flow was a haunting melody in its own right and spoke to her soul. Sprays of water splashed against her skin, cooling her off.

I never thought listening to the sound of rushing water could be so peaceful, Nthanda said to Kai who had come and stood beside her.

It's dangerous too.

I know. Nthanda touched the top of Kai's head.*Go hunt. Find your dinner. Stay close, Kai. Something lurks in the trees. Watching us. Be careful, friend.*

I will be safe, witchling.

"WHAT WAS THAT?" NTHANDA turned around searching for where the noise came from. A loud screeching sound grated her nerves and sent her heart in a frenzy of thumps and speed. A loud howl accompanied the screeching and the hairs on her arms stood straight up. *That was no animal she ever heard of.* She walked to the edge where the forest started again. She looked around but couldn't find anything. Kai was still out hunting, and that didn't make her feel any better. She would be much better if her cat was standing next to her.

"I've no idea and I don't like how it sounded. We should leave this place. Do you know how to swim?" Nessya asked.

"Not really. Besides, I'm not leaving without my familiar." She wanted to call out for her but decided against it. If something or someone was preparing to attack, her yelling could give their location away.

"I understand. We will wait. I can show you how to swim. The basics until she comes back. It's easy," Nessya said.

Kai leaped out of the wooded edge and growled when she skidded to a stop near Nthanda.

We cannot stay here. Daemons are hunting the Cabal men who follows us. They caught our scents!

"Mother Goddess that is not good news."

"What is wrong?" Nessya asked, seeing the alarm on Nthanda's face.

"The Cabal picked up our scents and followed our trail. The sounds are the daemons hunting them. We've got to go. Now!"

The group gathered their things, packed them tightly back in the bag and secured them. Nessya handed hers to Nthanda so it wouldn't get too wet.

"I don't think you are too heavy to get on the back of your animal. I know large cats can swim the river. We must cross and now."

I can carry you, witchling.

Nthanda peered down at her cat. "Are you sure?"

I am very sure. Now hop on. We must depart.

She did as she was told and hopped onto the back of the snow leopard. They waded into the cold water and Nthanda grumbled to herself about how cold it was. Nessya took to the water like a fish and swam across. Kai followed the young woman, making sure not to drop her witch into the water. The river currents were strong and more than once it carried Kai off course but she always righted her position. Not soon enough did they make it to the bank on the other side. Nthanda slid off the cat and embraced her neck, hugging her.

"Thank you for everything you do. I love you."

You're mushy right now. I should do that more often if I receive more hugs, neck and head rubs.

Nthanda laughed out loud and scratched behind the cat's ears.

Across the waters, two men, dressed in the black of the Cabal, stepped into the clearing they had just vacated. The men spotted them and pointed in their direction. The taller of the two men whose hair was in a topknot on top of his head began to pull from his stores of power and aimed his hands towards them.

Nthanda turned in circles, searching for shelter to hide but found none. Just when a stream of golden light left his hands, creatures jumped out of the trees, ran towards the two Cabal members and attacked. The light didn't get far before fizzling out. Nthanda had never seen them before but it was obvious who the creatures were. The tang of the Evernight wafted off the two daemons in dark gray tendrils. The pull of their power was strong and called to her. She wanted to go to them. They wouldn't her harm.

Bright Star, Stop! Kai cried out but Nthanda kept going. Her feet moved on its own accord. Kai bit at the cloth on her leg and latched on, jerking Nthanda in hopes it would wake her. *Please stop, Witchling.*

Nthanda stopped, shook her head and looked down at the cat. A sharp tingle shot up her leg from where Kai bit her.

"Why did you bite me?"

You had a glazed look in your eye and started walking to the water. I couldn't stop you so I bit you. I am sorry.

Nthanda took a deep breath.*It's fine. I don't understand what came over me but I think it may be them,* she said, pointing to the daemons.

The more human like daemon stood over seven feet tall. He had smooth reddish brown skin with markings on his chest that reminded Nthanda of her own. She absentmindedly touched her Goddess blessed mark as she watched him. The creature turned his face towards her and bowed his head. The daemon who stood on two legs, his eyes were like the flames from a blaze of fire, his hair was black as the darkest night and hung low on his back like the jungle dwellers. His fangs dropped and glistened under the moon's light. Nthanda wasn't surprised. Taught the hierarchy of daemonology a year before she turned twelve winters, this one was a high ranking daemon. He and his black furred hound, who was bigger than Kai, was there to protect her.

How in the Evernight did they summon a high-ranked daemon? The daemon turned to the two Cabal witches. The black hound went after the other man while, the fanged one went after the one who used his magic. She wanted to turn away from the gruesome sight but she couldn't. She had to watch because they killed for her. Done in her name. The carnage, she was no stranger to, and she would honor their sacrifice.

"We should leave." Nessya whispered, not able to take her eyes off what she witnessed.

"No. They shed this blood in my name. I will honor it," Nthanda said. She stood tall as the trees that surrounded them and she watched the carnage that took place across the river. The hound didn't take its time but instead rushed in and tore the screaming man from limb to limb. Blood splattered everywhere. The fanged daemon took a more leisurely pace and played with the man like a child plays with its food. He let the male witch get a hit in but in the end, there was no competition. The daemon reached with its clawed fingers and ripped the man's heart out. A bestial sound erupted from its mouth before he clamped down on the still beating heart in his hands.

Nthanda turned to find her friend on her knees retching up what little she had to eat. "Are you all right?"

Nessya continued to gag before she could speak. Her stomach was empty and the only thing she could do was dry heave. She flipped over and sat on her bottom. The sight of all that blood and the way they tore into those men, she couldn't help but vomit everything out of her system.

"Now I am. What in Elios name was that? How could you stand there and watch without getting sick?" Nessya rubbed her face with both hands. "That was brutal."

"You come from a land where sacrifice to Elios is as common as a man saying his morning prayers yet you gag and get sick at the sight of blood? Calling it brutal. That is only life. We live and we die."

"I wasn't sick at the sight of the blood but sick at the sight of how they ripped those two apart like *falis* bread! They're daemons!"

Nthanda smiled at the young woman. "Yes, they are daemons. Sent here by my family to protect me and mine. They didn't come this way. You see that the more human one bowed in reverence. We all will die sometime. It's just blood. There is power in blood. Knowledge in blood."

"Just blood," Nessya shook her head. "You really believe it's just blood. It's wrong how they did that."

"You have your sacrifices, we, the children of Enxyias have our rituals in blood. The same thing in my world. We have spells that are powered by blood. It is part of the old ways. You are learning the old ways, have you not figured that out? Don't look down on what we do because you don't think it is right or natural."

Nessya had no response. She stood and walked away, instead.

If it makes any difference, I thought what the daemon did was fantastic. I should take lessons on how he ripped the heart out so perfectly, Kai said, licking her paw.

Oh Kai, you keep me amused dear friend.

I try.

"I want to bathe in the shallow end of the river. I can't go any further smelling like dead carcasses. Can you stand watch for me?"

Of course, witchling.

"You know I am no longer a witchling, Kai."

You will always be my witchling.

“HOW MUCH FURTHER DO we need to go? I feel like we have been running for days on end,” Nthanda asked. The sun was up and her feet hurt like never before. “I miss wearing shoes.”

Nessya chuckled. “Shoes you miss? Of all the things you miss, you miss shoes?”

“Well, yes. This running and walking barefoot has gotten to my poor feet. They are rough. I’m used to wearing soft fur boots. It’s cold in my homeland. Everything is iced over and snow lunam round. Well, except for the three months of mild weather.”

“Lunam?”

“An ancient Enyxian word. Our way of how we mark a full year. A new lunam starts on the winter solstice. Your people call it Solis or a year. My people interchange the word year with lunam. Depends all on how the word spills from your mouth at the moment.”

“Ahh. Yes, and the year starts on the summer Solstice.”

“Which is odd to me. That’s backwards type of thinking.”

“Are you calling my people backwards?”

“Yes, I am. But you know this already.”

Nessya’s body shook from laughter. “If you say so. We are close to the city and the harbor. We will leave these lands by boat.”

"Boat?" Nthanda wasn't ready to get back on a boat. She remembered the long and arduous journey of sailing on one when she first came to these forsaken lands.

Nessya turned to Nthanda. Panic flared in Nthanda's eyes and fear clawed up her throat. Nessya really didn't know how to make it better. She sensed trauma involved and the only way was to get over it on her own.

"You will be fine. The boat is not too small, so a smoother ride. Plus, we won't be on the seas long. We are going to the desert lands. The Kingdom of Roshan. There we can properly rest."

"I don't want to go there. I want to go home!" Nthanda shouted.

"And you will go home. But I have business that takes us to the desert lands first. We need supplies and I need to speak with a few people there. We won't stay long. I promise you, I will get you home where you belong. You just have to bear with me. We cannot get caught. We will have more freedom to move around but not much. The Kingdom of Roshan is a human kingdom but has strong ties with my people. We believe in the same gods and have the same festivals and holy days but their laws differ only a little. They won't hesitate in turning us over to the Godspeaker."

"We don't want that. What shall we do?"

"Just follow my lead. The town is not that far ahead. Another candlemark," Nessya said to her. "Our passage has already been paid for."

Chapter 24

The boat swayed gently to the left then to the right like a child rocking in a bassinet. Unlike Nthanda's first time on a ship, this one was much more relaxed, and she was thankful for it. Not locked up in a room, unconscious, made much of the difference. Nthanda thought back to when they finally reached the coastal town of Cebi Harbor almost two weeks ago. A quick and urgent decision was made by Nessya to dye Nthanda's hair a darker shade. Her unruly white and black wavy curls would have given them away.

Soon as they arrived into town, they spotted a wanted flyer for both of them posted on the side of the door at the Black Snake Tavern, near the docks. Quickly retreating to the alley beside the tavern, both Nessya and Nthanda had to come up with some plan to not get caught. Nessya didn't want to use their magic while in Cebi because she didn't want to trigger any magical detection spells that she sensed hidden everywhere. Guards and other people wouldn't look twice at the color of Nthanda's skin because she matched plenty of others who visited from the Kingdom of Roshan, but her hair and eyes screamed 'Here I am!'

Cebi's daily hustle and bustle at the docks was filled with old and young fishermen. Sailors from all walks of life gathered in their circles, eyeing women who walked past their way. Whistles and laughter created a song of everyday life in the tight-knit community. Soldiers patrolled the area, watching every person who passed. Searching for the fugitives on the wanted posters that hung everywhere.

Not taking long, Nessya spotted the ship they were to embark on. A large vessel with sails the color of burnt red sand. Painted on the side, in large block letters, was the name *Sea Serpent.* Sailors moved all around the deck, shouting to each other as the crew prepared to leave the harbor. The group needed to become clever and find a way on board. Taking too long, they almost didn't make it. Nthanda was glad Kai could hide in broad daylight. It made her sneaking onto the ship much easier.

The Captain was a friendly man who always told a joke or flirted with Nessya. Which paid off because he let the women have one of the three cabins on board. Nthanda and her companions shared the not too small cabin space, which included two hammocks to sleep on. Kai slept near the door, ever on guard.

The trip had been easy now they neared the end of their journey. Nthanda thoughts about traveling by the seas slowly changed. She stood on the starboard side of the boat, watching the night sky as they sped along over the azure sea. High in the sky, millions of stars shone bright as diamonds and the comforting silvery light of the full moon called to her.

Rhythmic sounds of lapping waves, pushing and pulling against each other, and of the sails flapping when the wind hits them just right calmed her mind and soul. She no longer stood on the land of the jungle dwellers. The place of oppressive heat where even the plants and the smallest insect could kill you with just a tiny touch. She was closer to home and for Nthanda; it was a win and all she ever wanted.

"Lady..." a male's voice interrupted her alone time. The rich baritone voice distracted her from the calm place she found herself. Curious to find out who it belonged to, she twisted to the side to find a beautiful man watching her. His sandy brown hair fell to his shoulders in tight coiled twists. His eyes were a golden honey brown and his smile spoke of mischief. "Why are you out here alone and not resting below?" He asked with the thick accent she couldn't put a place to. "Where is your friend who always hang by your side?"

"Are you trying to find her or are you wanting to speak with me?" Nthanda responded with raised eyebrows. Challenging the man. His deep belly laugh was the relaxing music on a stormy night and she didn't know how to take that.

"I want to talk with you. Tell me your story?" he asked, leaning against the thick pole behind him.

"Why would I do that? What do I get out of it?" She shifted on her feet and crossed her arms across her chest.

The man's smile got wider. He was shirtless and the muscles in his chest and arms moved fluidly underneath his dark brown skin. "You will have discovered a new friend. You can never have too many of those."

"I have plenty."

"I can assure that you don't have any like me. So tell me, what is your story? I am positive it's an interesting one."

"You are right, but I am not telling you."

A chuckle escaped the man as his eyes raked over her, "Too bad. I think you would make a great one."

She noticed how the man kept his eyes on her. She may have been cloistered off from people most of her life, but she wasn't oblivious to what happens between a consenting man and woman. No doubt the man was beautiful and she could have plenty of fun with him, but that would have to wait for another day. If she decided to give him that chance. For now, she had other more important concerns to deal with.

"You can tell me your name though," she told him. "That is what friends do first, don't they?"

The man was quiet and kept his gaze on her face before saying anything. "Yes. They do." He reached his hands out for her to grasp. "They call me Etosh."

Nthanda was taken aback. His name sounded so close to her fallen guard, Ekon. Sad and mad that she hadn't thought of him much since that fateful night. He fell to protect her, and she killed for his vengeance. Her first kill and even now; she wasn't surprised at how much the act didn't bother her. Forgetting him bothered her to no bounds.

She clasped his outstretched arm as she sounded Etosh's name out loud. It rolled off of her tongue easily. "Etosh, are you from Roshan or elsewhere in the world?"

"Born in a tent and raised out in the sands. Roshan is my home through and through. My family are horse traders!"

"Then how come you are out here on the seas... horseless?"

"I follow where the wind calls my name. When I hit my majority, the winds led me to the waters. I broke tradition. I was training to take over the family business but with my first taste of the salted seas, I knew that I needed to be out here." He placed his hands on the edge of the ship and let his sight fall on the rolling waters. "There is something about the water. When she is hungry enough, she can claim you for her own and there is nothing you can do to stop her. The vastness of something so pure and dangerous but gentle and calm. There's balance out here." He looked at her from the corner of his eyes. "Life without balance is no life at all. At least that is what my mama always taught me."

Nthanda understood loud and clear what he meant. The word balance struck again. Over the course of the days leading up to and after her escape, the word made an appearance too many times. Life and balance. There was a message for her but she didn't know what the message was. Or why it was for her. Thinking no further, she decided she liked this Etosh. There was something about him. Something more he was hiding, and she wanted to know what that was.

"Yes, life without balance is no life at all. I agree," she said to him. "My travel companion prefers to stand in the sun and hang out here during the day. But I find the serene of the night and the moon more to my liking. Which do you prefer?"

He glanced her way and the charming smile he wore only gotten wider. "You are no fool are you? You see more than what most see."

"What do you think I see?" she cooed.

Etosh straightened and leaned into Nthanda. His lips almost touched the lobe of her ear and whispered, "Mother Goddess watches over all of her children. Even those who live in the bright desert sun."

Nthanda turned and faced the man, meeting eye to eye. He touched her shoulders lightly.

"Have a good night my new friend. If you need help with anything, don't hesitate to come and find me. It would be my honor to help you."

Nthanda watched as he strolled off leaving her to her own devices again. There was definitely more to the man than just being a sailor.

THE SEA SERPENT HAD docked, and the crew was busy unloading the cargo from the ship's hold. The cadence of footsteps beat a fastidious song above them. Nthanda and Nessya still in their cabin, prepared to debark the vessel while Kai kept going in circles in their cabin.

Frustrated and tired of being cramped up she was in the worst mood. *Bright Star, I need air. Hurry up.*

We are leaving. Have some patience.

I have some. Being cooped up in this room for too long makes me fussy.

I understand and I am sorry, Nthanda said, scratching behind the large cat's ear. *I'll make it up to you as always. I promise!*

The loud purrs coming from her familiar's chest was enough to know that her promise was acceptable.

"I have lodgings here in the city. We will stay there for a few days while I conduct my business then we can be on our way. Make sure you keep your head covered with the wrappings you had in your bag. The plant mixture I used earlier has worn off."

Nthanda had the wrappings in her hand and covered her head the way Nessya showed her. “I have no clue where we are, so I will follow your lead.”

Nessya opened the cabin door and stepped into the small hall before going up the stairs. Nthanda didn’t know what to expect from the new place. It wasn’t home, but it wasn’t the oppressive jungle either. She read about the desert lands in her studies as a child and always wanted to visit. The lands belonged to the humans, but they didn’t discriminate against witches, light or dark.

Before her mother took over duties as High Priestess from Mama Jia’ka she traveled far away from the cold winter-lands to the hot desert sands. She was able to pull that much from her mother one day. A time and place in her mother’s youth that she didn’t speak much of but always had a smile when she did.

Once topside, the multitude of unique sounds from the city reached her ears, and wrote its harmonic tune on the staff of the fresh sea air. The chord struck Nthanda’s heart. She stood at the top of the ramp looking out at the harbor. Mesmerized by the busy port. So many new sights and animals she had only read about. She wanted to touch, taste, and immerse herself fully into the fracas.

“Lady, can I help you down?” Nthanda remembered who that voice belonged to and turned to find Etosh standing there with an open vest and matching linen pants that came down to his calves. Brown strapped sandals covered his feet. His arm was outstretched for her to take. Nthanda smiled and took it. “You never gave me your name. I thought we were friends!” He frowned before smiling again.

"I haven't decided if we were friends yet or not."

"But our kind must stick together," he whispered to her. "Doesn't matter if you tell me or not. I already know who you are."

Nthanda stiffened and took a hard swallow. She forced herself to keep a straight face. "And how is it you know who I am if I didn't give you my name?"

"Words traveled far from the motherland. I remember learning your story when I was just a boy. That a girl was stolen from the citadel during an attack. For our people to be on the lookout." Etosh grinned. "To meet the girl with purple jeweled eyes. Never expected that. For the longest time, I thought it was just a story. You must be someone important for the High Priestess to send out the word like that. Who are you, really?"

Nthanda took a step back from the man. "Don't fret. I will not harm you. You are safe with me."

"Have you told anyone?"

"Why would I do that? Give myself away as a Child of the Moon too. We may be welcomed here, but doesn't mean they like us." Etosh sighed. "I would like to be a friend in a time of need. That's all. I can help you and your friend. Get you back to Enyxias."

"Why should I trust you?"

"Lady, I could have turned you in for the hefty sum the Godspeaker is rewarding the people for your return. I didn't even let the Captain know you were her. Now, let's move off this boat before they notice those beautiful eyes of yours and destroy your cover."

Etosh led Nthanda down the ramp and right into the ruckus of the harbor. Nessya wasn't far ahead, still within touching distance.

Kai, go ahead of me and I'll be right behind you.

He's nice looking. I won't eat him, Kai said and moved next to Nessya.

Nessya saw everything from afar but said nothing to the man and she didn't question why he was there. She glanced at Nthanda. "Stay close, the streets get busy here during mid-day."

Nthanda nodded. She said nothing else to Etosh, but she liked his closeness. Being near someone like her differed from being around Nessya. He could understand because he was her people.

The streets of Alikesh were wide and paved with cobblestone. Everyone traveled in all modes of transportation. From horse-drawn carriages, to the camels and people on foot. Food stalls sat outside of two and three-story buildings. Tantalizing aromas wafted her way, causing her stomach to growl in response. Everywhere Nthanda looked, there were colors everywhere. Golds and blues, reds and yellows. From the flower beds to the tiled mosaics in the bubbling fountains. It was beautiful to her. Different and new and she couldn't stop staring.

Nthanda was like a wide-eyed child wandering in the foreign streets of Alikesh. She wanted to touch, smell and taste everything. Every time she tried to venture off, Nessya brought her back and told her they would take in the sights all in due time. After traveling four long blocks along the winding canal and turning down multiple corners and streets, they finally stopped in front of a large two story sandstone building.

The walls surrounding the place were tall and imposing, hiding the dwelling behind the whitewashed enclosure. The large, expansive home was the last building on the block and took up the whole end. Men with swords on their hips and cream colored turbaned wraps that covered their hair, stood at the tall gates. Fierce scowls was a permanent fixture on their faces. On their chest was the sigil of Nessya's family but a little different. A sunburst but with what looked like a phoenix entwined around it.

"This is my family's home on my mother's side here in Roshan. She inherited it long ago and always kept it up. The Godspeaker does not know about this place. Father ensured that it would never get into his scrolls. The Godspeaker-likes to keep close tabs on his Te'Mak's. In my lands, women don't inherit. Only the men. Since mother is originally from here, the rules of inheritance don't apply here. There's always someone here. We keep the place occupied by distant relatives who won't say anything of our stay. It's like a resting home, an inn, while traveling. They haven't seen me since I was younger. We will be safe."

Nthanda trusted her this far, why not trust her on this? She relaxed her shoulders. "If you say we are safe, we are safe."

Nessya smiled then looked to Etosh. "You will not speak of us and where we came today will you?"

Etosh bowed with a huge grin on his face. "I promise. We all have our secrets. I do not want the Gods to come and hunt me down for breaking my word."

"Thank you," Nessya said to him.

"I will be on my way. I have things to do before I move out to the desert. Will I be granted the presence of your company from you two lovely ladies again before I depart?"

"Aren't you the charming one?" Nthanda said. "I will need a guide to the city, I am sure we will meet again Etosh."

He grinned wide like a young boy. "If you need horses and I mean good horses. The kind bred for the sands with speed, come to the market and ask around for me. I will hear and come find you. Until we meet again, may the sun of Elios forever warm your skin." He dipped his head and went back the way they came in while the women watched him go.

"He's quite the charmer isn't he?" Nessya asked.

"That he is."

"Do you trust him to keep his word?"

Nthanda waited and thought about the question before answering. "Surprisingly, I do. He knows who I am, and I said nothing to him about who I was. He could have turned us in long before we left your jungles."

That was news to Nessya. She would have to learn more about him just to be on the safe side. She walked up to the gates with Nthanda following her. She gave the guards the correct phrase to enter her home. They opened the gates and let them in.

Chapter 25

Nthanda wandered the house admiring the beauty of the place. It differed completely from the homes in the jungles and her home back in Enyxias. Tapestries hung on the walls, telling stories of Nessya's family history. Everywhere she turned, vivid colors of purple lilacs, white and pink lilies, and verdant green broad-leafed plants were everywhere. In the corners. In vases on tables. Wind chimes and its soft melodies pierced through the silent walls. The sweet scents of perfumed jasmine mingled with the warm and spicy fragrances of incense, filled the house telling stories of its own. Not needing to be told, Nthanda was in a whole new world. No wonder her mother always had a smile when she thought of the desert and its people. A genuine place of mystery and magical enchantments.

Kai walked beside her, invisible to everyone but her. She wanted a bath, and the house was grandiose and important enough to have its own private bath house. A servant showed her where it was earlier but she waited until Nessya left to visit. She wanted to relax in the heated waters and let her mind drift and do its own thing without being questioned about the man from the ship. Far too often did her mind wander back to the honey brown eyed man with the charming smile.

Nthanda also didn't feel well. The symptoms started the last few days on the journey over the sea but she chalked it up to being seasick. One of the many reasons, she kept going topside to the deck at night. Hoping the fresh, cool air would help. Now, back on land for the second day, she had gotten worse. Willing to try to anything, she thought a hot bath would help sweat the impurities out of her system. Another reason she waited until Nessya left. She didn't want her to know she was falling ill.

The private bath house was just past the courtyard and had three sections. One for the cool and warm water and the other for the steaming hot water. She walked up to the entrance and the attendant at the door let her in. A shorter, older woman, with graying hair and a few creases around her eyes waited on her once inside.

"This way, Lady-" the attendant let her words trail. Nthanda gave a false name, not wanting anyone to know who she was. The Godspeaker had her name and it should have been enough to put the fear of his god in his heart. Instead, he became infuriated. Since then, he pulled out everything in his hunt for her.

"Lady Jia" Nthanda responded. The older woman nodded and stepped towards a door.

"Well, Lady Jia. This is the changing room. You cannot wear cloth into the waters. You must step into the waters naked as the day you were born." She chuckled amused at herself. "Not only is this a cleansing ritual, but we see it as a communing with our inner selves. Find the time to find your center. I sense you need it most."

Nthanda looked at the woman and nodded, agreeing with the woman completely. The woman opened the ornate doors and stepped into an immense room with curtains for a person to change behind. The floor was another tiled mosaic of blues and whites. She couldn't keep her eyes off it.

"Here," the older woman said, pointing to a folded robe. "You put this on as you go between the hot and cold. Take it off before entering the waters. You can leave your clothing here. No one will touch them. We respect our bathing times."

"Thank you so much."

"If you need anything else, ring the bell. There's one in here and one in each of the bathing chambers." The older woman bowed and stepped quickly out of the room leaving Nthanda to herself.

Once alone, Kai made herself visible. Nthanda rubbed the cat's head in her favorite spot and she purred loudly.

I hope this helps you, Kai said.

Me too. Nthanda was more worried than she let on and nervous Kai would sense her mood through their bond.

She stepped behind the red and gold curtain and undressed. She put the robe on that was next to the chair and stepped from behind the curtain. Made with a soft cloth and not too thin, the robe was perfect. She moved towards the chamber for the hot bath and went inside. Full of steam, the minty aroma of eucalyptus with soft notes of jasmine and rose filled the air. The eucalyptus and the steam had medicinal properties she knew could help.

She expected the chamber to be dark, but it was full of light. Nthanda looked up to find the curved ceiling painted with bright colors in a garden scene. Massive sized glass windows high on the walls let the sun's rays fill the space, giving plenty of natural light. Nthanda disrobed and waded into the waters from the shallow end. Slowly moving deeper until she was chest deep into the heated waters. She almost moaned at how good the water felt to her and her muscles.

Kai moved around and found a spot away from the steam but within close enough distance to see her. Nthanda submersed herself completely and came back up. Wanting to sit and rest, she waded her way to the underwater stone bench and sat down. Low enough, the water still came to her neck while sitting. Nthanda closed her lids, rested her head back and let the aromas take her away.

NESSYA WAS TIRED, BUT she completed everything she needed to do and did it quicker than she expected. She had a full day to rest and relax before they departed for the next part of their journey. Another voyage on a ship but this time, the trip was to take them across the shores to Enyxias. Finding a vessel that headed that direction was hard, but she found one.

Walking through the gardens gave her hope that everything would be all right. They were mostly safe and far away from Namansii, her homelands. She would miss her family but she would find them again someday. She prayed to Elios they survived the sundering their society would go through.

Sudden shouting alerted her, and she ran inside to find out what was going on. She flew through the screened door and found Kanish, the older woman who attended the baths frantically pacing back and forth grabbing things. Nessya ran to her and grabbed her, hoping she would calm down and tell her what was going on.

"Kanish!" she shouted. "Kanish! What is wrong?"

"The woman who came with you. Something is wrong."

Dread filled deep inside of Nessya. "Explain? Is she gone or still here?"

"No, she is still here. But I can't wake her. She needs a healer."

"Take me to her. Now!"

Nessya traveled the maze like hallways, following Kanish to the private baths. On the way, she ordered the servants to stay away and not speak of anything they may have seen or heard. Rushing through the opened doors into the hot baths.

Sprawled out face down, Nthanda was partially in and out of the water. Nessya didn't know where Nthanda's familiar was and prayed the giant beast didn't make an appearance. Just in case the cat was still around she needed to make her intentions known, loudly.

"Kanish go stand by the door. I'll see what I can do to help," Nessya said. She checked Nthanda's wrist and found a slow pulse. Her skin was cool and clammy even though they were in the hot room.

"Yes, Lady," the woman nervously said and sped across to stand by the door.

Nessya made sure her back faced Kanish and spoke low so the woman couldn't hear her. "I know you are in here. I promise I won't harm her but we need to get her to a healer quickly. I am here to help as I've helped since we left my homeland. You can trust me."

She hoped the creature believed her.

"Kanish, bring me a robe and help me with her. We need to get her to her bed quickly."

Kanish did not hesitate and moved fast for an old woman. Together they put the robe on Nthanda and tried lifting her to no avail. A nearby guard came and helped, averting his eyes at Nthanda's near nakedness. Thankful their set of suites weren't far, they didn't have to move a long way to place her into bed.

Once the doors closed, Nessya groaned and sat at the foot of the bed. She had no idea what to do. She couldn't just invite any healer into her home. They were still wanted fugitives, and the Sun King was happily helping the Godspeaker out. She discovered that tidbit of news while conducting her business in the market. If the wrong person came into her home and recognized who they were, she had no doubt the city's watchmen and guards would pound at her door wanting to be let in.

She rubbed her eyes with the bottom of her palm and sighed. Not able to stop glancing at her friend, she was lost on how to help. Nessya didn't move from the bed, but sat there thinking of all the ways she could help the woman and none of them sounded remotely right.

The bed slightly moved, startling her but quickly realized it wasn't Nthanda moving. Nessya twisted around to only come face to face with the fearsome creature when the white beast materialized before her eyes. If anything, she wished she could speak to the large animal. Sadness permeated the crystal ice-blue eyes of the cat as she laid its head on her witches' stomach.

"I really wish I understood you. Maybe you have a few suggestions to help your witch."

A soft grumble came from the animal then she closed her eyes.

"Think Nessya, think!" Every healer she thought of were beholden to the Sun King and the Godspeaker. She stood and paced back and forth in front of the bed. She did not understand what was wrong, but they needed to figure the problem out soon as possible. Nessya didn't know how long Nthanda was unconscious or what possibly caused her to pass out.

Nessya made her way to the bedroom door when the city bells began to ring. Her whole body froze. Those bells weren't the standard bell toll but the toll of war. Warships was spotted on the sea. Chills ran down her spine and her heart tapped a quick beat in her chest. Everything inside her screamed at her to run as far as she could.

She turned to the cat, "You stay here. Do not let anyone in here unless it is me. I will announce myself at the door."

Nessya left the room in a hurry. Her long hair rippled down her back as she moved. She stalked down the halls full of purpose and one thing on her mind. Finding out what was going on.

The servants was scattered everywhere in the halls and her guards were at attention when she walked passed them. She stepped outside the doors to her home to be accosted by a blended chorus of people shouting and animals braying. The raucous noise traveled over the walls and drifted to her. Nessya made her way to the entrance to find the man from the boat outside of the gates arguing with the guards. He caught her eye, and she ran to find out what the ruckus was all about.

"Stop! He's here for me," she told her guards. "Let him in."

They did as commanded and Etosh moved inside the gates, ignoring the looks her guards gave him. She wanted to know why he was there and out of breath.

"What is wrong?" she asked leading him into the gardens, away from prying eyes and ears.

Etosh took two big gulps of air before speaking. "Warships on the horizon."

"I know. The bells are ringing."

"No. They are the Godspeaker's warships. He and the Sun King have come to an agreement. This land is no longer safe for my people."

"Your people? What do you mean?"

Etosh glanced around before whispering, "Children of the Moon."

Realization hit Nessya. *No wonder Nthanda took a liking to him. They were the same somewhat. That was why Nthanda said she trusted him. That he had plenty of opportune times to have told on them long before they left her lands.*

Relieved, "That is why she took a liking to you. No matter. She is sick and needs a healer. I don't know what is wrong. Lucky you found your way here just now."

Etosh eyes widened, "How long has she been ill?"

"No idea. I was away and came home to my bath attendant frantic. She discovered her in the bath unable to wake up."

"I know someone who can help but we can't stay here and they don't live here in the city. I will tell you more later, but know that once those ships docks, there will be a ban on travel and Alikesh will be locked down."

"How do you know these things?"

"I get around and hear things. Eyes and ears everywhere." He smiled. "Take me to her. Please."

"How do you know who she is? I only found out recently her name."

"She is important to my people. We have been looking for her for eight long years. And your people will regret the day they stole her away from our motherland."

"That is something we can agree upon. My people will regret that day and I have no sympathy for them."

Etosh was surprised to hear the woman agree. "You are not like the others. Maybe I can like you like she likes you."

Nessya laughed out loud. It felt good to laugh at that moment because she was full of fear deep inside.

"Well, if you're a friend to her, then you're a friend to me. My name is Nessya."

"Nice making your acquaintance. I am called Etosh."

NESSYA HAD ETOSH FOLLOW her through the house. She ordered the servants to prepare three traveling packs. The good thing about their private suites, was being located in the back of the house. Away from everyone. She trusted her household but if they were going to war, they wouldn't jeopardize their lives for two fugitives on the run. Their time had run out.

At the doors to the chambers, Nessya stopped before opening. She had almost forgotten about the large familiar guarding the room. She made Etosh step back and slightly pushed the door ajar.

"It's me and Etosh. We are coming inside."

A low growl came from within which she took as a safe sign to enter. "C'mon," she beckoned to Etosh. "I will have to warn you, don't be afraid of the large cat. It's rather protective of her."

"Don't worry. I've heard about her and the cat. I will be all right."

Nessya eyes narrowed and shrugged her shoulders. They walked into the room and found Kai crouched, ready to pounce. She stood down once she saw who came through the door.

Etosh didn't hesitate at seeing the big animal and rushed to Nthanda's side. Her skin was ashen gray and her breath was shallow. He touched her hand and withdrew it quickly. Cold and clammy. He glanced back at Nessya, fear on his face. "This is being caused by her magic. I've seen this sickness in young children when they first come into their gift. Where the power is wild and uncontrollable. She shouldn't be going through this. What happened? What has changed that is causing her body to react in defense to her own magic as if it's brand new?"

Nessya didn't want to tell the man, but he needed to know. Guilt poured out for her family's dealing with Nthanda.

"You must tell me, Nessya." Etosh pleaded.

She let out a sigh. "While she was a captive, they suppressed her powers. She wasn't able to touch them at all. Somehow, she broke the geas that had been placed on her and she immediately used her powers and nearly drained herself to the point of no return."

"What!" he shouted. "How long did your people suppress her magic?"

"Eight years. From the moment she was taken from the winterlands."

Etosh couldn't believe what Nessya was saying. He always thought the Children of the Sun were the true monsters. That they are what they claimed his people to be, but he knew better. *The Children of the Moon was nothing like those monsters at all.*

"Suppressing her power like that is dangerous. Don't you all know that? Especially for one of her caliber. When you block the gift, the magic always find a way to release itself. But hers is wild and dangerous. Our magic is a gift from our gods and goddess. And she is blessed by Enyxia herself. See her mark," he said pointing to Nthanda's mark on her chest. "The gift is sentient and knows our desires and wants. That's how we can bend it to our will. With our spells and conjuring's. What your people did is torture of the worst kind. No wonder she lay here almost dead."

"For what it is worth, I am sorry."

"Don't be. It's not your fault."

"No, but it is my family's fault and I take responsibility for their actions."

Etosh said nothing more but gathered Nthanda's surrounding clothes. "You dress her properly and I'll go get the horses. We don't have much time before soldiers start searching every house and home."

"Horses?"

"Yes, horses. I rode one and brought the second for you two to ride."

"How did you know to bring horses for us?"

"As I have said before. I have eyes and ears everywhere. Some in high places and they got word to me soon as they could. Does it really matter?"

"No." Nessya was in a state of shock and was just trying to piece everything together.

"My horses, they are around the way. Not too far from here. We can't be seen leaving this place. Discretion is imperative. Where can I meet you?"

"Meet us around the back. There is another gate that leads to a private alley. We will wait for you there. Hurry so we can depart this place. I have no faith in the Sun King and my house guards anymore. They saw you, her and I don't feel safe. Instincts is telling me to run."

"Sounds like you have good instincts lady." Etosh headed to the window to leave out the back way. "I will return in no time."

Nessya noticed and stopped him. "No, go out the way we came in. They must see you leave this place so they won't get suspicious too quick."

Etosh opened the door and glanced back. "Smart lady." He flashed her a smile and left.

Nessya groaned and sat down in the chair next to the bed. Kai's unnerving blue gaze caught her off guard and startled her.

"I hope this all works. For the love of Elios, they cannot catch us."

Kai yawned. Her fangs and sharp teeth glistened in the sunlight. The animal turned away from her, settling back on her witch. Nessya couldn't speak with her but she understood body language enough to know the beast agreed.

Chapter 26

Etosh found the alley Nessya spoke of. He tied his horses to the iron gate and crept in. The stone path he took guided him into another garden. This one was full of night-blooming flowers. He recognized the different species of plants and foliage on sight. Some were poisonous which made him wonder what type of witchery Nessya's family dealt with.

The hidden path took Etosh to a low inner wall and passed through a short gate. He made sure not to make any sounds. Glad that no guards patrolled while he crept through like a thief in the night. He kept to the shadows, sped across and reached the closest window. He peeked inside and found the room empty, dark. Etosh moved further down to the next one where he found the women waiting.

Etosh climbed in, speaking softly so Nessya knew it was him. She stood, looking relieved when he came through.

"Glad it was you and no one else. I can't lift her on my own."

"I know. That's why I came back. I can lift her for you." He nodded to the window, "Let's go."

Etosh and Nessya lifted Nthanda from the bed and placed her over his shoulders. Nessya grabbed the three bags she had made for them and locked the bedroom door from the inside.

"Now will be a fine time if you could do that disappearing thing you do," she said to the large leopard. Kai disappeared from sight. "Wish I had that ability," Nessya mumbled to herself.

Etosh went through the window first and Nessya tagged along behind him. It took them no time to go down the winding path and make it to the gates. He made it seem simple and easy with how quickly he put Nthanda on the horse. He sat her upright and got behind her.

He twisted around on the horse and peered down at Nessya, "I forgot to ask if you knew how to ride. It's not too hard."

Nessya smiled and hopped onto the horse. "Of course, I know how to ride. These are fine specimens."

"Yes, they are. My family is the only ones who breed this special type of horse."

"Nice."

"We have to ride out of the city proper. We'll move quickly. We bred these horses for top speed in the desert sand."

"Guess we better go. After you," Nessya said.

THE GROUP TRAVELED quickly through the crowded streets. The tolling of the bells had the citizens in a frenzy, wondering what was going on. *If only they knew that the Sun King sold them out*, Etosh thought to himself.

It didn't take long to reach the city walls and gates. High on the wall armed guards watched the goings and comings of everyone. Soldiers patrolled below and was at the gate checking people before they let them enter or leave. Nessya sidled next to Etosh and leaned over slightly his way.

"Are they closing the gates already, preventing the people from entering and departing?"

"No, they are searching. They must have gotten wind of what the fugitives look like." He eyed her then forward again.

Nessya understood what he was saying without him saying a word at all. "I will mimic whatever you do, Etosh. You are proving to be the expert at this already."

Etosh gleaming white smile glowed under his hooded cowl. "You should try an illusion if they have an accurate description of you and Nthanda. We're lucky her eyes are closed. They won't touch her hair since we covered it."

"Good point," Nessya agreed. She discreetly worked a small illusion spell over her face.

"If they try to stop us, keep going no matter what. These horses are fast enough to dodge their arrows. Whatever you do, just don't stop."

The group stopped at the tall, wooden gates. Two soldiers above focused on Etosh and Nessya as they indirectly aimed loaded crossbows their way. Nessya's horse snorted and sidestepped a little to the right. Two burly soldiers with long beards eyed the sudden movement. The soldier with a scar on his cheek, stepped to Etosh side. He checked out the horse and the unconscious woman in front of him.

"What is wrong with her?" the man asked with his thick accent. He took the handle of his sword and poked Nthanda in the side.

"My sister, she is sick. I am afraid she is contagious. We are trying to get her out of the city so it won't spread. Trust me. You don't want what she has."

"Humph. What she got?"

"The healer told us that her symptoms is the first stages of the *Sand Death.* The healer bade us leave without hesitation. If we stayed, it surely would spread." Etosh spread his hands wide in a fanning motion.

The scarred man jumped back at hearing what she had. He yelled at his comrades to move away from Etosh and Nessya.

"Open the gates!" he yelled to someone hidden, manning the gates. The creaks and groans of the old wood pushed the heavy doors aside, giving the group free rein to move. Nessya went first through the threshold, while Etosh glanced down to the man.

"Thank you, kind sir. You may want to have a healer check you out since you got near her. All of you actually." Etosh grinned and spurred his horse into a gallop then a full out run, catching up with Nessya.

Etosh was side-by-side to Nessya. "Stay close," he shouted then took the lead. They rode hard and fast on the road out of the city and into the golden desert. Etosh knew where he headed and didn't bother to check behind to see if the woman and the cat followed. He didn't lie about needing to get Nthanda to a healer as soon as possible. The woman sitting in front of him, slightly slumped over, needed the help.

There was only one person he trusted that could help heal her, and that was his mama.

Well known in the Kingdom of Roshan as one of the finest horse breeders and traders; merchant families, nobles, and even the royal family sought his tribe out for their horses. His ancestors didn't trust the humans and their pact of being okay with the Children of the Moon living free in the desert lands. Instead, his tribe and the other tribes hid their true gifts and the dark magic they practiced, letting everyone else believe they were just lowly nomads with a fine eye for horses. Etosh had to warn his family too. The only safety they could ensure was if they left Roshan altogether and found their way back Enyxias. War was coming. He wanted to make sure his family was secure and far away as they could be.

"Where are we headed?" Nessya asked when they slowed down and Etosh was able to hear her.

"To the Ta'zyk Oasis. Just north from here. My family tents will make the Oasis home for the next few months before they move on. We are a nomadic people. Never stay in one place."

"How far north?"

"With these horses, only a few candlemarks. We should arrive by dusk."

The duo kept quiet and to themselves as they crossed the arid desert side by side with Kai behind them. The sun beat down on the group but they kept moving. Stopping only a handful of times to let the horses rest and give them water. Time was of the essence and Etosh knew they didn't have much of it.

As the sun began to fall, the Ta'zyk Oasis appeared in the distance. Etosh slowed and stopped his horse, allowing Nessya to do the same.

"Why are we stopping?" she asked, placing her hands over her eyes to block the glare of the sun as she looked to the trees in the distance. Trees meant blessed shade, and she was already dreaming of its leafy coolness. The heat didn't bother her because her beloved jungles was nothing but trees, but the heat without shade was worse in her opinion. "We're almost there."

"I know but there are a few things I must go over with you."

Nessya shifted on the mare. The inner part of her thighs burned. They were rubbed raw. She really wanted to get off the animal. "Okay, like what? Or could this wait until we got there?" She jerked her thumb towards the dreamlike oasis.

"No. It cannot wait."

Nessya exhaled. She rubbed the sweat from her eyes. "Fine. Talk pretty boy."

Etosh brows shot up and grinned. "Thank you for noticing." Nessya mumbled under her breath. "My mother is the head of my family."

"As I figured."

"No, you don't understand. She is the head of my family and the desert tribes."

"Well, that's impressive. How big is your tribe?"

"The largest in the desert. We have forty different families in my tribe. But there are four other tribes in the desert that we interact with."

"So there is four different leaders too?"

"Yes, and they answer to my mother," he responded. He saw the moment the realization kicked in on Nessya's face.

"Wait... your mother is the head of all the desert tribes?"

"Yes, that is what I said."

Nessya reeled at the revelation. Etosh was more important than what he had let on. He just wasn't a sailor on the ship infatuated with Nthanda.

"You are royalty!"

"No. The tribes have no such thing as royalty."

"But you're important."

"I don't see how. I'm the youngest of five. The extra." He shrugged his shoulders.

"But your mother is still the leader over a lot of people. They answer to her. How come you were on our boat working if you don't have too?"

"I have my reasons. Besides, the seas call out to me. That's enough to want to be out on the waters instead of the desert."

"I see your point. The jungles can be stifling and I have always longed to come back here to the desert lands. Now that I am here, I don't even know if I want to be here again."

Etosh understood. He was born and raised out in the sands, but his soul longed for another home. "One more thing you should know. Unless my mother gives you permission to speak, don't. You are a stranger and not of us. I am already breaking rules by bringing you to our inner space. It will take a lot to convince my mama you are safe and not like the others."

"Why is that? I thought both light and dark got along in these lands?"

"We have until your people spirited her away. The dynamics have slowly changed towards my kind. And not for the good. Just remember, don't speak until you are told to."

"Duly noted."

"Come on, let's hurry so you can get off that horse. I can tell you are hurting. My mama have a fantastic salve for that." Etosh flashed his charming grin and spurred his horse into a full gallop. Nessya didn't need to be told twice to follow the man. The quicker they got to the oasis the quicker she could rest and hopefully find help for her friend.

Chapter 27

"My little Toshi is home!" A short stature woman said as she sauntered from inside the brown and black tent. Her grin was the same as Etosh and the familial connection between the two was obvious to Nessya. "What do you-" she drawled before stopping. She looked at the woman in front of him. "How?" She demanded. She stepped closer to his horse and touched Nthanda's face. "Bring her into the tent, now!"

The woman quickly turned and went back into the tent she had just come out of. Nessya jumped down and groaned at the soreness in her legs. She stepped closer to Etosh and Nthanda. She reached up to support her while he jumped off his horse. He nodded his thanks. Nessya helped him place Nthanda in his arms and went inside. She followed quickly on his heels, not caring if she should be there or not. This was her friend no matter the circumstances and she would be by her side.

"You should wait outside," Etosh whispered to her.

"You must be out of your godforsaken mind thinking I will wait outside. You have only known her for a few days, I have been her friend for years. I stay. So does the cat." Kai made her appearance, startling everyone in the tent. Including Etosh's mother. Nessya grinned and rubbed the top of Kai's head. She couldn't speak to her but they were in this together.

Etosh frowned. Nessya didn't care. She refused to leave her friend's side no matter what. Etosh stepped around Nessya and placed Nthanda on a cot low to the ground while his mother came to her. The woman's gazed raked Nessya from head to toe. A hissing noise emitted between her clenched teeth.

"Who are you to think you can come into my tent without permission?"

"Her friend. With her cat. If you don't like that, then I suggest you get over it. We are not leaving."

"You have a fire in you. Not unexpected from a child of the light." Etosh mother stared, saying nothing then turned, leaving Nessya standing there.

Nessya kept her gaze on the woman while she checked Nthanda's vitals. She ordered two women who stood in the shadows to bring water and other needed tools.

"You can stay. Sit in the corner over there and stay out of my way," the woman said without turning around.

A small victory nonetheless and Nessya would take whatever was thrown her way. Being around Nthanda was different, never once thought about who she was and where she came from. But surrounding herself completely with witches her family taught her to be evil her whole life was a little disconcerting.

She didn't know much about healing except the basics. With a childlike curiosity, she paid attention from the corner, as Etosh helped his mother along with her other helpers.

Nessya didn't care how they cured her, as long as they fixed her. She wanted to see Nthanda's face when she stepped back on the soil of her homeland.

A candlemark had gone by when Etosh made his way towards Nessya with a cup and handed it to her.

"What is this?" she asked, taking the cup from his hand. Filled with a milky liquid. She sniffed the contents and gagged. A strong sour scent wafted from the cup and made her want to throw up.

"Eh... a drink. Aren't you thirsty?" Etosh took a gulp from the cup she didn't notice he had in the other hand.

"I am but not enough to drink whatever this is."

Etosh shrugged his shoulders. "Not so bad. Actually, the drink is good for you. My people have drank this for generations. We're still strong and healthy. Just try it. If you don't like it, I will find something else for you."

Nessya sniffed the cup again and wanted to pour the milk out. But if she didn't try it, she would look bad in front of these people. She didn't want to show weakness. *How bad could it really be?* She lifted the cup to her lips, held her breath, and took a large swallow. The moment the thick liquid touched her tongue she wanted to spit it out.

Etosh stood there and watched as she tried the drink. He kept drinking from his cup and she knew she had to swallow. It was worse going down but she couldn't do anything but drink the weird milk. After she stomached the liquid, she wiped her mouth. She needed water, wine or anything to wash that out from her mouth.

"So what was that?"

"Camel's milk," he said nonchalantly. Etosh finished the cup of milk he held in his hand.

Nessya convulsed as if she would throw up.

"You okay?" Etosh asked.

The smirk on his face said everything Nessya expected. She couldn't reply because her body was rejecting the nasty she poured into it. She jumped up, covered her mouth, and ran out of the tent.

"It really is an acquired taste," he called out after her. Etosh chuckled and turned to find his mother frowning at him. "What?"

"You know what. Quit doing that woman like that and go help her. Then bring her back. We have things to discuss," she chastised him.

"Yes, mama."

Etosh stepped outside of the tent and searched around. Nessya could have ran anywhere in the large camp. Groaning, he set off to find her. He spotted dark fabric bent over near the side of the tent a ways down and went to her.

"Hey, are you all right?" She couldn't respond for emptying the milk she had just drank. Seeing her like that, he felt bad for not warning her. He moved closer to her and rubbed her back while she finished. She stood up eventually and groaned.

"I need water."

"I will get you some. My mother requested our presence back in the tent. Go on and I'll meet you back inside."

Etosh watched her go before going off to search for the well.

NESSYA SAT NEXT TO Kai. Etosh's mother lowered herself to the ground in front of Nessya and crossed her legs. The woman kept silent. Time moved all too slow and when Nessya thought she couldn't take the silence any longer, the tribeswoman spoke.

"I understand why my son brought the woman here, but why are you here? That part I can't grasp just yet." Nessya said nothing. She remembered what Etosh told her on the way there. Only speak when she is given permission to speak. The woman smiled. "My son taught you something of our ways. That's good. I have questions that need answers. You can give them to me. I allow you to speak here."

"The woman is my friend. I brought her here. I asked Etosh for help because I had nowhere else to go."

The tribeswoman tilted her head slightly to the right. Accessing and coming to a conclusion of her own deductions. No one had to tell Nessya the woman was intelligent. How else could be she the leader of all the desert tribes?

"How did you meet my son?"

"On our voyage here. On the seas."

"So you are from the cursed lands of Namansii? From the people who took her?"

"Unfortunately, yes."

"And how do you know her? How is she is your friend?" The woman drilled.

Nessya didn't want to answer truthfully but somewhere inside, she had an inkling that the woman could tell if a person was lying.

"It was my house. My grandfather who ordered my father to retrieve her as a child." Nessya's head hung low. "My father didn't want to, but he had no choice. He had to obey."

"He had the right to say no. Everyone in the world has free will. The choice to make their own decisions. That is the way the Mother Goddess created us."

"Godspeaker Nelioz was the one behind my grandfather's decision. We cannot disobey our leader. My family was on the line. If he didn't, we would have all died eight years ago." Nessya's voice rose with every sentence.

"I am aware of how that can be a problem. But a solvable one."

"My father's hands were tied tightly."

"Many people have died since that fateful day. If your family would have been sacrificed and died, then hundreds and hundreds of people would still be alive. It would have been for the greater good."

"But here we are. I still have breath and so does the Godspeaker. He is the one that needs to die. Luckily, she took his son out before she escaped. She sure made a dramatic exit." Nessya said sharply.

"The prince is dead?"

Etosh walked inside the tent. "Well, that explains a lot." He sat down beside his mother and crossed his legs as she did.

"What do you mean?" His mother asked. Her brows wrinkled in confusion. Lost, Mael wanted to know what was going on.

"Her leaving by killing the Godspeaker's favorite son. Rumors were flying swift as a bird, saying he was dead, but they never said how he died." He grinned. "She must have been really mad."

"You would be mad too if they imprisoned you for eight years then suppressed your magic for that length of time." Nessya spat out, quickly angered. Rubbing her hands over her eyes. Her body screamed for rest. Not realizing how tired she truly was until she sat down. "What is wrong with her?"

"She got the magic sickness. You suppressed her gift for eight long years. Her power sought to be free and broke loose from the weakened shackles. She is strong, and the gift is wild. Unstable. She has to get it in control. I stabilized her for now but she need a stronger healer than I. She needs to go to the temple."

"What temple?" Nessya asked. Both Etosh and his mother looked at her strange.

"Temple of Elios." Etosh intoned. "How long has it been since you last visited these lands? Everyone knows the best healers besides my mama here, is located at the temple."

"I haven't been here since I was a young child. My mother is from here. My father is pure Namansii."

"Ahh," the tribeswoman said, patting Etosh's knee. "Like he said, the best healers can be found at the temple. They will know what to do. You can leave tomorrow. Rest tonight. Eat. You could use it. The temple is only three candlemarks away. If you leave at first daylight, then you can be there before the sun is high in the sky."

"Thank you for your hospitality."

"No worries. What is your name?"

"I am called Nessya."

"Well, Nessya I am called Mael. The evening meal should be ready. Go to the center of the camp and ask for Lati. She is my eldest daughter. Tell her I sent you and she will know what to do. She will make sure you eat. Take the beast too. We should have a small goat around. We will be out shortly, we have further things to discuss."

Nessya understood a dismissal when she heard one and stood. Legs numb and tingly from sitting in the same position for that length of time. Kai did the same, stretching her back and legs. They left together out of the tent leaving Etosh and his mother, Mael, sitting on the ground.

Mael waited before she said anything to her son. She had to understand and grasp the situation completely. She made sure they were the only two left in the tent besides the young woman unconscious on the cot.

"How did you find them, truly?"

"It was how she said. On the seas. My voyage back home and they were on my boat."

"Mother Goddess led her to your boat. Praise her."

"I've told you since I was a child, Mama that I belonged to the seas. The waters. It was fate that I found her."

"Yes, you did." Mael smiled.

"They had darkened her hair, but I recognized her eyes soon as she boarded the ship. I said nothing to anyone. Not even my Captain. Soldiers were already in Cebi Harbor looking for the two. I couldn't risk them finding her. There's a hefty reward for their capture. A king's ransom."

"Hmm. A king's ransom. There is more to the story if they're offering that much. You observed from the shadows, I presume."

"Yes. Wrongly, I assumed they would have broken her spirit down to shambles, but they didn't. She is confident, strong, and enchanting. There's something about her that draws you to her. Pulls you in like the tides and I couldn't help but wade into the waters and speak to her."

"And how long did it take for you to gain that amount of courage?" She smirked.

Etosh held his head down and sheepishly grinned, "Two weeks. I approached her the day before we made the docks."

He smiled at the memory of the feisty woman he remembered from that brief conversation. Her jeweled eyes and the intelligence she exuded mesmerized him. She was beautiful and everything he ever wanted in a woman.

"I think my son is infatuated with the girl." His mother all-knowing gaze lingered on him. She had always been able to read him better than any other person could. He cleared his throat, cleared his mind.

"I am not infatuated," he denied. "She's interesting. When she wakes, you will see."

"Well, I won't be traveling with you to the temple. My duties lie here but you will go."

"That is not safe, Mama. They sounded the war bells. The Kingdom of Roshan is at war."

A gasp escaped Mael's mouth. "At war! With whom?"

Etosh hated what was happening in the world and didn't want to say but he had no choice. "They allied with the Children of the Sun and declared war against us. Us Children of the Moon. We are no longer safe in these lands. This is our home but we must seek safety elsewhere. Warships were on the horizon when we left and they should have landed by now. The city was on the verge of a lockdown when we departed. I had to lie to the guards and say she had the Sand Death. It is the only way they let us leave."

"That is not good news at all, son. We can't leave. Not yet. They don't suspect who we really are."

"They can tell. These lands aren't safe anymore Mama. War is coming and I can't lose my family. I can't lose any of you."

"You know as I do Etosh, that I can't make that decision on my own. We have to call a gathering of the tribes."

"That will take forever and a day to gather all the tribes together. We're so spread out."

"We are in luck. The Mother Goddess is working in her mysterious ways. The other tribes are not that far from this oasis."

"Are you sure? They could have moved on by now."

"We saw them on the way here. If we send the riders out now on our fastest mounts, they can deliver the messages tonight and be back with the other tribes by morning. We can have the gathering before you depart."

"I'll prepare my things. I can ride out with the others."

"You will eat first and I will pen the messages to a scroll. Come back to me with the riders after you have eaten, Etosh. I mean it. You look thin."

Etosh chuckled and stood. "You always say that mama. But I will eat something first. If Lati had cooking duty tonight, I know the food is good."

Mael smiled. "She took after her mama."

Chapter 28

Nessya sat in the back of the tent, hidden away in a corner with an invisible Kai. Mael and Etosh didn't know how well the other tribe leaders would take to seeing her. Out of sight, out of mind was their thinking and how they came up with the notion for her to hide. She was still able to listen in on the meeting and for her that was good enough. She didn't mind being away from the crowd because she was close to Nthanda.

She checked to make sure Nthanda's chest still rose up and down before sitting. Glad there were no major changes. Mael worked hard to keep her friend stable over the night, constantly checking on her and doing Elios knew what. Her skin wasn't ashen anymore, but it was still weird seeing her sleep and not knowing when she would wake up. If ever.

The way Mael explained magic sickness made sense and coincided with the actions of her father and grandfather. She prayed that it didn't lead to death. Nthanda had to fight it within herself. The magic warred with her life essence. Mael told her it was out of sync. Imbalanced. Suppression or a growth in power could set it off but that it generally happened with only young children. Not adults like Nthanda. The dark witch was the anomaly.

Mael stood tall in front of her peers with her hands clasped behind her back. The other tribal leaders didn't give any of her riders any trouble and came as soon as they could. If she called a gathering and sent riders to bring them back; it had to been bad. The normal way the tribes communicated was by leaving coded messages on trade and travel routes at the drinking wells and oasis. Urgency would be the only reason riders were sent.

All the leaders differed in age. Mael wasn't the oldest, but she wasn't the youngest either. Rhake was the closest in age to her and sat up close in the front cross legged. Rhake was a thin woman with graying hair and deep brown eyes. She wore the veil over her hair but not across her face. She wanted people to see her expressions when she spoke.

"Why the urgency, Mael? My people had to travel out of the way to come here today," Rhake said.

"Because I have news that cannot wait."

"Well, what it is? We're all here now." Enoksa said. An impatient man and one that Mael didn't like very much. She wished his family had chosen differently, but they knew what they needed and saw something in him that she didn't.

"War is coming," she said.

"I'm not surprised. It's been brewing since those sun witches took that child. Did they finally kill her? Is that why war broke out?" Seknyn asked.

Appalled at the thought the girl could be dead. Mael even told the man that. "No Seknyn. That girl is not dead. In fact, she breathes."

Seknyn being the oldest, moved slower than the others. He leaned forward like it hurt to just move. His muted grey eyes squinted. "How do you know for sure?"

"Because I have her here in my tent right now," answered Mael.

A collective gasp from the tribal leaders mingled into a hissing sound. Confusion, shock then wonder spread across their faces.

"Are you for sure it is her?" Milvono asked. The second oldest of the leaders, she was a timid and quiet woman. But never make her mad. Mael discovered the hard way after they chose her to lead them all.

"Because my son found her. She escaped her captors and is on the run. She has the jeweled eyes and the white and black hair."

"Can we see her?" Rhaka asked.

Mael didn't mind showing the girl to her fellow tribal leaders, but she had to warn them first. She didn't want her fellow leaders to think she harmed the woman. "Yes, you can see her but I must tell you, she is not awake. She is unconscious. She has the magic sickness and fights it. Etosh and her companion will take her to the temple soon as we are done here."

"Can't you help her?" Rhaka continued.

"I have done all that I can do. She needs better healers. Stronger magic. They can help her there at the Temple of Elios."

The group grew silent. Lost into their own thoughts and concerns. No doubt, they felt like she did. It was dangerous with war coming. The Temple of Elios was sacrosanct to those who worshipped the Sun God. Those who drew their power and strength from the Evernight was frowned upon. But it was a sanctuary to those in need and Mael hoped and prayed to the Mother Goddess that they would look past the woman's heritage and ancestry and give her a place to recover and seek help. She couldn't be lost.

"I don't have a good feeling about any of this," Milvono said out loud. Only mirroring what everyone else in the tent was thinking.

Mael shifted on her feet. "Before I show you the girl, she has a companion with her. One, not of our kind. She's from Namansii. The jungles across the seas. She claims that they are friends. That she helped her escape the clutches of the Godspeaker and brought her to these lands. She sought my Etosh for help when the girl fell ill."

The group eyed each other, but it was Enoksa who looked appalled. The man stood and stepped towards Mael. Face to face, their noses could touch. "Her kind is not welcomed here. They are the ones who started this," he spat.

"You know better than I that it was our own people who started this by betraying their own," Mael snapped. Enoksa sneered at Mael but stepped backwards from her. "Do you want to see her or not?" She asked, completely over Enoksa's attitude and superior thinking ways.

"I do. Then my family and I can go from this place."

Mael wanted to punch the man in the face but she was their leader and being civil won out. She turned away from them, leaving her back to the group and beckoned them to follow her.

Nessya heard everything and did not want to be seen by the elders. The animosity they each held was thick and she felt it from where she sat. Her hand was close to Kai's neck. The soft fur kept her calm. "If you don't want to be seen, I would suggest doing that disappearing thing you do," she whispered to the animal. "These people don't sound too pleasant."

Nessya wasn't stunned when the large cat disappeared from sight. She was somewhat jealous. She wanted the ability to hide in plain sight if she could. Instead, she was there, sitting in a corner, watching her friend sleep, oblivious to the goings on and shenanigans of the world.

The tribal leaders stood over Nthanda but said nothing. Once a few got their fill of examining her, they moved back to the other side of the tent. None of the men or women said anything to Nessya. Few even glanced her way except one. His eyes were cold and his face narrow. He had scarred markings under his eyes and his irises were the color an orange flame. Chills crept down Nessya's back as she looked at the man. He sneered and turned away.

"Enoksa, leave the child alone. She has done no harm to you or me. In that fact, any of us," Mael said.

Grateful for the woman even though she feared Mael at their first meeting.

"The Godspeaker has allied with the Sun King. They intend to purge the lands of our kind. Already, Alikesh and its harbor and the palace are being locked down. Homes searched, looking for our people. We are no longer safe in these lands," Mael told the leaders.

"Where do you expect us to go? These lands are our home. Have been for hundreds of years. We know of no other place to be safe," Rhake said. She was deeply troubled by the events.

"Yes, Mael. Where are we to go? How can we believe what you say is true? I haven't heard of any war news. I had riders just come back yesterday with the latest news," Enoksa grimaced. "None of the riders mentioned warships or an alliance. The only thing I can be sure of is that you have the girl here."

"Why would the Godspeaker declare war on our people? Besides the girl slipping through his fingers finally," Seknyn spoke out.

"She killed his favorite son. There's a king's ransom for her return alive. She must never go back. The sanctuary is the only safe place until she can travel to Enyxias."

"How will she get home? Do you know the way?" Milvono asked.

"There are ways. Meanwhile, your families need to know what is going on. Tell them. Give them the option to stay or leave for safety. That is all I ask. And do not tell anyone about the girl. Don't want the news to get back to the Sun King and the representatives of the Godspeaker. They would have the whole army in the desert searching for us because we hid her."

The leaders all nodded in agreement. The leaders were noisy as they left Mael's tent. Nessya didn't relax until they had gone. Mael came back and stood in front of her.

"You must get your things and go. Now! You will not be alone. Etosh already have the horses ready. You will leave together in a group. My children, Rihat, and Balash will ride along, creating a small caravan. I trust Rihat and Balash with all of my being to help guard," Mael rushed out. She looked back towards the tent's entrance and turned back to Nessya. "I don't trust all of my tribe leaders. Especially Enoksa. Soon as his family leave, your travel group will leave."

"Why don't you trust him?" Nessya asked.

"I can tell when a person lie. It's an ability I've had since a child. An annoying but useful ability that comes in handy when you're the leader of a group of people. Enoksa is hiding something. I don't care to find out what it is, so you all must leave. I don't trust him one bit."

Nessya didn't hesitate to move and gather her and Nthanda's things. She didn't want to be caught in anyone's grips.

"THERE YOU ARE, MY LITTLE star," a woman's voice rang out.

Nthanda turned in circles trying to find the source. Find where it was coming from but to no avail.

"Little Star, do you not recognize my voice?"

She remembered the voice. She would never forget that comforting sound and said as much. "I just don't see you. Where are you?"

Nthanda was back in the weird place from over a year ago. When her mother materialized before her, she couldn't stop the tears from falling out of her eyes. She ran to Chanda and hugged the woman, afraid to let her go.

"Mama, I am trying. It is not easy but oh so hard. I remember you said to come home."

"I know. Where are you now?" Chanda asked.

"Roshan."

"Be careful in those lands. Not all is what it seems. Hurry home." Nthanda wiped the tears from her face. Chanda flickered in and out.

"Mama! Don't go yet. I miss you and Mama Jia'ka."

"You will be with us soon enough daughter. Follow the stars at night, they will guide you. When hopelessness consumes your heart and mind, when you think you'll never make it back home," Chanda touched the necklace around Nthanda's throat and the markings on her collar, "Follow your instincts and heart. These will help."

"But where do I go? Who do I trust besides Kai? And Nessya, kind of."

"Who is Nessya?" Chanda asked, interest piqued.

"The girl who helped me escape. I wouldn't be here without her right now."

Chanda became quiet. She stared into Nthanda eyes then smiled. She flickered again. "My time is almost up. Bring her to me. I would like to meet this Nessya."

"Yes, Mama."

"I love you, daughter. Remember to follow the stars. They will guide you. Stay strong for us. For you."

Nthanda reached for her mother but she faded away. She slumped to the ground and let the tears truly fall. She was so lost and confused. Not knowing what to do. She was tired of life and just wanted to be at peace. In the comforts of her home with her family surrounding her.

Chapter 29

The small makeshift caravan definitely looked the part. Mael checked the wagon more than once. The girl was back there along with her giant cat and Yazi, Mael's youngest daughter. Nessya sat at the driver's seat next to her daughter Lati. Her boys Zaire, Ezael, and Etosh sat astride their horses. Rihat and Balash were two of her best riders, and they were to the side, on their mounts too. She trusted them like her own children and considered them family.

"Mama, we will be all right. Don't cry over us." Etosh said. He kept his eyes on her as she moved to everyone, saying her goodbyes. Mael walked to her youngest son and reached for his hands. With no hesitation, he reached down to her and grasped them.

"Ride fast as you all can. Stop for nothing. You all should have everything needed to make the trek." She kissed his hands and stepped back. "Don't forget the salt and spices to give as payment to help the girl. Ask for sanctuary if you need to. Never tell them you are of the moon. If anything, let Nessya speak with them. She is a daughter of the sun."

Murmuring words of agreements rang out. Mael wanted to go with them but she had to stand tall and be a leader of her people. She had to make arrangements with her tribe to leave the lands. Danger rode the fierce winds, and it was only a matter of time before the tribes would be touched by the raging storm. They were no longer safe.

The small caravan moved out. Refusing to leave, she stood there, at the edge of the camp, waving until her family disappeared from her sight. She made sure they left when all the families had left. If they kept a proper pace, they would reach the temple in three candlemarks.

"Mother Goddess who watches us all. Guide and protect my children and the girl. They need you now more than ever," she prayed out loud. Mael turned away from the shadows in the distance and faced the upcoming challenges her family, and her tribe knew were coming.

ON THE TRAIL FOR A little over a candlemark, Etosh told his eldest brother, Zaire to lead, and he fell back and peeked inside the wagon. His sister Yazi looked up and smiled at him. "She's fine brother. Still in the lands of Dreva. She walks with the Mistress."

"How can you tell where she walks? She might be with Mynhit, learning all about war and how to defeat those who goes against us."

"I can sense it. Even now, she dreams while her magic wars within. I bet she doesn't even realize what is going on but think the dreamscape is real. It truly is amazing how realistic the place can be," Yazi responded with a faraway look in her eyes.

Etosh wouldn't argue with his sister about the dreamscape. Since she was a child, she would get visions. She couldn't walk the dreams yet but she visited the dreamscape enough to know about it.

He grinned, "I trust what you say about the dreamscape. I will never know."

Yazi chuckled, "No because you prefer to battle and fight. Mynhit is the perfect choice as a favored deity for you, brother. Now let us be. The girl isn't going anywhere."

"Fine. As you wish." He bowed his head and moved to the other side of the covered wagon. He moved closer to Nessya and kept pace with the wagon and its driver.

"Anytime you want to ride, I'll switch places with you." He flashed her his charming smile and chuckled.

"I am fine for now. My legs still hurt from the ride over."

"Ah, you just need to ride more. It gets better. That I can promise."

"Hey charmer," Lati shouted to Etosh. "We should water the animals soon. The heat is unusually hot today. There should be a trail stop with a well in half a candlemark."

Etosh was glad to know that he wasn't the only one dealing with the heat. "I'll ask Zaire. See what he says. I'll be right back."

He galloped to the front of the caravan where his brother was riding lead. He looked over to him before saying anything a strong wind blew up from out of nowhere. Sand flew everywhere and got into his eyes. He gritted his teeth as the tiny particles cut across his face.

Etosh heart pounded a staccato beat and the horse under him went wild. An unnatural storm brewed right before them and they had nowhere to go for safety. Fear filled his heart, and he glanced to his brother who generally had a stoic face was distraught and panicked.

"Ride faster and harder. Try to outrun this storm if we can!" Zaire shouted. "Tell the others in the back."

Etosh turned his horse around and told everyone in the group he came across to ride fast and hard.

"What about the wagon? We can't go that fast. Too much weight," Lati said.

"Don't worry. I'll tell the cat to run with us. That should lighten the load tremendously."

"Do it."

The wind screamed and whipped around them faster, picking up speed. The cloths they used to cover the wagon snapped back and forth, threatening to fly away. The sky turned a dark and brownish color. Etosh hurried to the back of the wagon, opened the flap. "Hey pretty kitty," he said to the cat whose head rested on Nthanda, hoping the creature understood. "Things are looking rough out here. It would be great if you can run beside the wagon while we try to make it to safety. The wagon would go much faster."

The cat's blue eyes turned towards Etosh and growled. With quickness, Kai jumped out of the wagon and shook all over. Etosh closed the flap and hit the side of the wagon. Signaling his sister. Lati caught the understanding, and the wagon took off. Kai looked up at Etosh before padding towards the side of the wagon and trotted beside it.

The small caravan galloped and moved at full speed. The wind screamed loudly, piercing everyone's ears. The horses snort carried over the wind, and Lati's voice called to the horses to go faster. Etosh didn't blame them. Sandstorms were dangerous and a person could easily be lost when the sand came down on you.

The group had planned to stop at the nearest well and they should be close but with the storm, they couldn't see where they were going. Etosh rode hard, making sure they left no one behind. The screams became more pronounced, and a chill ran down his spine. The wind no longer sounded like wind. Shadows appeared then disappeared all around the group.

Ahead of them, a large sand funnel swirled and swirled, moving faster than any sandstorm Etosh had ever seen.

"This is unnatural," he shouted to everyone. "This is a witchstorm."

"What do we do?" Lati asked. "We can't go headfirst into that."

She was right and Etosh had no plan on what to do. They needed to ride the witchstorm out. Protect the girl in the wagon.

"Everyone stop and form around the cart," he yelled as he rode rounding everyone up. "We can't fight this and keep going too. We will face whoever is behind it!"

Zaire turned back to the group, and the riders followed pursuit. They formed a circle around the cart and Kai crawled underneath. Etosh removed the sword that hung on his back and pointed the tip in the sand. He drew a circle, encompassing everyone inside it. Once he went around, he went in the opposite direction and drew another circle. Stepping over both lines, he made it to the center with his family and closed the sand drawn spell circle.

"Project your energy into the circles and form a ward. Together, powering the circles, it should be strong enough to protect us!" Etosh shouted to everyone.

They listened, and each fed the circle with their magic. Multiple colors blending into each other to become one solid color. A loud snap crackled and then vacuumed silence filled the circle like they were in the void. A shimmering dome covered the group, protecting them from the raging storm just steps away from where they all stood.

"What in Athos is going on?" Ezael asked. He looked around at the frightened faces.

"This is a witchstorm. Powered by a strong witch. I think the storm is searching for something. Someone," Lati said. Her eyes roamed over everyone and stopped at Etosh and Nessya. "What is really going on? Tell us. We deserve truthful answers."

"I agree. Mama didn't tell us why we had to ride out with you to the temple but she commanded us to as our tribal leader. So talk Etosh. What kind of trouble did you lead us into now? This witchstorm has something to do with them." Ezael pointed towards Nessya.

"You are always getting into something, brother," Zaire chimed in.

Etosh hated when his siblings ganged up on him. Only person who ever stayed on his side was Yazi.

"Hey that's unfair. I didn't lead us into anything and definitely didn't make you all come. You could have said no. Or asked mama what was going on. I thought she told you, honestly."

"It's not his fault really," Nessya added with her soft-spoken voice.

"You don't have to take up for me," Etosh said. "But she's right. It's not my fault. If you want to blame anyone, blame the Gods for placing these two in my lap."

"It is blasphemy to speak of the Gods in that way," Yazi said, stepping out of the back of the cart. "But I agree with the girl and Etosh."

"You always agree with him," Zaire said.

"The girl is important and must reach the temple," Yazi continued. "She's the missing one with jeweled eyes that they have taught us about since we were younger."

The group stood there stunned. Then all at once, everyone began to talk. Etosh raised his hands and shouted at everyone. "We can discuss this later. Right now, we need to be prepared. Look," he said. His eyes looked passed everyone out into the desert where the shadows multiplied. They couldn't hear the screams but he knew those shadows.

"Those are sand daemons," Ezael said, taking a step backwards. Closer to the wagon. "Whoever summoned them can't be too far off."

"Then we will face them and fight," Zaire said, already getting into a fighting stance. "I won't go down today by some rutting reincarnated meat sack."

"You're always ready to fight," Etosh said as he got into his stance too.

The shadows got darker the closer they came to the group. Glimpses of snake-like eyes and forked tongues pierced through the wall of sand. The women got into the back of the cart with Nthanda except Nessya. She refused to cower and hide. She was the reason they were there. Both groups. She knew how to fight just as much as the men and would prove her worth to them.

She stepped closer to the warded wall and spoke a spell low to herself. In her left hand, a long whip made of golden, bright light formed and wrapped around her wrist and arm. She bent down and grabbed a handful of sand and whispered words over it. A flash of light came and went in an instant, and the sand in her hand moved as if the tiny grains itself were sentient and formed into a large dagger.

Nessya gripped the handle and twirled it in her hand, testing the weight, getting used to the feel. It's not what she normally would use, but she would. And she will. Smiling, she looked up to find the men with their mouths all gaped open wide.

"If you don't close your mouths, a horse fly will find a new home in it," Nessya said to them. Etosh chuckled.

Chapter 30

The sandstorm didn't let up at all. The whistling screams of daemons in the sand funnels pierced their ears. The force and strength of the wind battered at the warding, deteriorating the group's protection. Time was running out. Prayers to the Mother Goddess and Mynhit were muttered under the breaths of each one, hoping their dark gods watched over them. Nessya prayed to Elios to guide her. She didn't know the dark gods enough to pray to them but she hoped they answered the prayers of their supplicants.

The sand daemons were no longer hiding, and Nessya recoiled at the sight of them. The creatures looked as if someone was bored and pieced them together from different animals. The one most reviling to her was the one closest to them. The monster had the head of a snake, the upper body was humanoid and the lower body was that of a scorpion. She had always hated scorpions and to view one up close was enough to make her to shrink back in disgust.

"It's coming down!" Balash said from behind. His voice was rough and deep, different from Etosh and his brothers.

The shimmering barrier between the monsters before and the safety behind it was breaking. Spider web cracks crawled over the entire dome before shattering into a pile of magic dust. Whoops and screams of excited creatures became louder, and the ones who waited for the warding's downfall ran towards the group.

Nessya unwound the whip around her wrist and arm and snapped the weapon at the first creature who jumped at her. The monster fell down, and an unearthly growl escaped its chest. More monsters came her way, and she did the same, using a combination of her whip and dagger. She didn't bother to look around her to see how the others fared. Sparks and flares of light flashed here and there and she knew they were using their gifts to fight for their lives too.

The last beast she hit, bounced back up and attacked her again. Nessya didn't hesitate to dodge its advances. She flicked the whip around its legs and yanked the glowing coil. While still wrapped around the monster's legs, she pulled the daemon to her and leaped on top of its chest and sliced its throat. A thick black viscous liquid oozed from the wound and she almost gagged at the stench that emitted from it.

The Child of the Sun was in the fierce grip of battle and she relished the rush. Her legs and arms moved on their own volition. Natural body memories from the lessons she had as a child guided her along. At first stiff now loose and warmed up, Nessya quickly moved on to the next, leaving the group behind as she moved forward. Another daemon, smaller than the others, came at her. She yet again went ballistic and fought like she had no tomorrow.

No longer in the frame of mind to notice her surroundings. The storm became thicker the further she ventured away from her group. Nessya squinted to look for the others but couldn't see them. Only the unholy shadowed forms that gradually circled her in. Ears to the wind, she listened for their voices but the only sounds was the piercing, inhuman screams of monsters that didn't belong in the realm she lived in. She placed her hands over her ears, hoping that would help and mute the sounds. But it did little if any for her comfort.

Daemon after daemon attacked, and she fought back relentlessly. Her constant thoughts led back to Nthanda and that they mustn't find her. It was the only thing that kept her going. Nessya fought until she tired. A small creature, almost like the black hound that accompanied the daemon back in the jungles of Namansii, attacked her in the chest. Not seeing the beast come at her, she missed the other daemon as it attacked her once she hit the ground.

Nessya threw everything she had inside, but her well of power was nearly depleted. She could barely move. Exhaustion hit her hard. She recognized the signs she was in danger. The hound who pinned her to the writhing and shifting ground snapped at her face. She wanted to shove her dagger into his neck, but Nessya couldn't even move her arms.

An airy, light voice called out and for a moment, she was happy that the others found her but she realized the voice was speaking a language she's never heard before. From within the shadows a tall, reed thin woman, dressed in all black, walked towards her. Her face was the only thing uncovered.

Wisps of blonde hair whipped around the woman's face and her dark stormy grey eyes were cruel and cunning. Her thin red lips, parted into a wide grin that sent chills down Nessya's back.

"This one will do for now," the woman said to others that hid from Nessya's view. "Bind her. We will try for the others again later. We won't be able to move past the second wall they erected."

The woman with the cruel eyes bent down and squatted near Nessya's head. She took her gloved hand and caressed Nessya's cheek with the back of it.

"Godspeaker Nelioz doesn't like when his toys run away. Or being betrayed by his own people. Lucky for you, I got to you first. Sadly for you, he gave me free rein to do whatever I want. Only stipulation. You have to be alive when I deliver you to him. I promise you will enjoy my attentions. Then, you are going to have a great time with him," The woman cackled. She stood, leaving Nessya on the ground to the whims of the waiting people in the shadows.

THE SANDSTORM STOPPED just as quickly as it appeared. Etosh and his siblings looked around the area where they made a stand. Daemon carnage spread all around melded back into the sand. Out of breath, Etosh's chest heaved up and down as he struggled to suck in air. His eyes darted to each member of his party, counting to make sure everyone was there.

"Where's Nessya?" He looked around again to make sure he didn't miss her. He jogged to the cart and checked inside. Only his sisters who huddled together around Nthanda occupied the wagon. "Have you seen the other girl? Nessya?" The women in the cart shook their heads.

A buzzing noise started in Etosh head, followed by a ringing sound in his ears. He rubbed the nape of his neck, as realization dawned on him. He remembered when Nessya moved away from the group but he couldn't stop her. He was too busy trying to avoid getting killed by his own daemon. He rubbed his face and his shoulders sagged. They beat the daemons, but they lost the girl who was their way into the Temple. A failure before it even began.

Ezael moved closer to Etosh and rubbed his shoulders. "This is not your fault. We were ambushed and could barely focus on ourselves while we fought. She moved away in the heat of battle. I am sure she is still alive. If she was dead, we would have seen her body."

"Whoever created that witchstorm is the one who took her. We will find out who. But first we need to go to the Temple. We still have the girl in the back. There we can recuperate and make a plan of action," Zaire said.

Etosh nodded, agreeing with his brothers. Nthanda wouldn't forgive him or his family if they lost her friend. The girl was vital because she helped her escape the Godspeaker. They had to find Nessya no matter what, but they first needed to get Nthanda to a healer.

"Mount up. Let's get out of here before another ambush occur," Etosh said to the others. Lati jumped out of the cart and got into the driver seat. The cat hopped in the back next to its witch. Etosh untied his horse and got on. "We won't stop. We will move at a fast pace. Everyone keep up. The desert isn't safe for us."

"The desert has never been safe for us, brother." Lati said. "It is only visible to us now."

"Point made!" Etosh replied. He spurred his horse and took off in a trot before flowing into a full gallop leaving the others behind him. He had to clear his head from his mishap.

THE TEMPLE OF ELIOS never failed to awe Etosh. It was the biggest building he had seen built by man and witch in his life. And to him that was saying a lot. Out on the seas and the many ports he sailed into, he had seen plenty to compare. The Children of the Sun were prideful people. They wanted to reach the skies to be with one with their Gods so they built upward. Unlike his people, who worshipped in the dark spaces. The fully open spaces and underneath the light of a silvery moon. To a Child of the Moon, nature was their temple. Not some building one had to go to.

The temple was unique in its design. Sitting on an island surrounded by water, the only way in was to cross the bridge. The slanted roof had an opening in its center. It allowed the rays of the sun to illuminate the building inside. Two thick, engraved columns stood tall on each side of the entrance. As a person made the trek to the temple doors, they were watched. Silent statues of marble beasts lined the path. Stone creatures with the heads of an eagle hawk with sharp beaks, and bodies of a lion that had large wings on its back.

Etosh grew up with stories about the mythical creatures that once flew over the desert skies. The sacred creatures of Elios and how only a select few could fly on them. Seeing their likeness and the sheer size of them in stone put a few things into perspective.

The caravan came to a stop near the pair of griffins where two temple guards came out from a sandstone gatehouse. The shorter guard walked around the wagon, inspecting everything and everyone.

"Why are you here?" The other guard asked Etosh.

"We seek sanctuary and a healer."

"Why do you seek sanctuary? Who are you running from?"

"Only from ourselves and the daemons that are running freely in the desert right now. My companion, she is sick. My tribe's healer could only do so much. She suggested we come to the aid from the temple."

The guard called to his partner, and they discussed something in a tongue, Etosh didn't recognize. He prayed to the Mother Goddess that they would let them pass.

The taller man turned back to Etosh. "We take you to the stables. It's up to the priesthood on who they provide sanctuary to. From there, you must travel by foot to the entrance. You are on your own after we show you stables." He nodded to the shorter guard. "He will lead you."

"Thank you," Etosh said. "May the sun forever warm your faces."

Chapter 31

A Priestess of the faith stopped the group as they entered the temple. The priestess reminded him of the women who sold their wares and spices in the marketplaces in Alikesh. A native to the lands, the priestess was slender and wore the sleeveless gowns of the priesthood of Elios. Sigils and lettering that strengthened her magic marked her bare arms.

"How can we serve you?" she asked. Her voice soft yet backed with strength. Etosh could tell she was witchborn.

He turned to the others in his party but they all watched him. "We seek sanctuary and a healer for my companion here." He motioned to Ezael, who carried Nthanda on his shoulders during the long walk in.

The priestess moved around and examined the girl. "What is wrong with her? Will she not wake?"

"No, she won't. We tried."

"How long has she been like this?"

"A full day now. We had no one else to turn to."

The woman placed her hand on Nthanda's brow and closed her eyes. She stood silent, touching her for what seemed forever. Only a few breaths had passed. The priestess eyes shot opened, and she removed her hand.

"I will grant you sanctuary and I will heal her."

A flood of relief rippled through the group. The woman motioned to a young girl that stood only feet away from her.

"Take them to my chambers. I will be there shortly. Go through the passageway." The girl nodded. The woman turned back to the group. "Stay quiet and follow her. I need to gather a few things and be on my way."

The young girl didn't say a word as she took them through the inner corridors of the temple. The group glanced at each other but kept silent as the one who led them. It didn't get past Etosh that the priestess had the girl lead the group away from the rest of the temple and its inhabitants.

Gigantic cobwebs covered in dust littered the passageways. Obvious that the secret corridor hadn't been used in ages. Darkness covered the hallways, and flames came to life as they passed the sources of light on the walls. The heated illumination plunged the recently vacated hall back into obscurity once the group moved away.

Now and then, pockets of cold air would blast through, cooling the stuffy and humid halls. Etosh tried to remember the way, but they had went down so many halls and winding turns, he started to think the girl was trying to misdirect them on purpose. The young guide led the small group down another corridor, much narrower than the rest and stopped when a small entrance appeared.

She twisted around to face them, stuck a finger over her lips, advising them to be quiet. She pushed at the wall until a soft click sounded off then an opening appeared. She raised her hand, signaling the group to wait. She went in first, then a short time later she came back and ushered them into the room.

Etosh and his group followed the girl into an enormous chamber. The scent of fragrant flowers and incense lingered in the room. Candles burned everywhere. The girl scurried across the chamber to a door on the other side. The group was quick on her heels as they tried to keep up. She entered the smaller room leaving the others to decide who went in or not.

"Place her on the bed," the young girl told Ezael. She moved out of the way allowing Ezael to go through. Etosh found the space confining and wanted to hurry up and get out of the room. He was used to and preferred the open spaces.

"Why did we have to bring her here?" Etosh asked.

She shrugged. "That is for the priestess to tell you, not me. One of you can wait here, the other should wait in the chamber."

Ezael didn't hesitate, "You stay here, brother. When she wakes, she will need a friendly face that she recognizes. We will be out there."

"Thank you," Etosh said. The door clicked close as Etosh went and stood next to Nthanda's side. Her eyes fluttered underneath the closed lids. She was in a dream state. He prayed she would wake up. Etosh sat down and stretched his legs out before him. Letting his head fall back against the wall to rest, he shut his own eyes. His muscles ached and was sore to the touch. He wished he was at the hot springs in the cold mountains with food and sleep. In that exact order. Soon as he closed his eyes, he felt soft fur brush against him.

He opened one eye, to find the giant cat beside him with her head on the feet of Nthanda. If only he could talk with the animal, he would love to hear what she had to say.

Many days he wished he had a familiar but the Mother Goddess haven't seen fit to give him one yet. In time, if one was meant for him, it would happen. Much to his disappointment at his ceremony when he was younger, he still had hope. It's not unheard of gaining one while an adult.

Etosh didn't have to wait long before the priestess came into the room. He took a better look at her and still didn't couldn't figure the woman out. Why she was helping.

"Are you hungry?" she asked.

"I could eat something." At that time, Etosh stomach made its presence known by making loud noises. He stared at his stomach and frowned. "Guess I can eat a lot of something."

The priestess smiled, twisted her head towards the door. "Go. Eat and rest. You are safe here. She is safe here. I'll take care of her."

Etosh stood up slowly. Sitting down gave his muscles the chance to lock up and become stiff. He stumbled a bit, reminding him of the older men in his tribe.

"Thank you for everything," he said.

"I have done nothing," the Priestess replied. A puzzled expression crossed her face.

"But you have. You gave us sanctuary. You agreed to help her. All without intruding questions. You've helped more than you already know." Etosh turned and left the room.

The Priestess moved closer to the bedside and looked down at Nthanda.

"I will do my best to help the girl," she said to Kai.

The priestess placed her hands over Nthanda's chest and let them hover over her heart. She closed her eyes and let her mind drift into a space where she centered herself and focused. She searched for the point where the woman's magic took root. Slowly, she let her hands move on their own accord as she searched the girl. The priestess had a way to feel another person's magic and determined how strong they were.

From the moment she saw the group and the girl, she knew they all were in danger. One of the reasons she offered to help. Anyone else in the temple would have turned them away. With her eyes still closed, the priestess continued to search for the root of the problem. Not finding it in the center of her chest, she checked the woman's head. She placed a hand on each side of the girl's temple and felt around. She couldn't read the girl's mind or memories, but she could see where the discord happened.

The witch in her bed was unbalanced. The priestess got on her feet and brushed her dress down. "I'll be right back. I need to grab a few items that can help," she said to the large creature who followed her every move. Quickly, the priestess left the room and instead of going in the direction where the voices mingled, she went in the opposite direction. Checking over her shoulders to make sure no one lingered by, watching her.

Down the hall she turned right. A tiny wooden door loomed in front of her. She tested the handle and found it locked. She searched within the folds of her dress and pulled out a small key on a string and inserted it into the keyhole.

The door opened smoothly without a sound and she quickly entered the small den. Inside, flames on red candles flickered to life, giving the room ambient light.

Her eyes searched the intimate space, glancing to the shelving on the walls. High up were glass vials both large and small. Empty and full with a multitude of colors. But those were not what she came into the room for. Next to the wall on a table that came to her waist was the items she needed. She picked up a small leather pouch and opened it. Careful not to waste the contents, holding the pouch with care, she peered inside to find black sand. She had little in the leather bag but it would be enough to do what she needed to do. The woman closed the pouch and quickly departed the room.

Gone for only a few moments, there was no noticeable change in the witch. What she needed to do, she had to do it with speed. The girl was further gone than she wanted to tell the others. She couldn't fathom why, but she sensed both types of magic warring inside the young woman and they slowly drained her life essence.

The priestess opened the pouch and poured sand around the girl, forming a circle. Kai jumped down from the bed and sat on her haunches in the corner watching. Once the circle was complete, the priestess whispered words under her breath to close it. Her voice started out low and rose as she repeated a chant over and over again. The higher her voice got, the faster the words came out of her mouth.

A greenish glow formed around her hands. With the glowing left hand, she touched Nthanda's brow and with the right; she touched the center of her chest. She poured energy into her hands and let the healing tendrils flow from her into the girl. Seeing it clearly in her mind, the priestess guided the energy to the black, dark spots that blocked Nthanda's power, killing her.

It reminded her of a jumble of swollen veins and nerve endings. She found the knot in Nthanda's chest and tugged until it unraveled. The blockage dissipated, and the magic flowed like it should, but the one in Nthanda's mind was being stubborn. The priestess placed her hands on each side of Nthanda's temple. Her thumbs rested in the center of her forehead. The greenish glow around the priestess hands became brighter. Enough to light up the room. A low growl could be heard from Kai but the priestess ignored the woman's familiar. Her work was more important than dealing with the large animal. She found the entangled threads of Nthanda's power and pushed even harder to remove the life stealing knot.

She didn't know how long it took but she was done, and it worked. She was tired but the healing was worth her being exhausted. The working took more of her energy reserves than she expected, but if the girl is who she thinks she is, then they couldn't have lost her. Her hands shook as she removed them from the girl's head. The Priestess turned to the cat, "You can go to her. She will be fine." She bowed her head and left the room.

ETOSH GOT QUIET WHEN he saw the priestess as she strode into the room. She looked worse for the wear and wondered exactly what all she had to do and if Nthanda would be fine. The woman stopped in front of him. She looked as if she would tumble over.

"The girl will be fine. I found the disruption and freed it," she said.

"That is good news. Can I go see her now?"

The priestess shook her head, "Not yet. She is still asleep. Will be I imagine for a few more candlemarks."

"Oh," Etosh replied.

"Have the young girl showed you your rooms?"

He nodded, "Yes. You are very gracious. We all thank you."

"It was nothing. My chambers are very large. I have my own private baths and a set of rooms for myself, my servants and such. I only have the girl. I am sure you have plenty of food. Yes?"

"Yes, we do."

"Good. I wouldn't advise to leave from these rooms. You are safe here. Out there, not so much. Before you arrived, we had just received words from the palace about the new agreement. We are separate, yet my superiors like to favor the King."

Etosh glanced to the others before turning back to the priestess. "We are nothing but your everyday tribesmen from the desert. What goes on at the palace does not concern us."

"Yet you asked for sanctuary. I don't care why you asked for the safety of that but know, it's not safe out there or in here. I am the closest thing to safety you have right now."

"How do we know you won't turn on us?" Ezael asked. Etosh didn't realize his brother had moved and was standing beside him.

The priestess faced Ezael and smiled. "I know what you all are and the other priests and priestesses won't disturb me. I am a Seer. My word goes a long way and they leave me to my own vices. The way you came in, they do not know of it. If anything happens, go there and stay quiet. No one will find you."

Etosh and Ezael eyed each other. There was only one Seer at a time and she was revered amongst the witches of light. "Again, thank you," Etosh said.

"You're welcome. I'll return after I have rested. If you need anything, Vika, that's the girl, she can help. She's around here somewhere."

"And what is your name?" Ezael asked. Etosh elbowed him. If one didn't give you their name freely, you didn't ask that person for theirs. His people considered it rude and Ezael knew better.

A chuckled escaped the Seer. "I go by many names. For now, they call me Seer. Priestess. But you all can call me Zizia."

Zizia strolled out of the room, leaving the group staring at each other.

"Might as well get comfortable," Ezael said.

"Yeah, looks as if we're going to be here for a while. There's something she isn't telling us," Yazi said to the group.

Chapter 32

A soft simper came from Nthanda yet her eyes continued to stay closed. Her head thrashed back and forth to the side. She couldn't stay still and kept moving around. Kai moved closer to the bed and placed her head on her hand. Nthanda's eyes shot open to complete darkness, and she was confused why. She looked all over the room before sitting up. Her eyes fell on her familiar and a rush of calm hit her. She was safe.

Kai, she said through their mental link. *Where are we? What happened?*

You always ask a lot of questions. From the day we first met until now.

And you have a way to evade answering those questions. Kai chuffed at her and jumped into the bed, getting in between Nthanda and the cool sandstone wall.

A lot has happened, Bright Star. We are in some temple. We couldn't wake you. Nessya found the man from the boat and he helped with you. He brought us to this temple place so they could heal you.

Nthanda was speechless. Last she remembered was taking a bath in the private baths. She wasn't feeling well. Everything else was blank.

What is so great about this temple to have brought me here?

The man's mother was not able to heal you, so she said they could here. Said they were better than her. The woman took a long time, but she fixed you. Kai licked Nthanda's hand and purred loudly. *I kept a watchful stare on her to make sure there was no misunderstanding about helping you.*

The corners of Nthanda's lips tugged upwards. *You can't go around intimidating others by glaring at them, Kai.*

That's what you think. Works all the time.

Nthanda became quiet and withdrew into herself. Too many things happened while she was unconscious. *On the bright side, I actually seem much better*, she thought to herself. Better than she had in a long time. The fire in her chest was warm and the cold flames in her belly still smoldered. Both, no longer erratic. She didn't understand why her magic manifested in that way but it did.

She sighed deep and heavy and repeated the act. The repetition made her calmer. Then the hunger hit her. In fact, she was starving. Her throat was dry and scratchy.

"I'm starving," she said out loud. "I could use some water too. My throat is parched and dry."

The door to her room opened as she finished speaking out loud. A woman walked in and shut the door behind her.

"I can help you with you that." The Priestess heard Nthanda as she came inside the room. She flicked her wrist and the flames in the lamps flared up, brightening the small space. Nthanda didn't take her eyes off the woman who had a ceramic pitcher held firm in her grip.

The priestess smiled when she caught Nthanda staring at the jug. "I brought water. I'll bring you food next."

Nthanda sat up. Her body was stiff. She stretched her arms and couldn't wait to stand to stretch her legs.

"Food would be nice."

"I'll have Etosh and his family bring food later. They've been waiting days for you to wake."

Nthanda was confused. "Days? What do you mean days?"

"Since you've been here, a week has passed."

Nthanda's mouth flew open. A week had passed since she last remembered. She couldn't understand why Etosh was there and not her friend.

"Where's Nessya? I would like to see her first."

"Nessya? I haven't met a Nessya. The only women here with the group is Yazi and Lati."

Nthanda knew she looked confused. She had no idea who Yazi and Lati was. She glanced over to Kai.

Where is Nessya? she demanded.

A sandstorm came, and they fought. She was here then she was not. You must ask the man.

There was nothing more she would get from Kai. Nthanda needed to speak with Etosh. She wasn't friends with him like she was with Nessya. She noticed Kai didn't kill him, and Nessya sought him out, so he wasn't all bad. Nessya had to trust him enough to ask for help. To get home, Nthanda would have to trust those the Mother Goddess put in her path. Defeated, she scooted closer to the wall so her back could rest on its firmness.

"Tell me everything," Nthanda said to the Priestess. "All I remember was not being well for a few days before I passed out. I blamed the sickness on my heavy use of my magic after getting it back. I was in the bath and then I wake up here."

"I will. First things first. I am called Zizia. I am the Seer here at the temple."

"Zizia," Nthanda sounded out. The name sounded familiar but she couldn't remember where she heard that before and why it was so important. Her mind was too fuzzy. "What temple? I am afraid I have little knowledge about these lands."

"The Temple of Elios. The Sun God."

"Ah. Are we truly safe here? I don't want more people endangered because of me."

"Yes. No one knows you and your group are here." Zizia poured a cup of water and handed it to Nthanda. "I had their horses and carriage moved to a safe, undisclosed location. And I have relocated the guards on duty the day they arrived, far from here."

Nthanda listened and took a sip of the cool water. And another sip. Her parched throat was grateful for the wet reprieve. Before she realized, she had emptied the cup and was reaching for more. Zizia didn't miss a step and filled the cup again. Nthanda downed that one too.

"Slow down. Don't drink too fast or it'll come back up," Zizia said.

Nthanda sat the cup down on her lap once she was done. "I was thirsty. My insides felt like the lands when it needs a downpour."

"Happens with the condition you were in. Your magic was warring inside and draining your life essence." Zizia sat down next to Nthanda and continued. "You had the magic sickness. I normally see it in younger children. Rarely does it manifest in adults. I recognized soon as they came in with you."

"How do adults develop this? I never had issues with my magic before."

"Happens if you grow stronger. Which I can tell, you are and some. Your well runs deep I believe. But there's also another reason."

Nthanda eyes narrowed. "Because they had suppressed my magic?"

"Yes," Zizia answered without hesitation. She took a closer look at the young woman's eyes and face again. Nthanda reminded her of someone from her past and made her even more curious. "But also because you have both magics inside you." Zizia brows rose. "Who is your father? He cannot be a Child of the Moon. He has to be one of the sun."

Nthanda shook her head, disagreeing with the priestess. "No, that can't be true. I don't know my sire, and he was never brought up to me, but my mama always insisted he was a moon born witch. I think." She bit her bottom lip, deep in concentration. "In my lands, the father have no responsibility in the child's life, so I never thought it was odd he was never around. A man can claim the child is his, but that is all. Trust me, as a child, I overheard my grandmother try many times to draw my sire's name out of my mama but she never divulged. You really think he was sun born?"

"Yes. You have powers of both the sun and the moon. If they had your powers suppressed, the gift of the sun manifested during that time. Or the moment you stepped onto Namansii land and connected with it. From what I can tell, when you hit your majority, the powers broke free. It was too strong for the witch's geas they had placed on you."

What Zizia told her was news to Nthanda, and she really didn't know what to do with the information. She pulled Kai closer to her and kept quiet. The warm spark she felt was not of the moon but of the sun. What Zizia said was true; she didn't feel the heated fire until she stepped on the land of the light witches. At first, Nthanda dismissed the spark thinking it was the heat. Now and again a flicker would flare up when she was mad but still, she didn't recognize the signs for what it was.

Nthanda only thought her cold flamed, winter magic was manifesting in another form. Not once did she ever think she had dual gifts. And the news of Nthanda's father couldn't be true. Her mama wouldn't have a child with a light witch. A human... maybe. If Mama Jia'ka suspected, there would have been darkness to pay. She needed more information.

"This is quite a lot of information to take in after you just wakened. I couldn't risk discussing this in front of the others. The knowledge could cause problems."

Nthanda glanced at the woman, "Why do you help? Helped Me? You are a Child of the Sun. Their prized Seer."

Zizia brows crinkled in the center of her forehead.

"True Seers are very rare. If you're in the temple, your prophecies have been very accurate. And more than likely, the only Seer for the time being."

Zizia smiled at Nthanda's quick observations. "You are more than what you seem. But yes, I help because I've been expecting you. You are right, I am of the sun but I don't blindly follow the blind. Can you sense the change? There is something terribly wrong with our world. Ever since the first wars long ago, the world has been dying a slow death because of the imbalance. Scrolls point to the one who is attuned to the discord and can be the anchor that stabilizes everything. That person will be able to bring us back to the way our world should be, whether it's good or bad. I follow the gods will. I've been here for thirty years searching and learning as much as I can. To be a guide in a time of need."

"All I can sense is you believe I'm that person. Which I am not. I'm just trying to get home. The sooner I leave these lands the better."

"True. The Godspeaker hunts you."

"I'm not surprised. I killed his awful son. He deserved that and more. Wish I could have gotten the Godspeaker too."

"No remorse?"

"Athos, No! Lord of Death probably relished that soul. We live, we die. It's the way things are. Just do what you can to protect yourself. Your people have not been kind to me, so I don't have any regret for what I did. I would do it a thousand times over if I could," Nthanda said.

"What you probably don't know," Zizia said, "The reason your people in the other room requested sanctuary here is because these lands are no longer safe for the moon children. The day you fell unconscious is the day the Godspeaker and his soldiers landed on these shores. There is no reprieve. All dark witches are caught. Some are killed then or in a public display of burning or some other torturous way of his Cabal witches. The desert people are leaving these lands in droves. Most are going to the Winterlands, if they're not caught before."

"What?"

"The Godspeaker declared war the moment you left those jungles. Even the humans are not safe. But they're safer than your people right now."

"This is too much. Too much all at once."

"I understand. Now that you're awake, you must go. First thing once night falls. I'll arrange everything. The sun just rose. You'll have the day to prepare."

Nthanda nodded. "I am not ready to see Etosh yet. I'll come out when I am ready."

Zizia stood, brushed down her thin dress and looked at Nthanda. "I will tell the others and make sure they stay away. You should reconnect with your familiar. I am sure she missed you. Now that you're awake, she won't growl at everyone." Zizia chuckled. "I'll have Vika bring you some food. She's my personal maidservant."

"Thank you so much. You've done a lot so far. I'll remember."

Zizia smiled. "You should rest. Your journey is only beginning."

Chapter 33

Hunger now satisfied, Nthanda was ready to see the others. She didn't know who was all out there but Etosh. Kai told her she liked them. Especially Lati because she gave her extra goat the first night she met her. Leave it to her familiar to like someone based on how much food they gave her.

She opened the door and followed the sounds to the middle of the chamber. Lavishly decorated with bright and lively colors, thin veils of fabric and tapestries hung from the ceiling and the walls. It gave the suite a mystical appearance. A group of people who all favored Etosh stopped and stared at her. Her gaze went straight to Etosh as he stood and made his way directly to her. The way he stalked towards her made her feel a certain way and she didn't know how to respond. Nthanda refused to think about it and locked those strange emotions into a small compartment in her mind for later dissection.

Nthanda lifted her chin and straightened her back.

I still like him. He is perfect for siring.

Hush Kai. He is not worthy. I don't even like him like that.

Your scent says otherwise.

Nthanda's face scrunched up. Her animal always had a way to make her uncomfortable in the untimeliest of times.

"You're awake," Etosh said when he stopped in front of her. His gaze roamed over her before looking her in the face. "Are you all right? My mama told me you had the magic sickness and to bring you here. If not, we would have lost you."

Nthanda seen the worry and concern in his eyes. The sincerity rolled off of him. If anything, the man cared. "I am fine. Better than I have been in a long while."

"Did Zizia say why this happened?"

"They suppressed my magic for so long, when it finally broke free, the magic was all over the place. I am well now and everything flows as should." She didn't want to tell him the real reasons because she didn't know how he and the others who watched silently would react. A flash of relief crossed Etosh face and his shoulders relaxed. "Well then, let me introduce you to my family," he said with a smile.

"Before we jump into that giant snow pile," Nthanda said. She already searched the group for her friend but didn't see her. These people had some explaining to do. "Where is Nessya? How come she is not here?"

Etosh swallowed. The people behind him eyed each other before facing her again.

"Do not lie to me," Nthanda warned him. "Tell me everything."

"You probably should sit. Listen and eat. Come," he said. He turned and went back to the pillows where everyone else was. The group of people spread apart allowing her to sit on the closest pillow to Etosh. A low table was in the center of the pillows, laden with a spread of flat bread, fruits, strips of meat, and a mashed mixture of something she didn't recognize.

A woman picked up an empty plate and placed a piece of the flat bread on it. Nthanda eyed her sideways as she placed the food on the bread in an artful position then handed the meal to her. Nthanda reached for the plate, "Thank you. You didn't have to make this for me."

"I don't mind," the woman said. "Besides, if you start with the mashed laves and the goat with the bread, it tastes better that way."

Nthanda looked at her plate and nodded. "Etosh, explain. From the beginning. I need to learn your side of things. I am sitting and have food. Where is Nessya?" she demanded as she fixed the food the way the woman said.

"You are probably wondering how I came into all this?"

"I am."

"I have people everywhere. Especially in the palace close to Alikesh. That's where we docked. The capital city of Roshan. They knew I was back home and came to me soon as they could. They delivered information about the deal the King had made with the Godspeaker. I had to warn my people, you and Nessya. Once the Godspeaker landed on our shores, there would be no safety anywhere for our kind. The humans picked their side, and that's the side of light. Fools they are."

"Go on," Nthanda said in between mouthfuls. The dip and goat on the flatbread was delicious and flavorful. She almost groaned at the taste.

"I rushed to the house where I last saw you and her. I had horses for myself and you two. Nessya came out and told me of the situation. The only person who could help and not turn us in was my mother. This time of the year, I know where my tribe roams and where they rest. We were only a few candlemarks from the camp. We snuck out of the house because Nessya didn't trust the people in the house with everything going on.

The King and Godspeaker agreed to slaughter every single child, man, and woman who were dark witches. They say the world would be better without us. The cities across the land are on lockdown now. My mama did all she could."

"The priestess told me."

"But we're not safe. Even here our lives are in danger. No one else knows we are hiding. The Godspeaker's armies along with Roshan's armies are crossing the desert hitting all the cities, searching for our people. No doubt they will come here. Even the nomad tribes are no longer safe. We are neutral in these lands but no longer."

Nthanda understood the gravity of the situation but he still didn't say what happened to Nessya. She stared at him with his lovely eyes and charming features and became angrier. "If you don't tell me where Nessya is, I will punch you in the face, Etosh. Stop going in circles. I've already heard all of this from my familiar and the priestess."

Way to throw me into the fray, Bright Star. Kai grumbled. Etosh continued to speak. Nthanda heard him but spoke with Kai instead.

You will be fine. They won't do anything to you but feed you more goat.

Mmm. Goat is tasty. How come we don't have any back home? I will need to search the big rocks outside.

Nthanda's ears perked up and focused on Etosh when he said sandstorm.

"What do you mean sandstorm?"

"Here in the desert lands we have wind tunnels of sand that wreaks havoc on everything. They are dangerous and can kill you if you're not careful."

Nthanda's mouth formed a perfect O. "Sounds similar to our winter snowstorms back home."

"I've never seen a snowstorm but if they're anything and dangerous like our sandstorms here, then yes. But this sandstorm wasn't natural. This storm was witch born. Filled with daemons who came and fought us. Nessya refused to get in the wagon with the other women. She wanted to fight."

"She's an amazing fighter. She taught me a few things. It's not her way to stand by and watch."

"I saw. She was amid a battle rage and wandered off into the darkest part of the storm. We called out to her but she couldn't hear us from the loud screams of the daemons and the wind. Then everything all stopped. The storm. The screams. The daemons. We searched around and we couldn't find her. She wasn't in the sand. Whoever called that storm was searching for you and her we believe. They couldn't find you so they snatched her."

The anger and rage she felt. The entire situation horrified her. The warm flare in the center of her chest burned hotter while the cold fire in her belly became colder. Her magic played off of her emotions she noticed. "How come you didn't go after her," she said. Her voice was sharp and harsh. Etosh flinched at the new tone.

"We tried," he stuttered. "Their tracks were untraceable. We came to the temple instead. We knew your condition warranted immediate help or else we would have lost you."

Nthanda didn't want to listen anymore. She sat her plate down on the table. She was furious and hurt that she wasn't able to help the one person who helped her in her time of need. Standing up, she looked down at Etosh. His eyes never left hers.

"I vowed that we would search for her once you were safe and well. My brothers and I will find her. No matter how long it will take," he said.

Nthanda didn't need the promise. If the Godspeaker was on these lands, then she knew who had her.

"Don't worry about searching for her. I know who has her. If he wants war against my people. He will get it. The Godspeaker will regret the day he crossed me and mine." Nthanda turned from the group and left them. She needed a plan. There was a man to kill, and she needed to figure out how she would do just that.

ZIZIA WHISPERED WITH two women who were older than her just inside the door to her chambers. Nthanda could tell they were priestesses of the temple as well but they were covered fully with a head wrap and face wrap. She couldn't understand what was being said, but it wasn't good from how Zizia face contorted. She looked back at them quickly then back to the women.

Nthanda didn't have a good feeling about any of the situation. Especially the women who concealed their identity.

Zizia stepped into the main part of the room and stopped at the edges of the pillows where everyone stood. They were preparing to leave. Night had just fallen only a few candlemarks earlier ago, and more than enough time for them to leave.

Zizia opened her mouth to speak, but no words came out. An ominous, hollow sound reverberated throughout the temple, penetrating the walls. All the way to Nthanda's core, no one had to tell her it was too late for them to leave. The bells were a melodious warning. Deep and mournful.

"The armies are here aren't they?" Nthanda asked Zizia.

"Yes, and we must hurry. They haven't crossed the bridge. Not if the bells just begun. The army is too large. I am sure the Cabal will cross instead. You will leave through the back of the temple. A boat waits for you to cross the lake. Your horses and wagon waits on the other side. Filled with food and water skins. Do not stop for anything until you reach the western shores. There is a big enough ship to carry you across the sea to Enyxias."

"Why don't you come with us?" Etosh asked her. "If they found out you helped us and there are ways to find out such things, then you will be in far more trouble."

"I can't. I dedicated my life to Elios and this temple. Everything I am is here. Do not worry about me. I will be fine. Vika will show you the way out. Stay quiet." Zizia touched Nthanda on the shoulder. "I would help you many times over if I had to. Remember, everything I said. I'll be here if you have more questions. We have rooms full of tomes of records from over the years. All we need is a name and a time frame."

"I will remember. Thanks for everything you have done for me. For us. You are welcome in my lands if you ever find a need. Come to the citadel. High in the northern mountains next to Glass Lake. We will treat you with respect. Stay safe, Zizia."

A young, mousy looking girl no older than ten years came out of nowhere. Her hair was brown and limp. Short that stopped at her chin but her eyes told another story. There was more to the girl than her homely appearance. The girl hugged the priestess and moved towards the wall. She placed her hand on the wall and searched until she found what she was looking for. She pressed, and the wall opened a slip. Wide enough to let a single person go through at a time.

"Go with her and stay close to each other. The Cabal is hunting for you. That is the only reason an army would be at the temple gates."

Nthanda with Kai went in first close behind their small escort and the others came in behind her. The small tunnels were narrow and dark. The air was stale and spider webs were everywhere which triggered a memory of Serea and her Tindian spider familiar. The thought made her smile. Soon she could see her childhood friend who was the sister she never had. She wondered how the girl fared. Now a woman and more likely part of their coven as a full member.

The young guide stepped forward and moved quicker than Nthanda expected but she kept up. The healing she received and the rest her body received had done wonders for her overall health. The magic inside didn't war with each other anymore and for that she would be eternally grateful to the priestess. She thanked the Mother Goddess many times over that she brought the people she did in her times of severe need. If not, she would have been long dead, visiting the realm of the dead with Athos, the Lord of Death.

Like mice, they moved through the maze like hidden tunnels. The only sounds were of their breaths as they went up inclines and down the stairs. But she never tired. It was imperative they didn't stop. Nthanda tried to focus and pay attention to her surroundings but was lost soon after they departed the chambers of the Seer.

Her mind kept going back to the priestess and the conversation they had after she woke. Her having two types of magic and her father being a child of the sun. It couldn't be right. She couldn't imagine her mother doing something so horrible. Then a conversation she had with her mother a year ago tugged at her memories. She couldn't recall but it was something her mother said to her, and she remembered her father being mentioned. She hoped the memory came back because something told her the information was important.

The small group slowed down as they came to a hall with no exit. Nthanda looked around and didn't like the situation they were in. "What is this place? This feels like a trap." she whispered to the girl.

Vika twisted around to Nthanda and placed a finger over her lips. "Quiet. This is where we exit but something is out there. No one should know about this area."

Bright Star, I sense others outside these walls. They smell like rotten humans and witches.

"Vika, we can't go out there. Not yet. There's people waiting and they're not good."

"How do you know?"

"My familiar can tell if they are good or bad. She says they're rotten meat."

"Then prepare yourselves. We must fight to get out of here. The boat is close to here. If we run, we can make it there in no time. Fight only if we must. But keep moving towards the lake," Vika said.

"I don't know about the others but I am perfectly okay with this," Nthanda said. Her power surged and was on the precipice of breaking loose. She could call it anytime she wanted, and the gift would heed her command. But in extreme emotions the power did whatever it wanted. If the men or women outside the walls were the jungle dwellers, she had plenty of fire to give them. Her lips split wide open in a grin that put the fear of the gods in the others when she turned to face them.

Nthanda was ready to fight. "Let's show these fools that we Children of the Moon don't bow to anyone. Especially them."

Chapter 34

Vika pressed the hidden depression in the wall and slowly pushed. She motioned for the others to wait. Still able to hear the people on the other side, she peaked inside the corridor that led to the outside. The night's cool air hit her face. She stepped quietly over the sandy floor and reached her senses out to find where the people waited for them. Around the corner on the wall, she turned to go back to the others but found them right behind her. She pointed toward the soldiers and shook her head. She then pointed in the direction they needed to go.

The group stepped onto the soft sand and followed the small guide. They kept to the shadows, moving with quiet stealth, careful not to step into the light of the moon. In the distance, the lake loomed closer and closer. Half the distance from the temple to the lake a shout rang out across the area. Nthanda looked up to find men running towards them.

"They have spotted us. Move faster people!" She yelled to the group.

Everyone sprinted into a full run but the men chasing after them slowly caught up. The situation quickly became clear to Nthanda. They would have to make a stand. The group wouldn't make the lake shore without a fight. The young guide, Vika, ran as hard as the rest but still she wasn't able to keep pace with the others. Nthanda refused to let the Cabal take the girl.

Kai. Watch out for Vika. Protect her.

As you wish. Kai ran to the young girl.

Nthanda stopped in her tracks, twisted around and faced the men chasing her. *Might as well give them all I got!* She opened and closed her fists then spread her fingers wide. She called to the power within and brought it close to the surface. The magic lingered and would wait until she needed it.

As the men drew closer, Nthanda recognized their features and the colors of their clothing. They really were the Godspeaker's elite witches. His much feared Cabal throughout the kingdoms, was on a witch hunt for her. Not all was there, and she was fine with the odds. Four to her one. She refused to let the others fight her battles.

The biggest man came out swinging a thick, imbued rope made from the vines found in the Namansii jungles. Nthanda ducked, and the rope whistled over her head, barely touching her hair. She remembered a lesson from Mama Jia'ka when she was young about the power of the moon and its shadows. How they can strengthen a dark witch's magic and how it's even better with blood magic.

"Mother Goddess of all protect your sons and daughters. Give this one strength to do what is justified," she called out while staying the shadows.

Nthanda pulled energy from the Evernight, using the void as a source of power. The black and purplish tendrils her magic manifested as curled around her arms and hands.

Moving like a slithering snake across and around her body, waiting for her commands. The glowing colors of her magic pulsated light and dark.

The dark witch got up and ran towards the man who swung the vined rope and blasted a wave of energy at him. He couldn't stop the force even though he tried. The spell hit him so hard that he flew backwards. Nthanda didn't worry about the man getting up. She felt his life essence disappear soon as he hit the ground.

Another cabal witch ran towards the group while the last two came at her at the same time. She didn't worry too much about the lone witch headed the other way because Kai could handle it.

Nthanda spied a dagger on the hip of the witch coming at her. The two men wouldn't play fair. She needed to make the odds more in her favor. She didn't know what all she could do with her new powers but her creativity was never a problem when her magic was involved. The slender cabal witch tried to hit her in the chest but she sidestepped to the left, and grabbed the dagger from their hip.

The sharp dagger was in her right hand and Nthanda sliced her left palm with the blade. "This blood I freely give to you, Mynhit. Walk with me tonight." Her blood dripped freely and fast. The two light witches turned to face her, not realizing she had a weapon. She quickly flicked the dagger towards the one she stole it from and hit him between the eyes. He crumbled without a sound to the ground. That left the fight one on one and Nthanda liked those odds even better.

They circled each other, dark and light, waiting on the other to make the first move. Each not wanting to make a mistake. Nthanda wouldn't budge. She was a patient woman. She refused to die before she even made the trek home. The man's face was covered in dark fabrics, similar to what she and her companions wore. His flat, dead eyes caught in the moonlight. They crinkled and creased at the corner and Nthanda knew he was smiling.

"You are an abomination and deserves this sacrifice to Father Elios," the man said as he rushed towards Nthanda with long curved blades in each hand. She never noticed them on his back and didn't like that she missed that detail. She slapped her hands together, smearing the blood onto both hands letting the thick liquid drip. She had to work fast because the man came running to her with a speed faster than she expected. The blood spatter dropped to the ground and soaked into the thirsty sand.

Nthanda looked up and saw the man upon her with his blades aimed towards her. Without thinking, she stepped to the side and kicked him as she moved out of the way. Her foot connected with his upper thigh, and he stumbled. The few seconds gave her time to crouch down and draw a small circle with her bloodied hands in the soft earth.

She rose from her crouch and faced the man who turned and stared her down.

"Sacred darkness mimic my steps and movements," Nthanda chanted in a fever pitch.

The man moved closer to her then stopped in his tracks. His attention was fixated on the shadow that formed from the circle Nthanda drew with her blood. The shadow took her shape and rushed him. He sliced at the mimic but nothing worked. His blades went right through the shadowed mirror.

Nthanda crept behind the man while he fought her shadow. He no longer paid her any heed. Her shadow fought just as well as she did and that was enough for her to sneak behind him. She wrapped her hands around his neck and channeled her witchfire into him. The flames would start inside of his body and work its way outward. He couldn't fight back with the light magic. Her holy fire came from Mynhit. She let go when he began to scream. The haunting cry came deep from his soul. Her shadowed mimicry dissolved into itself and disappeared. Nthanda closed the blood circle and took off in the direction of her companions.

Not too far ahead, close to the lake's shoreline, a body lay on the ground. Nthanda ran at full speed, and barely eyed the lifeless man when she passed him. It didn't take much to catch up to her party, who waited beside a larger fishing boat. Most of the group was already in the boat while Etosh and the young guide, Vika, stood outside the vessel. Kai paced back and forth and stopped when she saw Nthanda.

Etosh checked Nthanda out. "Nice work back there."

"I can say the same," Nthanda responded. Etosh peeked over her shoulder to the dead witch on the ground behind her. He smiled.

"Oh, that wasn't me or my brothers and sisters. That was all her." He glanced down to Vika, and she held her head down.

Nthanda remembered her first kill at that age and was able to sympathize with the young girl. She touched Vika's shoulder.

"Was he your first one?" Nthanda asked her in a soothing tone.

Vika nodded then wiped her face. Her limp brown hair covered her eyes but Nthanda knew the girl was crying.

"Turns out, she can't go back," Etosh said to her.

"What do you mean?" Nthanda said as she guided the girl into the boat. They had to keep going. The other cabal members would recognize their friends never came back and will go looking for them.

"She's not one of them. She is a Child of the Moon."

Nthanda's head shot around, "Are you sure?"

"Sure as the sun sets and the moon rises. She is no light witch. Makes you wonder why she was in the temple."

"Yes." Nthanda didn't have time to wonder. There would be time for that later. She climbed into the boat. Ezael and Zaire was already at the oars.

I really hate these floating water crossing vessels, Bright Star. This one is much smaller than the others.

"Quit being a giant kitten and hop in or you will get us all caught."

Kai huffed and jumped in and the fishing boat dipped under her weight then righted itself. Etosh and Vika got in last and they took off. Nthanda watched as the temple became smaller and smaller the further they rowed away. Thankful for the blessing the temple was and glad they were closer to her getting home.

Ezael and Zaire steered the boat across the lake and reached the other side in no time. The group disembarked to find their horses and wagons ready for them. Void of humans, but there was a note on the wagon seat. Nthanda picked up the small paper and read so the others could hear.

Follow the North Star to the shoreline. We will meet again. Safe travels to you all.

Z.

Nthanda touched the necklace she wore and felt the pendant tingle in her palm. That was the first time it had ever done that. She knew they headed in the right direction.

"Can you ride?" Etosh asked her.

Nthanda's lifted into a smile. "Not since I was twelve winters old. I am sure it will come back to me."

NTHANDA SAT IN A CORNER of the boat with Kai curled around her to keep her warm. Everyone else was inside the cabin or sleeping. It was night, and the sky was clear. She preferred to stay in the corner with the open sky above her. Not in a dark space where it brought memories of her imprisonment to the forefront of her mind. She had enough of that. Up above with her head resting on her leopard, she glanced to the stars above.

She couldn't stop looking at the night sky and the moon above. It gave her so much comfort. To know she wasn't a captive any longer. She was free and the person who helped her getaway was back in the Kingdom of Roshan a prisoner. The vow she made was serious. She wouldn't leave Nessya to rot for years. She would find a way to get her out. She didn't know much about war, but she would learn. There were plenty of people she could learn from.

Etosh said it will only take a week to land in Enyxias. We must be closer. The air is colder, Nthanda said through the mental link.

The air feels great to me.

That it does. I missed the cold. It seems so unreal, coming back home. I never thought we would truly make the journey back.

Sometimes you have to have faith.

Since when did you become all knowing?

I have always been all knowing. You're just now seeing.

Nthanda chuckled. *If you say so cat.*

*How long have we been on this boat? * Kai asked as she yawned widely. *I'm wanting more than fish and dried meat. I crave a fresh kill. Where the warm blood fills my mouth and the meat still twitches as I bite into it.* Her long fangs glistened under the moonlight.

A little violent aren't we?

Look who's talking.

It has only been three days. When we see the ice fields, then we are almost there.

Kai let out a loud growl. Disrupting the quiet peace on the deck. The sailors close by stopped and stared at the cat. Nthanda saw the fear in their faces and body language whenever they came near Kai. She thought it was amusing and laughed each time it happened.

I hate all boats. Promise me we won't have to get on another one, Kai said.

Nthanda didn't respond immediately. Her thoughts turned to Nessya.

I can't promise you that, Kai.

A cat could only ask. I can sense it through the bond. You became sad just now. You are thinking about her.

How can I not? We wouldn't be here if it wasn't for her. She turned against her own people to help us.

I understand.

I refuse to let her pay. So no. I can't promise you we will never get on another ship.

Kai moved into a more comfortable position. *She was a good person. She would have made a good Child of Moon. Too bad she was wasted on the sun children.*

She is a good person, Kai. She is.

Chapter 35

"Etosh, I think it's time," Nthanda said. Back in his element, Etosh was all over the place. He helped the Captain and the crew who ran the large vessel whenever he had a chance. More relaxed and at peace on the waters than he ever was on land, he kept an infectious grin on his face since the group left Roshan. Nthanda was glad to see the transformation unfold in the short amount of time on the ship. The banter between each other became better after Nthanda realized she couldn't blame him or his family for losing track of Nessya.

He sauntered her way very much like the first time they met. Tall and sure of himself. Except this time, he was fully clothed. No bare chest for Nthanda to ogle. His smile made the butterflies in her stomach flutter at maximum speed and like every other time, she chose to ignore. She refused to fall for him.

The winter chill permeated everything ever since they passed the ice fields. The temperature had dropped tremendously at that point. Enyxias took some time to get acclimated to if you weren't born in its cold grip. Nthanda pulled her cloak tighter around her chest. Thanks to Zizia, everyone had cold weather gear to last until they made the port city. She had prepared for everything.

It was the first time Nthanda truly felt happiness since her escape. Since she was taken on that fateful day eight long years ago. She was close to home, according to the Captain. Only a day away before they make landfall and she couldn't wait to touch down on the ground.

"You think it's time for what?" Etosh asked. He stood next to her as she looked over the partially frozen sea. Ice formations jutted from the water, creating ice islands everywhere.

"To be properly introduced to your family," she said. She twisted her neck to the side and gave him a side smile. "I refused the last time and I've since realized that my actions can be considered rude."

"I am sure they understand. You had just wakened and the only person you knew was gone. You barely knew me-"

"I still barely know you," she interrupted him. "But we shed blood together. That warrants getting to know who you're traveling with."

Etosh placed his hands on the edge of the ship. "It does. I can agree with that. Let me gather everyone. They're all over the place."

"No, I will go with you. We can find them together. I could use the stretching of my legs."

"Very well then. Follow me."

Nthanda walked beside Etosh as he went below deck. Many families had escaped the purge and found refuge on the ship. Etosh and Nthanda walked to one such group where a woman was talking with a newly married couple and their young child.

"Yazi," Etosh called out.

Nthanda recognized the woman as the one who fixed her plate back at the Temple of Elios. Yazi turned at the sound of her name being called. She rose from the crouch she was in and waved. She said something to the young couple, then headed in Nthanda's direction. Yazi moved with grace and surety in her steps. Her smile never faulted. She had a glow about her and Nthanda found herself wanting to learn more about this sister of Etosh.

"How can I help you brother?" Yazi asked Etosh.

"She finally wanted to be introduced to everyone," he replied, pointing to Nthanda. "I'm just showing her around."

Yazi looked at her brother then to Nthanda. "Mmhmm. Sure you are," she said. Turning to Nthanda she reached out and gave her a hug. "I am called Yazi. I am this big head older sister but the youngest girl in our brood. I am also his favorite."

"Shhh..." Etosh hushed her. "Don't let Lati hear you."

Yazi's brows shot up. "Everybody knows, Toshi. Don't shush me."

Nthanda laughter's rang out. The easy going banter between each other almost had her envious for a sibling. She had Serea, and that was close enough for her. She couldn't wait to see her friend.

She smiled at Yazi, "I am called Nthanda. I am glad to make your acquaintance. And I also want to thank you for making my plate at our first meeting. I was rude and I apologize. I appreciated the gesture."

"No worries. I was excited to finally meet the missing child we have heard about for the last eight years." Yazi grinned. "You must be someone important if the alert to search for you came from the High Priestess and the council."

Nthanda was confused and it must have shown on her face. "I'm surprised my dimwitted brother didn't tell you." Yazi gave Etosh a look that made him retreat into himself. "The dark council sent word that you were stolen and to be on the lookout for the one with purple jeweled eyes. Never thought Toshi would be the one to find you."

"Oh. I had no idea," Nthanda said. She didn't want them to know the truth about who she was but she had to tell Yazi and Etosh something. "I am the friend to the High Priestess daughter. My mother and the High Priestess was best of friends growing up. My mother died in childbirth so I lived with my grandmother at the citadel. That's probably why she put the alert out."

Etosh believed what Nthanda said, but Yazi looked like she took Nthanda's response with a grain of salt. "That could be it," Yazi said.

Changing the subjects, Nthanda shifted on her feet. "Well, Etosh didn't find me. Our paths had only crossed. I had already escaped my captors."

"Mother Goddess led you to each other." Yazi smiled. "Think about that."

Nthanda never thought about it that way and she didn't want to think about it too hard either.

"I must go back. Continue helping the other families on board. Nice meeting you finally, Nthanda."

"Likewise, Yazi." Nthanda replied.

Yazi went back to the young family. Etosh turned to Nthanda. "One down, four more to go. Plus the two family friends who are like brothers to us."

"Well, guess we better get a move on. Lead the way," she said and playfully shoved him. Etosh nodded, and they went in search for the next one.

THE WEATHER HAD GOTTEN too cold above on the deck to sleep. The Captain insisted Nthanda slept below deck with the others. She didn't argue. His ship, his rules. The heat of the bodies nearby made it bearable, plus she had Kai beside her as a breathing blanket. She was warm aplenty. All around her people slept. The others had turned in long ago and Nthanda had a hard time sleeping. She enjoyed the quiet time because no one disturbed her.

The night had passed, and she was sure dawn soon approached. Her thoughts fell on the reunion of her mother and grandmother. How would they react? Would they even recognize her? Would they be mad at her for being caught? She didn't know what to expect. Nthanda was lost inside her what if's that she didn't notice the loud clanking noise above on the main deck.

People around Nthanda stirred at the noise and she got up to go find out what was going on. She took the steps up two at a time. Her breath stopped at what she saw. The ship was close to the harbor, but that wasn't what had a vise grip around her windpipe. The sound of the sea eagles screams as they hunted the waters for their next meals grabbed her. A pair not too far from where she stood called to her as she walked to the edge of the deck. The beautiful birds swooped and dived, dancing as they hunted. Oblivious to the people that watched their hunt.

In the distance, her beloved mountains soared so high that clouds covered the tips. Hills and flatlands were inland somewhere and she could picture them in her mind. To Nthanda's left, the mighty cliffs rose so high that she couldn't see over the majestic walls, as the frigid water sprayed its rocky shores below. The salted air was everywhere, and she inhaled all its salted sweetness in, loosening the vise grip that had a hold on her.

The whole scene was magnificent and beautiful. The ice and all the snow. Blinding white, powdery snow that covered everything. A sob escaped her, and she fell to her knees trembling. She couldn't contain the tears and let them flow freely. She didn't care who saw. She was home. She was finally home.

Kai found her witch and brushed up against her. The loud purr brought Nthanda out of her stupor. She wrapped her arms around Kai's neck and buried her face in her fur. She stayed like that for a few moments before she regained her composure.

We are home, Kai!

This cold brings me much joy. I can't wait to roll around the snow again. My fur missed it.

Nthanda giggled like a young child when they were full of merriment.

"Thank you, Mother Goddess, for watching over your daughter and bringing her home," Nthanda prayed. She slowly rose, keeping Kai close to her. "Looks like we're on the southern side of the land. That must be Nightfall Harbor," she told Kai.

"It is," an older man said from behind her. Nthanda turned to find the Captain grinning. "We will dock in the next candlemark. Got to unload, restock and head back out. As long as those heathens is purging our people, then we will run our ships, helping to get them out."

"What is your name? If you don't mind me asking." Nthanda asked.

He puffed his chest up with pride. "Don't mind at all. They call me Borza. Capn' Borza. I've been running this ship here for going on ten years. We carry supplies from here to Roshan and back. Now we're carrying our people. Never thought I'd see the day." He shook his head, clearly sad at his new type of cargo. "You don't have to tell me your name. I already know who you are. The priestess, Zizia herself came to me and paid for you and your group passage. We go a long way. Your identity is safe with me. Just know, I am glad I was the one who could bring you back home."

Nthanda stared. "I am just a just a native of the winter-lands who has been gone too long."

Captain Borza leaned into Nthanda and whispered. "I know who you really are. Don't worry. Your secret is safe with me." The older man winked.

"I have no words but thank you," she said.

"That is enough for me. When we land, I'll let you know where to go to find the best sled out of here."

"I would appreciate your help."

"You might want to prepare your things, we're almost there." Captain Borza left Nthanda on the deck and yelled to the sailors to prepare for docking.

Chapter 36

Nightfall Harbor was just as beautiful as it always been. The premier stopping point for any and all goods that flowed through Enxyias. The largest port city on the continent with grandiose buildings that stood high in the sky while ice sculptures dotted the common areas. The streets were full of people both young and old.

Infectious laughter rang out from a group of bundled up children as they ran past Nthanda and her companions. The city was famous for its covered marketplace where a plethora of goods was for trade or purchase. From tools that a witch would need to spices imported from other lands. Witches and humans both made the city run smoothly.

"That was kind of Captain Borza to lead us to a proper stable. These horses are sturdier than the ones we raise," Etosh said as he examined the horses they just purchased. "Our horses wouldn't last in this brutal weather." He shivered as a cold chill chased down his spine.

"I think it was sweet of Zizia to provide us with money to buy these things," Lati said. She brushed her fingers through the long silver mane of her horse. The pure happiness of being close to the animal brought upon a lazy smile on her face.

Nthanda kept quiet while Etosh and his sister fussed with each other. There was enough coin to supply everyone for the winter weather. She took a portion and found a fur trader. The people of her homeland would recognize her by the hair and eyes alone and she didn't want to be found yet. A disguise was needed, and she was proficient enough with working an illusion. She conjured one for her hair and face. Subtle but strong enough that it wouldn't dispel if she moved too much.

Kai did her invisible thing, disappearing, and walked beside her on Nightfall's streets. Nthanda had eventually found the merchant she was looking for. She went into the store and was promptly greeted by an older woman and an older man who was her husband. They were a friendly couple and helped Nthanda pick the proper furs that would keep her dry and warm. She ended up with Tundrean bear fur. Known for its white and grey thick fur.

The fur was already fashioned into a semblance of a coat, so she bought it. Nthanda tried the furred jacket on and the piece fit perfectly. Glad the coat was hooded, she could pull over her head anytime. She didn't have to be told it would come in handy when she became too cold. She asked the merchants if they knew where she could find a pair of daggers.

Nthanda remembered the smile he gave her. He had a pair but he wouldn't sell them to her. Instead, he gifted them to her. The daggers were in a carved box with initials on the front. When she opened the ornate wooden box, she gasped. He explained they had once belonged to his daughter long ago before she fell ill and died.

He explained she was their only child. The twin daggers were made of elk bone handle and the blade was a mixture of steel and obsidian. They were beautiful and refused any payments she tried to give him. He told her he's been looking for the right person to give them to and the moment he saw her; he knew she was the one. Nthanda knew not to argue with the man. She had gladly taken the daggers and left the old couple with a smile on their face.

Now, back with her companions, they prepared to leave. She touched the necklace she wore and was comforted by the warm sensation. The group decided against the sleds and would ride the horses. Not wanting to wait, Nthanda wanted to make the trek and head to the citadel. From Nightfall Harbor, the journey would take half a day on horseback. She couldn't believe they were so close and still so far away.

I will run beside you and hunt, Bright Star. I will watch from the trees and catch up. I just want to roam freely. Been too long.

Nthanda smiled at her familiar. "That is perfectly fine. Don't get lost."

I never get lost, Kai said. She brushed up against Nthanda then took off.

Nthanda watched her familiar go. She wanted to run free just as much as the giant cat did.

"Hey," Etosh said, interrupting her thoughts. "Where's the cat going?"

Nthanda smiled. "She's relearning the lay of the land. Besides, she's designed for this type of weather. The oppressive heat and wetness of the jungles along with the dry heat of the desert didn't do much for her coat or her mood. The joy I feel through our bond right now. Worth every moment of her going ahead of us." Nthanda blissful smile filled her face. "Don't worry about the cat. She will find us when she is ready. Let her hunt."

"As you wish. We should go. I don't know the land and don't know how dark this place gets."

"When night falls, we'll follow the northern star. The sun sets early here."

THE GROUP WAS QUIET as they traveled the road out of Nightfall Harbor. Only three candlemarks in, they were making great time according to the map Ezael had picked up. Etosh and his brothers didn't want to travel all night but Nthanda insisted they did or she would leave them and go on her own. All she had to do was follow the North Star and touch the pendant around her neck. The closer she got to being home, the warmer the necklace became.

An argument ensued when she said she would leave and then she made compromises with Etosh and his brothers. She agreed to stop a few times to let everyone rest since they weren't used to the weather. If that was satisfactory then they would ride all night.

Kai was still gone but Nthanda felt her presence nearby. Now and then she would see a white and grey blur streak through the trees. Thankful for her familiar, she enjoyed the joyous sensation of her friend as she bounded through the Dark Forest.

"We should stop soon," Zaire said. We need to confer with the map again.

"Fine with me," Nthanda replied. "A break to stretch my legs would be great."

The group went on for another half mark, searching for an open space. When they found one near a fork in the road, they stopped in the small clearing. Nthanda went over to the young guide.

"How are you holding up?" she asked the girl. Ever since they left Roshan and the Temple of Elios, she retreated into herself and kept quiet. Didn't say much. "Getting used to the cold yet?"

Vika messed with the furs she wore and looked up. "Yea, not so bad. I can get used to it. The sand and heat was not my favorite."

"Everyone thinks it never gets warm here, but we have mild weather. Doesn't get as hot, but we get to see the grass a time or two. Lasts for three months then the cold is back upon us. But those three months are the best. I think you will love it once we get past winter," Nthanda said.

Vika smiled. "I hope so. I like it here so far. The only thing I miss from Roshan is Zizia."

Nthanda wanted to know how a Child of the Moon came to live in the temple to the sun god. But she never found a proper time to ask the girl. "Can I ask how did you become Zizia's maidservant?"

"Sure. She found me in Mekech. That's the city next to the temple. I was no older than three summers. My birth mother abandoned me. I can't even remember her face. They took me to an orphanage, and I lived there for five summers. She came in one day, took one look at me, and adopted me from the orphanage. They didn't question why she wanted me, they were just glad to get rid of me. I wasn't like the other children."

"Because you are a moon born, that's why?"

"Yes, but I didn't know it then. She has been good to me and never treated me like a servant but as my mother."

Vika's demeanor change and Nthanda felt the sadness roll off the young girl. "You miss her?"

"Aye. She is the best thing that ever happened to me and if they find out what she did to help you, they will sacrifice her. You can't let her die. You have to save her!"

"Vika, I promise I will do my best," she said to the girl. Nthanda didn't understand why Zizia took her in but the girl loved her. Nthanda assumed Zizia expected they would take her. Vika nodded and stumbled off, leaving Nthanda standing by herself.

Bright Star! I found something! Kai said through their bond.

Where are you, Kai? Nthanda looked around but couldn't find the giant animal.

I'm coming. You're going to like what I have found.

Kai burst through the trees, alarming everyone. Ezael who was close to Nthanda, quickly pulled out a knife and went into a battle ready stance.

"You can stand down, Ezael. It is only Kai." Nthanda grinned as he tried to pretend that he wasn't scared.

Kai bounded towards Nthanda with what look like a giant stick in her mouth.

"What. Is. That?" She pointed to the white thing protruding from her familiar's mouth. "Kai. Drop it!"

Ezael and Etosh walked over to where she stood with Kai, looking down at the stick she brought to her. Nthanda went to pick the item up then stopped.

"What is it, Kai?"

Bone. I found it deep in the trees. Can't you feel it? Kai asked.

Nthanda picked the bone fragment up. Power still flowed through the marrow of whatever creature it belonged to. Not one of their world, but from the Evernight.

"I can. How did it get here?"

I don't know. Maybe how I showed up. One moment I am there. Next moment I am here. It's tricky.

Nthanda lifted the sturdy piece of bone. It was thick and almost as tall as she. The creature was powerful, that much she could tell. A fine gift. She already knew what she wanted to do with it.

"I thank you Kai for this fine gift you brought to me. I also thank the Mother Goddess for leading you to it. I will use it well." Nthanda kissed the top of Kai's head. She didn't realize the others had come to check out what was going on. Yazi looked at the long bone and smiled. "That will make a fine weapon," she said to Nthanda.

"Yes, it will. I just need feathers. If you find hawk feathers or even raven feathers, bring them to me, Kai."

As you wish. I'll follow through the trees. I just wanted to bring you this perfect gift.

And perfect it is.

Nthanda tied the large bone to the pack on her horse, making sure it wouldn't fall. She didn't dare lose the precious item. She climbed atop her mount and settled into her seat.

"What do you plan on doing with that?" Yazi asked. Bringing her horse side by side with her.

"I plan on making a bone staff. Like the one my grandmother had when I was a child. I always wanted one like hers. Besides, I need an item to help channel the flow of my magic. If I pull too much, the gift has a mind of its own."

"In time, everything will only move at your command," Yazi said. "The staff is a wonderful choice. Wield it wisely."

Yazi clicked her tongue and the horse she was on trotted off. Nthanda liked her. She differed from Etosh's other siblings.

NTHANDA COULDN'T STOP touching the pendant around her neck. It was too hot to keep next to her chest, so she wore the necklace over her furs. She knew they headed in the right direction because the necklace never cooled since they made it to Enyxias. The group had been on the snow-covered path for six candlemarks. Much longer than she originally expected. Nthanda was very tired but she refused to stop. Not yet. Not when she was so close to home.

Bright Star...

Yes, Kai Nthanda responded. She had gotten used to the random bursts of words in her head since they had left Nightfall Harbor. Kai had run around in the trees like a child on a fresh new snow day, but this time she sounded trouble.

I am ahead of you and the others. Soldiers are headed your way

How many? she asked. Alarmed, she rode to the front where Etosh and Zaire led with the map.

Nine. I'm coming back to where you are.

Zaire glanced over his shoulders and saw Nthanda trot up beside them.

He smiled then the smile disappeared. Immediately he caught the change in her demeanor. The slight fear in her face.

"What's wrong?"

"Soldiers ahead of us."

"How many?" he asked.

"My familiar counted nine."

"That's a squad,"

"I don't understand why they're out here this late but we are right on course to run into them," she said.

"Don't panic, we're just a big family going about our way. Unless there's a curfew we don't know about." Zaire's brow raised, silently questioning her.

Nthanda shrugged her shoulders. "I've no clue. I haven't stepped foot on these lands in eight years. We will keep the course. My only concern is being discovered. I'll have to wear an illusion."

"Why? They should be happy to see you home finally," Etosh chimed in.

"Last time I was here, my family was betrayed by those we thought friends. I won't take that chance again. Not while all of you are with me."

Zaire nodded. "I understand. Stay here behind Etosh and me."

Nthanda moved her horse directly behind the two men and they continued traveling on the path. Kai had caught up with them, melded in between the horses and disappeared from sight.

They don't seem vicious, like the other soldiers in the hot place. It's a mix of human and witches.

Well, that's good to know, Nthanda responded. *They are probably a scouting party. A larger troop may not be far off.*

I'll stay alert. Can't hurt to always be ready, Kai said.

Good point.

A curved bend on the road led the group right into the squad of soldiers. They wore the furs but their uniforms peeked through.

"Halt!" a man's voice shouted into the night air. Zaire glanced to the others and told the group to stop. "What are you doing out so late? Don't you know it is well beyond the curfew time?"

Etosh and Zaire eyed each other sideways before slightly glancing back at Nthanda.

"We are not from here. We didn't know," Etosh said with his heavy accent, which was thicker than normal.

The solider who spoke noticed Etosh's accent and bade them to wait. He went back to the other soldiers and spoke with another man who must have been his superior. The conversation went on and became heated but the superior had the last say. The soldier came back to them and eyed the group.

"How many are with you?" he asked.

"We are nine," Etosh answered.

"Well, you will have to come with us to the Keep. You are refugees right?"

"Yes. We have escaped the purge in the land of our birth. We were told we could have a new start here. That it is safe here."

"Yea yea yea. All refugees must go to the keep. The High Priestess and the council decides where you will go afterwards. We will escort you. We are only a candlemark away."

Nthanda was shocked to hear that her mother wasn't at the family seat but at the Keep instead. It didn't bode well.

Chapter 37

"What are you doing up here all by yourself? It is cold tonight," Mama Jia'ka said. The older woman had climbed the narrow stairs that led to the terrace that overlooked a small private courtyard. "You have been quiet all day and most of this evening during dinner. What is wrong with you? Are you sick?"

Chanda glanced over her shoulders, "Sick. Perhaps. My heart hurts, Mama."

Jia'ka understood pain of the heart. Hers hurt too. "I know, child. You aren't the only one who hurts."

"I had hoped and prayed to the Mother Goddess. Prayed she would be home by now. With the word of annihilation of our people in Roshan, I was sure she would have found her way home by now. What keeps her away?" Jia'ka stood beside Chanda and pulled her daughter close into her arms. "You don't think they recaptured her do you?"

"I don't know," Jia'ka whispered into the wind. "But don't give up hope. The girl is strong, yes."

"Yes, she is."

"She will find her way home." Jia'ka reassured her. "I often imagine what my Little Star looks like now. She was the most beautiful child I have seen besides you. She was a spitfire too. I wonder if she contained that fire inside her."

"From the dreamscape, her face was thin and her ragged clothes loose on her frame. Her captors didn't take care of her very well. Even with all the hardships she had to endure, it didn't take away from her. She was beautiful. Deep in those wide amethyst eyes, the fire burned still. She kept her head held high though her spirt was weary. You can tell that they could not defeat her." Chanda smiled. "I hope she gave them endless dark nights of trouble."

"Oh, I am sure she did. If she didn't," Jia'ka shrugged her shoulders and chuckled. "We didn't teach her properly. She is twenty winters now. Old enough to join the coven properly."

"That she is."

"And she is old enough to learn the duties of a High Priestess."

"But what if she is gone? I haven't been able to reach her anymore in the dreamscape."

"I believe she still breathes. We must have patience and trust the Goddess plans."

"Why is this so hard?"

"It's not meant to be easy." Jia'ka led Chanda to the closest bench and sat down on the cold stone. The sharp, thin air bit at their bare arms, making the flesh pebble like small stones one find on a rocky shore. Nighttime was always colder in Enyxias but also the time where the world was more peaceful.

Chanda leaned into Jia'ka and rested her head on her mother's shoulder. Jia'ka hated how their small family was destroyed. Yet she couldn't do anything about it. Once her Little Star was gone, no more was ever revealed to her about the child. For the longest time she thought her vision was lost. That she did something wrong and Dreva, her Goddess, was punishing her. But it wasn't punishment. Plans and more plans were in the works and she didn't have the privilege to view them.

Enjoying the warmth from her daughter, she wrapped her arm around Chanda. Holding her close was exactly what she needed. An old song from when she was younger came to Jia'ka's mind, and she began to hum the tune. The melody gently danced on the currents of the wind. Vivid colors of each note brightened before their eyes before disappearing into the night.

The song ended and Jia'ka and Chanda's soft breath broke the otherwise silence on the private terrace. Brighter than normal, the millions of stars in the sky beamed down on them. Watching. Observing. Hiding secrets of the world from time immemorial. Knowledge long forgotten, but the stars and the moon remembered. Jia'ka worried about the child as much as her daughter but it did them no good to worry about the girl. All things work out the way they were supposed to, but most days it seemed they always had to deal with the waste of the world. "Let us worry about things that we can control. Like the murder of our people. The God-speaker must die," Jia'ka said.

"That is something we can both agree on. His time is considerably overdue. His death was warranted eight long winters ago."

NTHANDA SAW THE FORTRESS Keep looming in the distance under the silvery tendrils of moonlight. Built on top of the highest cliff in Enyxias, the massive structure overlooked the southern portion of the lands. From the beginning, the Keep was used as the seat of power for the current High Priestess. Her grandmother came along and earned the title. She preferred the mountain keep as her sanctuary. Then her mother kept with that tradition, preferring the tall mountains to the north instead of the plain snowlands of the south. Got her away from the crowd of the people. The citadel was her sanctuary, her sacred space to commune with the gods.

Most of the population gathered near the southern borders. Some covens were nomadic like their ancestors and traveled all over the lands. Both places were close to magical ley lines underneath. Which was why they were built in those locations. As a child, Nthanda only went to the Black Keep for special occasions or during festival season for the temple.

Everyone was quiet. A glance here and there, while surrounded by soldiers on all sides. Afraid to speak out loud. Fear of what the soldiers might say or do. Nthanda kept her face hidden under the illusion. She was anxious and ready to be there already. She couldn't believe she was so close and yet still so far away. Time moves slow for the impatient. What seemed like many candlemarks had passed, was only half a candlemark.

Are we even close to being there yet? Kai asked. The cat still hidden from sight.

Almost. I'm excited and nervous all in one.

I can tell through the bond. You will be fine. I am glad to be back too. My fur prefers these lands.

Nthanda chuckled. * I do too. I just don't understand why we are going to the keep. I don't understand why she is not at the seat in the north.*

Perhaps something happened. Who knows? We will find out soon, yes?

Yes, we will find out soon enough.

Etosh scanned over his shoulders before turning back to the front. He moved his horse as close as he could to Nthanda and leaned her way.

"That's where you grew up?" he whispered. Clearly in awe. The gated twin pillars towered over the tallest trees straight ahead. The pillars were massive and could be seen from miles away. Flames in its open upper windows flickered giving it an ominous feel with the dark fortress behind it. Those gates were always manned even if the High Priestess wasn't in residence. Soldiers trained at the fortress and the dungeons is where they kept the most unworthy when they are set to die.

"No. I grew up in the citadel. Long ago before the last two leaders, this is where the seat of power resided. Now they govern from the citadel in the far north."

"So why are we coming here?"

"That is a good question. Your guess is just as good as mine, Etosh. I have no clue on why we are visiting this place. Makes me nervous."

"I'd be nervous too," he responded. "Looks like something that would come straight out of the deep depths of the Evernight." Etosh sat straighter in his saddle as they came closer to the gates.

The Lieutenant who led the squad of soldiers raised his hand, halting the group. Guards came out of the gatehouse and spoke with the leader. Soon after, the gates opened allowing the group to pass. The loud groaning and creaking metal of the gates screamed and protested and with a loud clanging, they shout. Inside, the group was led only a few feet before stopping. The lieutenant turned to face them.

"Law says that all refugees must come through here first. The High Priestess and council meet with everyone each morning before midday bells. Then if it calls for it, another session in the evening. Since it's late, we will have to keep you here in the holding area until the morning session. I'll alert the proper people so they know we have you here. Do you understand?"

"Yes, we do," Zaire said, speaking for the entire group.

The Lieutenant nodded. "Well come on, let's get you lot warm. It's colder than normal tonight."

JIA'KA AND CHANDA CAME down the stairs and into the receiving chamber when heavy knocks rapped on the door.

"I'll answer. Fix us some tea. My old bones could use a warm cup," Jia'ka said.

"The usual?"

"Always the usual love."

Jia'ka shuffled to the door and opened it. A soldier still in his winter furs and a guard bowed their heads.

"What do you want? The High Priestess is busy."

The soldier swallowed. People tip toed around Jia'ka, afraid of the old woman. Her reputation was fierce, and no one wanted to cross her. Or come across her path.

"I- I was told to inform you we picked up a large group of refugees just a candlemark from here," the soldier stammered out. From the corner of Jia'ka's eyes, she watched the soldier repeatedly open and close his hands into a balled fist.

"You know that we see the refugees during the morning. Why are you disturbing us with this news?"

"My... my Lieutenant thought you should know. Was a large group. Nine of them and the youngest was no older than ten winters or so."

Jia'ka grimaced. "I will inform her. Until then, place them in the holding area."

The soldier and guard bowed once more and left. Jia'ka closed the door and grumbled as she shuffled her way back to where the room was warm. Chanda had set up the setting for the tea and Jia'ka could smell the floral and spicy aroma from where she was.

"Who was at the door?" Chanda asked when Jia'ka sat down.

"Mmm, just like I like it. Thank you, daughter!"

"Mama, who was at the door and what did they want?" Chanda grew frustrated when her mother tried to protect her from anyone or anything.

"Just more refugees from Nightfall Harbor. They've been coming in like an unexpected blizzard," Jia'ka said. She picked up the cup of hot tea and let the aroma waft around her. She blew on the liquid, trying to quick cool it before taking the first sip. She moaned at the taste of the warm drink. It was her most favorite, and a treat anytime she got to drink it.

"Why would they be out this late passed curfew? They should have waited until morning to come here. It's dangerous crossing these lands at night. No telling what lurks out in the trees."

Chanda poured herself a cup of tea and moved closer to the fireplace, enjoying the warmth. She sipped the tea quietly as she tried to clear her mind.

"Doesn't matter. I told the soldier we will meet the group in the morning. During the time we have designated for the refugees. No point in changing things now. It's late."

"I really understand what you're saying Mama, but something doesn't sit right with me."

"You're worrying about things the council can handle. Sit down and quit pacing. Drink your tea in peace."

"You're of all people knows when I get a notion, I have to follow the trail."

Chanda sat the cup down on the table, strode to the heavy, Blackwood chamber door and opened it. Her personal guard saluted with a fist over his chest.

"Tell the Lieutenant I will meet those refugees tonight. Have them in the hall in the next candlemark."

"As you wish, High Priestess." The guard placed his fist over his chest again and took off down the hall.

Chapter 38

"At least they make the place cozy," Ezael said. He paced the large room they were in, making sure the chamber was secure.

Nthanda glanced around. "I think this used to be a recovering room. Like the ones in the healer's ward," she said.

"They're soft and warm. That's all I really care about," Lati responded. She had climbed into an empty bed and stretched out.

"I wonder if they're using the healing room for us since we are so many," Nthanda said. Kai behind her, moved into a more comfortable position on the bed she had claimed.

"I don't know but I like this thing," Ezael said pointing to the fire. "What do they call this indoor fire pit?"

Nthanda chuckled. "It's called a fireplace. Keeps the room heated." She stretched out on the bed, using Kai as her pillow. Beyond tired, Nthanda was glad she was home. She was also nervous. Worried what the next morning would be like.

"Ohh," Ezael responded. Etosh stood next to his brother and laughed at his ignorance.

Nthanda looked closely at the two men as they held a murmured conversation between each other. She kept staring and realized the pair was almost identical. Mad she never noticed until then. Mad at herself she just figured out what kept bothering her about those two.

"Are you two twins?" Nthanda blurted.

The brothers' head shot up at Nthanda's outburst. Ezael covered his mouth to hide his laugh but Etosh didn't care if she saw him laughing. Yazi came and sat on the bed opposite of Nthanda. "You are now asking this question?"

"Yes. How come you didn't say anything?" She asked the twins.

Etosh crossed his arms against his chest and smiled. "Because most observant people notice immediately. We never confirm if we are or not. Not in the desert lands. Twins are considered evil."

Nthanda mumbled, "Well, I wasn't fully myself."

"We remember," Yazi said as she placed a hand on Nthanda's leg. "That's why it's no big deal."

"You do realize twins are important to the Goddess. Considered sacred, revered and loved. Not evil." Nthanda told them. Etosh and his siblings eyed each other. Nthanda caught the brief glances. "Did you not know that? They teach this to us as young children!"

It was Yazi who spoke. "We did not. I am afraid our education of the true ways of our people has been diluted with traditions of the sun children and humans. Living in Roshan, we had to hide our true natures."

"We shouldn't be afraid to hide who we are for fear of reprisal. I am afraid things will get worse since the God-speaker is on the warpath," Nthanda told the others.

"That it will," Etosh said.

A soft silence fell on the room. Everyone, no doubt thinking about what Nthanda said. That things would will be worse before they ever got better. Nthanda was afraid for her people if they didn't fight back.

Someone is coming. Smells like a soldier from earlier, Kai said.

Nthanda turned to the door soon after Kai mentioned a visitor. She could barely replace the illusion for her face and hair before the door opened.

Thanks for the heads up!

No worries. Kai purred.

The lieutenant strode inside the room. Still in his uniform minus the furs, Nthanda got a better look at the man. He was of average height and build. His wheat colored hair was cut short on the sides and top. His posture was rigid and tight. He was a soldier through and through. He came to edge of the row where the beds started and stopped. He looked over everyone with a grimace.

"I don't understand why our High Priestess will not wait until morning. She has insisted on seeing you lot tonight. Prepare yourself and gather all of your things. I will be back shortly," he told the group. The Lieutenant quickly turned on his heels and left the room.

Everyone turned and faced Nthanda. Fear, nervousness, and anger all covered their faces. She raised her hands up. The same emotions warred within herself. "I do not understand why the High Priestess isn't waiting until morning."

CHANDA MADE HER WAY to the dais in the great hall. Jia'ka was in step next to her and Chanda's guards followed behind. Soldiers watched from the shadowed spaces, ever alert for trouble. Rules dictated she had the council with her to help place those new to the lands but she refused to wake them for this group. Chanda was the ruler of Enyxias and what is a ruler who can't do what she wanted, when she wanted. She couldn't rest. Her heart was heavy and her mind was full. Work seemed to be the only thing that helped relieve her troubles. Made them disappear.

As she approached the center of the dais, the obsidian chair loomed closer at the center of the dais loomed closer as she approached it. A cherished magical relic from when the Black Keep was first built. She sat upon the seat and let the cold seep into her. The seat itself was built into the dais and it tapped into the ley line that ran underneath the great hall. Amplifying her magic when she had a need for it. That alone was one of the many reasons her foremothers used the keep as their base of operations. Their home.

Jia'ka stood slightly beside her on the left and her guards stood at the foot of the steps that led up to her. Chanda sat up straight and rested her hands in her lap, changed her mind, then she gripped the arms of her chair. She didn't need to look imposing. This wasn't a trial.

"Bring the group in," she said to the guard next to her. With a fist over chest, he bowed his head and turned towards the door. He motioned to the guards with his fingers. The dark Blackwood doors slowly opened and the lieutenant who had come to her chamber's door earlier. Behind him a group of travelers followed into the hall and stopped a few feet away from the end of the stairs.

"You can speak Lieutenant. Who are these people and where do they come from?" Chanda's voice was strong enough to carry without being amplified for all to hear.

"We found them on the road. They didn't say where they were headed, but it was late and passed the curfew. They come from the Kingdom of Roshan but have no papers from Nightfall Harbor saying they're refugees. Figured we'd let you and the council sort the lot out so we came directly here."

"I understand. You can step aside Lieutenant."

"As you wish, High Priestess."

Chanda glanced over the weary group. "Who speaks for all of you?"

"I do," a deep accented voice said out loud. Chanda kept a guarded face as a man moved to the front of the group. His stride was smooth and confident. She took an instant liking to the man.

"And what do they call you?" she asked.

"I am called Etosh, and this is my family," he said as he pointed to the group behind him.

Chanda noted the name and memories rushed to the forefront of her mind. The name reminded her of her long-time friend, Ekon. She missed him so much and not a day had gone by that she didn't think of him.

"Etosh. I am the High Priestess and it is I who meet with all the people who is fleeing the land of Elios and find their way here. Why were you traveling so late? Did no one tell you about the curfew?"

"No, High Priestess. We didn't even know we were supposed to have papers. When we landed this morning, the Captain told us where we could find horses and supplies. That was it."

"Is there someplace you were trying to get to the reason you didn't stay in Nightfall Harbor this evening?" she asked. Etosh didn't respond but instead turned to someone behind him.

"Who do you speak to? I thought you were the speaker for your family?" Chanda leaned forward. Jia'ka moved closer to her.

"I do speak for my family. I was just getting the name of the town we were headed to." Etosh shifted on his feet. The priestess made him nervous. There was something about her that was familiar and he couldn't tell or figure it out.

"Hmmm..." Chanda said and got quiet.

"What do you want to do with them?" Jia'ka whispered. "Where would you send them? The men look sturdy enough, no need to send them away. I am sure we could find a use for their strength around here."

Chanda already had noticed the men. The women could be of use too. The child, her mother could train her. After of course, she tested the girl's skills. "I have some idea. Perhaps they could stay."

The High Priestess stood and took two steps toward the group. "Who was it you conferred with? Let that person speak since they apparently know the land."

Etosh moved to the side and Chanda's careful gaze cut to the woman as she pushed through the group to come forward. The woman stopped and didn't move anymore but

Chanda found her own feet moving forward. She glided down the stairs, and she didn't understand why the pull was so strong. She couldn't stop until she stood before the woman.

"Who are you?" she asked. Magic surrounded the young woman and Chanda recognized the working as an illusion spell. The tang of the woman's magic was familiar to her. "Reveal yourself!" She commanded.

The woman took her right hand and slowly waved it across her face, dispelling the illusion. "Do you not recognize your own daughter?" Nthanda's lips tugged upward into a grin while tears escaped her eyes.

A loud shout came from Jia'ka and Chanda took a shaky step back. She couldn't believe what she saw. The voice that was her young daughter's but matured.

"I prayed for this day," Chanda whispered. "I prayed every day for this moment."

"Is it really you?" Jia'ka ambled forward from where she was standing until she stood in front of Nthanda. "My Little Star, it's really you!" She reached out and gingerly touched Nthanda's face. As if touching her wasn't enough, she pulled her into a hug.

Etosh and his family was shocked as they watched the long-awaited reunion.

"Wait-" Etosh interrupted. Nthanda turned her head around to face him. "You mean to tell us you're the daughter of the High Priestess? The de facto leader of our people. Not the High Priestess daughter's best friend?"

"She is my daughter," Chanda replied not giving Nthanda the chance to speak.

"But for eight years not once did anything mention she was the missing daughter of the High Priestess," Etosh continued. He couldn't understand how the woman he helped was indeed the daughter of the most powerful woman in Enyxias.

"You have many questions young man but in time I will answer them all. We didn't want anyone to know my daughter was missing. Only a select few knew the truth of what really happened that fateful night. We had enemies everywhere."

Etosh raked his fingers through his coiled hair. "I understand."

"I don't know the story of how you all made it here but I will hear it on the morrow. For now, I give you sanctuary here in my home. You are honored guests because you brought my Little Star home."

Jia'ka motioned to the guards next to her. "Give them quarters in the eastern wing."

"As you command," the guard closest to Jia'ka said. He gathered the group and led them out of the hall.

Nthanda watched them and waved when Etosh looked back to her before going through the door.

"Did the little cat find you?" Jia'ka asked.

"She did." Nthanda touched what looked like nothing. Kai made herself visible to everyone.

Jia'ka laughed deep from her belly. "I knew you would find her. Thank you for watching over her. I know you must love her as much as we do."

Tell the old woman she is welcome, Bright Star Kai said through the bond.

"She says you are welcome, Mama Jia'ka," Nthanda said.

"I thank the Mother Goddess for this wonderful blessing," Chanda said. "There are no other words. I had to meet with your group tonight. I couldn't wait until morning."

"I have so much to tell you, Mama. You and Mama Jia'ka both," Nthanda said.

"We will have plenty of time for all of that," Chanda responded. "So much have happened and it must be set right."

"Yes. The betrayers of our own people have paid but the other culprits must pay," Jia'ka chimed in.

"The Godspeaker is the root of all evil who doesn't care about anyone but himself and his children. He has my friend. I can't let her stay there. Not after she helped me escape the jungles and the Godspeaker's cabal. I have to go back for her."

"You won't do this alone. We are family and take care of our own. Now that you're home and safe, there is only one option. We cannot be seen as weak. He wants a war, we will give him that. Except we have the Goddess of War and the Lord of Death on our side. They sanction our actions and we will sacrifice the lives of the Children of the Sun to our God and Goddess. We will bathe in our enemy's blood and laugh in their faces. For we are Children of the Moon and we will bring all the Evernight if need be," Chanda said.

"I second this," Jia'ka said. "We have no need for the council vote. We have a third who witnessed this."

Nthanda smiled. The first true smile she had felt since she could remember. "We are all in agreement then. The Godspeaker and his horrible followers must die."

About the Author

D.L. Howard is a cosmic traveler who embraces her weirdness. Never one to back down from a chance to get away, she is always traveling on a new adventure. Guaranteed to have a camera with her, snapping pics of her escapades. A lover of animals, (especially the cute baby ones) she is ruled by her psychotic cat overlord Sir Crookshanks! She finds comfort in listening to music, thunderstorms, dark and gloomy days, cold weather, curling up in a corner with a blanket and a good book. You can find her on www.dlhowardwrites.com, Facebook, Twitter, and Instagram. Don't hesitate to stop by and say hi. She loves meeting other cosmic travelers too!

Read more at https://www.dlhowardwrites.com.

Manufactured by Amazon.ca
Bolton, ON

17910465R00224